THE
COURAGE
of KINGS

DANA HALLIN

ILLUMIFY MEDIA GLOBAL
Littleton, Colorado

THE COURAGE of KINGS

Copyright © 2019 by Dana Hallin

Published by
Illumify Media Global
www.IllumifyMedia.com
"Write. Publish. Market. *SELL!*"

Library of Congress Control Number: 2019909533

Paperback ISBN: 978-1-949021-53-0
eBook ISBN: 978-1-949021-57-8

Typeset by Art Innovations (http://artinnovations.in/)
Cover design by Debbie Lewis

Printed in the United States of America

To my grandparents, Harold and Velma Hallin,
who not only poured their wisdom and love into my life
but taught me that all stories find their way to us from that
first, sacred story.

PROLOGUE

SOMEWHERE IN THE TRANSYLVANIA AREA OF ROMANIA

There were no warnings. Not a sound.

One moment, children were playing outside in the cool, feeble sunlight of an early spring morning, happy to be released from the stale air and cooking smells of a long winter spent indoors.

The next, they were falling to the ground. The playground was soon littered with crumpled little heaps scattered in the grass.

Two women, schoolyard attendants, stood chatting about neighborhood gossip and the challenges of getting their husbands to fix things around their houses.

As the children began to fall to the ground, the women's conversation slowed, sputtered, and finally stopped. They looked around, frozen in terror and disbelief.

Dear God, what was happening?

A shooter? A gas leak?

They slowly turned in unison to scan the fences of the property line, back to the little heaps and then up into the sky, their questioning thoughts hanging in the silent air, like frozen laundry left out on an abandoned clothesline.

Chapter 1

LOS ANGELES

Bree stared at the envelope propped up against the lamp at the corner of her desk. Yes, that was her friend Cynthia's impeccable handwriting. No need to open the envelope. Bree already knew what was inside.

The elegant handwriting on the expensive white parchment blurred in and out of focus as she struggled to keep control of her emotions. What had her grief counselor said? *When you have strong emotions, address the thoughts fueling them.*

That was it. She was supposed to address her thoughts. Thoughts that apparently only needed the arrival of a graduation announcement in the mail to come snaking out of the darkness, coiling next to her, hissing seductively, *"It's just an apple . . . Just one bite. One . . ."*

She shook her head, sending the bottom of her silky blonde bob sliding across the top of her collar. When she couldn't shake the dark thoughts away, she stood up and walked around the room, blindly skirting shelves and tables filled with exquisite urns, beads, pottery, and icons. The red soles of her shoes tapped out a muffled SOS as she paced across the corner of the Persian rug.

"Not now. Not now. Please, not now!" she pleaded softly with herself.

Suddenly she felt haunted by the mementos around the room, mementos collected during her—their—extensive travels. Each piece represented a memory or shared experience, and today, it was impossible to keep her mind from drifting toward those dangerous cliffs.

Another turn around the room. Bree could feel her pounding heart begin to slow as she fought to ground herself in the present. She took a deep breath and allowed herself to look around the room, taking in each personally chosen piece of furniture as if for the first time. Hers was an office envied for its distinctive style and design, something she had once valued so much.

She glanced at the envelope as she made yet another pass by her desk.

Two years. Had it been two years? She stopped in front of the bookshelf where his framed photos had once been. She had put them away because they had been painful to see every day, but now their absence seemed even more unbearable. Her knees weakened, and she blindly felt for the nearest chair.

There was no stopping it now. The floodgates had opened, and the waves she had so valiantly held back were now crashing up against her fierce resolve.

Another look at the white envelope and she felt herself slipping into memories of that night—and the white light in his hospital room.

♕

It is the light that is so unnerving. Bright and unrelenting. That and the noise. She hears the machines pumping their rhythmic clanks and beeps, heralding another precious second of life for Jayden. She is standing at the end of the bed, watching two members of the ICU post-op team hover over the unconscious form of her son.

Ben is standing at her side, and they are both dressed in expensive and now disheveled evening attire. The police had finally tracked them down at one of the many fund-raising social events that crowded their calendars. By the time they arrived, Jayden was already in surgery.

Now she studies his face. Is it a blessing that he is not conscious? She has no way of knowing. His head is swathed in dense white gauze, his eyes closed and barely visible as his lungs are pushed up and then down with each compression of the machines.

The authorities are calling it a "random gang shooting." Apparently, Jayden had been driving home on the 10 from a Lakers game. There was no evidence of any road rage. The lone eyewitness indicated that a dark-windowed sedan had sped up next to Jayden's SUV and shot him through the glass at close range. He was unconscious and in cardiac arrest en route to the hospital. Surgery was immediate. No time for her or Ben to weigh in on top surgeons or to access their concierge health-care facilities. They ended up in the Cedar Sinai trauma unit along with every other gunshot victim in LA tonight . . . and they are at the mercy of the Fates.

The initial trauma team has been replaced by an ICU team schooled in critical post-op care. They seem to be working on every part of Jayden. Bree wants desperately to touch him, but there is no space for her. She reaches for his one exposed foot. It's cold. Oddly manlike. When did her boy change into this man? An alarm goes off. More frenetic activity. More consultations. Still the bright light. Internal cranial bleeding. More surgery. She must let go. A nurse is pulling her away from the now-rolling bed. She hears a sobbing woman scream, "Ben! Ben! They are taking him! Do something! We can't let him go . . ." And of course, it's her own voice . . .

Bree heard a persistent buzzing. The traumatic images continued to swirl around her. The intercom on her phone still buzzed. Gradually she managed to pull out of the memories and regain a sense of where she was. Now. Today.

She and Ben *had* let their son go that night. He'd never survived the second surgery.

She couldn't move to respond to the intercom, and it eventually stopped. It was probably her assistant saying she was leaving for the night.

Bree sat rooted to her chair, emotions still ricocheting between memories from that awful night and the sight of Jayden's best friend's graduation announcement propped against the lamp on her desk.

It was so unfair. Why couldn't she be thrilled for Zach without being devastated by her own loss? Zach's story was a glorious one. His future so bright. Just like Jayden's had been. Why had this happened to her only child? What spinning cosmic needle of fate had landed on *her* son's life? She couldn't begin to answer this or any of the other questions that ultimately followed.

Bree felt ill-equipped for metaphysical quandary. She hadn't been raised that way. Her world and that of her parents had been created by calculated effort, not by introspective thought. Her father had drilled the concepts of focused objectives and self-determination into her psyche before she was old enough to make a conscious choice. She'd ridden those ideals from her first grammar school awards ceremony all the way to a Harvard MBA and beyond.

From her mother, Bree had inherited an equal drive for perfection and style. Her appearance, her home, her lifestyle, and even her family reflected Bree's carefully curated taste. There's no doubt that her choices had enhanced her position as CEO of the travel conglomerate she had eventually built. It was an accomplishment that had withstood the advent of the World Wide Web, the resulting thrust of e-commerce and, the crash of '08.

It had not survived the death of her son. She'd sold it the year after he died. "Taking the cash off the table" was how she had presented it to the world, but the truth was that it was her crushed spirit that was "off the table." She'd negotiated a two-year employment contract so she could keep working six days a week. It was the only way to keep what was left of her life buried under the weight of routine and order.

Not that it had done any good. Once again, she had been overwhelmed by relentless dark thoughts and emotions. No wonder she had stopped seeing that quack of a therapist. No one should have been better equipped to isolate and control negative thoughts and emotions than she, Breelyn Stanton. And yet, all it had taken was one envelope, and here she was, unraveling all over again.

Bree stood and picked up her Prada bag. Her last view of the office from the doorway was the desk lamp shining down on a symbol of the life she'd once had but would never have again.

Chapter 2

LOS ANGELES

Furious, Ben crushed the pages of the newspaper in his hands and slammed the wadded ball into the wastebasket by his desk.

This was always how it started. He'd be deep into a day of meetings and projects, and then some random thing, like coming across an article about three soldiers dying in Afghanistan, would trigger his grief and rage.

These were young men like Jayden. Jayden at the age he would have been today. So much promise. So much waste. Was Ben the only one who wanted accountability? Did anyone even have a clue at this point why the US was fighting in that godforsaken place? He felt like calling up his senator and asking her for a justifiable synopsis of the US position and military objectives for that interminable war. The only reason he didn't was that he knew he'd just get some politician-speak, filled with bullshit rhetoric that would send his blood pressure into orbit.

Ben looked down. Despite his best efforts, the names of the dead soldiers were still partially visible on the crumpled newspaper in the wastebasket. He took off his glasses and laid them on his desk, exposing his lean, angular face and intense blue eyes, now dark with the frustration and anger he couldn't seem to shake.

He leaned back in his chair, rubbing the back of his neck.

He thought about the parents of the young men and what they had gone through when they were notified of their sons' deaths. He'd once watched a documentary on the military protocol for getting dead US soldiers home. Even with decades of practice, there was just no good way to tell any parent their child was gone.

He knew that from experience.

He feels the air leave his lungs, doubling over as if he has been punched in the stomach. He grasps for the doorframe in order to stay standing. Bree is wailing, her body half on the bed as she pleads with Jayden to stay alive . . .

The police officer that night had crashed some "save the whales" (or dinosaurs) thing Bree had talked him into attending. How surreal to be dressed in a tux, holding a champagne flute, when you find out your kid is in critical condition in some hospital. The officer had launched into the details of Jayden's condition. He was still talking as Ben scanned the room for Bree. He spotted her across the room, deep in conversation, blissfully unaware of what she was about to learn.

He'd made his way through the crowd, then gently taken her arm and led her nearly to the exit door before uttering the words he never imagined he'd have to say: "Sweetheart . . . there's been an accident. Jayden is . . ." He couldn't say the words. "Jayden needs us."

The police had escorted them to the hospital under the protection of lights and sirens. Ben was grateful for the powerful engine of their Maserati sedan as they trailed the flashing lights through the LA traffic toward the hospital. Whenever he could, Ben had glanced at Bree. He'd silently willed her strength. *Bree, hold on, love; we will get there.*

Once they'd arrived at the hospital, Ben and Bree had rushed through the double doors, intent on finding their son. When they entered the trauma unit, they were not prepared for the sights and sounds of so many people caught up in a battle for life. Some people were grouped in clusters, arms around each other, seeking solace in hope and prayers.

Others were not so stoic, and their wails broke through the cacophony of conversation as doctors shared harrowing updates. Still others sat alone and silent, staring off with no one present to comfort them or share their sorrows.

As they stood frozen in the middle of all the human drama—Ben in his Armani tux and Bree in a floor-length, sequined gown—they'd felt like they had walked into a scene from an apocalyptic movie.

Eventually, they were escorted to a surgery waiting area on another floor, and finally, into a private ICU room. Jayden had lain motionless, barely recognizable under all the bandages. Ben had tried not to wince as his eyes followed the swollen shape of his son's head down to the ventilator that forced air into his lungs at regular intervals. His boy.

Oh my God . . . oh my God . . . oh my God . . .

The neuro and cardiac surgeons had funneled in and out, looking for positive responses or worsening conditions. Each took the time to inform Ben and Bree that they were dealing with a "worst-case scenario" and that the odds against Jayden's survival were minimal.

"I'm afraid it is only the heroic efforts of the first responders, and your son's incredibly strong heart, that have kept him alive this long," the cardiac surgeon had explained. "The next few hours will be critical in determining the outcome."

Ben and Bree could only nod, silent with the shock of what they were hearing.

"One more thing," the surgeon added, "and again, I'm sorry to have to discuss this right now—I need to let you know that according to his driver license, he has elected to be an organ donor. At some point, we may need to make decisions that . . ."

Ben hadn't heard another word the surgeon was saying. He could see his mouth moving, but not discern the words themselves.

Organs? Jayden's organs?

He and Bree had stood at the foot of Jayden's bed that night, watching as the medical warriors continued to fight. As the surgeon had predicted, that night had proved to be an epic battle for Jayden's life. Despite the Herculean efforts of every doctor and every possible medical response, they had lost him.

Much later, Ben had gone over every option, every possible scenario, looking for anything that might have changed the outcome for his son. He'd examined everything from Jayden selecting USC as a school, to transferring him to another hospital for different care and different surgeons. But in the end, it had been clear that there was nothing Ben could have done to prevent Jayden's death, short of keeping his son in a bubble. One thing he'd been sure of—neither he nor Bree would ever be the same again.

♛

Ben looked away from the wastebasket and up to the skyline beyond the window of his office. Not just any office, but a corner office, in a building he had designed and built himself. Bree had nicknamed it the Taj Mahal because of how puffed up he'd been over the international awards and recognition it had received. Having his name on this building had always meant so much to him. It still did. After all, he had bucked a privileged childhood filled with expectations and opportunities as the son of a renowned surgeon to become the senior partner of one of the top architectural firms in the world. His father had wanted him to follow in his footsteps, and as Benjamin Stanton III, he had in many ways. But, while both of them had felt called to work with their hands, Ben's patients had been steel and concrete instead of the human body.

There was something about creating a structure from nothing but raw materials that made him feel almost godlike.

But now, of course, he knew he wasn't anything close to that. He couldn't be. Mainly because he couldn't stomach the idea of standing around, twiddling his thumbs, while innocent people suffered and died, refusing to get involved. Oh, the explanation for the lack of any divine intervention was always cloaked under the guise of "free will" or some other kind of carefully crafted religious dogma, but he knew the truth. It was just another version of "pass the buck" rhetoric.

In the early days after Jayden had died, Ben had confronted God. "Either you're God or you're not!" he had yelled, pounding the steering wheel with clenched fists. "If you are, get in the game and quit letting this shit happen!"

Ironically, or maybe not, God had been too busy with the "twiddling" to answer him.

Irony. The word kept dogging him. Things just didn't seem to turn out the way they should. Not just God's absence or Jayden's death. Even before Jayden died, in fact. For example, there was the time Jayden had come home from some "do-gooder" summer trip and announced that he wanted to become a doctor. A *doctor.* He'd made the announcement over breakfast, prompting Ben to glance up from his coffee and paper. He'd given his son a scathing look, while mentally shaking his fist at his dead father. It had only taken one generation and Ben Sr. had managed to reach out from the grave to repay Ben for choosing architectural engineering instead of medicine.

Eventually Ben had resigned himself to the idea. After all, Jayden was a good kid. If he wanted to be a doctor, then let him. But it had been a moot point. A couple of joyriding gang thugs had made the final decision about his son's future. Poof. Done. No intervention and no explanation from the universe—or from Whoever claimed to be in charge.

In the two years since, Ben had been forced to reexamine his views about life and the nature of things. What he'd concluded was that he didn't like what he saw in the world. Just like the names in the journal today. Who would have thought that simply driving on a city street would have been as dangerous as fighting in Afghanistan? At least in war you could carry a weapon and defend yourself.

No matter how hard Ben tried to find an explanation that made sense, it didn't matter. In the end, nothing changed the outcome. Dead kids.

He was suddenly aware that his office was taking on the rich hues of the deepening purple sunset. He glanced at his watch, stood up, and grabbed the keys to the Maserati. Bree would be waiting, and he didn't want her to be home alone.

As he closed his office door behind him, he decided that all the untamed chaos and injustice meant one thing: a God with no balls *and* no logic.

And that wasn't good enough for Benjamin Stanton III.

Chapter 3

LONDON

"**H**ere's to all of the poor-paying acting roles you didn't get offered," Jules teased, holding up a pint of brown ale. Her slender hands and fine features were in stark contrast to her steely confidence.

"And here's to all of the news stories you were never asked to write," Rob countered, keeping the playing field level as he clinked his glass against to hers.

"And . . . ?"

"And . . . thank you for talking me into this gig," Rob said, giving Jules the win she was looking for.

They both laughed, and Rob signaled for the bartender to bring them the Dom Perignon that was waiting on ice. Every year they returned here, to their favorite pub in their old neighborhood, to toast the night fourteen years ago when they had "rebooted" their lives. That had been the night they'd decided to abandon their creative dreams and launch the business that had brought them their tremendous success.

As they watched the bubbles slowly rise to the surface of the champagne, it gave each of them time to reflect on their journey to this moment.

Sixteen years ago, Julie Hamilton had been a budding journalist right out of a state college, an academic whiz kid, and former student body president. Rob Bergman was supporting his equally budding acting career by working in the IT department of an insurance company in their Podunk hometown of Spokane, Washington. They were paying their bills but missing their dreams.

And that's when they hatched the idea of living abroad.

In the beginning, their London adventure had sounded so noble and highbrow.

"Well, blokes," Rob had said, in his best Sir Lawrence Olivier impersonation. "We're off to the bright lights of the BBC, in the land of Shakespeare, chips and eggs, and the House of Windsor." He'd made the speech at a party where friends and family had gathered to send Julie and him across the pond. Had he been paying better attention, he might have noticed the many eye rolls at the pie-in-the-sky speech.

But he hadn't, and after a small courthouse wedding, Rob and Julie had taken their meager savings, a love of fish and chips, and one solid work contact, and launched themselves into their dream.

The contact had turned out to be a bust, and they'd soon found the reality of subsistence employment in a foreign country to be as bleak as the relentless grey skies above. Julie had found uninspiring work in a clerical pool for an advertising agency, and Rob became a bartender with dwindling acting opportunities. The decision to create a "plan B" came to both of them as they were looking for yet a cheaper version of their cheap flat.

"Good God! Can they actually think we would want to slink down the hall to use a public water closet!?" Julie had exclaimed to their leasing agent on one of their many flat-hunting excursions. Julie had reached the end of her tolerance for tiny kitchens, poor plumbing, and old appliances. "And that stove! That's a life-threatening experience waiting to happen!"

"I'm not sure what you are expecting for the pittance you are able to afford," the agent had said with a sniff. "London has some of the most expensive real estate in the world. Unless you are willing to commute from outside this area, you are going to continue to be relegated to this level of properties. Certainly, you must be able to read those tea leaves!"

Both Rob and Julie could feel her condescension. When they parted ways, the agent, in her Chanel suit, had climbed into her equally impressive Range Rover and driven off, leaving them to wallow in their poverty.

"What a witch! Where did we dig her up?" Rob had huffed. "I mean, I know our budget is low, but come on!"

"Yeah. Who does she think she is, some Oxford grad?" Julie had said. "Let's go find a pub. I'm hungry and very thirsty!"

She'd marched down the street toward the entrance to the tube, with Rob trailing behind.

Julie still couldn't avoid the sting of what her father used to refer to as the place where "the rubber meets the road." The agent had only been the messenger—and she probably *was* an Oxford grad, for all Julie knew. The agent wasn't the issue. Julie knew that. The issue was reality.

An hour later, over pints of ale and bangers and mash, Rob and Julie had finally admitted their defeat.

"We aren't going to make our dreams come true, are we, Rob?" Julie had said, the ale toying with her pent-up emotions. She could feel the tears lurking behind the question, and she knew the answer before Rob could even respond.

"Nope, it hasn't turned out the way we thought it would. But hey, we've given it a damn good run!" He could feel the defeat at a deep soul level. There was no way to explain to Julie how inadequate he'd felt at not being able to provide for her.

But Julie wasn't wasting time on what hadn't worked out. Suddenly she'd had an idea.

"I could do what she does! How hard could it be to take people around to see places they can't afford?" she'd reasoned. "A little schooling and some weekend work. What have we got to lose?"

"We?" Rob had retorted. "Oh no. Don't rope *me* into this. No way am I going to spend my life in a suit, acting like those tight-assed people."

But in the end she had—and he had.

From the beginning, their plan had been simply to earn enough money to afford a better flat, and then a larger one, with working heat and hot water, and then maybe a family down the line. But before long, they'd found themselves the owners of a thriving real estate agency. They'd discovered they loved what they did and spent most of their waking hours engrossed in all aspects of their business. They became obsessed, the thought of having children, dogs, or even living plants a distant memory.

Julie, now known as Jules Bergman, managing partner of Bergman Associates, had become an international contract specialist handling complicated, multinational investment deals.

Rob, now Robert Bergman, had traded in his beloved jeans for suits, his beard for an expensively maintained goatee, and commuting on the tube for ownership of a luxury Range Rover. He handled all the backroom operations of the firm. His specialty was everything tech. As one of the early adopters of the web, he had taken basic programming skills and turned them into a niche expertise as he moved up the food chain of the tech world.

Together, they were a successful and formidable team that had parlayed their discontent into success.

Until the arrival of a new client changed their lives forever.

It had started with a breach in the firewall of their newly constructed website. At first Rob had been strangely impressed by the anonymous intruder and the level of sophistication he or they exhibited. Intrigued, Rob had engaged the interloper, inquiring about his or her identify and intentions.

The answer was swift and to the point. The hacker informed Rob that he needed a specific type and location of property and wanted the transaction to be untraceable. The payment the hacker offered would be twice what the Bergman agency typically cleared in a year. Rob had discussed the unusual request with Jules, and they had decided that, while it was enticing, they would pass.

Rob declined the offer and thought that would be the end of it.

The next day, the balances in the Bergman business accounts were zeroed out. The money had simply disappeared.

The hacker had suggested they reconsider. They had. Their accounts were restored, and they transacted the first of several clandestine acquisitions for their new client. These "off the books" deals were infrequent, sometimes as much as a year apart. Rob and Julie eventually stopped worrying about what their properties were being used for, and convinced themselves their client was probably just evading taxes. In the meantime, they continued raking in the money.

Over the course of ten years, they had become the go-to players for the kind of properties not discussed on their flashy website—strategically located warehouses, manufacturing sites requiring special build-outs, and safe houses—all involving bogus companies and pseudo-operations. What all these deals had in common was a deep well of deception and anonymity, coupled with a rich payload for Rob and Jules. They had finally learned to stop seeking answers and to accept what they didn't know—and would likely never know.

But their willingness to rationalize the danger of what they were doing had grown thin. They were plagued with a nagging sense of the dangerous side of their success. This current job made Rob finally admit what he and Julie had suspected for a long time—that their greediness had drawn them into a dark web of entanglement with increasingly dangerous players.

Together they had decided that as soon as this project—a warehouse they had outfitted in Budapest, Hungary—was completed, it would be their last gig. It was time to walk away, if they could—and a Swiss bank account flush with their ill-gotten earnings would help make that happen.

Fourteen years after their decision to go into real estate, they were on the threshold of a new life.

Rob looked at Jules across the pub table and raised his champagne glass.

"Here's to a new beginning," Rob toasted.

"A new beginning," Jules echoed, looking into Rob's eyes.

They both knew what that would mean.

"One and done!" Rob said, and they toasted again, their eyes locked in a determined pact.

Chapter 4

A WAREHOUSE SOMEWHERE IN BUDAPEST, HUNGARY

Three young Arab men stood around a table that held several computers and monitors. With intense fascination, they studied one of the oversized monitors displaying a livestream video of playing children.

Sitting at the table, a teammate used a keyboard to manipulate the flight of a drone more than five hundred kilometers away. The drone had moved into position and was now hovering over the unsuspecting targets.

With a few keystrokes, the man at the computer delivered the *coup de gras*, and the drone released its invisible payload, silent yet deadly over the small schoolyard and children below.

All four men began to cheer, excited in the way young men get when they are about to win a video game or a sporting event.

A fifth man stood apart, watching the live test as it unfolded. Amir, the leader of the operation, watched the younger men with amusement. They saw it as a thrilling accomplishment. Amir saw it as his life and his future. This weapon, once perfected, would usher in a new age of power in the war against the West. Most important, it would prove to his uncle, the great Al-Zawahiri, that Amir was the logical choice to lead the next wave of attacks on the infidels.

Amir's plan was nothing short of brilliant. And what better place to test a weapon than on an off-grid orphanage filled with children who already didn't exist to the outside world?

The orphanage and staff had been in such dire need, it had been ridiculously easy to win their trust. First, Amir had sent food and clothing, and then later the offer of medicines and vaccines. Of course, the director of the impoverished orphanage had no way of knowing that the vaccine had been embedded with a deadly, trigger-released bioagent.

And that trigger had just been delivered.

The vaccine had been developed in this very warehouse, which Amir had purchased through a London real estate agency specializing in off-record properties. This had enabled Amir to build a bogus pharmaceutical company, putting together a website, an IT team, and even a medical service van equipped with technicians to vaccinate the children.

Amir wanted his uncle to envision the idea of whole cities in the West, filled with "vaccinated" citizens, rendering them essentially mass hostages—without ever pulling a trigger or detonating a single bomb.

Amir smiled as he imagined presidents and prime ministers lining up to fulfill the demands of Al-Zawahiri before the deadly time bombs in the bodies of their citizens were triggered.

His uncle would have his every whim delivered to him on a silver platter: money, weapons, properties—not to mention powerful kingdoms brought to their knees before him.

And he would have Amir to thank.

The sound of cheering jolted Amir back to the warehouse. The young men were now slapping hands and backs as if their favorite soccer team had just scored the winning goal in the World Cup.

On the monitor, the images transmitted from the drone showed that the test appeared to have met with 100 percent success.

The playground was littered with dead children, scattered in lifeless clumps across the grass.

Amir stepped forward from the shadows to acknowledge the young men's success. Seeing their leader, the young men shouted, *"Allahu Akbar! Allahu Akbar!"*

For Amir, what they had just accomplished had nothing to do with pleasing Allah.

Chapter 5

An Orphanage in Rural Romania

Iona unlocked the double doors of the storage room and swung each one open wide, revealing nearly depleted stores of food and supplies. She hoped against hope that this month's shipment from the government would be one of the larger ones.

The delivery driver approached, pulling a wheeled pallet of bags of rice and a few cases of canned goods. Iona's heart sank. Her prayers had gone unanswered.

The man averted his eyes from Iona's as he wheeled the meager goods into the cavernous space. She signed the invoice, and he gave her a slight shrug of apology and then left.

The inadequate supplies shouldn't have surprised her; she was used to it. After all, she'd been the director of this orphanage for thirty years. It was just that with her decision to open a second orphanage in a neighboring village—without the government's approval—she needed this food to stretch further than it ever had before. Thank goodness for the gardens that had just been planted and for the unexpected help of a recent benefactor.

"Mrs. Dalca?" one of the young staff members spoke from the storage room doorway, interrupting Iona's ruminating. "You have a call."

"Can you please take a message, Marina? I need to get this food inventoried and separated."

"I don't think so, Mrs. Dalca. It sounds like an emergency . . . It's Elena, and she's very upset."

"All right. I'll take it in my office."

Iona swung the doors shut and locked them, another unfortunate but necessary precaution in a rural area filled with poverty; it was a sad irony that the children in her care were safer than their food supplies. She hurried into her office and picked up the receiver.

"Elena, what's wrong?"

Iona's question was met with sobbing and incoherent phrases.

"Elena, Elena, stop. I need you to calm down so that I can understand what you are saying." Iona steadied her hand, holding the receiver with her other hand to keep it from shaking against her ear. Elena was sobbing harder now. Something about children. The playground attendant sounded terrified. Iona tried again.

"What has happened? . . . Please speak slowly, I am not understanding . . . A child has died? Which child? Had she been ill? . . . *All*? What are you saying?"

Her legs weak and shaking, Iona dropped into the chair behind her desk. She could feel the effects of the adrenaline pumping through her body.

"Please repeat . . . Every child is dead? How? Was there an illness? Something more sudden?" Even as Iona voiced the questions, her mind was racing through possible scenarios. Were there children in this building in danger, too?

Between sobs, Elena explained that she and the other attendant had carried the fallen children inside and attempted to revive them. They had not been successful.

Twenty children, from five to nine years old, had dropped dead without any symptoms or warnings. This made no sense. And why hadn't the adults been affected? They lived in the same building, had eaten the same food, and were at the same playground at the time of the accident. Accident? Attack? Iona was too numb to know what to call it or what to do next.

"Elena, lock everything up. Don't let anyone from the village inside until I get there."

As she hung up the phone, she glanced around her office as if the answers to the questions racing through her mind would somehow be found tacked up on the walls or stuffed under the piles of paperwork. She was going to have to let her superiors know. Not just about the children's deaths, but about everything else.

Iona stood and walked on wobbly legs across the room to an old armoire. She cracked open a door, reached up to the back of the top shelf, removed a glass and decanter, and carried them back to her desk.

She didn't wait to sit before pouring a shot of the locally fermented *pálinka*. She swallowed it slowly, letting it burn its way down her throat before finally taking a breath.

Oh, mother of God, how has this happened?

Why? When all she had ever tried to do was save the very children that were now apparently dead? She had risked everything, yet that sacrifice had not been sufficient. If only she weren't facing this alone. If only she had someone to help her, someone who understood why she had done all of this.

She needed Jayden.

Chapter 6

Los Angeles

Ben kissed Bree as he took the glass of Cabernet from her hand. This had become the new ritual for them after they had lost Jayden. They would greet each other at the door like a couple of POWs, grateful for surviving another day, while at the same time inspecting each other for new wounds inflicted by the day's events.

"You okay, honey?" Ben asked tenderly, taking notice of Bree's troubled expression. "You look . . . well, not quite yourself." He hesitated, not sure how far to push her. "Did something happen at the office today?"

He scanned her face for information she was unlikely to share. Getting to the bottom of something with Bree was often like unraveling a complicated engineering puzzle. She was stoic in the way of . . . oh . . . Joan of Arc. The key had always been her eyes, but before he could get a good bead on them, she had turned away from him and started walking back through the house, another unspoken ritual.

After winding their way through the land mine of memories and quiet, dark spaces, they made it to the sanctuary of their outdoor living space. Bree had already spread a small table with more wine, stoneware, beautiful linens, and a charcuterie platter. Elegant yet simple, and so like Bree, Ben thought.

He looked around the patio. The space was jaw-dropping, filled with exotic woods, dramatic lighting, stonework, flowering plants, and the now-blazing fireplace. And the backdrop to it all was the spectacular LA skyline, illuminated by city lights against the darkening purple skies.

Ben marveled once again at what he and Bree had created together. The space was the talk of their social circles and the location of many events linked to the boards and causes they served.

Yet for the two of them, it had become the haven in which they could grieve, free from caring, concerned eyes. It was in this space that they could be themselves, breathe, and maybe even ultimately survive.

Ben sat in one of the cushioned rattan chairs, close to Bree, so he could hold her hand and get a clearer view of her face. There were definitely signs of a storm brewing in her expression. He studied her beautiful face, hoping to see some clue. What was he seeing? Anger? No. And not the usual mixture of resignation and grief. This was more like . . . fear. Fear? What had made his courageous Bree suddenly afraid?

Before he could ask, she spoke.

"Zach's graduation announcement came today."

"Wow . . . Already?" Ben searched for something—anything—to say. "It's been almost two years; I guess that makes sense."

Bree didn't respond.

He waited.

She was still silent.

He looked into her eyes.

He didn't like what he was seeing.

This was a new aspect of Bree's grief Ben had not witnessed before. It was unnerving to see her so shattered, almost like that first night in the hospital when she had been forced to kiss Jayden goodbye and let him go.

Ben was determined to take action. He cleared his throat.

"Listen, Bree. I've been wanting to talk with you for a while about us—about what to do moving forward with this. . . life we have now. We can't stay in this limbo forever. I know you are struggling. I also think you are getting worn out by trying to show the world that you are not. I can see it. We need to do something. Jayden wouldn't want—"

Bree held up a hand. "Please don't say what I think you are going to say, that you presume to know what Jayden would want us to do . . ." Her voice drifted off into the thin, emotionless air between them.

"I am going to say it, honey, because I think his may be the only voice we can hear well enough to help us. I have watched you with friends. I know how hard it is for you to be around Cynthia and Zach. I may not know your every thought or feeling like I used to, but I still know you. All the graduations and parties coming up this spring are going to be more than we can or even should get through." Ben made sure to include himself so that Bree wouldn't feel like some specimen under a microscope. But clearly she needed help, and he was the one to provide it.

She dropped her gaze to the flower pots artistically grouped throughout the patio. They were overflowing with thriving plants, with perfectly matched colors and textures. She was seeing them for the first time. They had clearly been professionally planted and cared for, and she wondered when this had happened. She felt so out of touch with her life.

Is this what grief does? Robs you of any sense of connection with your life? Leave you adrift in a sea of isolation?

Ben interrupted her musings.

"Remember that website Jayden was always talking about? A site where people exchange properties so they have a more authentic experience living abroad for a year? A complete lifestyle exchange, when you think about it. We aren't using our place in Big Bear, and I thought maybe—"

"You want to sleep in someone else's sheets and eat off someone else's dishes? For a year? That doesn't sound like you, Ben. You don't even like four-star hotels."

"Yeah, I know. But Jayden always wanted us to do something like this as a family and—even though things are, you know, different now—I thought if we did it anyway, now, it might help us feel more, well, comfortable or homey or something."

Grasping at anything that might cause Bree to engage with the idea, Ben added, "Jayden always told us we were missing out on authentic experiences by staying at those exclusive properties you always dig up. He kept saying we should get into the small places. The backroads . . ."

"Oh God . . . just the thought of the effort. We'd have to get pictures of the Big Bear property, and then do the website thing, the background checks, vetting candidates . . . Ugh. I can't even think about it."

"We still have all the Realtor's photos from when we were going to list it last year. Don't worry about the other details. I'll get it set up, and then we can decide if we want to move forward," Ben said, hiding his relief at the possibility that Bree was warming to the idea.

"So, let me get this straight. We offer our five-bedroom estate, located in some of the most prime real estate property in Big Bear, California, to total strangers. And we move to—what? Some one-bedroom, whitewashed, stucco cave without running water on some remote island? For an entire year? Just so we can show our dead son that we are not part of the 1 percent and that we can rub elbows with the masses?"

She was on a roll. Without waiting for Ben to respond, she continued her rant.

"And the magical result of this glorious plan will be meaning, purpose, and peace? Ben, I know you graduated summa from Stanford, but you can't really bullshit me into believing you are this simple at heart, right? Who have you been talking to—my mother? No, wait; this isn't her style—even at eighty-two she's more of a 'get back on the damn horse' person. Have you been talking to some touchy-feely, know-nothing therapist? I'm not interested in having another quack tell me how to—"

"Actually, none of the above," Ben said through a clenched jaw. Sometimes Bree could push his buttons, but he felt she was close to giving in, and he didn't want to derail the moment.

He took a deep breath. "Look, Bree, I was reading the *Journal* today, and the first thing I read about was three more dead soldiers in Afghanistan, all around Jayden's age. And I'm so sick and tired of hearing about the young men we are losing over there, and so fed up with how they are referred to as 'honorable sacrifices.' They seem like senseless and extravagant losses to me, considering we are sending them to die for a cause no one can even articulate." The veins in his neck were standing at attention, and he could feel the flush spread across his face. "And then I thought about you and me and the equally senseless loss we keep trying to survive, and it hit me like a ton of bricks. There's enough senseless loss in the world. I'm done waiting for some 'fate' or 'God' to drop the other shoe. And it will drop, Bree. Either you will lose me or I will lose you, and we will be sitting here wondering why we didn't hold on tighter."

"Ben, what are you talking about?"

I'm not going to lose you in a battle we can't—or won't—articulate. Every time we hit an emotional land mine like this graduation announcement, I see your resolve weaken. I see the light in your eyes dim a bit more. I feel like I'm losing you too. And today I decided that I—*we*—are not going down without a fight! I love you, and I am going to do everything I can to make sure we not only survive the loss of Jayden, but that we find a way to thrive—not *despite the loss* of him, but *because* of him. Jayden is the most tangible evidence of how special our love is, and it's for him that we need to somehow change direction." Ben felt a pang of guilt at having pulled out the "Jayden" card, but he brushed those feelings aside in his determination to save the woman he loved.

Bree had not been prepared for so much raw honesty. The graduation announcement had left her undone, and now hearing these words from Ben . . .

He did know her, damn it! He was the one person she couldn't hide from, although she thought she'd been doing a passable job of it these past two years. He was right. What alternative did they have? Did she really want to stay here and suffer through the graduation season, every weekend filled with parties and backyard barbecues celebrating their friends' children and their bright futures?

And if she couldn't? Then she'd have to make up excuses, endure the pity of others, and feel the loss more acutely than she already did. There was no way to navigate this without more suffering.

She turned and looked into Ben's beautiful blue eyes. They were Jayden's eyes too. Ben was right on the second point as well. There was a big part of her, a growing part, that wanted to just lie down and sleep until she was holding her son in her arms again. The only thing keeping her from that was this man, her love, trying so hard to keep her going. She just couldn't leave him holding the whole bag of grief and misery by himself. It was too selfish . . . but oh . . . how the snake hissed.

With sheer determination, she dragged her attention back to Ben.

"Okay, Ben. I'll give this a try. You are right. I can't go through this graduation season here. I thought enough time had passed, but it hasn't."

Ben stood and pulled her up into his arms.

Bree felt some of the tension in her body begin to ease. After a moment she asked, "But do you mind if we just tell people we are heading up to Big Bear for a while? I'd rather not share this whole vacation swap idea. People will think we've lost our minds!"

Ben was happy to say or do anything necessary to keep her moving forward. "Absolutely," said Ben. You find those property photos. I'll start working on a post for the website. I want to make sure our personal information is secured—you can't be too safe these days."

"Oh, brother. Now I *know* this is a crazy idea. Here we are, giving these strangers our house for a year, and you're worried about personal information . . . "

Chapter 7

CIA Headquarters, Langley

The third knock on the door finally broke through Mac's intense concentration.

He'd been reading a report about some kids who had died in a home for orphans in Romania, of all places. The facts weren't adding up, and in addition, it was triggering that "sixth sense" thing he was known for.

Reluctantly, he closed the file and shoved his chair back, slammed it against the wall, stormed toward his closed office door, and jerked it open. He knitted his bushy eyebrows together and glared into the eyes of a punk who looked about a third of his age with about a tenth of his IQ. From the official-looking packet in the kid's hand, Mac could only assume the poor soul had drawn the short straw in the HR department.

"Excuse me, sir, uh . . . Mr. McFarland . . . um . . . I'm here to . . ."

"Spit it out kid," Mac barked. "You're burnin' my daylight." Mac was both irritated and irritable, and this twit was standing on his last nerve.

"Here is your official transition package." The kid was starting to recover his equilibrium, despite the daunting image of the angry, disheveled man in the office doorway.

"Ha! Transition. Is that what they are calling it these days?" Mac could barely hide his contempt for the bureaucratic side of government employment. Transition?

He wondered if this was what Secretariat had heard after thundering to that magnificent win at the Belmont: "And here, sir, is a wonderful field of knee-deep green grass, Kentucky blue skies, and a hundred beautiful fillies waiting just for you." To an average horse, that would have sounded like the deal of the century. To *that* horse? Nothing close to the feel of the bars of the starting gate or the sound of thundering hooves in fast pursuit.

Idiots!

"Once you've had an opportunity to review the packet," the kid was saying, "please feel free to contact us for an appointment to discuss any questions regarding the information, separation dates, ongoing benefit options, etc."

Mac made absolutely zero response as he locked eyes with the kid, all the while wondering to himself which Ivy League institution had spit him out onto the payroll of the CIA headquarters in Langley, Virginia. As the kid inched backward into the hallway, Mac couldn't help thinking it didn't matter which school, because these kids were all coming out of the system with the same skinny-legged suits, weird-ass glasses, zero common sense, and not a set of rocks in the bunch . . .

"Uh, sir, one more thing," the kid stammered. "We have scheduled a small reception to honor your service and to celebrate this next exciting chapter of your life. It will be on your last formal day, also listed in the packet." He said these last words as he continued backing down the hallway toward freedom.

This last move made Mac grunt out loud. The kid couldn't get out of Mac's stall of an office fast enough. How ironic that in this world of covert operations—dealing with some of the worst elements of the human condition—it was "old age" that scared this young man the most! Ha. Well, didn't that just say something about this screwed-up generation?

"Idiot!" Mac muttered, as he slammed the door. Then he quickly opened it again, just in time to watch the HR/errand boy break into a sprint down the hallway. Shaking his head in disgust, Mac slammed the door again.

The world's in trouble if this generation is the one we are going to be relying on.

Getting this official notification of his "retirement" knocked the wind out of him. In fact, he'd become so engrossed in his work lately that if his bank account hadn't fluctuated every two weeks, he might have forgotten he was actually employed by someone. But clearly, the US government had not forgotten.

And not letting that employment go a day beyond the retirement cutoff was apparently far more important than letting him finish the case he was working on. *What's a little impending doom?*

As he made his way back to his desk, he tried to keep from thinking about the future, but it was no use. The thought of being forced to leave his life's work felt as abrupt as the end of a bungee cord drop.

Especially now, when there was so much at stake.

Mac was known for being a plodder. A workhorse. As a career CIA intelligence analyst at the Langley headquarters, he'd spent the last few years doggedly tracking an extremist organization. They were thought to have deep ties to one of the most brutal jihadist networks operating in the Middle East. Emboldened by recent terrorist attacks, this group continued to leave a trail of escalating carnage and mass destruction. The entire US military was on the hunt for their leader, Al-Zawahiri.

And now Mac suspected he was onto something.

Sliding his reading glasses higher on his nose, Mac returned to studying the Romanian report, looking for anything else that might support the theory he'd been noodling on before the knock on his door. He could sense something, and it was ugly. Not in the usual way of traditional warfare, but in the innovative way these terrorist groups kept finding to cause death, suffering, and destruction. They always seemed to be one step ahead of the good guys, kind of like a mutating "superbug."

Something wasn't sitting well with him.

He'd gotten his first real lead a couple months ago with an encrypted email referring to a warehouse lease in Budapest tied to a bogus pharmaceutical company.

Since then, he'd continued scanning intel around Budapest, to no avail—until he intercepted an email a few weeks ago containing coordinates of a small village in Romania and a vague reference to some kind of live test. Mac might not have pursued it—except for the fact that the encryption pattern had been similar to that of the email referring to the Budapest lease.

Then, this morning, he'd unearthed the report on deaths of the Romanian orphans. It was originally an internal report but had been released to the World Health Organization. The file described a catastrophic illness hitting a group of orphans living in a home on the outskirts of a small village. Usually, this kind of news would have been buried under governmental red tape. Especially since the home was being covertly used to hide older children who would have normally aged out of the orphanage system. Apparently, the director was trying to protect them from being sent to what amounted to government-sanctioned internment farms.

Something about the swift and deadly nature of this lethal outbreak must have made someone nervous. No wonder it eventually ended up with the World Health Organization. No country in this new "global family" wanted to get caught withholding information on a potential pandemic—as attested to by even the Chinese government's new openness concerning recent incidents of mysterious mutating strains of bird flu viruses.

"Mutating Chinese bird flu? Ha!" Mac said aloud, speaking to the corner of his office, as he sometimes did when there was no one around to listen to him pontificate. That wall was a better listener than most of the folks he knew.

"No surprise those folks keep getting sick, given what they are willing to eat. Monkey brains. Bird shit soup. But here I go again. Digressing. Or as my dear Gloria used to say, getting caught up in my 'bah-humbug-we're-all-going-down-the-toilet,' old-fart thinking. As if the world isn't going to hell in a handbasket. Of course, what did I expect, marrying an eternal sunshine-up-her-ass optimist. Gawd, I miss that woman. And look at me now . . . digressing from my digression, and no one to rein me in!"

He turned his attention back to the report. Apparently, there had been some type of toxic gas leak or airborne chemical that had overcome the children in a matter of minutes. The notes read like something out of one of those new sci-fi/horror movies the kids were all watching today. Horrific and unexplainable. Dozens of kids slumping to the ground in ghostly dances, dead in a matter of seconds.

In the movie, Mac would have expected aliens to land and a fight between good and evil to begin, only in this real-life version, there were no aliens. Just a lone wolf director of a kid's orphanage, writing with a pleading urgency in response to an eerie and inexplicable killer.

The report ended abruptly, the attached official government notes merely recommending "a review of sanitation protocols, including an order to establish additional guidelines for enhanced sterilization procedures for all nearby facilities."

"Whatever all of that rigamarole even means," Mac muttered.

There was no further word on any fallout from the report, or what had happened to the director once the report was filed. The fact that these kids had died on her watch while she was hiding them from the government couldn't have helped her case.

This is where Mac was grateful he had that stubborn streak his late wife had always complained about.

He just never gave up. And now it was paying off.

He thought about the encrypted email he'd intercepted a couple weeks ago. The one referring to some kind of live test. The one giving the coordinates of a small village.

He knew now from the Romanian report that the home where the children had died was on the outskirts of that very village, three hundred miles from the off-record warehouse in Budapest.

He noodled on that implausible connection for a while, pacing circles in his tiny office, trying to play the devil's advocate with himself. After wrestling with the pieces of the puzzle through lunch and most of the afternoon, he sat down hard in his chair, his heart heavy with resignation.

"God help us all if I am right—and I know I am," Mac said, swiveling in his chair and letting the corner of the room in on his most troubling thoughts. "What I need to know is where and when and how ugly!"

From what he could tell, it looked like his group of jihadist bastards had gotten ahold of some bad juju. It also looked like they had taken it for a test run on some unknown and unsuspecting children. This already told him more than he wanted to know about their psychological makeup. What it didn't tell him was where they were now and what they intended to do with the rest of their Kool-Aid.

And now, he had this blasted retirement looming, and he was pretty sure he was going to have to go "off the rez" to get a handle on this thing. Something was telling him it was going to be a wild ride. A swan song to end all swan songs.

Mac turned back to his desk, punched up a secure line, and dialed the oldest, most reliable source he knew.

Chapter 8

LOS ANGELES

The next morning, in his office, Ben logged on to his computer and googled "vacation property exchanges." He was shocked to see that there were literally hundreds of websites. When Jayden, Bree, and Ben had first talked about living abroad for Jayden's gap year between USC and medical school, there had been maybe a handful of sites to choose from.

Damn. Airbnb. Vrbo. Vacation villas. How am I supposed to choose?

He decided to start with the type of properties in which he would be willing to live. Bree was right—he really didn't like the idea of living in someone else's house. It wasn't exactly like he was a full-blown germophobe (his side of the bathroom vanity always looked like some kind of explosion had occurred), but he had an aversion to the germs of others.

But he had gotten Bree to say yes to this crazy idea, and he vowed to stay in the slums of Calcutta if it meant she was willing to go.

He found a site that handled the type and value of property he thought might make for an acceptable compromise between his taste and what Jayden would have said they needed to experience. The site was very detailed, with a large selection of location options.

He decided this would be a good site on which to post their Big Bear home. Working with one of the website's in-house designers, he put together a listing that looked so appealing he thought briefly about canceling the whole plan and just heading up to their own place in Big Bear!

But Ben knew that wouldn't take them far enough away from their pain.

He decided to focus on Europe and, in particular, the area around the Mediterranean Sea.

It's going to have to be far enough away that Bree isn't even tempted to think about graduations and neighborhood parties, he acknowledged to himself.

He found exactly what he was hoping to find.

A few nights later, after Ben and Bree had finished dinner and were savoring a glass of wine on the patio under the stars, Ben opened up his laptop on the low table between them.

"So, honey, I want to show you what I've come up with as a possible site for our home exchange adventure."

Bree looked so startled, Ben thought for a minute she was going to back out. A year abroad had sounded better a few nights ago, when the graduation announcement had just been delivered. But since the announcement had arrived, Bree had been unusually quiet, and that, along with the look on her face, made Ben forge ahead.

"The property exchange company has an excellent reputation," he said persuasively. "Higher-end properties. Great amenities. Our place stacks up nicely."

As he was talking, Ben had pulled up the website to show Bree the page that had been created to showcase their place in Big Bear. Ben made sure to click quickly through the photos showcasing their home, hoping the pictures wouldn't trigger painful memories for Bree, as they had for him.

Everything feels like a damn land mine these days . . .

Ben cleared his throat and continued his sales pitch. "They offer a concierge service that weeds out properties and locations that don't fit our profile. They will also be drafting the contract and doing the credit and background checks."

Bree seemed to be warming to the idea, and Ben felt almost giddy with relief. Over the next hour they paged through dozens of beautiful locations scattered around the Mediterranean.

"I like the idea of the Mediterranean," Bree admitted. "You know I love whitewashed stucco, fresh food, and the sun. I especially love the idea of lots of light and fewer people."

She drifted off in thought, and Ben watched her.

After a moment she spoke again, adding these last words as if from somewhere far away. "If we are going to do this, let's make it somewhere different but special."

"Okay. It looks like the Mediterranean is a winner," Ben said gleefully, interrupting her reverie with a high five. "Definitely something with a sea view, secluded but still with easy access to amenities. I'll get that information over to them."

Bree gave him a half smile, and it broke his heart in two. He realized for the first time how much courage it had taken for her to agree to this. He reached for her face and gave her a long, lingering kiss.

He filled her in on more details that night as they were getting ready for bed. "Oh, and by the way, it wasn't easy, but I kept my promise to you."

She tilted her head. "What promise?"

"To keep our friends from knowing what we're up to."

She laughed. "So, what did you do?"

"When I posted our property, I made up identities for you and for me." Ben gave her a furtive glance before continuing. "We are now Dick and Shirley Johnson. You are a teacher, and I am an engineer." Ben couldn't resist jabbing her with an old stereotype that they both knew didn't apply to her.

"Why can't I be the engineer and you be the teacher . . . that's pretty sexist!" Bree teased.

"Because if they asked you to solve a math problem, you would be outed!"

Bree slugged Ben and made a face that was so goofy and endearing that he almost cried out in shock. There it was; that glimpse of the "before Bree"—Bree before she had experienced the depth of pain that life truly could bring.

It was all the incentive Ben needed to keep going. Even as the playful look faded from her eyes, his hope remained. He knew now that it was possible . . . it was all possible. He could get her back. Maybe not *completely*. But enough to feel the warmth for life again.

Ben was determined to make it happen.

Chapter 9

THE ENGLISH COUNTRYSIDE
OF OXFORD

The bloody phone kept ringing and interrupting his thoughts. How many times had he read the same paragraph?

Who the hell is calling at this time of night—and on my private home phone?

Ian had been deep into an excellent new biography on the American poet Robert Frost.

Note to self: Unplug the phone after dinner!

The third set of rings proved to be too much, and he answered with enough of a growl and bark to make even the most insistent of intruders relent and hang up. Not so for James Dean McFarland— otherwise known as Mac—at the other end.

"Well, Ian, old friend, how many 'bloody hells' did I get out of you before you answered?" Mac chuckled, envisioning his friend in a smoking jacket, reading the classics, smoking a cigar, and sipping scotch.

"Bloody hells? Not nearly enough. Would you like to hear a few more now?" Ian's caustic response was tempered by his joy at hearing from his old friend.

"How long has it been, my friend? Thought you would like a call from your old intelligence partner . . . not to be confused with the bumbling group of idiots we each work for. Ha-ha!"

"Good point, JD. How the hell are you, old chap? Hanging in there without Gloria to kick your butt into gear these days?"

"Well, not to her standards," Mac admitted. "But I've managed to keep busy with the job and a few hobbies. I'm just hoping she isn't looking down at my housekeeping. How about you? Found 'the one' yet?"

Both Mac and Ian had a good belly laugh over the idea of "the one." It had been a running joke for the thirty years they had known each other.

Ian was a notoriously confirmed bachelor. No woman had ever managed to strip that title. The average tenure of those who'd tried was never more than a year before they ended up limping off, vexed by the challenge of unlocking his heart.

Mac and Ian had never discussed the reason with the exception of one conversation early on in their friendship. Over a bottle of scotch in a cold, dimly lit pub far from home for each of them, Ian had briefly divulged a story about a long-ago marriage, a beautiful young wife, and a sudden but deadly illness.

Ian was not interested in trying to re-create what he had lost with the love of his life, and was quite content to let the memories keep him warm at night. JD, as Mac was always known to Ian, had been respectful of that love and memory and had honored it by accepting his friend's decision to remain single.

As touching as all of that was, it did not preclude Ian from returning the favor by ribbing Mac endlessly about how "henpecked" he was. Mac's marriage had provided much fodder for Ian's quick wit and endless ribbing. Despite the jokes, and over time, Mac's late wife, Gloria, had morphed into a "wife" to both of them. She had badgered Mac into passing on messages to Ian about everything from housekeeping to cooking to making oneself "presentable to the opposite sex."

She had not known of their true connection as operatives for their sovereign countries, or if she had, she never let on. To her, Ian knew, he and Mac had been just two fishing and golfing buddies with a penchant for suspense novels, cigars, and scotch.

After Ian and Mac finished laughing, Ian gave the same answer he'd been giving for the past thirty years. "'The one'? Not yet, but things are looking up What's new in your world, JD? You've been pretty quiet for a while now. Are you working on something?"

"Working on it and being put out to pasture at the same time! Idiots!" JD grunted into the phone.

"Clueless, bloody idiots!" Ian ranted in empathy. Of course, this was Ian's favorite response to everything from a hangnail to his close friend's unwarranted retirement. "When's your last day, so I can raise a glass of port and finally get you over here for a visit?"

"That's why I'm calling. I need your help on this case. And before you say you aren't in the spook game anymore, I'm not sure it would really require that level of involvement."

"Okay. Well, I'm not really, nor was I ever, anything but an Oxford professor—"

"Cut the crap, Ian. Just listen to my analysis, and then you can discuss medieval literature or whatever the hell you teach these days."

Ian smiled on his end of the phone.

Mac launched into the details of his hunch.

"I've been tracking some interesting real estate deals in Hungary. Off the grid–type of transactions. I believe they are tied to a jihadist group that has been responsible for escalating violence in the European sector. These bastards seem to have access to high-level resources that makes me think they could have ties to ISIS . . . and even possibly Al-Zawahiri."

"That's quite a leap and quite a big fish. What makes you think they are related to the real estate deals in Hungary?"

"Let me tell you this part first. A few weeks ago, I got my hands on a report from the WHO about a bunch of kids who died at an unknown orphanage across the border from Budapest in Romania. Not a mark on them, no illness detected, no cause of death. They all drop dead while playing outside." Mac stopped so that Ian could digest the information.

"Witnesses?"

"It gets strange here. The playground teachers are left unscathed, even though they witnessed the whole thing. They can't remember seeing or hearing anything. One minute the kids are laughing and playing, and then the next minute they are down and gone." Ian could almost feel Mac's blood pressure rise as he recounted the information.

"Gas?"

"Nothing detected."

"Poison?"

"The teachers outside and workers in the school all ingested the same meals. These were kids that lived there and were never out of the care of the adults."

"What are you thinking? What is the connection with this group in Budapest?"

"We intercepted an email a couple of weeks ago that gave the coordinates of the Romanian orphanage and referenced a live test of some sort." Ian could hear Mac's breathing slow, probably in an attempt to keep his emotions from affecting his story. "Ian, you don't do a test like this because you have some deep-seated hatred of Romanian kids," Mac went on. "And if you're looking to do mass damage, you could have hit a public school anywhere in the world and garnered exponentially higher hit numbers—"

"You do this because you think it will go unnoticed," Ian cut in, "and you will have test data to analyze for . . . God knows what!"

"My thoughts exactly!"

"What do you need me to do, JD?"

"You speak Romanian, right? Don't answer that; I know you do. Any chance of you talking with the director of the orphanage? This was some off-grid place she had created outside of the government's reach. She clearly reported the deaths at risk to her own security. I'm assuming something scared her about this and that there is more to the story."

"Sure, I'll just pop right over to . . . where? Romania?"

"Transylvania, to be exact. A small village outside of Alba Iulia. I'll send you the location and the name of the director. Go easy on her, Ian, she's been through hell over this." Ian could tell Mac was feeling unusually uncomfortable about drawing her further into what could be a dangerous situation.

"Actually," Ian joked cheerfully, "and quite coincidentally, that was exactly the next place on my bucket list of vacation spots to visit before I die."

"Now, that's the smart-ass Ian I know and respect!"

"Bloody hell, you say? And it's Renaissance literature, chap!"

"Medieval. Renaissance. Let's just hope it isn't apocalyptic, my friend."

Chapter 10

LONDON

Rob carried his third pint of ale into his office, sat behind the desk, and logged on to his computer. Again.

Still no response from their client. The prearranged time of the follow-up contact and payment had come and gone.

He tried not to let himself panic. The first half of the money had been deposited on time, and it was a huge sum. It wasn't the money that was bothering him. It was the silence.

This client never misses a deadline.

The promised payout for this particular job had been huge. That could only mean that it was either illegal or dangerous, or most likely both. He remembered that both he and Jules had sensed danger from the start. In fact, it had been the first time they had truly argued over a job.

"Rob, are you sure we should do this? I mean, when is enough, enough?"

"Honey, I just want to make *sure* we have enough. Because when we leave, we aren't coming back."

As far as Jules could tell, they'd been "leaving" for the past ten years. They had purchased a house on an island in Greece ten years ago for this very reason. They'd also been amassing their "getaway" money for years and had long passed the point of needing any more deals. Their island getaway had been paid for long ago. This had nothing to do with the money.

"Do we really need this?" Jules had repeated, "Or is this an ego thing for you? I'm starting to think you are addicted to the thrill of this stuff."

"Oh, come on. That's not exactly fair! We BOTH walked into this with our eyes wide open, Jules."

"Well, now I'd like to shut them while lying on a secluded beach in the middle of the Mediterranean. Preferably while still alive and without needing an army of bodyguards to keep me that way."

They had gone back and forth, pro/conned it, and spent a restless night apart, but Jules had finally given in. Rob had assured her this would be the last deal. And he'd meant it.

At first it had seemed like an average deal. The contract required them to secure warehouse space in Budapest, Hungary, and to retrofit it to specs for a pharmaceutical company. Rob had tried not to think about why a drug company needed a covert laboratory. There were no comfortable answers. Jules had been right. There was something about this cloak-and-dagger stuff he couldn't resist. Maybe it was a throwback to his thespian days. He'd hire a shrink to help him figure that out later.

On the surface, everything appeared legit, but Rob knew—and his client knew he knew—that this was undoubtedly a bogus company with suspicious intentions. And that knowledge could spell trouble for Rob and Jules when they tried to walk away. And that's what was troubling him now.

The last transmission he had received from the client had been over two weeks ago with instructions to have everything dismantled and "cleaned." That meant Rob was to make sure all evidence of the client's existence was erased.

It was a pretty standard request coming from this client, but Rob hadn't been able to shake the growing feeling that he was going to need some leverage. Something to keep Jules and him from ending up in the bottom of their beloved Mediterranean.

The whole scenario had an eerie feeling to it, but he chalked it up to watching too many *Breaking Bad* episodes.

He called someone he trusted to "clean" the building but instructed him to take detailed photos of the lab and all its contents before making everything disappear. Those photos were now safely stored in a bank safe.

And now, with the missed deadline for the second half of the payment, Rob had a feeling those photos would soon be needed.

Sitting at his desk, studying his computer screen, Rob broke into a sweat. He thought of Jules. *Do I tell her what I suspect and get her worried, maybe over nothing . . . or do I try to first get the upper hand with these guys?*

His plan was to send an email to the client with a zip file containing copies of the photos, along with the information that another set of photos existed in a package addressed to London's MI6. He would tell them that as long as he and Jules were left unharmed, that package would not be mailed.

Rob doubted this would keep them safe in the long run, but he hoped it would buy them some time.

After drinking the last of his ale in one large gulp, Rob took one more look at the email he had just composed describing his demands. Then he attached the zip file containing the photos.

He took a deep breath and hit the send button.

Almost immediately, he received a notification. Staring at his inbox, he saw that his email had been returned as "undeliverable." His heart dropped into his stomach. He double-checked the email address, retyped it to be sure, and sent the message again. Once again it was returned as "undeliverable." For the first time, he felt real terror.

Whoever his client had been, he had disappeared as quietly as he had appeared . . . and Rob was left holding a very exposed bag.

It took a few minutes to let the truth of the situation sink in.

Holy shit . . . we're in trouble.

He'd always known this day might come but, like a gambler, he'd thought he could outrun the odds.

The last job. We were so close. If only I'd listened to Jules . . .

Now he had no choice but to implement the second half of his plan, which was a self-designed witness protection plan of sorts. He would need to tell Jules there would be no Greek island in their lives for right now.

Instead, they were going to need to find some unsuspecting American couple to take their place at their island home. Rob wanted to find Americans because he and Jules would need to assume their identities. Not difficult considering their Spokane roots.

Jules was not going to be thrilled.

Chapter 11

THE DIRECTOR'S OFFICE, THE ROMANIAN ORPHANAGE

Iona was standing with her back to the door of her office, attempting to calm her nerves and prepare herself for the visitor. She was glad that one of her staff had warned her about the strange car in the driveway.

The sound of footsteps stopped at the threshold of her office doorway. As she turned around, she found herself wishing she had never sent the report. A man stepped forward and introduced himself, and she was surprised by his cordial demeanor.

"Ms. Dalca, allow me to introduce myself. I am Alexandru Vasile. I am here on behalf of the National Directorate for Child Protection regarding a report that you submitted to us describing recent events—"

"I know why you are here, Mr. Vasile. I was wondering when you would come. I have been waiting for some kind of response from your department," Iona said crisply, determined not to be disarmed by his obvious attempt to soften her resolve.

♛

Ian was caught off guard. This woman was nothing like the cloistered spinster he had been expecting. Far from it. He was impressed by her sense of presence and her unwavering eye contact. He noticed that she had surprisingly beautiful blue eyes, even if they were steely with determination. Without the need to float any further credentials, he got right down to business.

"We have reviewed the report in some detail and have a few additional questions, if you would be so kind," Ian said, and as he did, he was again struck by the strength of her gaze.

"Yes, of course. However, as you have read, I was not present during the . . . incident. I'm not sure what information I can add that I haven't already provided."

"Let's start at the beginning, if you will, please. Why was this satellite orphanage undisclosed to the Directorate? How long had you been operating this second location? And more important, why?" Ian hoped the rapid-fire questions would prompt unrehearsed responses.

"Why? That is an absurd question, Mr. Vasile. You of all people should know of the fate of children in my orphanage once they reach the age of five. I was not wanting to ship them off to those new farms you people have created, where I can only imagine they are put to work and utterly forgotten." As Iona spoke, her words came out in a rush. She continued. "I realize the new system is a small price for Romania to pay for joining the EU, but certainly a high price for these children!"

"Forgive me, Mrs. Dalca, but are you really trying to blame the government's entry into the EU for your decision to deceive and manipulate the Directorate and the regulations?" Ian asked.

As Ian looked on, the director—what did she say her name was? Iona?—grabbed the back of her desk chair for support and looked like she might slip to the floor. When she spoke, he could hear the raw pain in her voice.

"I thought I could make a difference in their lives by keeping them in the village—but what a sad difference I have made. Now they are dead, and I have killed them!"

Ian watched Iona's shoulders sag under the weight of the haunting words she had just spoken. It appeared to take all of her strength and several deep breaths for her to regain her composure. Ian was moved by her sincere distress and wanted to reach out to comfort her, which was an odd feeling for him. He almost regretted pushing her so hard. He decided to take a different tack.

"We can assess liability at another time, Mrs. Dalca. Please tell me how you were able to run this second orphanage off the grid. How did you provide for the basic needs of the children without having the overages detected in the accounting department?"

"First of all, Mr . . . Vasile, is it? I did all of this to save these children. You must believe me. They are my life's work. If I'd thought that anything like this could possibly have happened, I would never have done this!"

"I'm sure you had good intentions, Mrs. Dalca."

"It was really because of one child. Her name was Maria, but we nicknamed her Molly. I had a special fondness for her . . ." Iona stopped and quickly wiped at a loose tear.

Ian stepped forward and handed her a perfectly ironed handkerchief from his pocket. She accepted it and took a moment to examine it, as if she had never seen one before or even knew what to do with it.

"Thank you," she said, still looking at the handkerchief.

"You were saying . . . ," Ian prompted.

"Yes, as I was saying, after Molly turned five, I kept her here with me. But then there were several more children nearing the age of five, and I knew I needed to do something. It's a long story that involves a group of visiting Americans, but their help and love for these children inspired me to do something to save them. One young man in particular helped me draft a plan that enlisted the help of a few people I knew in a nearby village, which is approximately twelve kilometers from here. But of course, you know all of this from my report!" She threw an exasperated look his way.

She reminds me of Ingrid Bergman playing Joan of Arc, Ian thought. He couldn't help but make the comparison as he listened to her impassioned explanation. He could clearly see how the loss of the children, and especially the girl named Molly, had left her brokenhearted and at the same time mad as hell.

"Of course we know this from your carefully detailed report, Mrs. Dalca. The problem is, we still can't explain what happened to the children or why, so please continue."

"There was a small home on the outskirts of the village that was not in use. My friends who live in the village agreed to help get the house set up, and to staff it as well. They provided whatever they could from their small gardens. My staff here also made extra pots of soup and sent them over. We were always struggling to have enough. Enough food. Enough clothing—but the alternative was unthinkable. And health care? It was almost nonexistent. At least until we received a special grant from a pharmaceutical company from Budapest. "

"A pharmaceutical company?" Ian asked, suddenly alert. "A pharmaceutical company showed up here . . . all the way from Budapest? Didn't you think that was a bit odd? How did they find you?"

"I'm not sure how they found us initially," Iona answered slowly, as if trying to remember. "I think it was through the son of a woman in the village. In fact, I know it was. The son of a friend of mine had gone off to the big city in pursuit of work, and came back to the village for a visit. He told us a pharmaceutical company had a program to help underprivileged children, and he told them about us. Soon after, a small, white van arrived filled with food and medicines. It was like the heavens had opened and blessings had poured out." She smiled wistfully before adding, "You have no idea what an impact they made in the lives of our children that day."

Ian could imagine the mixture of joy and relief this dedicated woman must have felt at being able to provide for her children, ALL of them.

"What happened then?" he prompted.

"Well, they made several visits—here and to the home—over a two- or three-month period, each time addressing an essential need that we had. The last time they came, they provided vaccines. I had not been able to provide vaccines to any of our children, even after several urgent requests to your department, Mr. Vasile."

She looked pointedly at Ian before continuing.

"As you also know, tuberculosis, scarlet fever, and now HIV have made inroads into this vulnerable population. So, you can imagine how grateful we were for the help of this company."

"How did they administer the vaccines?" Ian probed.

"They came with a medical team."

"Anything unusual about the process, other than it was *free*?" Ian asked. He emphasized the word "free" hoping Iona would get the bigger picture without his having to ask the obvious question that begged to be asked: *Lady, do you think most drug companies are roaming the back roads of Transylvania, looking for ways to give away free drugs?*

The woman squinted her eyes in thought. "Unusual? No, nothing unusual. Just that they were very insistent that the vaccines were meant only for children over the age of five, and that every child at that location had to be present and vaccinated at the same time. There could be no exceptions."

"How did they communicate with you to let you know when they were coming and about these restrictions?" Ian asked calmly, but he could feel silent alarms going off in his head.

"Through emails."

"I'd like to see the emails if possible." Ian kept the authority in his voice but had softened his tone. It was clear that this director had been through a lot.

She nodded. "Of course. Unfortunately, our computer is not working and hasn't been for a while, which is why I sent the written report instead of an electronic copy. In fact," she added, "it stopped working around the time of the medical visit from the drug company."

This was all the information Ian needed to connect the dots. He couldn't wait to fill JD in on all the details. From what Ian was hearing, his friend's instincts were right on. This director and her children had certainly been victims of at least a scam and very likely a heinous mass murder.

Iona was tired, and it showed in her eyes. She suspected from the official's line of questioning that she was not going to be allowed to stay on as the director of the orphanage. *And why would they let me stay? I clearly circumvented the rules. How could they ever trust me again? How could I trust myself?* She sighed before saying, with very little hope, "Now, if you are through with your questions, Mr. Vasile, I still have an orphanage to run . . . and children who need me."

Vasile bowed slightly, thanked her politely and walked out.

It was only after Iona heard the front door close and the car start that she removed her shaking hands from the back of the chair and slumped down onto the seat.

Once again, grief washed over her, creating such overwhelming despair that she could hardly breathe. She gave in and allowed the tears to flow down her face, eventually letting her head fall forward and resting her tearstained face on her folded arms. It seemed like it would never stop, as wave after wave of anguish flooded her heart and she sobbed out the pain she hadn't till now allowed herself to feel.

As the late afternoon shadows crept across her office walls, she finally lifted her head and allowed rational thought to crowd its way into her awareness. She stretched out her arms, cramped from being pinned down on her desk, and noticed she was still clutching Mr. Vasile's handkerchief in one of her hands. She examined the expensive cloth and held it up to her nose, noticing the now familiar and elegant scent.

Why didn't he remove me from my position? she wondered. *He clearly had the facts and the authority he needed.*

"Was it mercy? Or just the slow bureaucratic process?" she murmured to herself, turning to stare vacantly out the window. The children were all playing in the yard.

Only Molly was sitting quietly by herself on the single swing under a shade tree.

Chapter 12

ALBA IULIA, ROMANIA

Ian didn't waste any time contacting Mac. As soon as he had driven his car down the long driveway from the orphanage and onto the main road, he pulled over and used his satellite phone.

"JD, it looks like your suspicions were well-founded," he said as soon as Mac answered, skipping any formal greeting. "Most of what I discovered will support your theory. However, I don't think you are going to be pleased!"

"Nothing about this scenario is pleasing me," Mac growled. Ian could hear the irritation in his friend's voice. He glanced at his watch. No wonder. Where JD was, it was 4:07 a.m.

"How did they get to these children, Ian?" Mac went on.

"I'm not sure of the mechanism yet, but it is very clear that it was an orchestrated attack," Ian responded. "This was not an accident or a friendly fire situation."

"I was hoping it might turn out differently, but I'm not surprised," Mac said. Did you learn enough to help us back up our theory if we need to move forward?"

Ian wondered if Mac was thinking ahead, and perhaps of involving someone else within the CIA. "I believe so," he answered. "Thanks to the director, I have uncovered a potential source—a young man in the village—who could lead to exactly what we'll need. I'll get to the details of why I believe this, but there is another troubling issue, and that's the question of how long I'll be able to impersonate an official before the real folks show up."

"Well, from what I read in the version of the report submitted to the WHO, the officials have already weighed in with a stack of changes in hygiene protocol. It looked like they weren't intending to take any further actions."

"Let's hope so, JD. Mrs. Dalca, the director, was scared to death to see me. I've never seen such a mixture of dread and reticence on anyone's face. She clearly was expecting to be let go immediately. Once she realized I wasn't there to remove her from the orphanage, she was amazingly candid, opening up about the children's' deaths as well as why she was running another orphanage in the first place. And she feels quite responsible for everything."

"Responsible? Mac echoed, seemingly caught off guard by this remark. "Was she directly involved?"

"No. Like you suspected from her report, she had been hiding the older children at a house in a nearby village instead of letting them be shipped off to an institution. She was struggling to provide for the children at both locations."

"How did she get tangled up with our jihadists?"

"Apparently, a son of one of the villagers had given details of her dire situation to someone he knew at a pharmaceutical company located in Budapest. Even though Transylvania is technically in Romania, most of the population is Hungarian, stemming from the post–World War II border revision between the two countries," Ian explained, clearly in his element as he threw in a history lesson along with his intel.

"You really are a professor, my friend."

Ian could almost hear the smile of admiration in his friend's voice.

"The story this pharmaceutical company gave her was that they wanted to provide food, clothing, medicines, and sample vaccines as a part of a 'give back' program for these Hungarian descendants," he informed Mac. "They provided all of this free of charge, even sending 'nurses' to administer the vaccines. Interestingly, they had an age threshold of five, which, as you and I now know, limited the recipients to that second, off-the-grid facility. They also required every child at that location to participate without exception."

As Ian finished his recap, a horse-drawn cart filled with hay passed by his car. It was an idyllic image that was in sharp contrast with the horror that had occurred just a few kilometers away.

"Every child," Mac repeated. "No exceptions. Of course. How else would their data be credible? Good God, what a setup. Although, to our unsuspecting Mrs. Dalca, it probably appeared to be manna from heaven, right?"

"Actually, you are close," Ian answered. "Her exact words were that 'blessings from heaven had been poured out.' It looks like the ultimate manipulation of people in true need. Of course, the company's 'goodwill' ended when the last child was injected with their evil cocktail. There has been no further communication."

"Let's get a bead on that villager. Besides the director, his could be the first reliable set of eyes on our Arab attackers. You agree?"

"I'm with you. I'll make his identity a priority during my next visit."

"Just curious. How long before the incident was this stuff administered?" Mac asked.

"Weeks." Ian's abrupt answer sounded ludicrous, even to himself.

"Let me get this straight," Mac blurted out. "These kids get free vaccines and for weeks walk around perfectly normal, no symptoms and no reactions, and then out of the blue one morning, while running around a playground, they all fall dead within seconds of each other?"

"Yes. It is beyond perplexing," Ian agreed. "But it's got to be the vaccine, JD, because the adult staff were with these children at all times, both on and off the playground. They were left completely unharmed. The vaccine is the only variable specific to those children."

"Any identification or communication we can use to tie these guys and their vaccine to the warehouse?" Mac asked.

Ian could hear the gears shift in his pal's thought process. *He's probably already got a plan*, he mused. "No," he answered. "Nothing. According to the director, 'computer problems' hit soon after the company's last visit to administer the vaccines. In fact, her report to her superiors was actually handwritten. When I was in her office, I tried to get a close look at her computer setup—the PC is beyond archaic, and the make and model something I've never seen—possibly Russian."

"Also not surprising. Their last communication probably delivered a computer virus along with the vaccines." Mac paused for a moment, as if pondering something. Finally, he said, "The computer virus was probably added insurance. I'm guessing they thought she'd never report the deaths at all, since it would reveal to her superiors the existence of the hidden home for older kids."

"It was her integrity that compelled her to write that report, something these bastards know nothing about," Ian said with obvious disdain.

"And thank God she did," Mac added. "That report may be our first lucky break. Our Arab creeps aren't likely to know about it—or some old fart out of Langley getting his hands on it."

Ian nodded, forgetting that his friend couldn't see him. He had always admired Mac's ability to get into the heads of whoever he was pursuing. That talent was precisely what made him such a formidable analyst. He took a deep breath and then said, "I'm already on the task of getting someone out to go through the computer equipment. I will have something to give you the next time we chat, JD."

"The sooner the better. I'm nervous about letting the trail get too cold."

"One more thing, JD. I couldn't get over the feeling that there was something the director wasn't telling me. Not about the attack, per se, but about something else. Something more personal. I sensed not just sadness, but also a fierceness, like a mother bear. It could be tied to the fact that she lost a child she loved in the attack. Could be grief, but I don't know. Overall, the orphanage was a pretty bleak place. Gray and dreary. But enough of me waxing poetic. Nice lady. Dignified." Ian lapsed off into silence.

"If anyone can figure it out, it's you, Ian," Mac affirmed. "In the meantime, I'm going to have this phone with me at all times. Don't worry about time zones. I don't sleep a hell of a lot anymore anyway. Let me know when you have the analysis from your computer team."

"Now that I've seen this place firsthand, I'm only too glad to help." Ian felt a strange and unfamiliar surge of emotion.

"I appreciate it. In the meantime, I want to leave you with this: There's something we aren't getting here. If you inject something into a kid and a month later it kills him and every other kid injected at the same time, was it growing inside of him or lying dormant? And if it's dormant, what triggers it? And most important, what could provide a soundless, noiseless, simultaneous trigger? And finally, who are the evil sons of bitches that would do that to innocent kids?" Mac's voice went from deadly quiet and analytical to impassioned and determined.

"The kind of sons of bitches we have been nailing for the last thirty years, JD. Bloody hell! You know they always up their game. But I'm with you. This one looks as frightening as anything we've come across, simply because it appears to act like an undetectable ticking time bomb."

Ian took a breath and then unloaded something that was weighing on his mind.

"You and I both know the fastest way to confirm any of this is to exhume one of those children's bodies and have our professional experts perform some significant analysis."

"I'm glad you brought it up, Ian," Mac responded, without hesitation. "I'm in total agreement."

"Unfortunately," Ian went on, "I keep thinking about that director and her willingness to put her own professional and personal future at risk in an effort to shield those children. She'll need some help in coming to accept this idea. Now that I have met her, I'm sure it will require earning her respect and trust. I've got work to do. I'll be in touch."

Ian ended the call without any further discussion. He could feel his blood pressure climb. *The world has a few too many bastards these days, and I'll be damned if I am going to let them win!*

He turned the key in the ignition and pulled his car back onto the main road. He spent the rest of his drive making mental lists of contacts and equipment necessary to unearth the perpetrators of this heinous attack.

He hoped that the gods or fate or whatever would give the good guys enough time and a little luck.

Chapter 13

THE ORPHANAGE IN ROMANIA

After Mr. Vasile left her office and Iona finally gave in to her pent-up tears, she felt stronger somehow. Her emotional breakdown seemed to have released an untapped reservoir of inexplicable energy.

Reprieve or pardon, she thought to herself, setting her jaw, *I'm not going down without a fight!*

Over the next few days, she systematically cleaned her way through the main building of the orphanage, bringing order to the storage room, kitchen, and classrooms. Once she was satisfied that the staff had the children organizing their own sleeping areas, she turned her focus to her office.

She stood in the doorway, surveying years of accumulated paperwork, books, and children's artwork as if for the first time. *This room looks like it belongs to a stodgy old depressed woman,* she thought. *Is that who I've become? Maybe. But is that who I want to be?*

She was embarrassed at her own question. As she tore into the piles scattered around her office with renewed vigor, she let herself think about last week's visitor. Alexandru Vasile. He certainly wasn't what she had been expecting. He had been authoritative, yes, and she had no doubt that he was used to being in charge. But he wasn't condescending. In fact, he had treated her with an unexpected mixture of kindness and chivalry.

She stopped cleaning and walked back to the desk, where she had placed his freshly laundered handkerchief. She gently unfolded it, feeling herself blush as she remembered her emotional response to his compassionate act.

As she began to fold it back into its original shape, the faint monogram at one corner caught her attention. Why hadn't she seen this before? IAD.

She was puzzling over the initials when her office phone rang.

"Good afternoon, Mrs. Dalca. Alexandru Vasile here. I hope you are well and that my visit last week did not overly disturb the remainder of your week," the caller said.

"Thank you, Mr. Vasile. I am recovered. In fact, I was just wondering how to return the handkerchief you so graciously lent me." Iona could feel the warmth spread across her cheeks once again, embarrassed now at letting him know she had been thinking about him.

Her caller didn't seem to be aware of her discomfort. "I have good news," he said. "I've managed to find some updated computer equipment and would like to have it installed at the orphanage tomorrow. Would that work with your schedule?"

For a minute, Iona was too stunned to answer. She quickly recovered and stammered out, "Why, yes. I'm very grateful. You are very kind. Especially given the recent, um, circumstances . . ."

"Wonderful. I'll be by in the late morning and will bring both the equipment and an installation technician. Perhaps you will have time for a cup of tea?"

After they had agreed to a time and hung up, Iona was more baffled than ever. Surely, he would have filed a report soon after his initial visit to the orphanage, confirming her guilt and setting up her departure as the director. What was he doing, installing new computer equipment and wanting to sit down to tea?

She spent the remainder of the afternoon and evening alternating her attention between decluttering her office, theorizing about her future, and pondering the mysterious Mr. Vasile. Underlying everything was her worry about the impact all of this could have on Molly.

The next morning, she walked down the hallway feeling a sense of pride and accomplishment. The whole building reflected a lighter, more refreshed energy.

I'm ready for whatever you dish my way, Mr. Vasile.

She heard a knock at the front door. His knock. She felt her bravado waver.

Iona swung the door wide and forced a smile for both Ian and the stranger next to him. "Good morning Mr. Vasile."

"Good morning to you, Mrs. Dalca. I hope you are well. Glorious day, isn't it?"

He must have realized how ludicrous his question sounded, because his face reddened slightly, and he looked around, as if embarrassed. Iona followed his gaze around the dingy front yard, with its dry, sparse grass, then up at the cloudy sky, and finally, back to her face. He cleared his throat and continued.

"As I mentioned on the phone yesterday, after I reported on your dire technical circumstances, the district authorities agreed to supply newer equipment to replace your worn-out system. This is Vladimir"— he nodded to the man standing slightly behind him—"and he will be installing the new equipment."

"How do you do, Vladimir?" Iona said politely. "I'm Mrs. Dalca. I'm still not quite sure how our little orphanage warranted such an extravagant gesture."

"Actually," Mr. Vasile said smoothly, ignoring his partner, "technology is changing so quickly that it's not quite the expense it used to be. This simple upgrade should only take an hour or two of your time. In fact, if you would be so kind, is there a place we can continue our conversation while Vladimir gets started?" He smiled persuasively.

"Of course. Gentlemen, please come inside." Iona motioned for them to enter, then led the way to her office. "Vladimir, here is the equipment that is no longer working. I'd like to add, 'Let me know if you need any help,' but we know that's highly unlikely."

Both men chuckled at her attempt at making a joke.

"Mr. Vasile, if you would like to follow me, I have tea set up in a small private dining room so that we can continue discussing your concerns, although I have no idea what I could possibly add at this point—"

"Details, Ms. Dalca, details. I had time to review the notes from our discussion, and there are a few areas I'd like to revisit."

They began walking down the hallway.

"I hope you don't mind," the man continued, "but I took the liberty of bringing you a small gift. It's a bottle of my favorite port as a thank-you gift for all of the trouble I am causing you."

"Well, we have little to go with port, but thank you for the lovely thought. Come. Let me show you the dining room."

♔

In the meantime, unbeknownst to Iona, Vladimir had already begun dismantling the archaic machine while searching the entire room for electronic bugs or other findings that would be useful to their cause. He quickly installed the new, high-powered equipment he'd brought with him—a Dell computer retrofitted with every kind of sensor, spyware, and camera he could cram into the area at such short notice.

But the real prize was the old equipment he hauled out to the panel van in the driveway and immediately began scanning. As he was fond of telling agency newbies, what thugs, scammers, and terrorists always forget is that they are as vulnerable as the weakest part of their electronic security.

In this case, while the terrorists had some skilled hackers on the payroll, as soon as they'd interacted with the director of this orphanage, their security had been reduced to the level of this old, basic machine and its antiquated software.

Any minute now, he would be able to access their email communications with Mrs. Dalca and, from those, very likely trace their location.

♔

Mr. Vasile and Mrs. Dalca sat across from each other, sipping soup while covertly sizing each other up.

"Mr. Vasile, I don't quite recognize your name or your accent. Are you from this area? I certainly would have heard about you long before now. This district is not very large." Iona was thinking about the initials on the handkerchief.

"Mrs. Dalca, with all due respect. You have been running this orphanage for thirty years, immersed in the lives of your charges twenty-four hours a day, seven days a week. It is not surprising that we have not met before. Other than the villagers, have you met anyone in all of those years?"

Iona felt like she had been slapped in the face. "These children have needed me, Mr. Vasile, and it's a good thing I *did* run this place, although I suspect that now you are intent on discrediting me so that I will leave. I am ready, sir, and you don't need to do any more belittling of me to coerce my resignation!" Her face flushed and her eyes flashed with fury as she stood up abruptly from the table.

The man stood as well. "Mrs. Dalca, is that why you think I'm here? For your resignation? I can assure you, no one is asking for your resignation—"

"Mamma! Mamma!" a small voice cried out suddenly from the doorway. A young girl of around eight or nine came running into the room and threw her arms around Iona before she could stop her. The girl's face was lit with excitement as she looked up at Iona through a mop of wild, black curls, totally oblivious to the man still seated at the table.

"Molly!" was all Iona could muster as she tried to unclamp the girl's arms and at the same time send a message with her eyes to stop Molly from saying anything else. But Molly did not pick up on the desperately stern look.

"Mamma! You can't believe what I learned today from Miss Corina. I wrote my story about Jayden completely in English, and I didn't miss a single word! I got a perfect score!" The little girl beamed, and Iona, without even being consciously aware, beamed back with what could only be described as a mother's love.

♔

It had taken Ian only about a minute while observing this loving exchange to put two and two together. He now understood the vibes he had been picking up from the director. Clearly, this was not just another orphan. For one thing, she was older than the other children. Also, the emotional connection was very obvious. Here was the secret Iona had been hiding behind the sadness in her eyes. It also explained the mother-bear fierceness in her demeanor. Ian had jumped to the conclusion that this child had been lost in the attack. But clearly Molly was very much alive. How the hell had that happened?

♔

It took a few moments before Iona would dare meet Ian's gaze. But when she saw his startled surprise fade into gentle compassion, she decided it was safe to introduce him to Molly.

"Mr. Vasile, this is Molly. Molly, this is Mr. Vasile. He is visiting our orphanage as a surprise today. You mustn't let any of the other children know about his visit."

"Hello," Molly said in Romanian with a small, shy smile.

"Hello, young lady," Ian responded in English, much to her delight.

"You are English speaking!" The child clapped her hands with delight. "Did you hear about my homework?"

"I did, and I am very impressed. Your English is excellent. I would very much like to read your story sometime," he said encouragingly. Iona watched as this stranger took in Molly's curly black hair and piercingly blue eyes.

♔

What a charming child, Ian thought. But who was this Jayden she had mentioned? It seemed like an American name, and somewhat out of place in the orphanage. He would ask Iona when they were alone. Ms. Dalca interrupted his reverie.

"Molly, say goodbye to Mr. Vasile. We have some more work to do, and you must return to your school activities. Please tell Miss Corina that I will come for you when I am finished here."

"Goodbye, sir," the child said with a small curtsy and a fleeting glance to the director before dashing out of the room as fast as she had dashed in.

"Goodbye, my dear," Ian said with a wink. "Good luck with your classes."

After Molly left the room, an uncomfortable silence settled in and seemed to go on forever as Ian tried to think of a way to move them past this very personal interlude. It was evident to him that Ms. Dalca was thinking the same thing. She was the first to speak.

"Mr. Vasile . . ."

"Please, Ms. Dalca, isn't it time you call me Alex? As I was telling you when your lovely daughter came into the room—"

"Oh, Mr. Vasile—I mean, Alex—it is my turn to say please. First of all, you may also call me Iona. But second, we both know that I am far too old to be Molly's mother. She is a child I have grown to love. And I believe she has grown to love me too."

"And she has grown fond of this Jayden too," Ian said gently and quietly. He realized that he was mining some deeply painful emotional ground here and walked forward carefully.

"Yes, his name was Jayden Stanton. He was just a teenager himself when he came here. Molly was four, and they had an instant bond for the month that he volunteered here. They were inseparable, really. It was the most amazing thing to watch. She became his shadow and adored the very breath of him. Well, actually, now that I think about it," Iona gushed, "I adored him as well. He was the kindest, most compassionate, most beautiful young man you could ever ask to meet. I also felt an immediate bond with him, and I must say, at the time, I had grown hardhearted and cold. Not from choice, but Mr.—I mean, Alex—you cannot see this constant wave of despair and loss and pain and not have it take some kind of toll."

She paused, seemingly lost in thought, then said, "I really wasn't aware of the toll until Jayden came into our lives. He thawed my heart and helped me drop my guard and believe in goodness again. It was quite remarkable. He was almost like . . . well, you will think this kind of strange, but almost Christlike. I don't have any other words. Anyway, when he went away, it was like a light had left our world."

She stopped talking and blinked to keep the tears from falling.

"Is this the young man you referred to in our earlier discussion, the one who helped you establish the second orphanage?" Ian was not usually so quick to fill in the answers for someone he was questioning. But Ms. Dalca—er, Iona—was drifting off into some strong emotions and memories, and he was losing time to complete the story.

"Yes. It was his relationship with Molly that started both of us down the path of activism. In fact, by the time he left us, he had decided to become a doctor so that he could come back and help the children in a more significant way."

"Where did he go, this Jayden? Did you ever hear from him again?" Ian asked, ever so gently.

"Oh yes!" she brightened considerably. "He wrote often and sent funny things, little presents for both of us from the States! This went on for about three years. He completed high school and enrolled in college, still planning on completing medical school and returning to us. It was of course, an impossible dream on our part, but still, I believed and hoped."

"Are you telling me it never happened? Do you know why?"

"One day he just stopped writing. I'm assuming he either found a girlfriend or school became all-consuming. I don't blame him at all. We had three years more than we hoped for after he drove away so many years ago." She shrugged her shoulders and let out an audible sigh.

"And so Molly became one of the children you saved?"

"Molly became the first child I saved, and the reason for creating the other orphanage. I wanted her to be here for him when he returned. And when he didn't . . . she became my reason for, well, everything." Iona choked out the last part of the sentence, apparently too emotional to continue.

Ian moved closer and put his hand on her shoulder. "Iona, I'm so sorry for the loss of the children and all they meant to you."

He had failed to notice until now just how lovely her shoulder was. She was a handsome woman. More to the point, she had an inward combination of beauty and honesty that was quite disconcerting. He quickly lowered his hand and, embarrassed, walked to a window and pretended to gaze upon the stark landscape.

"I do have a question I must ask you, and I hope you will trust me with the answer as you have trusted me with all of this story."

"I will try Alex, but you must see that I have carried these burdens by myself for so long that trust is not easy for me."

"I fully understand that. I once lost a beautiful young wife to a savage and abrupt illness. I remember packing up my heart that day and putting it into cold storage. I trusted no one, but I'm realizing more than ever that my barriers have not served me well. I think that your barriers may not be so different."

The woman reached out, as if to comfort him with a touch, as he had for her, then as if having lost her courage pulled her hand back and instead, simply nodded.

He wished the moment could continue without the question he had no choice but to ask. But he had to plow ahead.

"Iona, do you happen to know . . . was Molly vaccinated at the same time as the other children?"

He heard her gasp. Then she shook her head in quiet disbelief. "Oh, dear God," she whispered.

She began to weep with deep anguish. Instinctively Ian moved back to her side and put his arms around her. She cried into his shoulder for a long time.

With Molly alive, they now had a living incubator, and the possibility of identifying the embedded bioagent. But Iona's deep sorrow only made clear to Ian the steep human cost of that knowledge.

We have to solve this. Not just for Molly and Iona, but for everyone else that will experience unimaginable suffering if we don't.

Chapter 14

CIA Headquarters, Langley

It was 2 p.m. as Mac paced around his tiny, windowless office, waiting for Ian to call him with an update. He'd never really cared about the size of his office before—hardly even noticed it half the time—but today, it was getting on his nerves. He felt like a POW, crammed in a cell, pacing to keep his fight-or-flight impulse under check.

Mac watched the clock on the wall tick off precious seconds. *What is taking Ian so long? Who the hell knows where those bastards are now, or who they are injecting with their cocktail of death?*

He saw the light pop on his desk phone and slapped his hand on the receiver before the first ring registered.

"MacFarland," he barked into the phone.

"JD, you sitting down? God, I hope so!" Ian's impassioned voice boomed from the receiver.

Mac slid into the seat of his desk chair. Ian had always been the calm one. This couldn't be good news.

"I'm sitting now. What do you have?"

"Everything you suspected and more. My guy Vladimir did an excellent job of retrieving and deciphering the email communications. It wasn't too difficult. Perhaps, instead of spending all of their time in the lab, they should have been focusing on their internet security." Ian let the sarcasm hang in the air.

Mac grunted.

Ian continued. "They were indeed masquerading as a pharmaceutical company. Vladimir was able to trace their emails back to a warehouse location in Budapest."

"A lease in Budapest? Too unusual to be a coincidence, right? That's gotta be our Arabs!"

"Exactly. That's what I thought the moment I saw it," Ian agreed. "I already sent an MI6 operative we had in the area over to the warehouse location, and, of course, it's been totally dismantled and professionally cleaned. We aren't likely to get anything from whatever went on there."

Ian had clearly already done much of the legwork.

Mac was impressed. "Next step, we find the source of the lease transaction," he said.

"Already on that as well. It appears that some middleman out of London worked the deal, but they've been difficult to trace."

"Your own backyard," Mac added.

"Exactly. The point is, everything seems to support your original theory that the terrorists, operating out of the Budapest warehouse, took a chemical weapon for a test drive on these kids."

"Any more details from the director? What about moving forward with a forensic analysis of one of the dead kids?" The question sounded a bit harsh, even to Mac, but he was feeling the urgency this new information had created.

"I'm getting to that part. This is why you need to be sitting down. Turns out, there was a child who was sick the day of the attack and did not go to the playground. She did, however, receive the original vaccine along with the others. The point is, JD . . . she is still alive."

It took a minute for Ian's words to sink in. Once they did, Mac came out firing.

"What the hell?" he bellowed. "So, she has the thing inside of her? And she's still alive because she wasn't out on the playground when the bioagent was triggered."

"It appears that way."

"Okay," Mac continued, "let's walk this through. According to the report, the caretakers on the playground with the children insisted there were no sounds, no planes, no helicopters, no smell, no clouds of gas, so I'm thinking it had to be—"

"A drone."

"Exactly. What else could have delivered the trigger?" Mac was noodling at a hundred miles an hour now, and knew Ian was as well. "But how do we get to the composition of the trigger?" he mused aloud. "Think anything is left in the playground yard? Could we get samples of the grass or dirt?"

"We can go back to the playground, but the odds of anything having been left behind isn't high. I did talk Iona into letting us take samples of the girl's blood, which I have shipped off to our lab in London."

"The girl who survived."

"Yes. Her name is Molly."

"Hmm."

"The lab will start working on isolating and identifying the implanted bioagent, if it's still even in her blood. When we get those results, we may have some clue as to what was in the trigger compound."

"Great work, Ian. Just dandy work." Mac was grateful his friend had taken the initiative.

"In the meantime, JD, this little kid could be a ticking time bomb. Not to mention the potential danger she'll be in once these bloody jihadists realize she's still alive."

Ian's voice sounded pained. Mac was incredulous.

"Okay, Ian, old boy, is that emotion I'm hearing in your voice? You, the lifelong bachelor and emotionless wonder?"

"JD, let's get these bastards," Ian said firmly, unwilling to take the bait.

"You are right; we have to stop these monsters. Now, I'm going to float something by you that you probably already know anyway. Stopping these bastards may require us to do something neither one of us is going to like, and that is to use the girl to smoke these guys out." Before Ian could protest, Mac added, "You know I'm right."

There was silence on the other end of the phone.

Mac went on. "We may need to leak the news that she's alive. Use her as a lure."

"I bloody well knew that before I dialed the phone, JD."

"Ian, we can do this and still keep her safe."

The line went dead.

Mac wasn't sure if Ian had heard that last part or not.

He got up and started pacing again. He could feel his heart pounding with anticipation and a sense of renewed energy. The CIA might be putting him out to pasture, but he was going to kick a few shins before they got him there.

Chapter 15

YEMEN

Amir bowed as he kissed his uncle's hand.

"*Sabah alkhyr. Ayuha aleamu alkarim.*" he said smoothly, wishing his honored uncle a good morning. With his words, Amir had both recognized his uncle's great status and reminded him of their familial connection. The older man eyed him suspiciously. His nephew seemed nervous . . . but eager.

Al-Zawahiri was no fool. He understood the unbridled ambition that lurked beneath his nephew's ingratiating salutation. He regally motioned Amir to the chair across from his own.

A man from the shadows instantly appeared with glasses of Al-Zawahiri's favorite mint tea. As Al-Zawahiri took the first sip, he gazed at Amir over the rim of the glass, sizing him up. His nephew was undoubtedly here to lay the spoils of his latest crusade at Al-Zawahiri's feet. So be it; he would give the young man his due.

"I am here to give you good news, Uncle," Amir said. "Our new weapon is like none other. The live test was profoundly successful. The targets were eliminated with 100 percent accuracy. We are ready for the next step!"

Al-Zawahri already knew that Amir had the fierce heart of a warrior. But what he couldn't determine yet was whether or not his nephew had the cunning and courage of a leader. Leadership was a different game altogether. Al-Zawahiri would have to test the young lion further.

He looked piercingly at Amir. "I already know that test was successful, and I am pleased. But you did not tie up the loose ends. The couple who served as conduits must now be eliminated." He let his words hang with just a slight tone of disappointment.

This was not the test he had in mind for Amir, but it would keep his nephew occupied while the true operation continued to be put into place. His only son was in charge of the implementation, and it was going well. Al-Zawahiri wished in this moment that he could meld Amir's fierce heart with his son's brilliance and intuition. But alas, he knew it was not to be. There would come a time for him to choose a leader, but it would not be today.

"Yes, Uncle," Amir said with a slight bow. "I will track them down and thank them for the services they provided." He said this with a sneer that reminded Al-Zawahiri of a pirate in a cartoon movie.

"Let me know when this task is accomplished." Al-Zawahiri motioned his nephew out the door, relieved to have such undisciplined ambition away from his presence.

He could not shake a sense of foreboding. It clung to the air as he heard the outer door slam. That type of myopic greed could be useful, but it almost always brought turmoil along as its companion.

Chapter 16

LONDON

Rob took a deep, ragged breath, willing his pounding heart to slow down so that he could concentrate on the computer screen in front of him.

All right, ole chap. You've got this. You've always known you might need a plan B. Well, here it is. Rob silently coached himself so he could focus.

It didn't take long for him to find the exchange listings for couples seeking homes in Greece. He narrowed the search to couples coming from the western United States. Being able to assume the identities of an American man and woman was essential to throw off any potential pursuers.

He kept passing and then returning to one particular profile for a couple listing a home in Big Bear, California. It seemed close to perfect: a world away from London, close enough to the amenities of LA, and yet isolated enough to allow him and Jules to blend in without having to fit in.

The website listed the owners as Dick and Shirley Johnson, which he assumed were fake names created for the website. He knew people, and judging by the location and value of the Big Bear property, these were careful people with assets and reputations. It didn't take Rob long to research the property itself and find the true identities of its owners. It turned out that Dick and Shirley were actually Benjamin and Breelynn Stanton III, a couple in their late fifties. Rob did a few Google searches and discovered that Bree was the owner of a large corporate travel company and Ben the senior partner of a prestigious architectural firm. The couple seemed to spend a great deal of time at fund-raisers and social engagements. They appeared to be distinguished and monied without being part of the pop-culture scene of LA.

Perfect.

Rob also discovered that, sadly, their only son was killed in a freeway shooting a couple of years back. The articles he found online were filled with the details of both his death and the plea bargain and sentencing of the gang members responsible for the shooting. Rob and Jules didn't have children of their own, but he was nevertheless moved by the story of these grieving parents. Rob wondered if a desire to escape the daily reminders of their loss was propelling this couple to Greece. He had a moment of remorse and thought about choosing the property of a different family, perhaps people he hadn't learned so much about.

But time was pressing in on him.

Rob studied the most recent pictures of the Stantons published in the society column of the *LA Times*. Jules looked enough like Bree that with some hair dye, a change in hairstyle, and dark glasses, she'd probably be okay. His transition would be more difficult. He stood up from his desk and walked over to a nearby mirror. *Oh boy. I'm going to need to lose a few pounds, jettison the beard, go salt-and-pepper, and add some designer glasses. No sweat!*

Rob hadn't waited for Jules's approval. She wasn't going to like any of this anyway. He'd best deliver the plan as a fait accompli and get them safely on their way to the US. He'd just have to deal with the fallout from her later.

He clicked on the link, indicating his interest in the property.

By the end of the week, it was a done deal. The transaction had gone easier than Rob had assumed. For some reason, his and Jules's Greece hideaway had been just the thing these two Americans wanted for what they had described as a "year abroad." Rob had made similar declarations about the "US mountain" experience. The exchange of properties, along with the contracts and necessary legal documents, was transacted through dozens of emails and several conversations.

Rob ended up telling Jules what he was doing as soon as the property deal looked serious.

Every time they were on the phone with the Americans, Rob and Jules had shared breezy tidbits of local flavor, favorite beaches, food, and sunset-viewing options. Their descriptions seemed to promise the "Johnsons" everything they were looking for. Similarly, the Americans had shared enticing details about their Big Bear home with the Bergmans. As soon as the arrangements had been finalized, they all settled down into relative silence, with only the occasional sparse email.

Rob had suggested that, due to the length of the exchange, it would be good to meet in person. He hoped that physically crossing paths with the Stantons would ensure the success of the identity swap. The two couples decided to meet up in Rome in a few weeks.

Soon after the contracts were signed, Rob and Jules quietly disappeared from their rented flat in London. Weeks later, they resurfaced—sporting their new looks—and checked in to a hotel on the Via Veneto in Rome, under their new assumed names of Ben and Bree Stanton, using the black-market passports Rob had purchased for this portion of their trip.

Jules took a moment to look around the stunning chandelier-lit lobby at the detailed art deco decor of the hotel.

"Rob, this place is truly amazing. Look at the curved marble staircase and the inlaid marble tile floor," Jules said, stunned by the details of their small, boutique hotel.

"Yep, it's all great. Jules, let's go over to that restaurant pronto." Rob pointed to the far side of the lobby and then took his wife's arm, steering her toward a small but expensive-looking dining area.

She raised an eyebrow.

"I mean, Bree," Rob corrected himself. Then he groaned and added, "I could literally eat a live elephant, I'm so starved." He had held to the plan of shedding fifteen pounds, but it had nearly done him in. As they passed a mirror in the hallway of the hotel, he had to acknowledge that the work had paid off. From a distance, he and Jules could pass for the Stantons.

"I gotta say"—he turned to Jules—"I'm loving your new blonde look. Is it true about blondes having more fun?" Rob asked the question more as a whispered suggestion.

"In this gorgeous hotel? I'm pretty sure we are going to find out. Especially since I'm going to bed with Ben Stanton—whoever he is!" Jules dug her elbow into her husband's much-leaner side.

As soon as they were seated, Rob sadly ordered a small bowl of broth and a salad. In an act of solidarity, Jules ordered the same before turning to Rob and posing the question she had been wanting to ask for the past few hours.

"Explain it to me one more time. They are us and we are them?"

Rob had already walked her through the answer several times. He knew she was still nervous. To help calm her—and also to keep his eyes and mind off the huge plate of pasta pescatore being served at a table nearby—he explained their plan and his preparations one more time.

"Yes. You got it. They are us, and we are them. I've left a digital footprint the size of the Grand Canyon out there, including some photos of us sporting our new looks. As far as the internet and any public records reflect, Rob and Jules Bergman must be experiencing a midlife crisis, because Jules has gone blonde, Rob has lost a few pounds, they've sold everything, and are about to retire to their beloved Greek getaway on the island of Folegandros. In the meantime, they have reserved a room at the Hotel Hassler for a short holiday before heading to the island."

"Where the Stantons will be checking in today."

"Exactly. I told them I reserved a room for them in our name, and paid for it with our credit card."

"So if anyone is looking for us . . . ," Jules said.

"They'll trace us to the Hotel Hassler, find Ben and Bree, and assume that they are us."

Jules nodded.

"In the meantime, we will be boarding our nonstop to LAX and beginning our new life as Bree and Ben Stanton." Rob could hardly contain the pride he felt in pulling off such a coup.

"Rob, do you worry about these people? Ben and Bree? They seem so nice. I mean, this could put them in danger."

"We've talked about this ad nauseam. It's them or us. Do you want to make a different choice?" Rob was getting frustrated with this endless moralistic discussion. They'd crossed the line quite a while ago when they started taking on shady clients. And now they were facing the idea of living in hiding for the rest of their lives. Rob had worked through every possible option, and he was convinced there was no other viable scenario.

"No," Jules answered with resignation. "I understand." And Rob knew she did. She understood everything and always had. Now he only hoped that, just this once, the universe would decide to go easy with the karma.

Chapter 17

ROME, ITALY

"This doesn't seem real, does it?" Bree asked, closing her eyes and taking a deep breath, letting herself relax for the first time in a very long time. She was sitting across from Ben in the shade of a tree along the winding Via Veneto. It was a sultry July morning, and the two of them had just finished their second round of cappuccinos at one of their favorite street cafés in all of Rome.

Bree, having finished her croissant, reached absentmindedly for the rest of Ben's.

The famous street was beginning to fill with the sounds and movements of the impeccably dressed, monied, and gorgeous as they began their daily rituals. No one could drip class like the Italians, Bree thought, whether they were sipping an espresso or just walking the dog. Their sense of style was sewn into the seam of everything they did.

It didn't hurt that as a huge movie buff, Bree knew the history of this street. Once, it had been the all-night party scene of the glamorous stars of the '60s, with their miniskirts, sports cars, and wild affairs. They were living "la dolce vita"—the sweet life. Bree couldn't help wondering if she and Ben would ever say they had the sweet life again. She had no idea. But for now, this seemed the perfect place for the two of them to start rebuilding their lives.

Bree wasn't sure how the simple desire to escape graduation season had turned into selling their home and businesses and moving abroad.

Or maybe she did. The truth was that she had wanted to flee not just the painful memories and the familiar routines, but pretty much everything about the life she and Ben and Jayden had built together.

And once she and Ben had started letting their lives unravel, the impulse to continue to pull at the loose threads was unexpectedly intoxicating.

Bree stole a glance at her husband as he sat in the morning sunshine, reviewing their bill.

He had been right. Now that they were getting older, the other shoe could drop at any moment—he could lose her or she could lose him. She didn't want to just sit and wait for it to happen, like some helpless victim. Let fate chase after them, but it would have to be on a dead run to catch up.

In fact, her new motto had become "Time to thrive at fifty-five!" When she'd shared it with Ben, he had been miffed, because he was immutably three years older, but she had offered to "grandfather" him in to her "thrive" club. She'd let him know that the secret initiation was a tequila shot. There was nothing Ben hated more than tequila, especially with the lime wedge. Bree laughed out loud at the memory of how ridiculous he had looked knocking down the shot and shuddering over the lime.

Ben broke into her humorous reverie.

"Does it seem real?" Ben pondered the question Bree had asked a moment ago. "No. It really doesn't. Especially when you think about what we've done in the past three months to get here."

"You were right, Ben. This does feel . . . different. More hopeful. And yet somehow . . ." Bree added wistfully, "I thought it might give us . . . more direction. I'm still not sure exactly where life is taking us."

"It will come, Bree. Just give it time. Leaving the past doesn't make the future magically appear—it just gives us a clean canvas and the chance to create it."

♛

Ben had said the words with true conviction, but part of him could hardly believe the stuff coming out of his mouth these days. He thought to himself, *That sounds like something Oprah would say. Oh well. Whatever it takes to keep Bree moving forward.*

He felt a twinge of embarrassment as he caught the eye of a man sitting a few tables away. The man was staring right at them. He looked like a rich Arab. Ben could only assume the guy probably had ten wives, who, when added together, couldn't have taken as much energy as Ben's one wife did.

This whole scene is probably that guy's worst nightmare. Ben decided he'd had enough humiliation for one day and stood up, dropping some euros on the table.

"Oh, Ben," Bree said with delight, standing up and kissing him hard on the mouth. "A clean canvas? You are so full of it! Where did you read that? In a magazine at the dentist office?" She punched him playfully in the shoulder and turned to head up the sidewalk ahead of him. "I'm going to Harry's Bar for a Bellini, and I don't really care if it's only 10 a.m. You coming?"

Ben sighed, shaking his head and glancing up at the blue sky through the leaves of the trees lining the street.

"Of course," he acquiesced, "but I'm telling you right now, I'm not sitting around drinking Bellinis all day!" He knew before he'd even finished protesting that it was exactly what they would end up doing.

Harry's was the perfect place to drink and watch the rich and famous, and people-watching was one of Bree's quirky passions. She was insatiably inquisitive and adventurous. She had an amazing spirit, a crazy side that could take his breath away, and it was one of the many reasons he had fallen in love with her, and it was the reason he wanted to rescue her right now.

At least, that had been Bree before their world had caved in on them.

As they walked up the hill toward Harry's, Ben thought back over the past several months. It was a miracle that they hadn't both backed out of the plan. Naturally his partners had thought he'd gone crazy.

"Are you absolutely nuts, Ben?" one of them had asked. "You have four projects on the docket and a dozen more in the works! What are we supposed to do? You know these clients don't want to work with anyone else. They came on board to work with *you*."

Aaron Goldberg, Ben's partner and closest friend, had waffled between being exasperated and furious. He'd been upset enough that at one point he even considered staging an intervention.

But in the end, Ben had managed to talk Aaron off the ledge, explaining his concern for Bree and about the graduation announcement. "Aaron. I don't have any other choice. I can't let her go through this graduation season. I really don't think she would make it. Hell, I'm not sure I would make it. Staying here is digging up too many painful memories."

Aaron knew Ben well enough to know he was not going to budge on the decision, and he'd eventually agreed to the potential sale of the partnership, as well as to the idea of someone else taking over Ben's projects. In the end, Ben had managed to negotiate a win-win, giving most of the responsibilities over to his most senior project manager, who had been patiently waiting in the wings for the opportunity.

What Ben hadn't told anybody, not even Bree, was that he secretly hoped this stopgap measure might buy him some time until Ben could really decide if this was a forever decision.

Their house had been a different matter. With its unique architectural design and stunning outdoor space with sweeping LA views, it had sold within a week. After an intense bidding war, the final cash offer had been 30 percent more than what they were asking. And with a cash offer, there'd been no need for any inspections or lender requirements to appease. This had allowed them to spend more time clearing out the accumulation of twenty-five years. As they'd worked their way through their troves of priceless objects, they'd ultimately discovered that without a house to put them in, they weren't really that "priceless."

The new owners had purchased some of Ben and Bree's artwork and furniture, including the entire outdoor patio collection. Ben and Bree had given other favorite pieces to a few close friends, and the remaining items had been sold in a large estate sale. Finally, the truly priceless things—which ended up being mostly Jayden's boyhood items, family pieces from their parents, or collectibles from their travels—had gone into a storage facility. The essentials they'd wanted with them in Greece were sitting in a few trunks on some dock in Santorini, waiting for them to arrive.

It was during this massive clearing-out process that Bree had found a journal of Jayden's that she'd never known existed. According to the dates, Jayden, then seventeen, had kept the journal during the summer he volunteered at an orphanage in Romania.

When she'd shown it to Ben, he'd seen something fragile resurface in her eyes.

"Bree, honey," he'd said, reaching for the journal and taking it gently from her hands, "let's save this for Greece, when we can take our time and really digest it. I'll read it with you; I promise!"

She'd watched his every movement as he'd placed it in one of the packed trunks heading to Santorini; then she had reached in herself to make sure it was protected by some clothing. When Ben had closed the lid and secured the lock, she'd caught her breath. Days later, he'd seen her rub her hand across the top of the trunk as she walked by, as if to place an invisible "mother seal" over the precious cargo. He'd glanced at his watch to check the date, wondering if they would make it out of LA before another wave of uncertainty hit her.

Ben had kept them inching forward, and finally they were here, in Rome, spending a few days to unwind and rewind. The only thing left to do was meet up with Rob and Jules, then ship out to Greece.

The Bergmans. Something about them seemed a little off. Ben was interested to see what these folks were like, even if just to get a quick face-to-face before turning over their property. The easy way they had acquiesced to whatever Ben had wanted still nagged him. And now they had suddenly thrown in a boat and paid for Ben and Bree's very expensive room at the Hassler. Who did that kind of thing without a motive?

Ben and Bree had been walking up the Via Veneto to Harry's Bar and now, as he watched Bree waltz onto the patio, he pushed his unsettling thoughts aside.

I'll just wait and see what I think after meeting them.

Bree seemed very focused as she picked out the perfect table close to the sidewalk, with a full view of the avenue and a stone's throw from the walls of the Galleria Borghese.

Turning, she beckoned to Ben. "Look! The perfect spot!"

He smiled as he made his way to her side. He got there just as a waiter arrived to formally seat them.

"Oh, honey," Bree exclaimed, "I'm so glad we decided to take a few days before getting on the boat to Santorini. Did you see that Lamborghini over there?" Without skipping a beat, she addressed the waiter. *"Due Bellinis, per favore."*

As the waiter left to retrieve their drinks, Ben chuckled and shook his head. *What's a day spent drinking thirty-dollar drinks?*

He'd have bought her Harry's bar itself if it kept her from remembering their reason for being here.

Chapter 18

ROME, ITALY

Nazir stood in the shadows across the street from the café, watching the couple as they sat at one of the outside tables, enjoying a languorous morning breakfast.

As if in direct contrast to their easy, calm idyll, he struggled to keep his anger from boiling to the surface. This was supposed to be Amir's job, but he had been mysteriously called away on more pressing matters. Al-Zawahiri had asked Nazir to do it. His father never did anything without a hidden agenda, so Nazir figured it was some kind of test. It wasn't as if he couldn't succeed at the task—it was just that he hated being constantly scrutinized by his father.

Now, just ruminating on all of this made it difficult to concentrate on the couple.

Turning his attention back to them, he watched incredulously as the woman ate her own croissant as well as her husband's, washing them down with at least two or three cappuccinos. He wondered how she could remain so slim. His eyes lingered on her tall, thin frame before moving up to her blonde hair, green eyes, and endless tan. She definitely had what he would have described as the quintessential California look. The husband was also tall and tan, but with darker, more chiseled features. Neither were what he expected Rob and Jules Bergman, two sun-deprived Brits, to look like.

Something isn't right.

Nazir crossed the street, casually seating himself at a table near the couple. After ordering his own espresso, he unfolded the newspaper he had carried with him in feigned absorption as he attempted to catch their conversation. It wasn't their discussion, but their American accent that startled him, making him momentarily lower the paper.

What the hell?! These people aren't even British.

Unfortunately, the movement brought him eye to eye with the husband, something he didn't want to have happen at this juncture. Luckily, the husband only made brief eye contact. He seemed preoccupied with the bill and trying to half listen to his wife's stream of conversation.

Damn. Why did my father ask me to do this? Nazir thought again to himself. *I'm a highly educated and respected diplomat. What am I doing tailing people, like a private investigator?*

He could only think it was more of his father's weird philosophy of training him to be some kind of "king."

For some reason, thinking about his father jarred an early-childhood memory and brought it to the surface of his thoughts. He remembered his father reading a poem to him as a child, over and over, as if the secrets to life were hidden within its stanzas.

The poem was about a prince who didn't want to be king, despite the fact that it was his destiny. Hiding among the peasants, the prince ran from his responsibilities and his father's wishes, until circumstances intervened.

The poem hadn't made sense to Nazir at the time, especially because he wasn't a prince, nor did he know any kings.

He only knew then, as he knew now, that it was imperative that he never disappoint his father.

Unfortunately, his father's point of view was difficult for Nazir to understand, let alone go along with. Al-Zawahari was determined to embrace an ancient jihad dating back to Abraham. And that stubborn position had set Nazir and his father on a course of inevitable conflict.

For example, while his father and cousin were busy running tests that required the murdering of innocent children, Nazir had been using his intellect and following his instincts. And his instincts regarding the London contacts had already been proven to be correct. Nazir had suspected the British couple they'd been working with would run once the second payment had been missed, and they had. It hadn't been difficult to trace their steps as they'd emptied their bank accounts and their Chelsea flat, tried to change their looks, and moved their assets to a Swiss bank and their possessions to an island near Santorini.

Nazir hadn't been surprised by any of their actions.

Until this morning, when the Bergmans appeared to be a couple of American tourists.

As the husband looked down at his bill, Nazir took the opportunity to stand and quickly step behind a waiter walking by, moving with him until he could duck behind a group of Japanese tourists moving as a herd along the sidewalk, and finally disappearing down a side alley. He stopped in the shadows for a moment, catching his breath, again silently cursing his father.

A moment later he spotted the woman. She marched past the alley entrance, heading up the sidewalk, her husband following behind, shaking his head and laughing. From the brief bit of conversation Nazir overheard as they passed by, he learned that they were headed up to Harry's Bar, and that she, at least, intended to stay there for a while.

Nothing that he had observed in their conversation or demeanor fit a British couple on the run. He decided his best option was to head over to the Hassler and figure out where he had lost the other couple's trail.

Chapter 19

ROME, ITALY

"**I**'m sorry, sir, but there is no message from a Rob or a Jules."

The front desk clerk of the Hassler had delivered the news with the imperious air of the president of Italy himself, looking at Ben through glasses perched on the tip of his nose.

Ben was beyond irritated. Feeling the effects of a few too many Bellinis at Harry's wasn't helping. "Are you sure? Please check again. We're supposed to meet them here tomorrow morning."

Ben was mentally preparing his jousting armor when the clerk dramatically cleared his throat.

"I *said* there is no message from Rob or Jules. There is, however, an envelope addressed to you and your wife. It was delivered by courier, earlier today. I have no idea who it is from."

Ben bristled. Luckily, Bree stepped in.

"Thank you." Bree thanked the clerk, taking the envelope, while Ben attempted to separate his irritation with the clerk from his true disappointment in not meeting the Bergmans.

Ben had really wanted to meet this mysterious couple. Not just because of a nagging doubt or two about the swap, but also because they had been easy to talk to, and Ben and Bree had both sensed the potential of a growing friendship. Who knows? Rob and Jules Bergman might have turned into the first friends Ben and Bree would make on their new journey—new friends, who didn't carry any memories of the Stantons' former life, or their devastating loss.

As Ben looked on, Bree stepped away from the front desk and opened the envelope. "It's a note from Rob," she said, "explaining that a family emergency has come up, and apologizing for not being able to connect in person." The envelope also contained some other documents, he could see. The look on Bree's face told him that she thought something was odd about them.

Ben joined her, holding their hotel key with its heavy ornate tassel, and they headed toward the elevator that would take them to their room. After yesterday's long flight from LA, a restless first night in the hotel, and now a day spent drinking Bellinis, they were both ready to readjust their internal clocks.

In the elevator, Ben took the envelope from Bree, turning it over and back again, looking for a clue that would help explain their hosts' sudden departure. Ben didn't buy the family emergency excuse. As the doors slid open on their floor, he made a mental note to revisit his questions as soon as he and Bree were settled on the island.

Chapter 20

ROME, ITALY

"Oh my God, Ben! I do looooooove this city!" Bree exclaimed, clearly feeling like a new person after a full night's sleep. She took in a deep breath and exhaled with a look of complete bliss.

They were wandering the cobblestone streets of Rome, enjoying an early-morning walk, as they took in the intoxicating aromas of espresso and pasta sauce. Seeing Bree so relaxed confirmed to Ben that they had made the right decision to begin their journey in Rome.

"I think it's weird that the Bergmans didn't show up," Ben mused aloud. "I mean, after all of those phone conversations, and how excited they seemed to be to meet us, doesn't it seem weird to you?"

Bree didn't seem surprised by his question. After all, it must have been more than obvious to her that he'd been stewing over the no-show since the conversation with the clerk yesterday evening. Ben was afraid his funk was starting to interfere with their new commitment to live la dolce vita.

Bree grabbed his arm and gave him a loving hip check.

"Hey, mister. You did extensive background checks on both the website and the Bergmans. They clearly have money. Look at that boat they threw in at the last minute. Besides, it's not like they can just pick up our mountain house and cart it off!! Relax. We came here to forget . . . and to let go, right?"

Ben was silent.

She's right, he thought to himself. *Why the uneasiness? Everything is fine. It's not like I've given them access to our life savings or anything. Besides, we'll probably meet another time.*

He was just feeling on edge. On edge about spending a year on an island he'd never been to, and maybe—if he were honest as he glanced up at the imposing shadow of St. Peter's Basilica—on edge about still feeling stuck in purgatory, a halfway place where he'd left the past but hadn't really found his future. Their future.

"Okay, Miss 'Gelato and Espresso Before Breakfast,'" he said, determined to change the subject and shake off his mood. You're going to have a dilemma this morning. Gee, which one will you have first?"

Ben's question was meant to tease her, but they both knew it would not deter Bree in the least. Her passion for strange food combinations was something he had been in awe of since their first date. This woman could eat. And not just eat, but eat the strangest things without the least bit of trouble. Ben had always stuck to bland basics on their travels, and even that had rarely protected him. But Bree could eat raw fish, washed down with ouzo, followed by fermented horse milk, and laugh and smile through the whole damn meal, without an antacid tablet in sight!

"That's the whole point, Ben. I'm not going to choose!" she laughed, letting go of his arm and nearly sprinting to the gelato shop a few doors down.

And so began another blissfully happy day together.

There were moments when their past life threatened to creep in, but they both seemed to sense those moments, refusing to let memories or sadness steal their fledgling joy.

"Okay, my dear. Any ideas on what you would like to do today besides eat gelato and drink endless cups of espresso?" Ben asked as they sat relaxing at a table outside yet another newly discovered espresso bar.

"Drink!" Bree said slyly and with that come-hither look that could still rattle him.

"I can make that happen, madam." Ben said as he claimed her hand. He dropped euros onto the table, then stood to stretch from sitting too long under the Italian morning sun, pulling Bree up with him. He kissed her with more passion than he remembered ever having in his youth, and they were both surprised and silenced by it.

"Actually, I think I've changed my mind," Bree responded breathlessly, giving him another sly and beguiling glance. "Take me to bed or lose me forever." She smiled as she whispered the famous line from one of their favorite movies.

She didn't have to ask twice. Ben took her hand and pulled her close, wrapping his arm across her shoulder. The walk back to their hotel felt like the most delicious foreplay of their lives. Ben was aware of the fragrant blooms on the trees, the sight of ancient ruins mixed in with modern chic shops, the sound of scooters and taxis vying for road space—but mostly aware of the beat of his own heart. He hoped Bree was too.

Bree walked ahead of Ben into the high-ceilinged, ornate lobby of their hotel. Distracted by anticipation, Ben nearly tripped over a woman's luggage and her small yapping dog. As he caught himself and regained his balance, something caught his eye. It was the Arab man from yesterday, sipping an espresso in the hotel lobby bar, intently staring back at him.

What the hell is this guy doing in the lobby, and why is he looking at us? Ben wondered as he followed Bree into the elevator. Before the doors could close, Ben looked for the man to return the stare.

He had disappeared.

The doors closed and the elevator began its smooth ascent.

Ben shook his head, kissed the back of Bree's neck, and took as deep a breath as his lungs would take in. He let it out slowly. He'd seen the man twice. Big deal. Probably just a coincidence. He was undoubtedly a guest at the hotel. Ben vowed to think about it later. First, he had some exploration to do with one of the most sensuous bodies and deepest souls he had ever known.

There was something profound about that afternoon spent loving each other in their hotel suite. It was as if a supernatural bottle of warm oil had poured down over them, wrapping them in a heated, soothing balm of love—taking them beyond passion, beyond connection and even beyond pleasure.

"Ben. What just happened? Did you feel that?" Bree said, half-crying and half-laughing at the same time. They had always had a strong physical connection. and sex had never been disappointing or boring for them.

Still, there had been an increasing number of times when they were busy and tired from their demanding jobs—and most certainly after they lost Jayden—when they just couldn't bear the thought of trying to pry open their hearts. In those moments, making love had felt too intimate and, at least for Bree, it seemed to Ben, even frightening.

Ben wasn't able to speak. He was trying to find words and to make some sense of his feelings at the same time.

"I have no idea. Wow. What time is it?" As soon as he asked the question, he trapped Bree's arm before she could lift it to see her watch. "Wait—don't answer that. I don't want to know the time. I just want to hold you and never let you go. I don't even want to move, honey. Just stay right here. I feel better than I have in a long time . . . healed . . . lighter . . . I feel . . ."

"Hopeful? Broken open somehow?" Bree was softly crying, the tears leaking out of her closed eyes and running down onto his arm that was cradling her neck. His were falling unnoticed into her hair. It was as if each of them was trying desperately during the moments of silence to make sense of the emotions that had been released after so long.

"I thought I had lost you, Bree—at least your heart. You seemed so contained, so distant." Words began flowing now that Ben had allowed to well up.

"I think it was just my way to survive, Ben. At least I thought I was surviving. Right up until the day Zach's graduation announcement arrived. Then I knew I wasn't doing well after all. And it scared me, because for the first time since Jayden died, I was honest enough to admit that I knew I was never going to be okay. That's why I agreed to your plan. This plan. I knew in my heart I was about to give up."

As Ben listened, he was hearing the old Bree. The remoteness was gone, replaced with that soulful, compelling openness that had always been her trademark.

"Promise me one thing, honey," Ben whispered. "If you find yourself sliding back to that place—and unfortunately, I think we still may have some dark days ahead—promise me that you will walk *toward* me instead of away from me. Let me be your strength, Bree."

Bree let the silence hover for a minute, summoning up the courage to finally own her path forward, then said, "I promise. I'll try. But I also don't want you to have to carry me, Ben. Part of being a parent means being one even when a child is lost. I'm still Jayden's mother—whether he is physically here or not—and I want to keep moving forward, for him. He would have wanted that more than anything." She whispered these last words against Ben's forearm, as though she were unconsciously using his body as her sacred place on which to vow her new intentions.

They spent the rest of the afternoon and evening talking, sleeping, and making love, each experience lifting more of the heaviness from their hearts and bringing a healing balm to the deep chasms of ache buried so deep within them.

Silently and without their awareness, a divine presence greater than themselves hovered over them, weaving shimmering threads through their entangled limbs and around their bodies, binding up the broken shards of their hearts, soothing their wounded spirits, and, lastly, intertwining their souls once again.

Chapter 21

BIG BEAR, CALIFORNIA

"**R**ob! I had forgotten what the forests of the West really looked like—and smelled like!"

As Rob watched his wife, he could see that Jules could barely contain her enthusiasm. It had been so long since the two of them had been someplace so rugged and beautiful. No wonder she was like a kid in a candy store.

They were drinking their morning tea at dawn on the elevated deck of the imposing mountain home, looking out over the surrounding forest.

"I'm thinking maybe we made a good choice after all," Rob said with a smile. "The island was certainly stunning, but always felt a bit confining to me. This place makes me think of infinite possibilities."

"I love the Stantons' place. But I have to say that now that we're here, I'm still feeling a little guilty about luring the Stantons to replace us on Folegandros, Rob. I mean, they didn't really do anything to deserve . . . well . . ." Jules's voice trailed off.

"Yeah, I know," Rob admitted, taking a sip of tea before continuing. "But Jules, there was a high probability we weren't gonna make it out of there alive. You know that, and so do I. What other choice did we have? Besides, maybe—since we never alerted the authorities or demanded the second payment—our clients will decide we aren't going to cause trouble and leave the Stantons alone."

Rob hoped he sounded more optimistic than he actually felt. This place did seem a world away from the stress and danger of their lives for the past decade. He was breathing a little easier now that they'd poured their first cup of tea and were safely ensconced in such a remote and beautiful place. Unfortunately, Jules was not ready to leave the subject behind.

"I'm just sorry we didn't get to actually meet them," she said. "They seemed so nice and so sad at the same time, losing their son and all." She paused in thought, taking a deep breath of the clean mountain air before adding, "This place is certainly stunning. I'm afraid they're going to be slightly disappointed when they land at our place. I'm really glad you threw in that amazing boat. They may want to sleep on that!"

Rob knew she was picturing the owners of this ginormous home walking into their small villa in the Mediterranean.

"Like I said, Jules, we don't know how this will play out. We certainly haven't heard anything yet, and after all, they have been in Rome for a few days. In fact, they should have taken off for Greece already. Let's let some time go by. If we get any inkling that they are in danger, we can always try to alert the consulate or something. In the meantime, what do you say we drive into town and try to acquaint ourselves with our new surroundings?"

At that very moment, a man emerged from the shadows of the trees at the back of the property. He was wearing a medium-sized backpack and had a rifle slung over his shoulder.

Both Rob and Jules were startled. Jules, still in her bathrobe, dropped her cup on the table and grasped to close the front over her nightgown.

Rob wondered if dropping in on your neighbors before the sun was fully risen was some kind of mountain etiquette that they weren't aware of. He thought to himself that the man looked like a cast member on one of those reality TV shows about duck hunting and survival.

"Hey, sorry to bother you two this morning," the man called out, standing still so they wouldn't be afraid. "Name's Ed. My car broke down a few miles back. You have cell service here? I'd like to call a tow truck!" He finished on a slightly louder note than was fitting for the situation, as if he thought they were hard of hearing, or maybe he was nervous.

Rob motioned him to the deck and took a minute to size him up while he crossed the yard. Ed looked to be around six foot two and was wearing hunting camo, heavy boots, and a stocking cap. He looked to be in his midforties, had a pleasant face, and looked like he was in good shape. Rob noticed that he seemed slightly agitated, but who wouldn't be after breaking down and getting lost in the woods? That would have gotten anyone rattled, Rob thought.

"Nice to meet you, Ed." Rob reached down over the side railing and shook the man's hand. "Sorry to hear about your troubles. We can offer you a cup of tea and some breakfast, but unfortunately, this place doesn't have cell service. To make matters worse, we can't seem to get the internet working either," Rob added with a shrug. "We were just headed into town to get some supplies and figure out the cell situation."

"Naw, no thanks to the breakfast," the man said, fidgeting. He set down his pack, his eyes darting around. "I don't need anything except to get the hell out of here. Too bad about the cell coverage. I sure would like to use your facilities, though, and then maybe hitch a ride with you into town if you don't mind?" He seemed to be making an effort to calm himself.

Rob and Jules exchanged glances, but Rob wasn't picking up any bad vibes. Didn't seem like Jules was either.

Rob shrugged. "Sure. Come on in."

Jules added, "Excuse the suitcases. We just arrived yesterday from London and haven't really unpacked yet."

"London? What are you folks doing in Big Bear?" Ed asked nonchalantly, readjusting the rifle on his shoulder as he started up the short flight of stairs to the deck.

Rob noticed that he'd left his backpack propped up against the bottom railing and caught the first sense of danger. He looked desperately around for something to use as protection, but the butt of Ed's rifle hit his temple before he had time to react. The last image he saw was Jules' horrified face as he fell to the ground and the world went black.

In some ways, it was good that he never saw what happened.

♛

Jules' expression went from disbelief to horror as she stared down at her husband. As far as she could tell, he wasn't breathing. She wanted to go to him, but she heard the sound of the rifle being pumped and knew she would be next.

How did they find us so quickly?

Strangely calm and without looking over at the man, she turned and simply walked down the stairs into the yard. The man behind her yelled for her to stop. She didn't bother to turn around. Instead, she kept walking toward the shaft of sunlight coming through the trees, those beautiful trees she had hoped to spend a year getting to know.

She never heard the single shot.

The end was quick. The killer carried the woman's body back up to the house, and then went back for the husband. He did indeed use the facilities and catch some sleep before setting off the explosive device in his pack. The resulting fire and smoke could be seen for miles around, but the inferno was so intense that it would take days before an inspection team could determine that nothing remained of the bodies of Benjamin and Breelyn Stanton or their mountain home.

Chapter 22

CIVITAVECCHIA PORT, OUTSIDE OF ROME

Ben and Bree walked up the ramp toward the yacht, feeling every emotion under the sun.

They had decided to take a short, four-day mini cruise on their way to their new island home.

Unlike the big cruise ships, with thousands of passengers and intensely crowded ports of call, this small European yacht only carried a hundred passengers. That meant it could meander through the Mediterranean to smaller ports, like Elba, Capri and other small island idylls, before finishing in Santorini.

Ben brushed Bree's arm with a caress and smiled. "After yesterday, I'm kind of digging the idea of a remote island."

Ben winked as Bree blushed ever so slightly.

"Well, sir," she said coyly, "I hope you packed your vitamins!"

"I packed so many I had to leave my clothes behind. So, get ready, gorgeous lady. I think we will be turning back the clock a little."

The plan was to pick up supplies in Santorini, then take a much smaller ferry to their island, Folegandros, and begin their new life. The Bergmans had already arranged for a caretaker to show them around, help them unload supplies, and orient them to the property and their new boat.

All in all, this was turning out to be the perfect extension of what Ben was now calling "Honeymoon 2.0."

As they entered the lounge of the ship, they were met by a steward holding a tray of drinks. Ben grabbed two glasses of prosecco and handed one to Bree. Then he raised his flute in a toast to their journey, both past, present, and future.

"Here's to everything we are together!" he said adoringly.

"Thanks, honey. I can't imagine my life without you."

Bree took her first sip of the prosecco and felt a sudden, odd shiver as the bubbly liquid moved down her throat. *What's that about?* she wondered, moving closer to Ben's side, seeking the reassuring touch of his arm against hers.

My life without you. Had she really said those words out loud? Had she foolishly revealed her deepest fear to the universe?

After a few minutes of mingling with other passengers and meeting the crew, Ben steered Bree over to windows overlooking the Mediterranean.

"Do you remember on our first honeymoon at the Hassler, when the room butler showed us to our suite and opened that bottle of Dom Perignon and poured us two glasses?"

"Oh my God, Ben, we were so concerned about what the bottle was going to cost that we forgot to enjoy the toast!"

They both laughed so hard they almost teared up.

"I still remember how relieved I felt when I looked at the final bill and discovered that the bottle had been gratis!" Ben said, shaking his head.

Bree chuckled, remembering how naive they had been back then. But naive or not, they had shared something deep and passionate from the very beginning. "We shouldn't have worried about the cost," she teased. "Think of all the money we didn't spend on food!"

That was an understatement, she thought, almost before she'd finished her sentence. She and Ben had hardly left the room.

"But," Ben responded, and this time he got close enough to her ear that only Bree could hear him whisper, "I would trade all of those days of heated passion for what we shared yesterday, my love."

And without hesitation, Bree let yet another chunk of her painfully constructed guard fall to the floor. All she could think about was the light of the love she saw in Ben's eyes. This man had been the best decision she had ever made, and would ever make, in her life.

Chapter 23

SANTORINI, GREECE

Santorini glittered in the early morning sunlight like a rare sapphire set in a crown of diamonds and gold. Ben and Bree watched breathlessly from the bow as the yacht sailed into the beckoning harbor and anchored under the shadow of the cliffs.

"My God, this is glorious!" Ben said, taking a deep breath of the warm, salt-soaked morning air. "I know we have said that at every port in the past four days, but, baby, this one is really something, isn't it?"

Ben had been holding Bree by his side, and he took a moment to give her a hug and quick kiss before turning to pick up their carry-ons to head back inside.

As they took their first steps onto the narrow gang plank leading from the yacht to the dock, they paused to take in the expansive view of the sparkling harbor and the rugged cliffs that rimmed its busy docks.

Even knowing that the curve of the island was actually the outward shell of an extinct volcano did not prepare them for the magnificence of this ancient harbor, with its steep cliffs rising straight up out of the dark blue water. High above, they could see the famous white stucco structures dotted with blue-domed roofs, pinned in clusters along the edges of the rocks.

Once onshore, Ben and Bree did a quick perusal of the long lines for the aerial gondola used to ferry passengers up to the clifftop village.

"Come on, Bree. Let's live a little. Let's skip the gondola and climb the path. It's not like we are on a clock or anything. You game?" Ben gave Bree's backside a playful pat while pointing to the stone pathway that zigzagged up the side of the cliff and ended at the village perched at the top. He knew that challenging Bree was the way to get her to do anything.

Once they had stored their bags and had confirmed their tickets for the ferry later that evening, Bree was off to the base of the path. Ben snickered. Bree was obviously trying to show him that she was still the fit mountain goat he always called her whenever they hiked.

Halfway up Bree, gasping for breath, stopped to lean against the stone walls that lined their ascent. "Ben, what were we thinking?" she sputtered. "There's more donkey dung on my shoes than there is sole!" She looked down at her shoes and then up at the steep road above.

Suddenly, Ben grabbed her, pulling her back against the stone wall, barely in time to avoid a thundering herd of donkeys racing past them on their way down to pick up the next group of waiting tourists.

As soon as she caught her breath, Bree said, brushing the dirt of the stone wall off the back of her white jeans, "I can see now why most people stand in that long line for the gondola or ride a donkey up this beastly path!"

"Come on," Ben said, taking her hand and steering her back up the steep incline. "It's good for our hearts. We've been eating and drinking our way across the Mediterranean, and it's starting to take its toll on us—well, on me at least!"

He jumped when Bree turned and pinched the small love handle that had begun to form just above the top of his shorts.

Despite the chaotic mix of heat, elevation, people, and donkeys, they eventually made it up the Z-shaped path to the village of Fira, thirteen hundred feet above the Mediterranean. Laughing and gasping for air, they staggered straight to the nearest bar. Soon they were seated at an outdoor table, the breeze blowing gently as they attempted to absorb the incredible beauty of the harbor below and the far-off islands in the distance.

"If the Greek gods actually existed, they must have spent all of their time on top of this island, don't you think?" Bree murmured.

A breeze suddenly curled around them, like a caressing presence, as if to whisper, "*We still do.*" Ben shivered and wondered if Bree had caught the message of the breeze.

"Yeah . . . ," he answered dreamily as the waiter delivered an iced bottle of Assyrtiko and two glasses. "I could stay here all day," he added, feeling relaxed in a way he hadn't felt in years. Once the white wine was poured, he raised his glass to Bree and then swung it out to the cloudless skies and finally down to the harbor, glistening below their clifftop perch.

"Here's to you, my love . . . to our grand adventure . . . and to this intoxicating place."

Bree rewarded him with a big smile, and his heart did a somersault. Life suddenly felt . . . possible. He hoped Bree felt that too. They poured another glass of wine and spent the next hour letting the intense beauty and energy of the island nurture their bodies and their hearts.

After the views and wine had satiated their spirits, Ben and Bree left their table and wandered hand in hand through the narrow stone streets. The day flew by as they picked up some last-minute provisions, checking items off their shopping list one by one. Much too quickly, it was time for an early dinner. Their time in Santorini was drawing to a close. After dinner, they were scheduled to board the small ferry for their island.

They chose a restaurant that the Bergmans had suggested. It was known for its exquisite preparation of the local fish caught daily from the Mediterranean. Ben stuck with his usual salad and gyro meat. Bree, however, enthusiastically embraced the "while in Rome" theme she'd always lived by, and started with a plate of freshly caught calamaries, marinated and laying on a bed of lettuce. In between bites of his familiar and safe pita bread, Ben was subjected to the vision of legs or tentacles or whatever they were disappearing into her mouth, her eyes closing with each bite, as if she were in sheer ecstasy.

"Oh my God, Bree. I've never understood and will never understand how you can eat all of this stuff and not have a freakin' huge stomachache." Ben said the words with love and delight, laughing as he looked down at Bree's second course as it arrived. Who the hell knew what that stuff really was? He looked up again and this time caught the moving shadow of a man right behind her head—a shadow that looked familiar and caused a cold chill to run down his neck even in the heat of the early evening.

"Tell me it ain't so," he said under his breath.

"What, honey?" Bree asked as she sat hunched over the piping-hot dish of eggplant souvlaki in front of her.

"I'll be right back!" Ben said, pushing himself away from the table.

He hurried toward the restaurant's only exit, hoping to confront the man who seemed to be stalking them. Forced to slow down long enough to let an older couple get up from their table, Ben didn't make it to the door in time, and the man managed to slip out. Ben tried to follow but was blocked by a new group of diners coming in the doorway. He turned quickly and headed to a balcony overlooking the street. Peering over the edge, he spotted the man slipping down a narrow alleyway and disappearing around a corner.

It was the same guy, all right. This was the third time Ben had spotted him. He could no longer tell himself that this was a coincidence.

Who the hell was this guy, and what could he possibly want with them? Bree wasn't loaded down with expensive jewelry, and it wasn't like they were dropping wads of cash everywhere. They were seasoned enough travelers to make sure they kept low profiles when abroad. It just wasn't making sense. Ben couldn't shake the bad feeling he had about this guy.

And now, to make things worse, he and Bree were headed to an island and setup that were completely unfamiliar.

Ben headed back to the table, mulling over their options. If they got on the ferry tonight, their chances of slipping away were much higher than if they spent the night in a hotel and left in broad daylight. But if, by chance, this guy knew where they were heading, he would find them regardless, and they would be more vulnerable on the small island.

Bree hardly seemed to sense that he had been gone, already perusing the dessert menu. As Ben sat back down, he tried to recapture his previous sense of enjoyment, but he couldn't shake the unnerving feeling of being watched.

"Okay, I'm definitely going with the pecan baklava!" Bree announced, clearly in her element. "It looks amazing. And then I'm thinking some of that great coffee with a shot of—"

"I hate to do this, honey," Ben interjected, "but we either need to leave now to grab the gondola to the harbor so we can catch the ferry, or we'll have to spend the night here and try it again in the morning. What would you like to do? My vote is to leave now."

"Oh, you're right. I can't keep eating like this. Besides, with our supplies purchased and waiting for us on the dock, it makes sense to jump on the ferry and get going. I can always find baklava in Greece."

The waiter appeared and Ben paid the bill; then he stood up to leave. Bree put on a fresh coat of lipstick, then gathered up her purse and her sunglasses and stood up to join Ben. Just as they stepped away from the table, Bree felt a tap on her shoulder. She turned to find the waiter had returned from the kitchen. He held a small box.

"Madame, in honor of your great passion for our food, I would like to give you this complimentary baklava to take with you." Bowing, the man handed her the gift.

"Thank you, Andreas. I have so enjoyed the meal!"

With Ben pulling her arm, Bree waved goodbye, and they both stepped out of the restaurant.

"You do live right, baby," Ben said, shaking his head. "The food gods follow you around and pour blessings all over you."

"Food gods? Very funny. You are going to thank me tomorrow morning when I pour you a cup of instant coffee on our tiny little patio overlooking the neighbor's giant satellite dish and hand you a perfectly delectable slice of baklava," she teased, her voice mellow after the relaxing day filled with good food and wine.

"Knowing you, I doubt that stuff lasts halfway through the ferry ride," Ben rejoined. "And speaking of that, we better bust a hump or we will be spending the night on that dung-strewn harbor sidewalk!"

With that, he hurried her through the crowded narrow streets toward the entrance to the gondola.

The ride down was steep and swift. At the dock, Ben hired a couple of dock hands to load their supplies onto the ferry, which turned out to be a hybrid between a jet boat and a large fishing boat. It might only hold a few dozen passengers, but it had plenty of horsepower.

The man following them was nowhere to be seen, and not among the few passengers. It gave Ben the breathing room he needed to calm his racing heart.

The engines rumbled to life as the ferry slowly pulled out of the harbor. The sun dipped low on the horizon, finally disappearing as its last gasp of pink and gold light danced on the gentle waves. It was a gloriously surreal moment for both Ben and Bree, who were standing at the bow, arms entwined. To anyone watching, they could have been two ancient Greek statues, locked together, and worn to an alabaster smoothness from the winds of suffering.

The softness of the moment brought fresh thoughts of Jayden to both of them. Bree found herself wondering why Jayden had been so insistent about taking a gap year and traveling together, and wishing with all of her heart they could have shared this trip with him. Ben found himself questioning the quixotic nature of any God who could create such beauty and yet allow such senseless and horrific things as Jayden's murder.

Instinctively, they tightened their embrace, trying not to let their unanswered questions pull them into an emotional abyss. But it was no use. As the boat cleared the edge of the majestic harbor ridge and headed out to sea, it was as if Ben and Bree had also cleared some kind of safe harbor and were heading out to rough, unchartered waters.

As the bow sliced through the swells, strains of an ancient mariner's song could be heard wafting across the darkening waters, whispering a plaintive reminder:

Come, walk these ancient islands,
and learn from this azure sea,
all that is of healing . . .
the song of life . . .
eternal call . . .
Love.

Chapter 24

SANTORINI, GREECE

From the shadow of a building near the harbor, Nazir watched the couple run to catch the small, inter-island ferry bobbing in the darkening water. As he had confirmed before their arrival, their destination was the nearby island of Folegandros.

Discovering in Rome that these people were not the British couple he was supposed to be tracking had changed everything. Instead of dealing death to these two, he needed only to set up a means by which to watch them for any suspicious behaviors.

It had only taken money and resources to replace the original caretakers at the island home with his own team. His standing instructions to his people now posing as their staff were to attend to the couple's needs, and to report back to him anything suspicious or of interest. He had seen no reason to expect that he would hear from them.

Nazir sighed and walked out from the shadows over to one of the lampposts, to get a better view of the ferry as it started up and turned to head out of the harbor. He had no interest in spending any more of his own time chasing these two, especially now that he realized they were most likely just clueless pawns in the bigger picture.

In fact, these two appeared to be nothing more than restless, wealthy Americans in search of an experience living abroad. They seemed to have inadvertently crossed paths with the Brits, who had made a valiant but unsuccessful attempt to switch identities, intending to use them as unsuspecting decoys.

Unfortunately for the British couple, their elaborate plan was relatively easy to unravel, and just as easy to rectify. In fact, Nazir had already received the text from Amir indicating that the California assassin had been successful.

Nazir felt an odd lurch in his chest as he thought about the dead couple. He wondered if he would ever get used to the idea of taking the life of someone else. His approach, had he been in charge of this plan, would have been to watch and wait to see if, in fact, the Brits intended to cause trouble. Maybe they would have disappeared without saying a word. But his father had wanted absolute resolution, and Amir had evidently found a way to bring swift results.

These two Americans don't know how close they came to being killed. They were just damn lucky the Brits ditched them in Rome, Nazir thought, shaking his head at the near miss and the whim of the Fates, of which the American couple were unaware.

Leaning against the post, he reached up to light a cigarette, his Rolex glimmering in the light from the lamp above his head. He was still musing about the role of fate in the grand scheme of life and death when his phone vibrated. With one fluid movement, he turned away, simultaneously taking his first drag and lifting the phone, to scan the incoming message. He was being summoned back to Yemen.

His breath caught at the thought of the magnitude of the attack that was about to be perpetrated on the Western "infidels." Nazir wondered if, after all his father's years of planning and sacrifice, this would bring Al-Zawahiri what he was expecting. Nazir was not so sure.

He turned back to the water and watched as the ferry cleared the breakwater at end of the harbor. Nearly every passenger had crowded to the stern of the boat order to catch a last glimpse of the stunning harbor and cliffs, the last bastions of land and security before heading out into the deep Mediterranean beyond. So, it was odd to see the American couple standing at the bow, holding each other and looking out to sea. He wondered briefly about their story, and why they had no interest in looking back.

He watched until he could see only the faintest outline of the boat. It was only then that he turned and walked down a wooden ramp to a nearby dock. There, an unmarked powerboat sat idling. The driver looked to him for an order, which Nazir quietly issued in Arabic as he stepped down into the boat.

On the other side of the island, a yacht waited. On the yacht was a helicopter that would whisk Nazir to a jet, which would then take him directly back to Yemen.

Chapter 25

FOLEGANDROS, GREECE

There is the proverbial "morning after," and then there is the first time you wake up to the sun-drenched morning that can only be found on a small Greek island in the middle of the Mediterranean.

So it was for Ben and Bree.

The ferry ride over to their new home had been too short to allow them the time needed to process the flood of emotions they felt as they left the safe harbor of Santorini. Once they'd reached the island, they found the caretakers to be very nice and more than understanding, insisting that they unload all of Ben and Bree's supplies, bags, and the trunks that had already been shipped.

Ben and Bree had been only too grateful to turn the logistics over to their hosts and fall into bed, overcome with an exhaustion that was sudden and overwhelming.

Which was why the midmorning sunshine woke them at almost the same instance and with such a jolt.

"Ouch. Who turned on the solar oven?" Ben croaked, his throat dry as he rolled out of bed and stood on the cool floor tiles. He headed toward what he vaguely remembered as the master bathroom and was again blinded by the light coming in through the window. The open shutter not only let in the intense light, but also revealed a glimpse of a blue sea, the color of which he struggled to name. *Azure? Lapis?* What had that travel book called it?

"My God, Bree . . . I don't know what the rest of this place looks like, but I'm about to pour a glass of wine and just hang out in here!" He yelled the words toward the bedroom, only to turn and bump into an equally blurry-eyed Bree, both of them laughing at how out-of-it they were, and yet how delighted at what they had discovered. The place had turned out to be amazing!

"Ben, I'm good with everything you said, but could we start with coffee before we move on to wine?" Anyone who knew Bree knew that coffee was the essence of life in her world, and that nothing of significance could be allowed to happen without a cup of steaming dark roast in hand.

"Lucky for us, I paid close attention to the instructions last night on how to work that amazing thing they call a coffeemaker. You go splash some water on your face, and I'll attempt to get something brewing. Meet you in the kitchen in five."

Ben went off to make magic in the kitchen, leaving Bree to do exactly what he suggested.

Bree looked into the mirror with a little shock, as usual. Not because the last two years had clearly taken their toll on her face in terms of its previous fullness and light, but because she was always slightly surprised to see that grief hadn't killed her. Here she was, not only alive, but slightly happy and waking up in the sunshine of a glorious morning on a Greek island. And then the inevitable dagger of thought stabbed her conscience before she could stop it.

What right do I have to be here when Jayden isn't?

The searing power of that thought always made her catch her breath. It was abrupt and surprising every time, like accidentally touching a hot stove.

Will I ever get to the point where I don't have this whiplash? Where the momentary joy of forgetting isn't followed by the crushing pain of remembering?

She turned away, pulling her robe over her shoulders and making a concerted effort to move past the thought, when she walked into Ben, holding two clay mugs of steaming coffee.

♕

"Coffee has arrived!" Ben said brightly, masking the concern he felt seeing Bree struggle as she tried to face this new day and new life. He knew it was a replacement life and not the one she had hoped they would be living, and for a moment, he wondered if doing this thing without Jayden had been a wise idea. In all the frenzied planning and preparation, he'd forgotten that they would have to actually live— just the two of them—a year that had been meant for the three of them.

He looked over at Bree, her mask now firmly in place as she smiled back at him and reached for the coffee mug he held out to her. It took such courage and strength to choose to move forward, and he felt a rush of love and compassion for her.

Ben also knew it was going to be a lonely battle. He could only do for her these small things, like coffee or hugs or teasing. The mother's heart she was attempting to heal was her own—one he could not heal for her. The thought made him sad, and for the first time in his life, he wondered if he should have gone into medicine after all. Maybe if he had, he would know of some other way to help her.

All he had this morning to give her was his love, a good cup of coffee, and that sea he had glimpsed from the window. He hoped that would be enough, at least for today.

♕

Bree saw the waves of concern and love wash over Ben's face. As hard as it was for her to face this day, she could only imagine what it was like for him. This man, who could build, analyze, and engineer anything, could not fix the hole in their lives.

The frustration and pain must be agonizing for him, she thought, silently vowing to try to work harder at her part.

Just then, a newly minted and fleeting thought crossed her mind. *What if there is still something purposeful for us? Something we can only find or understand on the other side of grief?*

Ben spoke and interrupted her thoughts. "What say we drink this out on that lovely patio with that crummy view and come up with a plan for our first day here?"

Bree responded by looking deep into his eyes, beaming her love to him as warmly as she could.

"Deal."

They had more than a couple of mugs of coffee, and then quickly dressed and headed out into the sunshine, determined to explore the beach below, as well as the small village nearby. For anyone watching—and there were several pairs of eyes trained on them—they appeared to be happy-go-lucky tourists, holding hands, and laughing as they walked along the path toward the sea, oblivious to anyone other than themselves.

Chapter 26

CIA HEADQUARTERS, LANGLEY

After pacing for several minutes, Mac returned to his desk, still trying to wrap his mind around all the details from Ian's call.

A child who had been targeted was still alive!

It was a miracle, considering that these extremists had gotten their hands on something so deadly—and effective.

The other thing Mac couldn't wrap his head around was the sheer magnitude of the potential outcomes.

How far along were they in their plan? Who was the next target, and how were he and Ian going to find that needle in a world of 8 billion haystacks?

Think, Mac! Put yourself in their shoes. Pretend that you want to test a new level of terror, so you stick some crap into a vaccine, inject it into a bunch of orphans in a remote Romanian orphanage, and kill them all. Who are you targeting next?

The ominous question made Mac's chest feel like it was being compressed by a cosmic vise.

Day cares? Schools? Hospitals? The list is endless. He could feel his blood pressure rising.

Again, he returned to his computer screen, looking for any new intel or chatter, but the whole region had gone eerily silent. He made a

119

few exploratory calls to the CDC and WHO, looking for anything new or alarming. They had nothing suspicious to report. Finally, he scanned through what he knew were special geographic regions of interest, meaning places where there were active NSA or CIA operatives dealing with Middle Eastern terrorist groups.

Still nothing.

He drove home that night feeling defeated. *Maybe I'm just not as smart as I think I am. These bastards are getting the best of me, and I don't like it! Maybe I* should *be put out to pasture . . .*

That evening, as he sat in his worn leather chair in front of the TV, nursing his one scotch while halfheartedly watching the news, he could feel the heavy sense of dread building in his chest again. What were these crazy terrorists up to? The ruminating got so bad that at one point, he had a fleeting thought about asking his dead wife for some "divine help."

Gloria? Any chance of helping out down here?

Mac stopped himself before he actually asked the question aloud.

Probably not a great idea to get her in hot water over my problems.

Mac wasn't sure the tentative detente he had reached with God over his wife's sudden death was solid enough to call in favors. Besides, he was pretty certain that after his initial tirades, his number had been moved to the Old Man's "do not call" list.

He decided to turn back to the news.

There was a story about a rogue LAPD cop who had been implicated in the death of a wealthy California couple. Apparently, he had been in the grip of some PTSD episode, probably related to a couple of tours in Iraq. Something had tripped his trigger, and he'd blown up a private residence in Big Bear, resulting in the two deaths, before he had taken his own life.

Doesn't bode well for the good guys when one of our own goes off the deep end, Mac thought to himself. *Poor fella.*

The next news story featured more dire economic updates, alluding to the potential for yet another looming financial crisis and stock market crash.

Great. So now that I have to retire and live on a fixed income, my money is not going to be worth crap!

Mac stood up and grabbed the remote with disgust, pointing it at the screen, ready to call it a night, when another story caught his attention. Apparently, the Gates Foundation had launched distribution of a new vaccine in tandem with the CDC. Folks were calling it a game changer because it was the first effective immunization against malaria. The reporter went on to say that it had been fast-tracked through the usual maze of FDA approvals in order to expedite its use among the general population.

This wouldn't have typically caught Mac's attention, except the vaccine was slated for worldwide use, even in areas not currently at risk for contracting malaria, like the USA.

"What quack decides that a vaccine for people who aren't at risk makes sense?" Mac muttered to himself.

As if answering his question, some PhD from an Ivy League school came on to extol the virtue of fighting epidemics, pandemics, and a bunch of other "-emics" using broad-based vaccines. In his best doomsday voice, the professor went on to cite statistics that indicated it was only a matter of time before a pandemic hit the world population.

Mac moved closer to the TV, his attention now on full alert. A scientist was taking the idea one step further, talking about the vaccine's crossover effectiveness in potentially warding off the West Nile virus and Zika, which were becoming more prevalent in the North American continent and, in particular, the US.

Mac shook his head, bewildered. He was all for being prepared, but to vaccinate Americans when half the world really *did* need the vaccine seemed a stupid use of resources, in his mind.

So, we convince folks in Podunk towns across America to line up and get a shot in order to avoid something they are never likely to be exposed to . . .

Alarms started going off in Mac's head before he could even finish the thought. "Holy shit! That's it!"

He looked up toward the ceiling and blew a kiss to the only angel he knew by name and drained his glass.

Glancing at his watch, Mac quickly calculated the time difference, deciding the news was too important to worry about Ian's beauty sleep.

Mac sat down and picked up his cell phone. Then he dialed his friend's number.

On the sixth ring, Ian answered. "This bloody well better be life-or-death!" Ian barked into the phone.

"More than you will ever know, my friend!" Mac answered.

"I imagine you're calling at this ungodly hour because you just saw a news report about the launch of a worldwide vaccine."

Nothing like being out-spooked by another spook. It always annoyed Mac when Ian got the better of him—which he often did.

"I'm not even going to ask how you knew already," Mac said, too excited tonight to take Ian's bait. "More important, do you think it makes any sense as a possible connection? How would this terrorist group have learned about this vaccine distribution without some pretty high-level intel?"

"To answer your first question, we are just starting to put the picture together regarding our 'friends' in Budapest. My guys in London just finished cleaning the hard drive from the orphanage and have started tracing the emails back to their sources. There is quite an intricate network involving that bogus pharmaceutical company. It was clearly a front for a jihadist operation of some type, and it's becoming very clear that the attack on the children was indeed a trial run for something much larger and more catastrophic."

"When are we going to know about the implanted bioagent and whatever trigger was used?" Mac asked, his impatience starting to bleed through in his tone of voice.

"Nothing identifiable so far. In the meantime, I want to tell you about the real estate transaction involving the warehouse. This could be the missing link we need. Apparently, our terrorists used a third party to secure and retrofit properties. We had a hard time finding the identity of the third party—or I should say identities."

"Identities?" Mac asked. "They were working with more than one party?"

"Turns out they were working with an American expat couple living in London who have been doing these under-the-radar transactions for shady operations for years. Seems the couple got a tad skittish after this contract, because they decided to retire to some small Greek island in the middle of the Mediterranean."

"What scared them?" Mac pressed.

"Who knows?" Ian continued, "but it was an abrupt departure. Their flat and offices were cleaned out, as in *cleaned* out. But here's where it gets odd."

"It's already odd," Mac grunted.

"They're obviously pretty savvy, having been involved with fairly sophisticated clandestine activities for years. Then suddenly, they lay down a pretty obvious trail to a Greek island, where they plan to retire."

"That doesn't really fit the profile, does it?"

"Right, ole boy. I have someone headed to that damn island, looking for them, and I should have some better intel the next time we speak."

"We also need to know where the CDC vaccines are being manufactured, right?"

"Already on it," Ian assured. "But we also have to be open to the possibility that the bioagent isn't being introduced at the time the vaccine is manufactured. It could be added at any point along the distribution channel."

"We also need to identify where the first batch of CDC vaccines is headed," Mac said. "What makes this vaccine so appealing to the terrorists is the breadth of its intended use. Highly unusual to get half the world's population lined up as potential victims without firing a single shot."

"Unfortunately," Ian added, "which half and when is anybody's guess!"

Both men recognized the agonizing complexity of the situation.

Mac had a thought but didn't know how it was going to be received by his old friend. "We have that kid, Ian. What say we take a shortcut and make the bastards come to us? I know you don't want to use a kid as bait, but we may not have a choice." Mac hoped to appeal to his friend's logical nature. For some reason Ian had gone soft on this one.

"I'll bloody well send a handwritten invitation with my mother's picture and address before I string a child out to dry, JD. She's a nine-year-old orphan!"

"Yes, but she is the best chance we've got, and you know it! I'm not wanting to get her injured, but I'm also not above the idea of the 'good of the many'—and neither are you!"

Mac knew that Ian would have given him the same lecture if the roles were reversed.

Silence.

"JD, you got me by the balls on that one." Ian's voice had gone quiet and cold. "I'll compromise with you and leak something about the surviving child. But first, I'm going to need to fortify the place without getting children or the director suspicious. She already thinks I'm bad news. I'll call you when it's all in place."

Ian slammed the phone down without so much as a goodbye.

Mac got up from his leather chair and, rather uncharacteristically, walked over and poured another scotch. It had indeed been one of those two-scotch evenings, and he had more thinking and mulling to do.

Chapter 27

Yemen

The driver made a sudden turn into a dark, narrow street, jolting Nazir out of his brooding thoughts. As Nazir looked out his side window, he could see that the car was moving along the familiar high stone wall of his family compound. It looked as impenetrable as the inky black sky above it. He felt his heart rate pick up speed. This always happened when he was about to see his father—it was one of the great ironies of his life.

In Washington, DC, Nazir could push this life into a locked room, thinking only rarely about its details. There, he was a well-respected lecturer and consultant, the go-to source for interpreting and understanding the Arab culture. As a constant behind-the-scenes face on Capitol Hill, he was often asked to be involved in the latest congressional peacemaking or crisis-solving agendas for the Middle East. The respect he garnered had also earned him a high-level diplomatic clearance status and, eventually, relationships stretching all the way to the White House.

It was all part of the great Al-Zawahiri's plan for Nazir's role as his son and heir apparent. Nazir had been groomed to play the role of "Nazir Akbari," the ruse made believable by a pseudo-identity, degrees from Ivy League schools, and strategic diplomatic connections purchased by his father's money. Al-Zawahiri had meticulously orchestrated Nazir's life down to the smallest detail. Not out of love for his son, but out of a desire to bring down the Western infidels from within their own walls.

But now, it only took the smell of the desert night air and the feel of its desolation to bring all of Nazir's childhood memories roaring back. Even now, dressed in his expensive suit and sitting in the back of a chauffeur-driven car, he could taste the loneliness and isolation of his youth. He could also feel the heat of his father's constant opinions—the endless history lessons told through the lens of Al-Zawahiri's worldview—meant to mold Nazir's young, impressionable mind.

But he had also been the product of his mother, Al-Zawahiri's first wife, known for her serene beauty and calm spirit. While his father had believed in teaching him through discipline and strength, his mother had taught him through quiet courage and, in the end, dignity. Nazir rubbed his forehead. He still could not think about her death.

For him, this inevitable flood of memories always took him on a conflicted journey, one that was littered with emotional and philosophical land mines. Reliving these memories never brought him resolution and, just like now, he was inevitably left with feelings of confusion and unrest.

As the car cruised along the exterior wall of the compound, Nazir tried to push his thoughts aside. *Tonight, I must be at the top of my game,* he reminded himself.

A few minutes later, the driver flipped the headlights off and on twice, then slowed the car, turning through a set of gates that seemed to slide open only long enough to swallow the vehicle before closing again. Nazir had traveled by private yacht from Santorini to Tripoli, by air to Yemen, and finally by car to this heavily fortified compound. And yet, with all that time to think and plan, he was still trying to figure out exactly what he wanted to report to his father.

Dealing with Al-Zawahiri always resembled an intricate dance, and Nazir inevitably found himself weaving between respecting his father's authority and making stealth moves of self-protection.

The car rolled to a stop. Nazir tapped the driver on the shoulder and stepped out of the car. At that moment, the heavily fortified door of the main building opened as if on cue.

Nazir took a moment to straighten his suit coat and, more important, his shoulders, and then walked swiftly through the entrance into the main hall. Several servants stood along the walls, as silent and stiff as statutes, waiting for orders from their master. One of them stepped forward from the shadows and, with a slight bow, greeted Nazir and then motioned for him to follow.

They stopped in front of a set of heavy, ornate doors, and the servant knocked softly before stepping in to announce Nazir's arrival. Al-Zawahiri, wrapped in the same style of robes and headcover worn by his ancient ancestors, sat on a large, cushioned chair that reminded Nazir of a throne.

How apropos, he thought cynically before raising his expressionless eyes to his father's face.

Al-Zawahiri looked up from something he was reading, his eyes equally dark and impenetrable. He took a moment to assess Nazir's expensive suit, Italian shoes, and coiffed hair, the slight tightening of Al-Zawahiri's jaw the only hint of his disapproval. He wished silently that his oldest son had less of his mother's beauty and sense of style, and more of his cousin's intensity and ambition.

He got straight to the point.

"The elimination of our concerns in California appears to have been handled with great success by Amir and his team. What is your assessment?"

He didn't wait for Nazir's answer before continuing.

"And what are your observations of the Americans who are staying in the Bergmans' home near Santorini?"

"*Alsalam elaykum warahmat Allah wabarakatuh.* May peace and mercy and blessings of Allah be upon you." Nazir greeted his father with a slight bow, despite Al-Zawahiri's typical disregard for personal greetings.

His father ignored the gesture.

Nazir continued. "Whatever arrangements the Americans made to exchange homes with our British couple, they appear to have been left in the dark as to the Bergmans' true identities and occupations. As we now know, the rendezvous in Rome was a ruse on the part of the Brits, intended to confuse us into believing their identities were in fact those of this American couple. Of course, they had no way of knowing how much we already knew about them and that there was little chance of us following this bogus trail, especially once I was able to observe the Americans."

Nazir looked for any response from his father and, when there was none, he continued.

"As you have heard, the Brits were eliminated in an arson incident perpetrated by an LAPD officer who supposedly 'snapped.' That officer was eliminated by Amir's team once he had completed the required tasks. We did leave his family untouched, as negotiated, although I had some difficulty in convincing Amir that it made sense to do so."

Nazir wanted to add something about his concerns regarding Amir's increasingly unstable nature, but one look at Al-Zawahiri's face told him the timing was not right.

Nazir continued with his assessment.

"As Amir has undoubtedly told you, the ongoing investigation has already ruled out terrorism. I am confident the case will close soon." Nazir delivered this last statement with a rush of words that mirrored the increasing pulse beating in his chest.

Fear was the control factor of every encounter and interaction with his father. Nazir had learned early in life that there was no accounting for the mysterious "will of Allah," which apparently only his father could interpret and dispense.

"Unless something changes, we will leave the clueless Americans alone for now," Al-Zawahiri commanded, standing abruptly to his feet, which caused the servants to stand at attention, alert and ready to serve. "Our focus must be on the creation and implementation of the greatest death blow ever delivered to the infidels. Allah has cleared our pathway with the successful test on the orphans, and we must now swiftly move toward our destiny. I will discuss the plan in detail with you tomorrow, once we have both rested."

Without another word, Al-Zawahiri swept out of the room, his robes, the sound of his purposeful stride, and his dark energy swirling after him. The audible exhale of every remaining person in the room came unprompted at the sound of the closed door. The collective sigh echoed the sound of the wind outside as it blew over the sands around the compound, relentless and without mercy.

Nazir watched his father's grand exit before stepping back and turning around toward the larger main doors. He motioned the servants away, not wishing to fall back into the habit of having grown men unpack his things, run his bath, or fill his water carafe. Instead he picked up his own bag and walked toward the suite he always used when visiting, wondering briefly if his father had ever experienced the simple pleasure of doing anything for himself. Had he ever run freely as a young boy, playing in a world of imagination and creativity? Or had he always been at the mercy of a myopic drive for power and control? Nazir was fairly certain there would never be a time or place when he could ask his father questions like these.

Once he'd shut the outer door to his rooms, Nazir could feel the walls closing in around him, pushing and shoving his emotional resolve around as if he were still a child.

Why does this place still make me feel like a defenseless little boy?

As if to drive home the point of his hard-won independence, he lay down on the bed fully clothed, exhausted but unwilling to undress. His last thoughts were of tomorrow's plan, wondering what his father would require of him.

Meanwhile, sitting quietly behind the closed doors of his private rooms, Al-Zawahiri reflected on how pleased he was at having masterminded such a vision for himself and for his people.

His chemists had already stockpiled the bioagent destined to replace the vaccines that would soon be en route to six targeted cities. The plan was for his men to intercept the vaccine between the CDC's sanctioned labs and the distribution points in each city, replacing it with vials of bogus vaccine spiked with the bioagent. So seamless was the planning and organization that it was difficult for him as a zealot of Islam to keep from praising Allah in advance for the success of such a powerful and visionary jihad.

He refused to accept any concept of guilt or wrongdoing. Any mantle of responsibility for the lives at stake would fall on the shoulders of the American leaders. If they chose to negotiate and hand over the power and wealth he would demand, no drone triggers would be sent . . . at least not right away.

He had no intention of keeping any promises to which he would agree.

Eventually, he would send the drones.

Let the foolish infidels trust Islam for a while and see what it was like to experience persecution and discrimination. Let them be mocked for their spiritual beliefs and their cultural idiosyncrasies. In the end, they would be dragged once again to the proverbial Coliseum to be slaughtered, crying out to their God in vain for mercy.

And then there would be only one ruling nation, one caliphate for Allah.

Chapter 28

FOLENGANDROS, GREECE

"**B**en, are we really going to keep walking up and down this one beach all day?" Bree asked as they passed the same beach café, with its distinctive blue-and-white-striped awnings and umbrellas, yet again.

Ben laughed.

Folegrandros had ended up being a much smaller version of Santorini—huge cliffs with villages perched on top, with only a few accessible beaches dotted here and there.

"Well, we've already had our coffee, completed three crossword puzzles, swam laps in the pool, climbed up to the church of the Virgin Mary, gone around the entire island by boat"—Ben paused to glance down at his watch—"and it's only three forty-five. Our dinner reservations are for eight. Any other ideas?"

Ben's sarcasm wasn't lost on Bree. He was just voicing the same sense of island ennui that she was feeling. The island was excruciatingly small. They'd only been there five days, and it felt more like a month.

The third time walking past the café was their undoing. For some reason, as they looked at the café and then at each other, it struck them as so funny that they lost all control, laughing hysterically and staggering toward the water to avoid the stares from customers sitting at the outdoor tables.

Moving farther away from the café didn't make things any better, as they continued to struggle for control, holding their stomachs, doubling over, and eventually sinking to their knees in the sand.

At first, the laughter felt liberating for Bree. She couldn't remember the last time she had laughed so hard or for so long. But it also felt frightening. When she tried to catch her breath and couldn't, she felt a growing sense of panic. Somewhere in the few minutes that followed, her tears of laughter turned to real tears and then—unable to hold in the agony she had carried for so long—deep sobs of despair.

♕

Once Ben realized what was happening, he rolled up onto his knees and grabbed Bree's shoulders, taking her into his arms and sheltering her from the curious onlookers who were beginning to look their way. He held her as wave after wave of anguished, convulsive cries racked her body.

As Ben continued to hold her, he was astounded by the sheer power of the grief as it exploded from deep within her. He murmured softly against her temple, rocking gently, unconsciously moving with the sound and tempo of the waves rolling onto the shore in front of them.

Finally, after his legs had cramped and gone numb, he could feel Bree's knotted-up body relax and then go slack in his arms. He laid her gently down on the sand and then stretched out beside her so that they were holding hands but lying on their backs, gazing up at the late afternoon sky as it rolled its way toward the purple dusk at the end of the horizon.

"I had no idea all that was inside me," she whispered, her voice barely a dry whisper. "Or maybe I did, and I was just too afraid to face it." She seemed to add this last thought slowly and haltingly, as if it had just been newly born.

"I'm sorry it had to come out like this," Ben said, "but maybe it was time, honey. You have been so brave for so long. This needed to happen." He caressed his wife's arm as they continued to let the warm sand soothe the ache they had both experienced.

Ben rolled over onto his elbow and looked deep into Bree's eyes before adding, "I know, because I had my moment like this not long after the accident. I didn't tell you, because until you let yourself grieve with that kind of primal intensity, it's kind of hard to describe."

"I didn't know. You didn't tell me."

Looking at her now, Ben sensed that Bree suddenly felt vulnerable, as if his decision to protect her from his experience had somehow separated them when they had most desperately needed each other.

"I didn't want to pile my pain onto yours, honey," he said in defense. "It was early after Jayden had died, and neither of us was doing well."

"You didn't tell me," Bree repeated herself, processing the thought.

Still propped up on one elbow beside her, Ben leaned over and kissed her softly. "I was in the car on the side of a road. It started with me yelling and pounding the steering wheel, and then it moved to that same agonizing, gut-wrenching sort of guttural thing that feels like your insides are being torn out through your heart. It took a while before I could make enough sense of my surroundings to drive home."

Bree blinked back new tears, tears over Ben's pain, and not her own. And with those tears, the feeling of being separated from him dissolved. In fact, she had never felt closer to him—to anyone. Except, of course, to Jayden at the moment she held him in her arms while the doctors unplugged the machines and she felt him drift away.

Looking at Ben, she thought, *How strange that death would bring this soul-deep connection between us.*

Still lying on her back on the sand, she looked up at the sky and tried to make sense of the irony of receiving such a gift from such an agonizing loss. Even more ironic was the fact that she had stumbled across the word "soul" as a way to connect these events together.

What does that mean, exactly? she questioned. *Do I really believe we have immortal souls?*

Bree shook her head, willing herself back to the present, not wanting to get stuck in the painful memories and the questions they raised.

Sitting up, she brushed the sand out of her hair and off her shoulders and then looked over at her beloved husband. Bree reached for his hand, gathering it into both of hers and pulling it to her heart. She wanted him to feel how much she loved him in that moment.

"Ben, love, I'm so sorry that you went through that without being able to tell me. But truthfully, I think I've been in such denial of my own feelings that I would have been incapable of understanding or even accepting your emotional experience. In fact, I'm grateful you didn't tell me when it happened, because I would have probably considered it to be weakness and judged you for it."

Ben was amazed at Bree's new level of candor. She could be a tough critic of others but rarely of herself. He stayed silent and waited, not wanting to interrupt her introspection. He didn't have to wait long.

"But, Ben, even though I get what grief does now," she said, "and I understand how emotions can get caught within us—and I do feel better—I'm still terrified."

"Of what, honey?" Ben wasn't sure where she was taking the conversation.

"It's not like our good intentions, money, accomplishments, charity work—or anything else we've relied on as measurements of our success in life—kept us from experiencing our greatest tragedy. We still lost our only son. We couldn't keep it from happening. Ben, *we can't keep bad things from happening*! And that terrifies me. There doesn't seem to be anyone in charge. Which means something horrible could happen—again."

"Hey, hey, hey," Ben said soothingly, pulling himself up so that they were both sitting and he could see Bree's face. "Let's lay this down for today, babe. This has been a tough time for us—new territory we've never traveled—and never expected to. I think we are doing pretty darn good. We have each other, and we have this beautiful place. Let's make that enough for right now." He reached out to caress her cheek, then laid his hand on her shoulder so that she would feel him with her.

♕

Ben was right. All of Bree's questioning had merely evoked more of the anxiety she had just unloaded. As terrified as she was to move forward, she could not imagine going backward into what she had finally escaped.

They stood up and in the rose-tinted light of the fading sunset, took a moment to kiss and hold each other, the emotional intimacy they had just shared forging a new bond between them. Their love had been strengthened along with their resolve to continue choosing to move forward.

Arm in arm, they slowly retraced their steps back to their new home.

To anyone watching, they would have appeared to be the same happy, loving couple that had spent the day sauntering along the beach. But in her heart, Bree knew that a major tectonic shift had occurred—for both of them. Together, they had mined a new and deeper level of honesty and awareness.

Most important, the iron doors of grief that had held Bree captive had been pried open to reveal the tender flesh of a heart, yearning to be free of the loneliness of loss and sorrow.

Chapter 29

FOLENGANDROS, GREECE

As is often the case with emotional or physical healing, what starts out as an impossible hope, in time, becomes reality and—eventually—a milestone in the rearview mirror of life.

As soon as Bree's emotional dam broke open, her body and heart began to heal, which in turn freed her to begin processing things in a whole new way.

It wasn't that lovemaking, swimming, cooking, or sightseeing weren't enjoyable pursuits. They were. It was just that after those two or three hours were over, there were still twenty-one more in each day. She and Ben were trying to fill those hours on an island that was roughly twelve miles around with a population of 650 people. Being relatively young, Ben and Bree were also relatively restless. And now—and she could tell Ben was feeling the same way—they were . . .

Bored.

One night, while Ben was engrossed in a soccer match on TV, Bree decided it was time to go looking for Jayden's journal. She located the specific trunk in the guest bedroom, reached inside, and dug around until she felt the smooth, worn leather. It felt comforting to her touch, even before she pulled it out. She wondered briefly why it had taken her so long to do this. Maybe it was because she was just now feeling strong enough—and more curious too.

She needed to know what had happened at the orphanage. *What about his experience there impacted Jayden so much that he journaled about it every day, but didn't bother to tell me or Ben?*

From the little she had read in the journal before Ben put it in the trunk, it seemed Jayden had grown fond of the director of the orphanage. He'd also found an adoring little fan in a five-year-old girl. But most important, Jayden had written about some kind of encounter with a spiritual being, perhaps an angel.

Bree had just started reading about that unnerving encounter when Ben had packed the journal away.

Now she needed to find those pages again.

She sat cross-legged with her back against the trunk and flipped through the journal. Some pages contained nothing more than lists of projects Jayden was doing around the property. On other pages, he described sightseeing trips they had taken as a group. She leafed past those, vowing to read them at a later point. It wasn't long before she found a dog-eared section that seemed to be what she was looking for. She took a deep breath and began reading.

According to Jayden, from a distance he'd seen a flickering light and movement within the chapel and had gone to check it out. Once inside, it spooked him a bit.

She skipped through his thoughts about what he thought God's role should be regarding issues like poverty and suffering. Apparently, he'd wanted to know the answer to the age-old question about why bad things happen to good people. (*Don't we all?* she thought.) The point is, Jayden had acted exactly like she and Ben would have, putting God on the stand and holding Him accountable until He answered.

But whatever conversation the two of them had started out having, Jayden soon encountered something—or Someone—so powerful and mind-blowing, he had ended up on his knees, bowed and sobbing.

Bree slammed the journal shut. She didn't even pretend to understand, and she certainly didn't want to read about any weird, mystical encounters that involved her dead son. Truthfully, it frightened her as well. Sure, she had been to church—on Christmas and Easter

Sundays—and knew the general outline of the Christian story. But it didn't translate into *this*. She'd never experienced anything like what Jayden was describing.

Was there something unique about the orphanage chapel? The Transylvania location? Was it her son, specifically?

♔

When Ben walked in an hour later, he found her still sitting with her back against the trunk, in near darkness, looking like she was a million miles away from Folegandros.

"Bree . . . good grief! What are you doing in here?" he said before he saw the journal in her lap. He felt a brief flash of anger at not being around to run interference for her as she read it.

"I was feeling restless and thought I'd dig Jayden's journal out. I wanted to know about that orphanage and what he experienced—and never bothered to share with us."

Ben was having trouble deciphering Bree's mood from her comments. She wasn't exactly sad. It was more like a mixture of confusion and jealousy.

"Ben, he saw something in the chapel. Some weird spirit or something. Talked with it. It really affected him. I needed to know what it was."

"Bree, I don't know. It could have been the wind blowing through the rafters, making weird noises that he thought were voices. He was a seventeen-year-old kid with a huge imagination, remember?"

"I know. But somehow, his life was changed by the experience," she countered. "You even commented on it when he came home, although we didn't know what had happened."

"I remember saying that I thought he had grown up and become more mature, more thoughtful," Ben defended himself, but he did wince at the hazy memory of being half-worried his son—suddenly so touchy-feely—was gay.

One look at Bree's face and he knew he wasn't going to bring any of that up!

"How far is that orphanage and city from here?" she asked, attempting but failing to sound nonchalant. Ben pretended not to notice her failure. He only shrugged, unsure of the answer. She continued.

"We talked about doing some traveling, and I'm thinking I'd like to visit this place, since it was so important to Jayden. Besides, admit it: you are going stir-crazy on this tiny island. We need an adventure . . . or something."

Ben could also tell from her contrived casualness that this was not a suggestion. When Bree got it into her head that she wanted to do something, it usually meant you'd better just acquiesce.

"Okay, Bree. I'll look into it. Some sightseeing might be a good idea. I know we've always wanted to visit Croatia, and I'd like to see Budapest."

At least he would try to add some interesting diversions into this dismal prospect of a trip. He could already tell Bree was pinning way too much hope on this journal and that orphanage—as if retracing Jayden's steps would somehow explain the actions of a gangbanger halfway around the world.

Chapter 30

FOLENGANDROS, GREECE

"And what are we going to say to these people in Romania when we show up at their doorstep?" Ben asked the next morning.

He and Bree were enjoying their usual morning repose on the small patio. They wore sunglasses and held steaming mugs of coffee as they watched the intense morning sun climb slowly up from its sleepy ocean bed to blaze another day into their lives.

As Ben felt the warmth of the sun literally climb up his body, he thought about last night. In the light of day, their decision to set off on a journey to unearth details about their son's spiritual awakening seemed oddly impetuous to him now. If he were honest, he had agreed based more on Bree's sudden emotional meltdown than his own heartfelt desire to visit the orphanage.

And now here they were, discussing logistics.

"What's there to say, really?" Bree laughed. "Let's just knock on the door and introduce ourselves!"

Ben could tell she was not about to let him cast doubt on her plan to gain a sense of who her son had become—and why. Reading his journal had clearly knocked the wind out of her, and Ben was smart enough to realize she didn't like the feeling. This was about regaining her equilibrium.

He lifted a fist and pretended to knock on some invisible door. "Hi. You don't know us," he quipped, "and we don't know you, but can you point us to the old haunted chapel? And while you're at it, can you call up a couple of token spirits and have them meet us there?"

👑

Normally, Bree would have howled at her husband's ability to dish caustic humor, but she was lost in thought, wondering what unintended havoc this journey could cause.

What am I really trying to accomplish? What if I meet the people and visit the place Jayden came to love so much, and it makes everything hurt more? What if this trip makes me feel even more separated from him? What if I discover things about my son—or even myself—I'd rather not know?

That strange twinge of jealousy and sadness hit her again, and she nearly let Ben talk her into staying put.

Nearly. But a mother bear is a sight to behold in any culture, and Bree's nagging need for closure won the argument.

With even greater resolve, she turned to her husband.

"Ben, I know this whole thing is not your cup of tea. I get that whatever took place in that chapel could be attributed to the imagination of a seventeen-year-old boy. But I need this, pure and simple. I can't get closure without at least trying to understand this part of Jayden's life. Something obviously happened at the orphanage that deeply impacted him. If I can't make sense of everything, then I can't move on."

👑

As usual, Bree's articulate explanation of both her needs as a mother and what she needed in order to heal left little room for argument from Ben. He thought about saying "Yes, dear," but knew better than to throw gasoline on these smoldering mama flames.

"Okay," he conceded, "Romania it is. I'll warn you, though, I'm intent on doing some sightseeing along the way. You know I've wanted to see Croatia, and especially the island of Vis." He stood up and teasingly kissed the shoulder blade peeking out from beneath the strap of Bree's negligee. "All you need to do is pack about four bikinis, a toothbrush, and some walking shoes, baby. We are off to find either Dracula or Jesus, or maybe both!" Ben stood up and went inside to their computer, to figure out the logistics of their trip.

After several hours, it became obvious to Ben that it was going to be somewhat more complicated than simply hopping the first flight out of Santorini. He called the caretakers and asked their opinions on the various segments of travel and, while they were very helpful, the whole thing was starting to sound like a John Candy film: a boat, a bigger boat, an airplane, a car, another boat, another plane, a donkey . . .

Oh, well, he reasoned. *It's not like we're in a hurry to get back to real life.*

That evening, just before he drifted off to sleep, Ben found his mind wandering. If he were completely honest and nowhere near Bree, he'd say he still thought about waking up and discovering this was all an elaborate dream, like a soma trip dreamed up by Aldous Huxley.

In his mind, exchanging homes with the Bergmans—and now this trip to Romania—were just ways to fill time. His son was gone and, with him, Ben's legacy, as well as any desire to live his old lifestyle of intellectual and business pursuits. It had become easier to simply drift through endless sunrises and sunsets saturated with either coffee or wine, distracted by the occasional "bat in the belfry" idea, like going to Romania. As he fell asleep, he wondered whether this new life would ever feel like home.

At some point in the middle of the night, the caretakers emailed Nazir about this new development. Typically, their daily reports consisted of recounting the Stantons' routine activities and conversations. This time, however, they had more to report: the news that the couple was planning a trip to eastern Europe.

About the same time, another man was on the phone with *his* superior, filing his own daily report regarding the American couple. The gentleman, a British chap, had made contact with Ben and Bree earlier that day. He had positioned himself at an adjacent table as the couple ate lunch in the village of Chora. Under the guise of being a fellow tourist looking for information about local points of interest, he'd successfully engaged the Stantons in casual conversation about the island and, eventually, about themselves.

"These folks are not from England, sir," he explained over the phone. "They are simply bloody Americans spending a year abroad, like half of the US seems to be doing these days. It was pretty damn difficult to get them to talk much. From what I could ascertain, they know almost nothing about the people whose house they are leasing. Well, not leasing, really; more like vacation-home swapping. They have some place in California, funny-sounding place. I thought they'd said Wolf something until I reviewed the tape. Turns out their home is in Big Bear, California. They were pretty proud of it."

Ian was quick to fire back a response. "So, there was nothing that made you think they were hiding out or covering something up? Bad debts? Legal trouble? Anything?"

"No. They didn't show any nervousness at all. There was one thing, and I'm not sure how relevant it is, but they mentioned a son. Got the impression he may be deceased. The wife was clearly having a difficult time with the subject. They talked about starting over. Moving on. But then they asked me if I had ever driven up the Croatian coast. Seems they want to go to a small Romanian village where their son had traveled."

The field operative heard Ian mutter a "Bloody hell!" before issuing some curt instructions. Then the phone went abruptly dead.

Chapter 31

CIA HEADQUARTERS, LANGLEY

Mac stood in front of the link chart he had compiled on the wall of his office. The fact that it involved an entire world map was an ominous reminder of the magnitude of what was at stake if he and Ian failed to connect the missing dots.

Without turning around to look, he could hear and feel the clock on the wall of his office ticking away the seconds, signaling how little time he had to identify and nail the terrorists.

Mac could literally feel the urgency of his short-timer status. He was being subjected to an increasing barrage of well wishes, jokes about being put out to pasture, and endless references to fishing trips. Meanwhile, visions of poor Secretariat wandering round and round a barricaded pasture, being chased by a bunch of horny fillies, danced in his head. It was all excruciating for Mac, because the idea of a purposeless and boring "retirement" scared the shit out of him in a way that a terrorist group never could—not to mention that the whole "happiness ever after" scenario was never likely to happen for anyone if he and Ian didn't get this case solved.

The ring of his phone interrupted Mac's morose thoughts. He picked it up on the first ring. It was Ian.

Ian cut straight to the chase. "You can't write this stuff, JD. There's no bloody author that could think this crap up! Those people on that godforsaken island are not our people!"

"What do you mean, Ian?"

"They're not our Brits. These two are bloody Americans who exchanged their mountain home in California for a vacation home on Folegandros that just happens to be owned by our British couple. Which means that our Brits are wandering around California without a single pair of eyes on them and up to who-knows-what kind of jackass trouble."

"Trouble, for sure. Have you figured out the location of the Americans' California home? That's where we'll likely find the Brits.

"As a matter of fact, we have. Big Bear, California."

Ian's answer took a full twenty seconds to fully register with Mac. That's when the warning sirens fired up in his brain.

"What the hell did you just say?"

"A mountain town called Big—"

Mac didn't even let Ian finish.

"God help us, Ian. They already fucking took out our potential witnesses!"

Silence.

"I'm not . . . following you," Ian said finally.

"Last week, an LA cop went rogue. He loaded up with weapons and explosives, headed for Big Bear, and blew up a mountain home— with two people inside—before taking his own life. Or at least that's the story being circulated. The media is reporting it as an episode of PTSD triggered by stress. No terrorism involved. But from what you're telling me now, I bet if we had our hands on the forensic reports, we'd be finding the DNA of our British couple in the charred ruins of that burned-out home. AND I'd be willing to bet my first retirement check that those Americans no longer have a home in Big Bear!"

"Holy crap!" Ian bellowed.

"Do you think the Americans have any idea about their home at this point?" Mac asked his old friend.

"Not likely. I think they would have said something. My guy on the island says the conversation was centered on trying to move on after the death of a child."

"Okay, Ian. So where do we go from here?"

"Here's where it gets eerie, JD: These folks are going to be traveling up to Croatia and Hungary and finally to Romania—and specifically to an orphanage in the Transylvania area. Apparently, their dead son had worked there one summer."

"Orphanage? *Our* orphanage?"

"It's gotta be. Just how many orphanages in Transylvania do you think there are? Take a wild guess. Better yet, let me answer this one for you. ONE."

Mac was unconvinced. "How the hell are these people involved?"

"Iona told me about a young man that was very involved with the orphanage a few years back. I didn't think anything of it at the time, but now I'm guessing he may be this American couple's dead son. If so, this young man knew our girl Molly."

"Molly? The girl who survived the attack? With the bioagent still in her body?"

"The very same."

Mac let out a low whistle.

"At some point we're going to have to decide what to tell Iona," Ian mused. "She doesn't know that the young man is dead. She'll need to be told."

"Eventually, yes," Mac agreed. "And not only about the young man, but also about our plans to leak information about Molly's survival in order to draw out the terrorists."

"You know I still loathe that idea."

"I understand, old friend. But how else are we going to lure the deadliest Islamic terrorist group known to mankind back to the middle of godforsaken Transylvania? And don't forget we now have a couple of Americans thrown into the mix. Add to that the orphanage, the director, and the pending annihilation of the Western world."

Mac was certain that would keep the phone line quiet for more than a few minutes.

"Well, I might have a plan . . . ," Ian said at last.

"Now, *that's* what I was hoping to hear."

Chapter 32

Transylvania, Romania

Ian's heart was pounding as he knocked on the orphanage door for the third time in as many weeks. He was suddenly dreading what he was about to do. Inside, he was wrestling with how the news about Jayden would affect Iona. Would she be relieved to know the boy had not willingly forgotten them, or would the horrific ending to his life be the last straw to break her spirit?

I've forgotten what it's like to care for someone else, he realized. *Well, hell, old chap, not just "someone else" . . . a woman!*

While waiting for someone to come to the door, Ian looked around at a handful of children playing in a dusty side yard.

What a godforsaken place.

Yet, at least by the front door, Iona had worked hard to interject spots of cheerfulness. There were flowers in a recently painted pot, and he could smell soup cooking on the stove inside. And while the children playing were clothed in older and obviously worn clothes, they seemed clean, healthy, and relatively happy.

The door swung open abruptly.

A smiling Iona stood in the doorway.

Ian thought she looked attractive in the morning sunlight, and he felt an uncharacteristic rush of warmth as he stretched out his hand to greet her.

"Hello, Iona. Good to see you again. Thank you for seeing me on such short notice."

"Good to see you, Mr. Vas—I mean, Alex."

"I know you are extremely busy, and I appreciate the time. As I mentioned on the phone, I have some news I thought best to share with you in person."

Iona gave Ian a quizzical look before motioning him inside. "Would you like a cup of tea or anything else to drink?"

Knowing what he had to share, Ian thought briefly about asking for a stiff shot of something much stronger than tea, but decided against it.

I doubt she has anything around the orphanage that would come close to what I could use right now.

He politely declined the tea, and they began the short walk toward Iona's office. As soon as they'd crossed the threshold, Ian launched into his speech before he lost his nerve.

"Iona, I'm afraid I have some rather sad news for you. Unfortunately—and I have now been able to confirm it—your young man, Jayden Stanton, was killed in an accident." He paused to let the initial information sink in.

Iona's cheeks paled as she let out a small gasp. Ian could see she was struggling to grasp the full meaning of his words.

"It happened a couple of years ago on a freeway in California," Ian added gently. He'd been able to review the police records as well as the court documents for the case. He deliberately chose to omit the details of the shooting. There was no need to create unnecessary trauma. The idea of using Molly as a lure would be traumatic enough.

Fighting tears and clearly overcome with emotion, Iona slumped into a settee near the window, then turned to stare out at the children playing in the yard. It took a minute for Ian to realize she was looking at Molly, who was twirling on a rope swing hanging from an old, gnarly tree.

When Iona finally spoke, it was with a voice heavy with weariness. It made Ian realize she had placed more hope in the young man returning than she had let on during their earlier conversations.

"So . . . that is why we stopped hearing from him. He didn't stop caring; he just couldn't . . ." She struggled to contain emotions she had likely held at bay for the last few years, maybe more. It appeared to be a Herculean effort, and Ian's heart went out to her.

As strong as he knew she was, he wished he could take back his words and somehow keep her in a cloistered and protected place. But then he roused himself from that utopian ideal and reminded himself that these terrorists had already robbed Iona of her safety and peace of mind—and robbed her of the children to whom she had dedicated her entire life.

The only thing he could do for her now was kill the bastards before they did any more damage.

"I'm sorry to be the one to tell you. Actually, I'm not sorry to be the one." He walked to her and put his hand gently on her shoulder. "I am, however, sorry for the news. I cannot imagine what you must be feeling after hoping for so long that he would return," he said. He sat down next to Iona and took her hand in his, making sure she was looking at him before he continued.

"I wish that I could leave our conversation here, so you could grieve privately and for as long as you need. But unfortunately, I have much to share with you and not much time to do it."

Iona nodded at Ian's earnest plea.

"Iona," he went on, "our paths have crossed at a unique juncture in time, and I need you to bravely listen to a plan I am asking you to be a part of." Ian then began speaking softly in Iona's native Romanian tongue, explaining all that had happened, including some of what he and JD assumed was about to happen.

His explanation grew a little more emphatic, and Iona's response more resistant when it came to Molly, but having seen the devastation the vaccines had wreaked on her innocent children already, she eventually agreed that the only solution was to lure the terrorists into the open using Molly.

"Alex, I understand. I don't want to, but I do. However, I don't want to put any more of these children in danger. I just can't," she said, as emphatically as Ian had just spoken. "Can you tell me how you plan to make sure that doesn't happen?"

Ian nodded his agreement. "It was the first concern my team had when coming up with this proposal. I promise that we will do everything humanly possible to protect your children, starting with relocating all of them—with the exception of Molly—to another location where there is no possibility of further injuries."

"Thank you. You have been both kind and honest, Alex, and you have won my trust. I'm convinced, from all that you have shared, that unless we stop these monsters, more innocent people will die. I couldn't live with myself if that were to happen and I didn't do everything in my power to prevent it!"

"I was counting on your amazing strength and character, Iona. Thank you."

Ian opened the file he had brought with him. Then he and Iona burned the midnight oil, refining a plan that would hopefully ensure the protection of not only Molly and the remaining children in her orphanage, but many lives in the future.

Chapter 33

ROMANIAN VILLAGE

"Twenty children are dead," Iona spat, fire in her eyes. She was standing over a cowering young man sitting at a kitchen table in one of the homes in the village. After her discussion with Ian, Iona had gone straight to the home of the young man who had put the bogus pharmaceutical company in touch with her orphanage.

The boy attempted to return her stare, but he was no match for the pent-up venom she had for what his treasonous act had done to her children.

She delivered a withering assessment of her friend's son—a traitor responsible for the death of innocents. "The weight of their souls now rests on your shoulders," she hissed. "You have disgraced your family's name and betrayed your entire village. I knew you as a decent, young man, Tamas, and now I am ashamed to say I know you."

Ian watched this interaction in awe. He could see the young man wince as Iona let the truth of what he had done wash over him.

This was a side of Iona he had not seen before. When she had called Ian with the news that she had located the snitch who had informed the jihadists about the orphans' secret home, at first he had been skeptical. But she had, indeed, located the young man. Who knew that Iona Dalca, spinster orphanage director, would in fact provide the linchpin to their whole plan? Ian couldn't wait to tell JD this one.

Her courage and trust in him also made Ian realize it was time for him to be completely honest with her. On the drive to the village, he had revealed his true name and identity.

She hadn't seemed surprised in the least.

"Ian, I may have lived in relative seclusion for the past thirty years, but I know the difference between a Romanian and a Brit. Did you notice that I always offered you tea instead of coffee? Not to mention that the monogram on your handkerchief was a dead giveaway." She'd smiled a knowing smile.

Ian had grimaced at his own lack of attention to details.

"Iona, I'm sorry that I had to deceive you. I had no idea who you would be or what I would find at the orphanage." Ian felt genuinely contrite about having lied to her.

"We are so fortunate that you even heard about our tiny home and the deaths of our children, Ian. I understand why it was necessary to lie. I am just grateful to you and the others involved, and I am determined to make the children's deaths matter," she'd responded.

Now, as Ian watched her grill the informant, he realized that without Iona's intervention, the young man would have likely gone undetected. There was no question that Iona had played a pivotal role in the investigation.

And she wasn't bad at interrogating, either. Ian could tell that her questions were touching a deep nerve in Tamas's young psyche.

Ian patted Iona's hand before stepping in.

"Here's the point, Tamas. We don't have time to start at the beginning to try to understand why you decided to betray your family and village by informing for these terrorist bastards. You made your choice, and you will pay a steep price for that choice. But I do want you to understand that far from being heralded a hero, your jihadist friends are right now plotting your death . . . and it won't be as a martyr."

Tamas straightened up in his chair, showing his fear for the first time.

"I can't protect you from the torture and mutilation they are planning for you unless you help me with the details of what was done to the orphans and how you were involved."

When Tamas remained silent, Ian stood up and pulled a phone from his pocket.

"There is an MI6 counterterrorist team waiting in Alba Iulia for my signal. They'll be happy to get this information from you."

"I didn't do any of this on purpose; you have to believe me," Tamas blurted out.

Ian didn't look impressed.

"I wanted to go fight in their war. I didn't know they were going to attack my own village. I love my parents. I didn't want to hurt them."

"Go on."

"They said they wanted to try out a new vaccine for kids. I told them about the home where the orphans lived."

Whatever chord Ian had struck, the idea of being interrogated must have done the trick. Tamas couldn't get his words out fast enough.

"I had no idea what was in those shots. I know . . . now it sounds stupid. I only found out about the bioagent by accident. One of the guys who had sent in the drone asked if I wanted to see a video. I was shocked. I didn't know the children would die. All I wanted to do was prove myself to them."

"Well, you certainly did that!" Iona broke in bitterly.

Ian pressed Tamas for more details. "Do you know now what was in the vaccine or how they triggered it?"

"No. Once the attack happened, it's like I didn't exist. I haven't heard anything. I came back to the village because I got scared. Scared that they will do something to me because of what I know and maybe because I saw that video."

"You proved yourself useful to the jihadists, and see how it turned out for you?" Ian asked, shaking his head at Tamas's obvious naivety. "Well, now you are going to prove yourself useful to us. Can you still make contact with this group?"

Tamas nodded silently.

"Good. I want you to send them an update on an unexpected development regarding the attack, and I am going to tell you exactly what to say."

Ian dictated the exact message he wanted Tamas to convey. It was simple and to the point. A little girl carrying the embedded vaccine was alive and at the main orphanage. She had missed the day of the attack due to a fever.

Ian instructed Tomas to add that a government official had come to the village to ask questions.

He wanted to make the terrorists uncomfortable with the idea of letting the child live. If they thought someone was snooping around, it was more likely they'd come back to finish the job.

As soon as Ian and Iona left Tamas and headed back to the car, Ian got Mac on the cell phone and got straight to the point." The worm is on the hook," he told his friend. "Now let's see if the big fish takes the bait."

Ian and Iona spoke little on the drive back to the orphanage, each lost in their own thoughts, emotionally drained by the events of the afternoon.

Ian pulled his car in front of the main building and walked Iona to the front door.

"Thank you again, Iona," he said. "You have helped us tremendously. Let's talk tomorrow. It will be necessary to move these children to safety and begin laying out the larger trap of our plan."

Iona nodded somberly.

Ian patted her on the shoulder, then turned and walked back to his car. He waved at Iona before heading out the driveway.

Chapter 34

YEMEN

Amir knocked again on the ornate door leading to his uncle's chambers. This time, more forcefully. His first knock had gone unanswered. Convinced of Al-Zawahiri's uncanny ability to hear across thousands of miles, he could only imagine that his uncle's unwillingness to answer was an ominous sign.

Inside his chambers, Al-Zawahiri was engrossed in reviewing his plan and not interested in being interrupted. He thought he heard a knock, but knowing his servants would never enter without his bidding, he returned to his review.

After the successful test on the orphans, he had continued to move his teams forward with the plan. From his sources within the CDC, he knew the organization had started distributing their combination malaria/Zika/West Nile vaccine. The number of American cases of Zika was increasing, and they represented an unacceptable threat, at least for the American psyche. The Americans could not tolerate the idea of mortality at any level, and thus, the expedited release of the vaccine.

For Al-Zawahiri, this panic was a gift from the hand of Allah. Al-Zawahiri's lab—operating covertly within the US—had already created at least a million doses of the bioagent.

Initially, the doses of bioagent would replace only a few thousand vaccines distributed by the CDC. His people would intercept the vaccines in transit, make the switch, then complete the delivery as scheduled.

His team would focus on a small segment of the distribution areas within two major Southern cities: Miami and Houston. The combined populations of those cities numbered in the millions—but for now, he would need only to kill a few thousand people for mayhem to ensue.

Al-Zawahiri heard another knock on his door, this time more insistent. He turned his back to the sound, thinking, *Whoever it is, they will benefit from a time of contemplation.*

He returned to his plan.

He would use the hysteria following the attack as the ultimate negotiating tool. His goals were domination and control, not annihilation.

He stood and began pacing.

The American officials would not be told which cities and populations had received the vaccinations containing bioagents. That unknown would render the entire population of the country, or at least everyone who had received the vaccine, vulnerable. The weak man-child who called himself president would have no choice but to give in to Al-Zawahiri's demands. There would be no target for the American military forces to retaliate against. Every attempt would result in more deaths—silent, inexplicable deaths. America, the once-proud eagle, would kneel as a little sparrow.

BRILLIANT!

Al-Zawahiri fought to keep his heart from racing with pure exhilaration and anticipation at the thought of his own genius, fueled, of course, by the favor of Allah.

The visitor knocked a third time before Al-Zawahiri was roused from his self-absorption. His patience suddenly thin, he barked an order as he returned to his gilded chair.

"Alaistiedad li'iieta' hayatik." Prepare to give your life! He was fairly certain it was one of two visitors he was expecting, and each man deserved to have his loyalty questioned.

Al-Zawahiri was not surprised when Amir strode across the threshold, looking as if he was, indeed, prepared to die, and bowed.

"Most excellent one, my uncle." Amir remained bowed in front of his uncle.

"I have summoned both you and Nazir to Yemen because I have received some rather interesting news," Al-Zawahiri said with a dismissive tone. "However, I am waiting for Nazir to arrive before sharing it with you both. Sit to the side and wait, Amir, and perhaps wrestle with the question of why I might have sent for you."

Al-Zawahiri looked up to the ceiling, shaking his head as if to include Allah in his frustrations in finding an heir to his throne. He glanced over at Amir and thought about all the tedious hours of teaching and training he had expended in raising him as if he were his own son. From what Al-Zawahiri had recently learned, it would appear that even with all of that effort, Amir had failed to develop a disciplined mind or a true understanding of his calling. Was it too late?

Amir could feel the heat of his uncle's penetrating stare. He looked away and then down at his feet. As hard as he tried, he could not think of any reason he might have been summoned. Actually, he couldn't think of anything at all—except his burning desire to sit in the gilded chair that Al-Zawahiri now occupied.

Maybe I am going to be given new responsibilities, he thought hopefully. But even as the words formed in his mind, he knew they were unlikely to come true.

A furtive glance at his uncle convinced him further. There was something about the set of his uncle's jaw that made Amir think for the first time that he had somehow fallen out of favor.

If he could have read his uncle's thoughts, Amir would have bolted from the room.

Make no mistake about it, Amir. You have earned my disfavor and lost my trust. Once you complete this new task, you will pay for such laziness. It is the way of Allah.

Chapter 35

CIA Headquarters, Langley

Mac sat in his office—or as he liked to call it now, his government-issued horse stall—and stared up at the link board. It had gained several more lines of connection since Ian's last call. The countdown to his "Secretariat Gala," as Mac was now euphemistically referring to his retirement party, was so close that he could hear the horses lining up at the starting gate. He was running out of time!

He was going to need help in pulling this off. Including getting surveillance on the village rat, more on the surrounding area, intel on all frequencies of communication, some firepower on the ground, and an arsenal of drones to hit whatever targets were generated once the full diabolical plan was unearthed. Mac's dilemma continued to be whom to tap for these resources without having to go through a lot of rigamarole to get them.

He settled on a buddy who had risen up the ranks of the CIA. Randall Edwards had started in the same freshman class with Mac, but he had ascended the agency ladder and never looked back. He was now the assistant director of the CIA. Lucky for Mac, he'd also never properly thanked Mac for covering his ass during a late-night rendezvous gone bad that would have likely killed his blossoming career—and still could. Mac was not one to hold on to leverage, but clearly, leverage was called for now.

He picked up the phone.

"Randall!" he said when his old friend answered the called. "How are things up in the rarified air of covert covertness? You probably don't want to know who this is."

"McFarland. Now, here's a voice from my long-forgotten past."

"More like your worst nightmare."

"You're still tickin'. Go figure."

"I managed to keep myself alive by clinging to a wimp-ass desk job, of course," Mac said, then heard Randall's muffled chortle.

"Listen, Randall, I've come knocking to collect that favor."

Hearing only silence on the other end, Mac could only assume his old classmate was trying to figure out a way to throw him in the brig for blackmail. Mac comforted himself with the thought, *Hey, I'm getting put out to pasture. What the hell else can they do to me?*

"What do you want, MacFarland?"

Mac was encouraged by the fact that his boss's boss's boss was at least still on the line. He decided to cut to the chase.

"The bad news is, it's a short trigger, and I don't have time or evidence to go protocol. The good news is, if it works out, it could get you the final seat at the table in the oval, as in Oval Office, if you catch my drift." Mac knew his only ace was to play to Randall's notorious ego and his rumored political aspirations.

"You've got about three minutes to explain whatever ridiculous scheme you've cooked up." Randall said it in such a way that Mac was pretty sure nothing was going to happen beyond this phone call.

Mac launched into the details of the suspected scenario, its wide-reaching implications, and the urgent need to take action. Once he had his listener's attention, he provided the general points of Ian's plan, along with the logistical requirements.

As he'd hoped and expected, Randall took a big, frenzied bite out of the apple Mac held out.

Great! Now we're off to the races! Mac thought, grinning to himself. Then, *Enough with the horse analogies, already. I'm going to need counseling to get rid of this horse thing once this is all over.*

Later on, Mac dialed Ian to let him know the supporting resources were committed and would be on their way soon.

"Ian, we've got the mother lode. I just got high-level approval for everything we need. Drones, hellfire, a Delta team, and surveillance equipment. All brought to you with compliments from the CIA." Mac couldn't hide his pride in getting the best of old Randall.

"JD, you never cease to amaze me. Good for us and bad for the invitees to our little soiree," Ian said. He didn't even question how Mac had managed it.

"Whoever the mastermind behind this despicable evil turns out to be," Mac said, "I suspect he's got an ego the size of the European continent and a brain the size of his left nut. When we nail him, he's gonna wish it was the other way around!"

Chapter 36

YEMEN

Nazir sat cross-legged on a Persian rug, with his back against the front of a brocade couch. Balancing his laptop across his legs, he finished the last of his bootlegged coffee as he responded to an email from one of his colleagues in Washington, DC. He was missing his life there, and more important, his stature among the city's elite. He glanced at his watch and decided to look at the rest of his emails later.

He shut his laptop and left his rooms for the long walk to his father's chambers. He'd come to think of it as being like a caged lion in a zoo, moving from his small sleeping cage to the larger, daytime cage, complete with gawking visitors watching his every move.

Nazir steeled himself for the inevitable diatribe from Al-Zawahiri about either the way things were, or the way things would soon be. If there was one thing his father didn't dwell on, it was the present.

Nazir knocked on the outer door and waited to be called in. This was one of his father's favorite manipulative tactics—making people wait. After a dramatic pause, he heard his father's gruff voice commanding him to enter. Nazir was halfway into the room before he realized that there was another visitor, sitting off to the side, in the shadows near the wall.

"Good morning, Father. Amir." He nodded to his cousin, who had stood and moved closer. Nazir took in his cousin's attire—the traditional robes his father favored. He also noted Amir's brooding countenance. Nazir was pretty sure he'd never seen his cousin smile, and it was all he could do not to laugh out loud at him. What was the cause of all of Amir's unhappiness? Nazir just didn't get the concept of choosing to live in a world clouded by constant, simmering anger.

As usual, his father, with only the slightest nod in Nazir's direction, launched into the day's agenda.

"I've called you both back to Yemen, because I've had some news I think you both need to hear. Apparently . . ." Al-Zawahiri paused for great dramatic effect, and Nazir's heart skipped a beat. It was never good when his father started the morning with theatrics. "I have been notified that"—again he paused—"there is a test child still alive in the Romania orphanage."

Amir could not hide his shock. "That's not possible, sir," he said, his voice shaky. "My follow-up drone showed no sign of life on that playground, other than the two old women!" He was clearly trying, with little luck, to keep his voice from rising with his emotions.

"Your drone did not pick up any sign of life, but did it count the bodies? Did you compare the number of children inoculated with the number of bodies on the playground?"

Nazir watched Amir's face go white, his expression reflecting a dawning realization of his own mistake. Before his cousin could think of a response, Al-Zawahiri continued.

"There was a girl who was inoculated but not present that day. She now contains an identifiable and traceable bioagent. I distinctly remember telling you, Amir, that there were to be no survivors!"

Amir was silent.

"I'm assuming it would not be too much to ask that you return to the area to make sure that this is accomplished," Al-Zawahiri said, his voice dripping with disdain.

It felt like the room temperature had dropped ten degrees.

"Where is this child, uncle?" Amir asked.

Nazir could tell he was buying time to think of a way to defend himself. He was rather enjoying watching his cousin squirm under his father's withering look of disapproval.

"She is at the main orphanage. It was confirmed by our informant in the village. He also confirmed that she had received the vaccine. She was sent back to the main location the day of the test, due to a fever. I am appalled, nephew, at your lack of attention to detail."

Amir, now flushed with embarrassment, simply bowed and nodded in shame.

"You know, of course, what must be done immediately. Get yourself and your team back to that orphanage and clean up the damage." Al-Zawahiri's words were clipped, each one a short, fierce staccato echoing through the high ceilings of his room.

"Yes, Uncle," was all Amir could manage.

"And one more thing, Amir. I'm assuming you know that this mission needs to be as quiet and covert as you can make it. It's one child. That's all. In and out, without any scene. Do you understand?" Al-Zawahiri was now speaking to Amir as if he were a child being sent to his room.

"Yes, Uncle." With a bow, Amir moved back to the shadows of the edge of the room. He had been dismissed.

Nazir kept his eyes averted, staring at the wall behind his father's head, silently thanking Allah for allowing him to escape his father's wrath.

As if on cue, Al-Zawahiri turned to Nazir and launched into the second half of his diatribe.

"And your Americans. The people you said were of no consequence. They have inexplicably decided to make a trip to"—his father paused for effect—"a Romanian orphanage."

Nazir's mind exploded with questions. Why would the Americans be going to the orphanage? What the hell was going on?

"I'm assuming you will be getting to the bottom of this nonsense. Clearly, they are not as innocent as you were led to believe. And, I am assuming that they will be taken care of."

Nazir nodded, much like Amir had done, minus the embarrassment. He knew he had not failed in his mission to clear the Americans as they related to the London couple. What his father was saying made absolutely no sense, unless there was some unknown factor involved—and there most certainly must be.

Al-Zawahiri stood up from his chair, his robes and countenance as imperious as ever.

"My original intention had been to pass the mantle to one of you after the completion of our glorious victory against the infidels. Now I find myself wondering why I would entrust my power to either of you. Perhaps you would like to prove me wrong?" He raised his eyebrows, giving each of them a pointed look, and then motioned for both men to leave his room, flicking his hand at them as if they were mosquitos and he wanted to be rid of their pesky presence.

The cousins bowed, turned, and exited as if they were performing a pas de deux.

Once outside, Amir turned to Nazir and began to bark orders. "I will head back to the orphanage, cousin. You go back to your island and take the Americans out. Clearly you miscalculated their involvement in our test in Romania."

If there was one thing that could push Nazir to anger, it was Amir's misguided sense of superiority, and the fact that he never wasted an opportunity to communicate it when they were together. Nazir, with all his education and cosmopolitan lifestyle, always found himself inexplicably wanting to coldcock his cousin, to knock some sense into his ego-fogged brain. Instead, Nazir took a few breaths, calmed himself, and then responded, "Amir, you take care of your loose ends, and I'll take care of mine."

As he turned away and began to walk back down the opposite hallway to his rooms, Nazir was already making plans to return to Folegandros. On his way, he tried to figure out how his father had discovered the couple was going to Romania. Why hadn't the caretakers informed Nazir? Perhaps they had emailed during the night. Now he wished he had finished going through his in-box before coming to see his father.

More troubling still was the fact that, for some reason, his father didn't trust him. And without his father's trust, Nazir knew he had far more serious problems than just the Americans.

Chapter 37

YEMEN & VIS, CROATIA

After his father's surprising edict and the confrontation with Amir in the hallway afterwards, Nazir was done having anything to do with his family's drama. All the way to his room, he could still hear Amir yelling orders after him. As soon as Nazir crossed the threshold, he slammed and locked the outer door, then reached for his cell phone and punched in a number.

"Hello?"

"I want the full story," Nazir barked without greeting. When he realized he sounded just like his father, his tone immediately softened. "Stephano, did you email me last night?"

On the other end of the line, Nazir's man posing as one of the caretakers in Folegandros, sounded nervous. "I didn't, sir. Since the couple is no longer here, I assumed you no longer needed the nightly reports—"

"No longer *there*?" Nazir interrupted. "And when were you going to give me THAT crucial bit of information?"

"But . . . but I did, sir! Two nights ago! I emailed you about their plans to leave the island! I even emailed you their itinerary!"

"Dammit. It never arrived." Or . . . perhaps it had, but a sloppy hacker had inadvertently deleted it after it was read. "Resend it please," Nazir ordered. "In the meantime, what were the motives for their sudden trip? Did they discuss it with you?"

"Yes, and unfortunately their story is a sad one. The Americans are trying to recover from losing their only son, who died in a gang shooting in LA. According to Mr. Stanton, Mrs. Stanton is not doing well in terms of recovering from the loss. After discovering a journal the boy kept, she read his entries regarding a visit to an orphanage in Romania, and now she wants to travel there, as some kind of pilgrimage."

This was not what Nazir was expecting. He tried to make sense of the coincidence of this family being tied to a Romanian orphanage. How many orphanages could there be in Romania?

Nazir was silent for a moment, then asked, "Any idea of when they will arrive in Romania?"

"It's in the itinerary, which I have just re-sent to you."

Nazir kissed his fingers and held them up to the sky, as if to thank Allah for such an unexpected gift. It would make catching up with the Americans so much easier than having to go back to Folegandros.

"Thank you, Stephano. Good work."

Nazir ended the conversation and sat down on a nearby sofa. He flipped open his laptop, eager to read Stephano's second email, the one with the itinerary. He'd have time to study it in detail later, but first he scanned the list to find the Stantons' destination in Romania.

There it was. Alba Iulia.

His heart sank. Alba Iulia was just a few miles from the orphanage used for Amir's deadly test.

The Americans' grief was pulling them right into the path of Amir's overzealous mission to clear his name. And Nazir's father had clearly known this when he ordered Nazir to follow the Americans, while ordering Amir to return to the orphanage to clean up loose ends.

What is he wanting? A showdown between the two of us?

The shot of adrenaline that hit Nazir's bloodstream was so intense that he jumped to his feet and began pacing before he even realized what was happening. As he circled the room for the dozenth time in as many minutes, he knew he needed to calm his mind and to unwind all that had occurred in the last hour.

They were all going to end up at the same place. Driven by different agendas, but that wouldn't matter once Amir arrived. The Americans had no idea the shit storm they were about to enter.

While Nazir packed his bags and made travel arrangements, he tried to work out a solution to the looming showdown at the orphanage. He had no interest in getting mixed up with Amir's agenda. No matter what Amir had promised Al-Zawahiri, Nazir knew when the time came, Amir was too much of a loose cannon to keep the mission on the lowdown. There would be collateral bloodshed, and probably lots of it. It didn't seem right that the Americans would be put in such unnecessary danger.

But Nazir could not think of a way to avoid it. In the end, he knew he had no one to blame but himself for continuing to play this spy game.

Damn my father. And damn you, Amir!

Two days later, Nazir was in the back of one of his father's sedans, being driven to a private plane headed for Dubrovnik. He was not surprised to see that his trusted friend and frequent driver had been replaced by one of his father's goons.

So, even while I'm off to do his bidding, my father cannot find trust in his heart for his own son? So be it. Then I must make sure I protect myself.

The idea that a jihad had replaced Nazir in his father's heart made him sad. For the first time since childhood, he could feel the sting of tears in his eyes.

Perhaps my father's obsession is the reason my mother was so unhappy.

Nazir caught up with the Americans in Dubrovnik, an ancient walled city in the southern part of Croatia. He spent two days watching them as they wandered through the stone city, sightseeing, eating, drinking, and taking pictures of an old castle, St. Lawrence Fortress. He knew the castle had been the location for filming an American TV show called the *Game of Thrones*.

While following the Americans as they toured the castle, Nazir found himself standing on the wall of the castle and looking out at the Mediterranean.

He couldn't ignore the irony.

Game of Thrones, he mused. *They should have called it* Nazir's Life Story!

He laughed out loud. It felt good to finally laugh at something that had dogged him his entire life.

From Dubrovnik, Nazir followed the American couple as they drove up the coast, visiting the small coastal villages and spending time in still more restaurants and shops, until they arrived at Split. Nazir had not been to Croatia before, and he found himself enjoying the respite from being in Yemen with his father and overbearing cousin.

This is a place I could live. The thought surprised him as he drove several cars behind the Stantons' rented sedan. *The people are kind, the views are stupendous—and most important, my family isn't here.*

While he kept tabs on the couple, he tried to work out a plan to avert their collision course with Amir. Unfortunately, from the conversations Nazir had listened to, the wife was becoming more insistent on visiting the orphanage. He was confident, though, that these two knew nothing about the dead children, or how the British couple had tried to assume their identities. And suddenly, he very much wanted to protect them.

👑

"Ben, can't you just see us living here?" Bree gushed as she flung open the shutters of their hotel room window and gazed out onto the city of Split. Everywhere she looked were red tile roofs, interrupted by the occasional steeple. And beyond the rooftops glistened the dark blue-green of the ocean.

"You have literally said that at every place we have visited since we left Rome, Bree!" Ben laughed, his head shaking. She was nothing if not easily delighted.

"I know, but I really mean it this time. The people are so kind, and look at these views. Plus, we don't know anyone here. The perfect place!" Bree rattled off the list as if it were just that easy to reinvent her life.

♛

Nazir, in a hotel room across the street, had been listening to the couple's conversation with the help of the sophisticated surveillance equipment his father's men had provided him. Now, hearing the woman's last words, he stood up from his chair and walked to the window overlooking the hotel where the couple were staying.

Didn't I just think the same thing she did? Nazir was unnerved by the connection he was starting to feel to Bree—he had even started thinking of her by her first name. He would be glad when they all arrived in Romania and he could leave this part of his life behind him. He was getting too emotionally attached to them—no, to her.

The next day, the couple was scheduled to take a ferry to the island of Vis. Nazir headed to the harbor early. Ben had seen him in Rome and in Santorini, and he could not risk another sighting. Once at the harbor, Nazir realized the ferry was too small. If he crossed over with the Stantons, an encounter was inevitable. He would have to lease his own boat.

While arranging for another boat, he saw the couple arrive, then hire a dock hand to help load their suitcases and purchases. Bree looked happy and relaxed and was wearing a sundress that, along with her hat, made her look like a thirty-year-old.

Looking at her, Nazir felt his heart skip a beat.

Fifteen minutes later, Nazir was seated toward the rear of a speed boat heading out of the harbor. The hired driver was steering closer to the ferry than Nazir would have liked. Seeing Ben on the front deck of the ferry, Nazir dropped his sunglasses down onto the bridge of his nose, hoping his casual clothes and hat would disguise him. As they came within feet of the still-idling ferry, he looked away.

Once past the ferry, he turned to watch as Ben and Bree settled into their seats on the bow and began taking pictures of the harbor. Nazir was glad that he would get to the island first. This would give him time to put his surveillance equipment in place at the villa that Stephano had arranged for the Stantons.

Once on the island, Nazir rented a nondescript sedan and headed straight for the villa. As he drove along the small road skirting the ocean, he felt a sudden rush of euphoria at the beauty he was experiencing. Nazir had never seen anything quite like it. The vibrant blue-green water sparkled in the morning light.

A few minutes later, as he entered the village, he slowed his car in order to navigate the cobblestoned streets as he took in the clusters of villas, alleyways, and walkways covered with bougainvillea and wisteria. He stopped to allow a small, orange tabby cat to amble across the road, completely oblivious to any danger in the midst of such beauty.

Even the cats know this is the place for "the good life"! Nazir thought, and he couldn't help chuckling. He felt free and happy here. He spent the rest of his drive smiling, just because he could.

Nazir pulled up to the villa, protected from the road by a six-foot stone wall shrouded with vines and flowers. He kept the motor running as he stepped out of the car and peered through an ornate iron gate. It was clearly one of the nicer properties in the town. The side patio had been made ready, complete with upholstered lounge chairs, a built-in kitchen, and uninhibited views of the harbor below.

"This is perfect for Bree. She will love this one." Nazir was unaware he had said the words out loud; he was so engrossed with the ambience of the place.

Seeing that no one was around, he quickly opened the gate, walked into the courtyard, and spent a few minutes positioning the listening devices around the patio and beneath windows. He left through the same gate, but not before glancing back one more time at the view of the water and the boats bobbing in the harbor below.

Yes, this is the place. I could live here, Nazir thought, then interrupted his own reverie with a painful dose of reality. *As if Al-Zawahiri would allow me to escape all the "destined to be king" stuff he has drilled into me since I was small. Who am I kidding?*

No, there would be no island of Vis in his future. Not in this lifetime, anyway. He turned and walked with resignation back to his car, then drove away from the villa and from his fleeting thoughts of fantasy. He'd better check into his own place and get something to eat before the Stantons arrived. He'd be back to watch and listen later.

A few hours later, Nazir was back in his car, parked inconspicuously down the road from the villa, quietly smoking a cigarette as he watched the couple juggle their suitcases through the gate. As he suspected, Bree kept stopping to look at the side patio, with all of its flowers and the view of the water below.

♔

"Ben, this is the best place we have ever stayed!!!" Bree gushed. "I'm never going to leave. In fact, I want to throw on my suit and get down to that water as soon as possible. Look at all of those gorgeous rocks. Who knows what I'm likely to find down there?"

Ben shook his head. Bree had been collecting rocks from every place they had ever visited since their first trip together. He could never quite understand her love of dirt, but apparently it made her happy and so be it.

♔

Nazir stepped out of his car and walked across the cobblestone street to the shadowed walkway running between the Stantons' villa and an adjacent home. From his earlier visit he had decided this would give him the best view of the patio and the stony beach beyond.

As Nazir watched, Bree walked out of the villa and down the steps to the beach. He found himself drifting closer along the shadows in order to observe her.

So sad and yet so beautiful.

As she meandered along the rocky shore, looking at rocks and obviously locked in memories, Nazir could only imagine she was thinking about the loss of her son.

There is something so different about how these Americans approach death, he thought. *They are always so shocked by it and unprepared, as if it were some alien concept dropped on them like a bomb.*

Nazir did not understand. In his almost forty years of life, he had seen much death. But in his culture, rather than hide from the topic, the idea of death was an ever-present and necessary part of life. In fact, he was taught to live life in preparation for a good death. That meant living and abiding by the ancient laws so that when death came, it would bring a peaceful afterlife.

If by chance he were lucky enough to die a martyr's death, well then, the party would begin at the end of his last breath. Nazir had always felt in his heart that his life would end this way. There would be no easy death for him. His only hope was that he would have the courage he needed when the time came.

In contrast, he knew very little about the Western thought of the afterlife. He'd obviously heard of the idea of a heaven that offered forgiveness of a lifetime's worth of sins. But it seemed fanciful to him, a Christian ideal that conveniently allowed for a life of excesses that were somehow forgiven at the last minute with some miraculous atonement.

Nazir could still hear Al-Zawahiri's warnings to him as a young boy about believing such nonsense. "*Nazir, when you attend school in the West, you will encounter a strange notion about life after death. You will be asked to believe that your choices in life are irrelevant because there is this great, benevolent god in the sky who will forgive them all. Don't believe it. When you die, you will pay for every sin you have ever committed. The grave will require it.*"

His father's words had terrified him as a young boy. Somehow, his visual of Allah had morphed into some kind of wrathful henchman, a dictator who could never be pleased. He certainly wasn't a comforting presence.

Nazir had never made peace with his father's words, and he wasn't sure about them even now. He shook the uncomfortable thoughts from his mind and returned to watching Bree walk along the beach.

It seemed clear that Bree, also, was not comforted by the Christian view of heaven. She did not seem able to let go of her son, even when he'd been martyred and had earned a good death.

Nazir was jolted from his thoughts by the sound of laughter as a father, mother, and two children approached from the road. He was forced to step out and around the edge of the wall so they wouldn't see him.

He had seen enough to know the Stantons would not be leaving right away. It was nearly noon. He took the outside walkway back up to his car. He could listen from there anyway.

He started the engine and drove the car to a spot where he could still see Bree's distant form down on the shore. It was enough. He could feel her in his heart.

Chapter 38

Vis, Croatia

Ben dropped his ball cap over his short-cropped hair, donned his sunglasses, and stepped out of their rented villa into the afternoon sunshine. He placed his beer and a book on a nearby table, then walked over to the edge of the patio and stood gazing out at this latest view of the Mediterranean.

Technically, he knew that this far north it was called the Adriatic Sea, but for Ben, it would always be the Mediterranean—the sea he'd been staring at since they left California. First from Rome, then Santorini and Folegandros, and now Croatia. Same sea, but different light and vastly different colors. Here, it was darker green.

He waved to Bree down on the beach and turned to walk back to his chair, feeling relaxed and surprisingly glad to be staying on a small island again.

He lay down and stretched out across one of the luxuriously upholstered lounge chairs. He was glad that Bree had talked him into taking this trip. As time fillers went, the trip so far had been spectacular, Ben thought. The cities of Dubrovnik and Split had provided a fascinating glimpse into the history and architecture of the region. But this place, the island of Vis, it seemed downright magical.

After taking a long, slow draught of beer, he languidly watched Bree as she slowly roamed the shoreline. Now and then she bent over, intently inspecting, selecting, and then rejecting rocks, as if the hundreds she had already picked up and put down somehow didn't quite fit her exact requirements. She looked so relaxed and content, like a young girl, really. He noticed that her skin was now a deep golden color from so much leisurely time in the sun. Her blonde hair was a stark contrast. Yes, the blessings of the gods of beauty had landed squarely on her shoulders, and Ben was still amazed to have her as his wife.

Even well into her fifties, he had seen men reacting to her beauty and her spirit as she wandered the streets and ruins in Dubrovnik. What grief had taken in terms of voluptuous curves, it had certainly added in alluring fragility. The crazy thing was that she was totally unaware of how attractive her vulnerability was to a gender whose DNA was steeped in "rescuing"—even in the twenty-first century, men still yearned to be heroes.

Ben let out a quiet "Oh shit," as he let the truth of his thoughts sink into his own life and agenda. This trip, their year away, and even his focus on vanquishing her grief, were in fact driven by that ancient need to be the hero of their lives.

Damn! So much for altruism.

Meanwhile, down on the beach, Bree was struggling with a different issue. She was trying to recall Jayden's face—and failing.

Even the shoreline had somehow blurred into a faceless gray canvas. It seemed to taunt her with its blank stare.

Trying to quell her panic, she remembered reading about this in one of the books on grief that someone had given her. It was one of the truly startling things about recovery. One day you can't breathe for fear of living without your beloved, and the next thing you know, you can't pull up a memory of the face and voice that have haunted you so relentlessly. It seemed a cruel and ironic twist to an already unimaginable loss.

As she continued to search for rocks, an unexpected puff of a breeze broke her reverie. It caressed her skin and delivered the faintest scent of the sea. That scent was somehow familiar, and both the feel and smell of the moment sent her traveling back to the memory of another time and another beach.

She is sitting on a towel watching Ben and Jayden toss the football. It's clearly a contest of distance and skill as they throw spiral after spiral as hard and far as they can. She shakes her head and laughs as she watches the familiar competition between her young son and the father he idolizes.

She can see the boyish grin on Ben's face as he throws the ball high into the sky and does what looks like an end-zone dance to celebrate an anticipated victory. She shades her eyes from the sun as she follows the ball through the bright blue sky until it lands in the intended receiver's arms. She slowly scans the raised arms down to the face, to find herself looking directly into Jayden's eyes. His beloved face, flushed from exertion and excitement, and his dark blue eyes, so beautiful and intelligent. Her son.

The relief of remembering his face shocked her back into the present, and Bree choked on the sob that had been lodged in her throat.

He is still in my heart. I'm not a horrible mother after all.

She stood up and in a single fluid movement, arched her stiff back and raised her face up to the sun, slowly turning to let its warm rays of light hit every angle of her body and heart.

As she continued to slowly turn, her arms stretched wide and her eyes half-closed, the warmth from her memory and from the sun— combined with the magic of the island—worked their way deep into her still-guarded heart.

At the same moment, she could feel something calling her to loosen her tight grip on the idea of how her life was supposed to be, to accept her loss of that romanticized ideal and to look forward. Jayden was gone. He was still in her heart, but not in her life. She'd had the gift of him for twenty years and those twenty years were hers forever. No one could take them. But now, she saw the need to move forward, the need to see what life wanted from her and what it still had to give her in return—the need for courage.

Bree opened her eyes, thankful for the insight and healing she knew she had somehow received. She turned to look up at the patio of their villa, searching for Ben and the reassurance that this had not just been a dream. He smiled and blew her a kiss.

She looked down at the rocks she had dropped into a pile by her feet. Why she had selected one rock over another was anyone's guess. In fact, who knew why she'd needed to collect any of them at all? Except that maybe she needed to do the same thing with this new life—carefully select the experiences, relationships, and values that would enhance her life, and consciously let go of the ones that no longer served her.

👑

As Ben watched the scene unfold, he had no idea what he was witnessing. To him, it was just another scene in a series of languorous island "beach days."

He suddenly felt drowsy from the combination of the beer and the sun. He slowly breathed in the warm, humid air and closed his eyes in anticipation of a relaxing nap. A sudden breeze blew onto the patio from the beach and swirled around his chair, carrying a strong scent of the ocean and the sand. The scent and feel were oddly familiar, causing him to stir and then to drift back into a memory he'd forgotten of a family weekend spent in Hawaii. And of him and Jayden, throwing a football, a pastime they'd both associated with every beach and every vacation.

The joy of the first glimpse of this memory was euphoric. Oh, what it was like to be so free from sorrow and to enjoy time with his son! He'd forgotten how easy life really was back then. Although if asked, he would have listed a dozen pressing work-related stresses he was feeling at the time. But now, looking back, he—they—had really been living an idyllic life.

Oh, to throw the ball with Jayden just one more time.

Ben was stunned by how quickly the memory had materialized and by the powerful emotions it had evoked. He could feel the tears in his eyes and the familiar rage that inevitably followed any memory of life with Jayden.

Why? he thought to himself. *What purpose has Jayden's death served? What the hell kind of God does this random shit?*

He had not noticed Bree stepping up onto the patio and moving toward him.

"Hey, mister, you wanna buy my jewels? Pretty and cheap." She let the sexual innuendo slide over her tongue, her melodic voice dripping with slow, heated meaning as she held out a handful of rocks.

It took Ben a few seconds to gather his thoughts as he looked up into Bree's shaded face. He struggled to conceal the emotions evoked by what he had just experienced, and she could see his obvious distress.

"Awww. Hey, honey, did something happen?" she said. He wondered what strong emotions she had just caught playing across his face. Anger? Loss? Guilt? Hopelessness? Hard to tell, but probably a bit of all of them.

Ben didn't want to ruin this island idyll by giving vent to his ferocious enmity with God. Besides, there was nothing to be done about it. If he believed that God existed, then Ben was pissed at Him. If he didn't believe in God, then Ben was pissed at fate. Either way, the long-term prognosis for a détente was not great.

"I want to bargain for those lovely jewels, lady. How much you want?" He sat up and softly caressed the back of Bree's thigh all the way up her bikini bottom to the small of her back. She gave him another thousand-watt smile, but he could tell she wasn't thinking of jewels anymore. She was thinking about how to get him to share whatever was obviously on his mind.

Before she could get her questions out, he stood up and pulled her toward him, kissing her eyelids, her nose, her mouth, and eventually working his way down to the soft indentation that pulsed at the base of her throat.

Bree caught her breath with a soft moan, and then in one fluid movement, Ben bent down, picked her up, and carried her into their bedroom overlooking the sea. Once there, he spent the next hour convincing her that her skin was the balm for every unspoken injury or painful memory he would ever have.

Neither of them saw the dark-haired stranger move away from the trees near the wall of their patio.

And neither Ben, Bree, nor the stranger were aware of the M16 drone as it hovered silently above, picking up their conversations and so much more.

Chapter 39

VIS, CROATIA

Bree looked over at Ben in amazement as he lay on his stomach, softly snoring and half wrapped in a tangled sheet, one arm around the bunched-up pillow under his head and the other thrown across her body.

Is there anyone more dead to the world than a man asleep after making love? she wondered with a smile.

She looked at the clock on the nightstand. It was only seven—too early for her to fall asleep for the night. She tried to move Ben's leaden arm from off her side. Unsuccessful, she tried to relax, hoping sleep would come despite the early hour.

She thought about how safe she used to feel with his protective arm draped over her, as if nothing in the world could touch her. But of course, it had, and while it wasn't Ben's fault that death had pushed its way into their lives, she felt differently about this visual now.

Instead of that sense of complete security, she felt more like a pioneer woman who needed to help her husband circle the wagons, pull in the animals, stoke the fire, and load the rifles in preparation for whatever they might encounter before dawn.

But regardless of how much they might prepare, she couldn't shake the feeling of wariness, the necessity of staying alert to danger.

In Bree's mind "danger" was embedded in the diminishing numbers of her family. Once there had been three of them, with the promise of more, and now there were two. Two lonely souls trying to stay connected to life and each other.

She brushed the hair away from Ben's forehead and closed her eyes. She tried to think of three things she was grateful for. It was a technique she often used when sleep eluded her. She'd picked it up from Oprah on her Sunday-morning show. Supposedly, remembering three things that evoked gratitude every day could help keep the mind and heart in the present.

Bree began her list.

One, Ben.

Two, the sound and smell of the sea.

Three . . . There used to be three . . .

She opened her eyes.

She couldn't fall asleep. Maybe it was the scare of forgetting Jayden's face on the beach, or maybe it was her growing misgivings about this trip. What if she was taking Ben on a wild goose chase? What if she found absolutely nothing of comfort in Romania? And then there was this foreboding sense that she was also heading for a showdown with Jayden's God. Was she prepared to deal with that?

She slowly slid out from under Ben's arm and shuffled quietly into the living room. She went straight to the love seat, where she had left her large satchel. She had slipped Jayden's diary into the bag before they left Folegandros.

Actually, if she were being honest, she would have to admit that she had been carting it with her everywhere—it was, after all, the sacred text of her beloved son. This was something she imagined Mother Mary might have done if the Gospels had been written soon enough after her Son's brutal death. Just like Bree, perhaps Mary would have carried His words around as comfort, using them to keep His memory close.

In fact, lately Bree had been wishing she'd been raised Catholic, if only to reach out to another mother of a murdered son. Bree longed to talk with someone who had lived through what she had, and knew the answers to the big questions that were still heavy in Bree's heart:

How can I forgive those responsible for his death?

How can I survive the thousand daily reminders of this loss?
How can I ever believe or trust in God?

But she wasn't Catholic, and she didn't have a personal line to Mary, so there would be no divine solace and guidance. All Bree had was Jayden' s journal about his experiences and her own thoughts and feelings.

Bree carried the journal into the guest bedroom so she would not disturb Ben. She settled into a large, overstuffed chair near the window, unconsciously stroking the cover of the journal as if it were Jayden's skin, yearning for the feel of him. She felt so unworthy of life. Aren't parents supposed to die first? She felt overwhelmed by guilt.

Taking a shaky breath, she opened up the journal.

She had turned to a page describing Jayden's impressions of a woman named Iona, the director of the orphanage. Apparently, she was a force to be reckoned with, a mother bear to all one hundred or so orphaned cubs. A woman who had devoted her entire adult life to the care of those children. The orphanage was run like a typical government institution: long on rules and short on comforts. Iona had tolerated the visits from the American kids in exchange for the labor and materials they provided.

It wasn't long before a friendship between Jayden and Iona had grown, Bree learned. Iona had come to rely on Jayden for help with the computer, the building remodeling, and the leadership of the other young people with him.

Reading Jayden's words, Bree could sense how proud he was of what he was learning, and how he was able to contribute. The group of young people he was leading had truly made a significant impact on this facility.

Smiling through tears, Bree felt her son's personality and spirit wash over her. Catching a glimpse of this part of Jayden's life was such an unexpected gift, and she was overwhelmed by the immense sense of pride she had in him. He had been such a good young man.

She read on, wanting to learn more about the little girl Molly. Bree was intrigued by their connection. Jayden had never shown much interest in children. In fact, as an only child, he hadn't been much of a child himself. With two overachieving parents who dragged him along on their career adventures, he had moved through childhood very quickly.

Yet, clearly, he had experienced something special with Molly.

As she turned the page, Bree noticed the edge of a photograph sticking out of the final pages of the journal. She pulled it out and found herself staring an image of a young girl, thin, stoic, and shabbily dressed. What really caught Bree's attention was the expression in the girl's huge blue eyes. She turned the photograph over and saw that someone had written "Molly, age 5."

While Bree had no idea yet what this little one had experienced in her life, its impact was already written across her face. Molly's soulful eyes immediately drew her in, making Bree ache to pick her up and comfort her. So precious and so grown-up at the same time. An old soul. Bree remembered someone using those words once to describe Jayden.

She wondered if by some divine intuition he had known he would die young.

Bree held Molly's picture in one hand and the journal in the other, glancing from the page to the picture and back to the page. At the time of Jayden's visit, Molly had been nearly five. Apparently, if orphans were not adopted by age five, they would be moved to a larger, more impersonal government institution.

According to Jayden's journal, he had been worried about Molly; he didn't want that for her and had worked with Iona to see if there was a way to avoid it.

In one of his entries and in the true Stranton overachieving family tradition, he had voiced frustration with his young age and his lack of real power. He'd longed to do so much more.

Bree turned the page.

Here was the dog-eared passage she had been unable to finish reading in Folegandros. She couldn't avoid it any longer. Now was the time.

Bree had known in her heart she would have to read this next part of Jayden's journal alone. It was as if he were calling to her; as if she could feel and hear him near her.

With one deep, slow breath and an even longer exhale, she began reading aloud, softly, as if Jayden were telling her the story himself.

Chapter 40

JAYDEN'S JOURNAL

I have been working hard for a couple of weeks to help set up the new orphanage. Nate and Corey really don't get my interest in this place. In fact, I think they think I'm just a suck-up. Whatever. There's no way I can explain it, and I'm not sure I know myself. I mean, there's probably some psychobabble stuff about being an "only child" wanting to protect a sister I've never had. I don't know. I just know that when I think about Molly having to leave this place, I don't feel good.

I mean, I can't lie that I haven't thought about asking Mom and Dad to adopt her, but when I think about when and how I'd bring that up, I just picture their faces over breakfast, both looking at me like I've brought home the plague or one of my eyes has fallen out. Or, maybe just *never looking up from their morning papers and iPads, other than to say, "Will you be home for dinner?"*

And then . . . drum roll, please . . . there's this thing I experienced last night in the chapel. I wasn't going to write about it, because even now, it sounds ludicrous! Crazy . . . like bat crazy. I woke up this morning and I'm pretty sure it all happened and not like in a dream.

I was done with my chores a little late and the others had already left to walk into the main part of town. They were going to the only internet café, looking to connect with friends and family and maybe score some snacks and sodas. One of the things I've been working on is repainting the huge iron fence around this property. Not sure why, considering how run-down the buildings look.

But anyway, as I was cleaning the paintbrush under the outside faucet, I looked up in time to see a light flicker through the stained glass window of the chapel at the far end of the property. The orphanage is in what used to be part of the church compound and housing for staff. I waited, thinking that the flash had been a reflection of something moving on the road. I saw it again and looked out to the empty road but I didn't see anything.

Did I mention that we are smack -ab in the middle of Transylvania? Dracula country! I figured I could outrun almost anything, thanks to soccer and my dad's penchant for throwing a football long and deep. It only made sense to go investigate.

The door was about twice as heavy as me, so it took a few tries to get it open and me into the church. It was late afternoon and so the light wasn't the best and the place felt kind of creepy. I'm pretty sure my parents and I had been to an Easter service in a church in the last ten years, but I really can't remember much about either the church or the service. And that's pretty much the total extent of my church knowledge.

It took a few minutes for my eyes to adjust and to decipher shapes and objects through the dust floating on the last beams of light coming through the windows.

My first thought was that this place was kinda plain. I'm used to seeing pictures of famous cathedrals, and this wasn't anything like that. This chapel had simple painted boards for pews, a few paintings, stained glass windows, and a rough cross up at the front with a figure nailed to it.

The whole scene was strange and kind of uncomfortable.
I remember looking up at the cross. That Christ did not look
happy or handsome. He was in pain, and he looked like any
other eastern European guy I'd seen on the street. He didn't
look like my idea of a god.

I must have chosen a seat about halfway up the aisle.
In order to slow down my racing heart, I decided to think
about all the experiences I'd had and the people I'd met
since coming to Romania. Then I started thinking about
Molly and what she had so unfairly experienced in her short
life. I was so sad. I might have cried a little, even.

I remember looking up at the Christ and saying,
"Well, that act was a complete waste of time for the real
world." I actually said it out loud. I wasn't trying to be
disrespectful—it just seems like the world is still a pretty
messed-up place. So how much could his death have helped?

More time passed, and I think I ranted about a few
more things I don't get, like my dad does after he's read
something that bothers him in the newspaper.

That's when I saw that flash of light again.

I instinctively looked down at my hands. Maybe I was

hoping some garlic and a stake would magically appear in them. I'm gonna say here and only here that I was too scared to look up to see where the light was coming from. I've seen enough Dracula movies to know what comes next. I could sense that something was moving towards me.

I was going to have to do something.

I took a deep breath and slowly looked up.

I don't know what I expected, but this was crazy different. Not really an angel, not really a person, and not really god with a big G. More like a combination of all three.

All I could think about was getting out of there before something even scarier happened. I stood up to leave.

Next thing I knew, I was on the floor on my hands and knees. This is the really weird part, and I'm not sure I would believe it if it hadn't happened to me.

Nothing had pushed me down. I didn't feel a hand or anything. I just couldn't stand up anymore. It felt more like energy against weakness.

The light that had started out as a flash was now so bright that I had to squeeze my eyes shut. It was not only intense, it had a sound to it, like a vibration or a hum. I could feel the sound and hear the light. I know. It sounds crazy.

For some unknown and insane reason, I felt compelled to repeat one of my earlier rants about the unfairness of God and how I didn't want to believe in or follow a God that allows kids like Molly to suffer so much. I might even have yelled something about God being unfair.

The hum of the light grew louder and more intense, and I tried to continue to talk but no sound or words came out of my mouth.

At the same time, the hum grew instantly knowable to me, like I had a built-in translator. I could actually understand the hum's intensity and frequency as words. It was so cool! I kind of forgot to be afraid and started to make sense of the words coming out of the hum. It was like I was having a conversation with it in my head.

"Jayden, you think I am unfair, uncaring, and that I am too busy to help the world."

"Well, put like that, I think sometimes . . ."

"I am God. Be still and know it."

And then, the coolest of cool things happened.

I was taken on a journey of some of the world's big events. Some of them I remembered, and others I had only heard about in history class. It was like a collection of YouTube videos. Each one seemed so real, it felt like I was actually there. But with each one, I was also shown that God had been present.

Then, I saw another video that showed the bigger picture that revealed how the event had played into other stories and people's lives. I could see that God didn't cause bad things to happen, but sometimes allowed them so that other things—good things—could happen. And you know what? Watching all this? It made sense. I understood. Like one of those silly memes on Facebook that begins with "behind every dark cloud, there's lemonade" or something like that.

It sounds stupid and trite to write this now, but at that moment, while I still didn't like the suffering, I kinda got the whole story.

Then the videos switched to my own life, and I felt embarrassed at some of the things I watched. They even included feelings and thoughts, which really made me feel weird. I saw both the good parts of me and the not-so-good parts. I watched myself do things that touched people and made me feel proud, and then I saw my actions and words that had done damage or made others feel bad.

I even saw my resentment toward Mom's and Dad's constant work. The fact that they never seemed to have much time for the three of us. The idea that God has been paying attention to stuff inside of me was mind-blowing. Seriously, it was something I had never even considered.

Strangely, all these exposed feelings didn't make me feel bad. It was like He was showing me my deepest feelings and thoughts, not to punish me or hurt me—or even judge me—but so I would know how well He really knew the deepest parts of me.

I'm not sure how long all of this took. It could have been minutes or could have been hours.

When I felt like I was in the church again, I was overwhelmed with love and I knew it was God. I was still on my face in front of the cross and my face was wet with tears that I didn't remember crying. The light was gone. Yet, I felt completely known and secure. I've never felt that way before.

I also felt this ache in my heart, like a deep need to help others find this place of overwhelming peace.

At the same time these thoughts were going through my mind, I was suddenly aware of a hand on my back. Someone touching me with such kindness. I could feel heat and energy (I know . . . it's crazy to even write this down).

The voice in my head identified the heat as God. I was to give myself to His purpose and design. And I was to trust Him. I remember saying out loud, "Yes!"

It was then that I heard Molly's voice and realized she was the one touching my back.

"Jay Jay! Yes yes! Jay Jay!"

It was all that her small English skills could help her say. But now I could feel her love and her terror at the same time. She didn't need words. I remember sitting up and grabbing her with a bear hug so tight, wanting her to understand through that hug that I loved her and would make sure she was okay.

I also silently vowed to get medical training and return to this place and these children. That shocked me. I thought I would be an architect, like my dad, even though I've never *felt the passion he does when looking at buildings.*

But this idea? Helping others? Helping them find God? I can get fired up about this.

I grabbed Molly and stood up, looking up at the cross and now seeing for the first time in the agony of Christ the incredible love I hadn't seen before. This Christ's death was not a "have to" act. It was a choice. A gift. My knees almost buckled with that knowledge, and I could feel the weight of my life lift off my heart and mind.

It felt like I had wings . . . I was finally free.

♕

Bree stopped reading, aware that she had been holding her breath and sobbing at the same time.

It was so inexplicable and yet strangely beautiful, God choosing to reveal this to her son. No wonder he had come back from this trip so changed and determined. It wasn't just the high of a summer trip; it was the interaction with God and the understanding that his life had purpose and design.

A darker thought also surfaced in her mind: Clearly, Jayden had not been shown how short his life was to be or the violent way his life would end a mere four years later. He must have assumed he'd be graduating now and entering med school in the fall.

Bree slumped back in her chair with an exhaustion she had not known since hearing the news of the shooting. At the same time, questions flooded her mind.

How was she ever going to make sense of this God of Jayden's, given her son's senseless death? How could God have taken her son without discussing it or giving *her* a video tour? Why didn't He bother to show *her* the comforting "bigger picture" during the weeks and months of intense mourning and grief? Why did mere humans have to wander around on this earth in complete darkness, experiencing horrific things, and having no answers or understanding? How could that be love?

Still pondering these and similar questions, she drifted into sleep.

It was Ben, gently shaking her shoulder and whispering to her, that woke Bree from a dreamless slumber. Wincing, she reached up to rub her stiff neck. As she stirred, the journal fell from her lap to the floor.

"Wow, honey. Was sex so bad you had to sleep in a chair on the other side of the house?" Ben asked, his tousled hair and sleepy voice a giveaway for how recently he had become aware of her body missing next to him.

It took Bree a minute to clear the cobwebs from her brain.

"What time is it?" she asked Ben.

"It's almost ten."

Bree slowly remembered why she was sitting in this chair and what she had experienced. As she glanced around, she felt inexplicably lighter, as if her heart had finally been freed from the fifty-pound anvil that had been crushing it for the past two years.

"Yes, you might as well know that it was awful," she teased him back. "I'm going to have to leave you." Then she reached up to give him a kiss that suggested a much different story.

Bree buried her face in Ben's neck as he picked her up and carried her back to their room. Oh, how she loved the smell of Ben's skin and the feel of it against her face.

There would be time later to share with him all that she had read.

Chapter 41

VIS, CROATIA

It was after seven o clock in the evening, and the intense sunlight was giving way to a rosy glow. Nazir was standing outside the Stantons' villa, wearing wireless earbuds.

He would have been more comfortable if he had stayed in his car, but something about the couple intrigued him, and he had been tucked in the shadows of the walkway beside their villa for several hours. Nazir had just heard their intimate moments, but it wasn't the sex that drew him in. It was something else. Something unfamiliar.

He couldn't deny that he was intrigued by the Americans. Ben demonstrated a tenderness toward his wife that was not something a man of Nazir's culture would think to express. This man Ben was not afraid to tell or show his wife how he felt about her. If Nazir were honest, he'd have to admit he'd never witnessed anything like this before, and certainly not while observing the imperious Al-Zawahiri with Nazir's mother—or with any of his father's other wives, for that matter.

The couple had been quiet for some time, so Nazir was surprised to hear Bree's voice begin to speak softly. He pressed his earbud close so he could hear what she was saying.

She seemed to be reading. He didn't hear the husband respond, which probably meant she was reading out loud to herself. It seemed an odd thing for her to be doing, but the listening devices he had planted on each side of the villa picked up her voice as if she were right next to him.

He grew still as she recounted what was obviously some type of strange fantasy story about someone meeting the Western "God" while still alive, as if that were possible.

Nazir could tell by the way her voice wavered, and how she fought now and then to regain her composure, that this was an important story to her.

It perplexed Nazir. *Is this about her dead son? Why else would she be so emotional? Could this be his story?*

Nazir felt himself drawn into the narrator's journey.

As he listened, Nazir tried to make sense of the story from his own perspective. In studying Islam as a young boy, Nazir was never taught about the possibility of a relationship with Allah—and he was certainly never encouraged to dialogue with him. Nazir was only taught about meeting the standards of Allah's imperious will, its secrets known only to Allah himself, and occasionally interpreted by certain important followers, like Nazir's father. Even then, the will of Allah seemed to be elusive, deciphered by open or closed doors of opportunity. If a door opened, it was Allah's will. If it did not, it wasn't.

As Bree continued to read and the story unfolded, Nazir was intrigued to find himself wondering if a more personal connection and understanding of God was truly possible. Rather than demanding a life of disciplined sacrifice in an attempt to earn a better death, what if God actually desired relationship? One built on interaction and compassion? A relationship in which weakness and surrender could trump strength and cunning?

These were strange notions to Nazir, like nothing he had ever heard before.

Eventually, the narrator spoke of a little girl who came to comfort him. Nazir wondered who she was. Something about this part of the story must have affected Bree as well, because Nazir heard her crying softly. It made him feel unsettled, and he felt unfamiliar emotions stir from somewhere deep inside of him.

Nazir glanced up at a single lighted window. He had been slowly walking along the perimeter of the villa compound as he listened to her read—now he was surprised to realize how close he stood to where Bree must be sitting. A glance at his watch told him it was now after eight. He'd been listening for an hour.

As Bree sniffled and fell silent, Nazir wondered again about the young man's story. Could the little girl be the one his father had ordered Amir to eliminate? Nazir hoped not but felt in his gut that this was not only possible, but likely.

What would the girl's death do to Bree?

More important, how would her son's God feel about it?

Nazir didn't want to incur the wrath of any more gods. He had enough trouble with his father and Allah.

These thoughts were interrupted by the vibration of an incoming text. He pulled his phone from his pocket and read the message. *Great.* His father wanted to speak to him.

He glanced once more at the window near his head and the sound of Bree's weeping. He gently touched the wall, and then turned and silently slipped into the darker edges of the surrounding property.

As he stepped from the shadows and crossed the back of the property, he stopped and turned one last time to glance back at the villa. Nazir did not want to leave her. Not when she was so distressed. The cell phone vibrated again, and he knew he had no choice.

As Nazir walked away, he felt something ancient flood up from his soul. Not just the usual pull between his Eastern sensibilities and the Western world. It was something more powerful, a sense of foreboding mixed with a more primal calling—a feeling that he could not begin to articulate. It felt as if the earth's surface were opening up and his ancestors were calling to him.

He could sense Abraham standing at what seemed to be a fork of a road, beckoning to him, asking him to choose.

But choose what?

♔

Above the troubled man's head, and unseen to his dark eyes, a drone hovered. Little did the Arab know that at the moment he had turned back to glance at the villa one more time, the drone's camera caught his face full on.

Chapter 42

ROMANIA

I an looked at his cell phone to see who was calling. It was his man following the Americans, and he was making contact six hours sooner than scheduled. This could only spell trouble.

Ian answered abruptly. "Ian here."

"Sir, I don't mean to interrupt your evening, but I didn't want to wait until morning either. Nothing to report on the Yanks in terms of their travel. They have been moving up the coast from Dubrovnik to Split and now to the island of Vis. Looks like they may be here for a few days."

"What's the pressing issue, then?"

"I picked up a tail on them."

Ian felt like he was watching a car crash in excruciatingly slow motion. He was unable to stop it, yet unable to tear his eyes away. There was no denying that these people were on a collision course with the snare he and JD were laying for the terrorists. It was difficult to admit that he had no effective game plan for handling the Americans' unique combination of cluelessness and unlimited discretionary income.

"Electronic or boots?" Ian got down to business quickly.

"Boots."

"CIA?" Ian didn't think Mac would be tailing the Americans after asking Ian to do it, but it didn't hurt to ask.

"No. I sent in a small drone. The tail was outside their villa wall. Definitely Middle Eastern. He was no novice, and clearly trained at avoiding security cameras or standard surveillance. It took a while, but we caught a lucky break. For some reason he stepped into the light and looked back at the villa. We'll see if it was enough. I've sent video up to get facial recognition but don't have anything back yet."

Apparently, the jihadists are already onto the Americans, Ian thought. The realization made him nervous.

Ian shook his head at this newly added wrinkle before giving instructions to the man on the phone. "While we're waiting for identification, I don't want them to catch as much as a whiff of us. Make sure you stay invisible. Let me know what you come up with. And sorry to say this, but now you have two competing assignments. Along with surveillance, you'll have the unenviable task of trying to protect these fool Americans as well."

"Yes, sir. I may need some help."

"Of course. I'll authorize additional support immediately. However—and I want to make sure you understand—the big picture still takes priority. If at any time you must choose between our operation and the safety of the Americans, I'm giving standing orders now to sacrifice them. I will deal with any fallout. Let's also step up our reports. I'd like contact through the same channels, but at twelve-hour intervals, or sooner for major developments. Well done."

Ian clicked the phone off and headed straight for the bottle of port.

With glass in hand, he paced the small, confined space of the home he had rented near the orphanage in preparation for the big showdown. What did JD call it? The OK corral, or some such western idiom. He decided to discuss the news of an additional gunslinger with ole John Wayne himself.

He punched Mac's number, despite the fact that it was five in the morning in Virginia. When his buddy answered, Ian said, "Sorry for the early call, JD. Just heard from my man tailing the Americans. Apparently, we aren't the only interested party."

Mac didn't seem surprised. "As soon as the Brits were eliminated, I figured our terrorists would need to confirm how much the Americans know," he said. "They're probably as intrigued as we are at the unexpected complication of this couple marching toward the orphanage."

Then, as if he'd realized something else, Mac suddenly added. "Great. Now we have to worry about the terrorists trying to knock off the Americans!"

"I'm in total agreement with everything you just said, JD. So far, our Arab 'friends' seem to be treating the Stantons in the same watch-and-wait manner that we are, but that could change at any moment, and I highly doubt we will get any warning. Not only does this mean it's going to get crowded, but the chance for collateral damage obviously increases. I have my MI6 field operative doing his best to control the situation, but he is going to need help if things get out of hand."

"Let me know what I can do from this end. We've been promised whatever resources we need."

"JD, just thinking. Any reason to inform the Americans and bring them in on this?" Ian hesitated to bring it up, as he was already managing the village kid, Molly; Iona; and the soon-to-be arriving Delta Team, as well as securing a hell of a lot of geography in the area. The idea of taking these tourists under wing did not thrill him.

"God no, Ian. I'd rather drug them and throw them in a cell than tell these grieving powder kegs about more dead children. No telling what they would do."

This was the exact response Ian had hoped for. No sense in getting these two worked up and acting out. Still, they were walking into the middle of one hell of a tsunami.

"Let's talk about what the jihadists know at this point. Or what we hope they know. I'm assuming you coerced the village canary into singing about the miraculous young survivor?"

"I'm fairly good at interrogation, but I have to say that once Iona got ahold of his ear and threatened his very existence, he sang at the top of his lungs, and directly to our target audience."

"Sounds like one tough gal!" Mac said.

"They've killed the Brits; they're onto the Americans. I think we can assume they know about Molly and are making plans to return for her."

"So, you think they're on the move."

"That's my gut instinct. I also think we should take a run at whoever is tailing the Americans—as soon as we figure out who he is. We're working on that now. He could know something that will help us before the showdown begins."

Ian promised Mac an update as soon as he had one. Then he called it a night.

Chapter 43

VIS, CROATIA

Nazir sat in his car, cell phone in hand. He wanted a moment to gather his thoughts before calling his father. As he looked across at the Stantons' villa, barely visible in the darkening sky, Nazir felt a sudden chill of loneliness.

I wonder what the hell I've done to displease him now?

He punched the call button.

A moment later, he heard his father's voice, sounding even more autocratic than usual, if that was possible.

"Nazir, I wanted to speak with you in person. As you are aware, Amir has exposed our jihad through extreme carelessness."

Nazir wondered where this was heading.

"My first choice has always been for you to one day take your rightful position as the leader of the faithful. In preparation for that moment, I believe you need to take a stand with your cousin. I want you to be the one to personally deliver Amir's 'reward' for his carelessness."

Nazir hadn't known quite what to expect, but it wasn't this. He was shocked. Was his father actually saying that in order for Nazir to prove himself, it meant killing someone who was not only a dedicated follower, but also their own flesh and blood? Granted, Amir was a pain in the ass at times, but death? Nazir's brain scrambled to find the words to calm his father down and buy some time. He also felt the first of several sharp points of dawning realization.

"I'm sorry to hear this, Father. Amir has been very faithful to you and to the jihad—"

"Faithfulness does not excuse ineptness!" Al-Zawahiri boomed. "His greater calling and allegiance is to the Caliphate, not to me. It is Allah who requires his sacrifice. An example must be made."

Nazir thought about the hundreds of other "examples" his father had helped Allah make. To his father, he simply muttered the obligatory "Allah is great" while secretly thinking, *Maybe not so much.*

At some point, isn't there some goodness that is supposed to come out of serving Allah? What about the compassion and love in the story Bree read about her son?

Realizing he could not dissuade his father, Nazir acquiesced. "I will arrange to meet up with Amir before he arrives in Romania." Then he added, "I am finished with my work following the Americans. Their pending visit to the orphanage is nothing more than a strange coincidence, a pilgrimage on behalf of their dead son. It has nothing to do with knowing about our purpose there or the prior attack on the children."

"You have confirmed this?" His father sounded doubtful.

"Yes. I am willing to stake my own life on it," Nazir assured his father, before really thinking about the implications of his pledge, or his father's uncanny ability to read his deeper thoughts. He was throwing down a gauntlet to a man who had already shown he was not to be trusted.

And I have just revealed that I care about what happens to the Americans, Nazir realized with a sinking feeling, knowing that he had just handed his father the sword that would lead to his undoing.

But Nazir knew there was no other way—he had to get both his father and Amir off the unthinkable idea of killing the Americans. Appeasing his father was foremost in his thoughts.

"I will handle Amir, and any other responsibilities you require, Father. I have sworn my allegiance to you and to the Caliphate."

The phone went dead, and Nazir sat for several minutes in complete darkness, unable to move as he contemplated this latest edict. As much as he disliked Amir's unrestrained penchant for theatrics and violence, he was still Nazir's blood, his cousin. Either his father was losing his grip on reality, or he had decided a fight to the death was the only way to reveal the rightful heir apparent to his grand jihad.

Nazir thought once again of Abraham, beckoning him to choose the road he would follow.

So, this is the choice Abraham has been asking me to make.

Chapter 44

CIA HEADQUARTERS, LANGLEY

Mac could hardly sit still, even though he was in the middle of his own retirement party.

He sat with one leg crossed over the knee of the other, staring at his left ankle and foot as they moved in circles fueled by complete and utter agitation. This bullshit was almost more than he could endure! If he detested being the center of the attention, however contrived and predictable the retirement party ritual was, he detested wasting precious time even more. As various office minions stood up to praise his "amazing work ethic," his "commitment to detail" and even his "years of service without missing a sick day" *(Twenty-seven, but who's counting?)*, all he could think of was getting on his way to Budapest.

In fact, at that very moment, a black suburban sat idling at the curb outside the building, ready to whisk him to an unmarked private jet waiting in a nearby hangar.

"And now, Mac, we'd like to present you with this plaque . . ."

The words jolted him from the list of operational details he was going over in his head. He stood up, walked a little too briskly toward the speaker (another bureaucratic horse's ass he had never respected), jerked the plaque from his hands, and uttered a couple of remarks through a grimace that never quite made it to a smile. Mac had intended to say something like "Thank you for this overwhelming and undeserved recognition. It's been an honor serving with you."

What he said instead was, "Don't let the bad guys win. Let's eat!"

The small crowd clapped, standing to their feet, already eyeing the buffet table. Mac knew this, because that's what he'd done as a member of this same herd many times over the years. He was half sad he wouldn't have a chance to dig into those barbecued ribs. But he'd be well on his way to the hangar by the time lunch was served.

He looked down at the plaque and the envelope that he knew contained some silly Orvis gift card he would never use. He vowed to give someone a heads-up on what a person with over thirty years of service would really like to hear and receive, but that would have to wait until his return.

In the meantime, he inched his way toward the door, shaking hands and collecting a few slaps on the back and hugs from the assistants' pool. Had he ever even seen half of these people? He had no idea who they were. Most of them looked like they should still be in grade school.

The only delightful experience of the day had been making eye contact with the young idiot who had delivered the retirement package to him. He couldn't help but laugh as he saw the kid inching away from any chance encounter.

Go ahead and run, boy, he thought. *You can't outrun Father Time. He'll come looking for you before you know it!*

And with one last piercing look, he turned and walked away from his lifelong career.

As he settled into the backseat of the black Suburban, his cell phone rang, and he picked up the call on the first ring.

It was Ian.

"JD, let me be the first to congratulate you. But I'm also going to tell you that your retirement will be as impactful to the CIA as taking a hand out of a bucket of water!" Mac could tell Ian was struggling to not crack up. Mac could only scowl at him from the other side of the world. "In fact," Ian continued, "I hear they are unbolting your name plate from the door and replacing it with the name of your successor even as I speak!" This time, Ian lost the struggle and uttered an all-out belly laugh.

"You aren't telling me anything I don't already know!" Mac barked back into the phone.

"Well, here's something you don't know. We have a make on our guy who was hiding in the shadows outside the Americans' villa in Vis. He is neither what nor who we thought he'd be. Turns out he's your diplomatic wonder boy, Washington's much-lauded authority on terrorism, Nazir Akbari."

It took a full thirty seconds for Ian's words to truly sink in.

"What the hell . . . ?" Mac could not get his head around this unexpected development. Like the ripples in a pond, after a stone is thrown into its once-placid waters, the ripples from this news had ever-expanding implications. "Ian, this guy has been all over Washington and on every news channel as *the face* on terror. He's highly educated, highly respected, and now—apparently—highly dangerous."

Mac was already mentally connecting the dots between Nazir's influence and his intelligence access. "If what you say is true," he said, "we have a mole at the highest levels of diplomacy with probable top-secret clearance!" The implications were making it hard for Mac to breathe. "How we failed to catch this one, I do not know. But this is game changer."

"Are you sure you can still trust the operational integrity from your end?" Ian asked. "Who else besides Randall knows? "

Mac didn't pretend to hide his annoyance. Ian was probably his closest friend—well, hell, probably his only friend—but this question got under his skin. "Yes, we are definitely cloaked on this one. I'll be ready to roll as soon as I get to Budapest. You just concentrate on your side of the ops. The team better be prepped and ready by the time I get there!"

Ian realized by Mac's tone that he had crossed a line with his old friend. "Sorry, JD . . . Didn't mean to imply anything but complete trust. This latest development obviously has everyone a bit jumpy," he said apologetically.

Mac seemed not to even hear Ian's apology. He changed the subject.

"More to the point, who are we really dealing with here? This thing is starting to move up the food chain, if you know what I mean. What if we have something much bigger, Ian? Is there even a slight chance that we could have inadvertently hooked into Al-Zawahiri?

Ian didn't want to admit that his friend could be onto something. But what were the odds that they had stumbled onto the machinations of the most powerful and elusive leader since Bin Laden? The thought was more than a bit chilling.

"Why would Al-Zawahiri risk such an important and successful mole on a simple tail operation?" Mac had raised the question, but it mirrored Ian's thoughts as well. Neither of them had the answer.

They both sat silent. Ian's mind was spinning like a GPS after missing a pivotal turn. He'd bet Mac's was too. Only, now this "redirecting" was taking on global proportions. The small orphanage drone test took on an entirely new level of threat in the hands of Al-Zawahiri.

Suddenly, Mac announced, "We just pulled up to the plane. I'll noodle on that one while I'm flying over the pond."

"I sent a packet of materials on ahead," Ian said, "regarding your cover. You can study it on the plane."

"Great. Homework," Mac muttered.

"You may want to leaf right to the story of David and Goliath."

"Who?" Mac had obviously failed to make the connection between the biblical story and their current predicament. Ian ignored his question. Instead, he asked one of his own.

"By the way, you don't happen to own a slingshot, do you?"

Ian didn't wait for an answer before ending the call.

Chapter 45

CROATIA

Ben stepped on the gas to pass a slow-moving car. He felt surprisingly at ease driving the unfamiliar Croatian roads. He had no idea, however, if he was obeying the traffic rules or even what they were, and that made him laugh out loud. He glanced over at Bree and she smiled back. Vis had changed her, somehow. She seemed calmer, more peaceful. He wasn't quite sure how to even broach the subject of what had changed.

Maybe I won't.

Whatever it was, it had been difficult to get her to leave their island villa.

"Please, Ben. Can't we just stay here forever?"

They'd been sitting on their patio that morning, enjoying their last cup of coffee and the early sunrise over the harbor. They could hear the fishermen yelling to each other and laughing as they worked to get their gear ready, and finally, one by one motoring their boats out to sea.

Ben had understood why she wanted to stay. It felt like they were living inside of a painting.

"Bree, you are the one who needs to get to Romania. I'd stay here for another month, no problem."

"I know." She had stopped to breathe in the heady perfume from the flowers blooming along the patio wall and in the pots scattered around the patio. Ben had smiled when he'd seen her nostrils flare as she inhaled the scent, mixed with the crisp early morning air.

"This place just has a special something," she'd said, smiling as if at a secret. Then she's gotten up from her chair and walked over to climb onto Ben's lap.

"You are right, honey. I do want to keep going. But promise me we will come back here someday."

Ben had literally felt the calmness that flooded from her green eyes. He'd marveled at how beautiful she looked, even in the early morning light and just out of bed. She seemed more the Bree before . . . well, everything.

"I promise," he'd said, and kissed her as if to seal the deal.

They'd packed and headed back to Split on the ferry. And now they were driving in a rental sedan, on their way north to Budapest.

Maybe this is the best we can hope for, Ben thought, *wandering the globe, going from place to place, experience to experience. It doesn't seem like a half-bad life. We could do worse. And Croatia, who would have thought?*

"Who would have thought that we would be driving through Croatia at this point in our lives?" Bree said, once again verbalizing what he'd been thinking. It was uncanny. Maybe the "two shall be as one" thing about marriage was true. Sometimes it felt like they really were two sides of the same coin.

"And on the right side of the road!" Ben laughed. And suddenly, they were both laughing as they reminisced about other driving adventures during their travels—now embellished with the passing of time—like driving in Ireland, and the many times they had nearly crashed.

"We spent half our time expecting a head-on collision at any moment," Bree said.

"Hey, what about the Philippines? Remember the *tuk-tuks*? Every time we jumped in one of those, it felt like we were risking our lives. Remember all the gasoline fumes from the engines pouring into the open cab while we were weaving in and out of traffic?"

"And the dust and dirt from the roads! Remember my white pants? I never did get that red dirt out of them."

"And China! My God, Bree! The sheer number and speed of the motorcycles and cars!"

Bree nodded. "A billion people, and every one of them on the road at the same time. Crazy!"

They really had shared some great travel experiences together, Ben thought. He reached over to touch Bree's hand. She was staring off with the kind of contented smile he had not seen in years. He was instantly sorry that his touch had interrupted whatever thoughts were causing her to feel so happy.

"Ben," she turned to him, suddenly serious. "When you found me the other night with Jayden's journal, I had just read the part about his experience in the chapel. I know we talked about reading it together, but it just felt like the right time." She paused for a moment, as if debating whether or not to tell him more. She didn't.

Ben could clearly see that she'd had an emotional experience with whatever she had read. He remembered finding her asleep in the chair, waking her up, and the journal falling to the floor. Her serene demeanor and obvious joy made more sense to him now, but they also made him nervous. It was so like Bree to create high expectations. After all, that was her business, selling dreams. But when it came to her own, she was a bit fragile and he had learned early in their marriage to make sure she was not disappointed.

It had been relatively easy because she was always so appreciative of his efforts. But this thing, this journal and the memory of their dead child, had the potential for disaster built into it. How could he control all these moving pieces? What were the chances that the orphanage director or the little girl even remembered Jayden? And if they did, what could they possibly offer so many years later that would make sense of anything he and Bree were experiencing? He could see that agreeing to this trip had set him up for an epic failure, and maybe for a giant setback for Bree as well.

She interrupted his thoughts before he could formulate a contingency plan. "I think I need to read a part of the journal to you. It's the part about Jayden's experience in the chapel, and I've been waiting for the right moment. Would you mind if I read it to you while we are driving?"

Ben took a moment before answering, wanting to lower Bree's expectations without dousing her hopeful joy. Finally, he said, "Sure. I'll listen. But I'm not likely to change my mind about this God thing based on my seventeen-year-old son's summer journal entries, especially given the circumstances."

There was that ever-present hard edge to his words that emerged whenever Ben connected the subjects of Jayden's death and God's existence. Bree remembered feeling the same way before reading Jayden's journal. For just a moment, she thought about telling Ben about her experience on the beach, when she'd been so afraid that she had forgotten what Jayden looked like, and then about the return of that glorious memory of Hawaii—a memory that had almost felt like a divine gift—but then thought better of it. She didn't want him to think she was going crazy. So instead, she simply nodded, then reached into her bag and pulled out the leather-bound book.

She opened to the page she had marked using Molly's photo, then began to read, letting Jayden tell his own story:

"'I have been working hard for a couple of weeks to help set up the new orphanage. Nate and Corey really don't get my interest in this place. In fact, I think they think I'm just a suck-up. Whatever. There's no way I can explain it and I'm not sure I know myself . . .'"

Chapter 46

THE ORPHANAGE

"Well, the place certainly feels different without your beloved children here, Iona," Ian said as he and Iona walked through the nearly empty orphanage.

The staff had relocated the children to the house in the village that had once housed the older children who had been killed in the attack. It had been an uncomfortable decision to make, given that experience, but there was no other facility nearby that was set up to handle and support that many children.

"I'm sorry we needed to do this," Ian added, "and believe me when I say that if there was any other way . . ." Ian stopped walking and turned to look into Iona's eyes. He knew she was understandably anxious about whatever would happen next.

There was no escaping the fact that this was ultimately about Molly. She was the bait, the lure that would hopefully draw the terrorists into their trap, which meant she had not been sent to safety along with the others. It had been another difficult but necessary decision. Molly had been told she could stay behind to help Iona welcome a new mission team that would be arriving soon to do renovations on the property.

Molly had been thrilled.

The same story had also spread throughout the town, as it always did when the potential for revenue and interesting encounters with Westerners was on the horizon. Every time a mission team arrived, the itinerary always included several visits to the village so team members could get a sense of what it was like to live in this part of Romania. Without being able to see it firsthand, it was impossible for these young people to believe that many of the villagers still had horse-drawn carts, cut their grass fields with scythes, and didn't own a TV.

The idea of bringing in the covert ops folks as a mission team had been part of Ian's brilliant plan. The team would consist of twelve men and women led by none other than JD himself, all covert ops and highly trained special forces. They would spread out over the property and village, performing actual renovations, while secretly securing the area with 360-degree surveillance, drones, and enough ground firepower hidden among the building supplies to level everything within a one-hundred-mile radius, if necessary.

Of course, they hoped it wouldn't come to that. Their objective, instead, was to capture at least one of the terrorists sent to kill Molly, and to extract from him the information they needed to stop the jihadists from using the bioagent in any further attacks. And if they were very, very lucky, they might even get a bead on Al-Zawahiri himself.

♛

Iona's hands shook as she tied the ribbon in Molly's hair and kissed her on the cheek. She could and would do this—for Molly, and for Jayden too. She looked over to see Ian watching both of them and felt a surge of warmth flood first her heart and then her cheeks. There was something about Ian that made her feel safe. As if caught with his hand in the proverbial cookie jar, Ian turned his face away, and Iona took the opportunity to study his profile. It was a profile she was growing to love—the face of a gallant knight who had come into her life long after she had given up hope for him. Ian must have felt her intense gaze, because he turned to look at her again. Embarrassed, she turned her attention back to Molly's hair, stroking it lovingly and adjusting the ribbon she had just tied to the dark strands.

♛

As he watched the tender scene before him, Ian felt a newly familiar mixture of admiration and emotion wash over him.

He could not comprehend the courage it had taken for Iona to have single-handedly protected the many orphaned children in her care all these years. He had certainly served his country, but it had not required this level of selflessness, combined with anonymity. Unlike Iona, Ian had enjoyed all the creature comforts of life, plenty of accolades, and intellectual stimulation. Her life had consisted—and still did—of such a quiet, lonely, and unrecognized heroism. She was someone he could . . .

He roused himself from letting his thoughts meander down that path. It was too soon to think of what he might want after all this was over. They were days, maybe even hours, away from an epic showdown, and it was going to take complete and utter concentration to keep them all safe.

Looking at Iona and Molly, Ian was more determined than ever to make sure that happened.

He smiled down at Molly, patting her shoulder. In English he said, "Molly, my girl, you look more beautiful every time I see you!"

She blushed and looked shyly at Iona, then gazed through the window at the chapel in the distance.

For some reason it made Ian wonder if she ever thought about Jayden. She never spoke of him, yet sometimes she seemed far away, as if she were locked in a memory.

He silently vowed to put more effort into getting to know her and those thoughts she kept so tightly bottled up.

Chapter 47

HOTEL GELLERT, BUDAPEST, HUNGARY

Ben and Bree had discussed the selection of a hotel in Budapest while still on the island of Vis.

Bree wanted a modern and vibrantly hip property she had researched online that had received glowing reviews for its *très chic* amenities. Ben, on the other hand, preferred the architectural wonders of a more authentically historical and grand property, like the Gellert.

It was a hopelessly one-sided discussion, because Bree had promised Ben that very thing in luring him to consider the trip in the first place.

She gave a half-hearted attempt at arguing but gave in at the first sign of resistance, and now they were booked at the Hotel Gellert, with a room overlooking the Danube. Bree was familiar with the pros and cons of the old property, as she had described them to many of her top clients. But she had to admit, there was a certain mystique about the hotel that defied its lack of modern amenities.

There was something indeed old-world about crossing the Széchenyi Chain Bridge over the Danube and their first glimpse of the stately grandeur of the Hotel Gellert. As they drove over the bridge, Bree pulled the hotel website up on her phone and read Ben a description of the history of the place:

"'It was built in 1911 in the Art Deco style of many of the palaces of the day. It was common to have royal visitors, with everyone from princes to maharajas teeming about in its grand foyer and elaborate gardens. In between its days of glory and due to its strategic location on Gellert Hill, it was also used as a military headquarters in invasions, uprisings, and ultimately, World War II. Now a bit outdated and worn with use, nevertheless, it holds an indelible and hallowed position in the skyline and folklore of Budapest and its increasing number of visitors.'"

Ben smiled. "I have a feeling we're going to love this place, Bree."

While Ben checked them into the hotel, Bree walked to the concierge desk to ask about booking appointments at the famous spa connected to the property. Apparently, the thermal baths and mineral waters of Budapest were world-renowned for their healing properties. Bee had no idea if any of the concierge's medicinal claims were in fact true, but soaking in a steamy, mineral-laden pool sounded heavenly— especially after the long drive and her and Ben's discussion about the journal.

Bree wasn't sure how she felt about Ben's reaction after she'd read the chapel entry out loud in the car. She didn't feel surprised, exactly— more like a little sad. Sad that Jayden's experience hadn't had the same effect on Ben as it had on her. It wasn't as if she were suddenly best friends with God, or even completely on board with the notion of a God. It was just that her arguments against His existence had been swept away along with the heaviness of her heart. She wasn't even quite sure how or why. She did know that for the first time in over two years, she had seen a morning sunrise without wanting to pull the covers over her head and retreat from the world. If she were honest, she'd have said that she had hoped it might have impacted Ben the same way.

Instead, as she had finished reading and looked over at him, he had seemed far away, his face a dark mask of simmering anger. She'd hoped for a discussion, but his response had been minimal as he retreated into his own thoughts and emotions, unwilling to even open the door on sharing his reaction.

So here they were now, less than a day's drive from the orphanage, and she was once again wondering if this trip had been a mistake. Bree was suddenly aware of the concierge.

"Excuse me, madame. Will this be for you only, or for you and your husband?" she asked Bree for the third time.

"Oh, I'm sorry. Yes!" Bree blurted. She had no idea what she was agreeing to, still caught in the fog of her heavy thoughts.

The concierge was clearly getting frustrated with her client's lack of concentration. "'Yes' for you only, or are we booking this for two?"

"Sorry! Two! My husband and me. We have had a long day of driving and are tired and . . ." Bree spoke in an overly pleasant voice, trying to smooth things over. But the hotel employee was having none of it.

Bree took the confirmation slip, thanked the concierge, and, eager to escape, spun around so quickly that she bumped into a gentleman, stepping on his shoe and nearly sending both of them to the ground. He braced himself and reached out to steady her, and they had a moment of eye contact and connection that unnerved them both. He seemed strangely familiar, which was crazy in her mind, because he was an absolute stranger.

"Oh, I am sooooo sorry!" In the span of less than five minutes, Bree had found herself apologizing for the third time for her uncharacteristically distracted behavior.

The man, still holding her elbow, seemed flustered. Not in that awkward, man-woman-chemistry way she sometimes sensed when meeting a man. More like a wish-you-hadn't-seen-me way, which left her baffled. It wasn't like she was with hotel security or anything.

"No need to be sorry, madame. It is I who should apologize. Are you steady enough for me to release your arm?" He said all of this in perfect, formal English while looking at her with the darkest and most beautiful eyes she had ever seen on a man.

It was her turn to become flustered, and she was pretty sure it *was* the man-woman kind of flustered. "Um . . ." was all she could muster.

The ambiguous answer seemed to keep them both in the awkward dance of not quite knowing what to do next.

"I mean, yes, I'm fine," she blurted out. "Thank you!"

The stranger let go of her elbow and stepped back from her. She could now see that he was both impeccably dressed and probably of Arab descent. It wasn't just his movie-star looks that held her mesmerized. It was something intangible, the way he held himself, a sense of presence. It felt as old-world as the hotel lobby.

She was about to suggest that perhaps they knew each other when he seemed to look past her at something or someone.

With a slight nod goodbye, the mysterious man quickly turned away and headed toward the stairs at the far end of the lobby, disappearing around a column.

Bree didn't hear Ben's approach from behind or his first question as she stood staring at the back of the retreating man's head.

"What are you looking at?" he asked, making Bree nearly jump out of her skin.

"Oh nothing, really," she answered quickly. "I just tripped over someone and nearly knocked us both to the ground. I was just watching to make sure he was all right." She turned and now centered her attention on Ben.

"Well," he said, "our room is ready, and the bags will be sent up shortly."

Bree noticed that Ben's voice still had a bit of a chill in it, and she felt sad again that their conversation about Jayden's journal and about God had somehow come between them.

"Great. By the way," she added, "get ready for an amazing experience. I've apparently booked us for some hedonistic pleasure palace thing that should turn both of us into a couple of wet noodles!" She laughed, knowing Ben would cringe at the thought of getting into a communal pool in the middle of Hungary with complete strangers. He'd do it, but he wouldn't be happy until it was over and he felt the results.

Maybe the minerals will get us back on even ground.

Chapter 48

HOTEL GELLERT, BUDAPEST, HUNGARY

Nazir had held on to Bree's arm for as long as possible. He'd only let go when he'd seen her husband moving toward them. At that point, Nazir had no recourse but to turn and walk away. He had headed toward the grand staircase at the far end of the lobby, climbing the steps two at a time to get as much distance as possible between himself and the other man.

At the top, he slipped behind a large pillar, disappearing from sight. After a couple of steadying breaths, he moved around the pillar, where he could get a clearer view of the couple—still standing near the concierge desk—while he remained out of their line of vision. There was something about the man's body language that seemed different from the few other times Nazir had observed him. A tension of some kind.

Nazir was fairly certain he hadn't been spotted by the husband, but it was hard to know for sure. Now the man was facing Bree, and they were discussing something, but Nazir was unable to get a clear view of his face or expression. *Perhaps it is a marital spat,* Nazir thought to himself. *That would mean their marriage isn't so unusual after all.* That idea gave him a perplexing sense of pleasure.

As he continued to watch them, he thought back to his brief encounter with her, especially the feel of her skin, the faint scent of her perfume, and the deep well of her green eyes. These were all unexpected treasures, like panning for silver in a river, only to find beautiful emeralds in the gravel instead.

Nazir felt an overwhelming desire to charge back down the stairs and pick her up and carry her away. She had a fragility that made him want to shelter and protect her. These feelings were new and unsettling, and he suddenly felt embarrassed.

Maybe it was having listened in on some of their intimate moments as a couple, but that didn't feel quite like the reason. In fact, he had always viewed sex as nothing more than a necessary physical release and nothing to be embarrassed about or to keep hidden or secret.

No, it had more to do with the story she had read out loud and the private anguish she had experienced and unknowingly shared with him. Her unguarded suffering had somehow pulled him into her life, and he knew it the moment he looked into her green eyes—eyes that truly were the window to her soul.

Nazir shook his head as if to loosen every errant thought from its hiding place. It was probably just the combination of his own weariness and his dealings with his father that were making him act and feel like this.

What am I doing? he chided himself. *Where do I think I am going with this notion of being in this woman's life? Where could this possibly go?*

It was time to clear his mind of all remnants of these insidious Western notions. For some reason, he thought again about the story his father used to read to him as a young boy. The one about the prince who had wanted to escape his destiny. He had run away, but in the end, he had given in to his fate of being king.

Nazir was fated for a story that did not include this woman or her suffering. Just like the prince, he could not escape his destiny.

That destiny included a meeting with Amir and the team tomorrow. Nazir had a lot of thinking and planning to do before then, both of which would require a clear and focused mind.

Nazir turned away from the pillar to walk to the elevators. He looked back at the couple one last time. Bree was smiling and linking her arm through the man's. Whatever tension that had existed between them had passed. They walked away. And regardless of his feelings, so must he.

Chapter 49

OVER THE ATLANTIC AND BOUND FOR BUDAPEST

As soon as he was buckled into his seat in the back of the Gulfstream, Mac looked around. He had never flown in a private jet before, and he had to admit, it felt pretty damn special.

No wonder people want this kind of luxury, he thought to himself, *and are willing to do almost anything to get it.*

The flight attendant interrupted his thoughts.

"Would you like something to drink before we take off, Mr. MacFarland?"

"I'd like a scotch—neat, please," Mac answered.

As soon as the attendant walked away, Mac opened the packet of materials Ian had sent. He pulled a thick pile of papers from the courier envelope.

He and Ian had analyzed every possible scenario. Mac was supposed to pose as a spiritual leader of some kind, which was why the packet included several selected readings from the Holy Bible. Mac read the first couple while sipping his scotch. For some reason, he was having a hard time making sense of what he was reading. Probably because he hadn't cracked open the Good Book since the day he'd lost Gloria.

It wasn't that he hadn't given much thought to the idea of God. He'd actually thought many times over his lifetime about the possibility of God's existence. After a lifetime of observation, if Mac were being given an exit poll, his honest answer would have to be "Maybe."

But Mac would have followed that with the caveat: "The guy clearly has too many balls in the air." The proof, in his mind, was in the fact that bad shit continued to happen to good people.

That belief had been solidified by Mac's wife's death. If God existed and He really was the purveyor of good and evil, why the hell would He have let her die and Mac live? It made no sense whatsoever. It also made him lose all respect for the guy. But that was another thing Mac didn't like to do—ruminate on the past. It did no good, and it wouldn't bring her back.

Mac forced his mind back to the plan at hand.

Much to his chagrin, the plan was for Mac to lead a group of misfits into the desert to wander around for forty . . . Wait. Wrong story. Actually, in Mac's story, he was supposed to be more like the Jesus character in the New Testament—a kinder, gentler version of God. In this version, they were going to be "renovating" the orphanage, feeding the poor, and doing good deeds throughout the area.

It was times like these that Mac wished Ian was a little less creative and a little more pragmatic. Why couldn't they just lure the bad guys into the orphanage and then drop a MOAB (mother of all bombs) on the building? That was more like the God he had an interest in representing. But no, instead, he'd probably end up having to wear a robe and sandals before this thing was all over.

The first time Ian had mentioned this part of the plan to Mac, they'd been on the phone. Mac's reaction had been, "Holy shit! Ian, you gotta be goddamned nuts!"

Ian had let Mac vent before launching into the grisly details. "JD, the first thing you are going to need to do is to drop all the expletives from your conversations. These people don't swear, and they take great umbrage at using God's name—or any iteration of it—in vain."

Well, Mac had thought, *thank goodness I can still say the word "nuts."* He had a feeling he was going to be using that word a lot.

"Mac, you are also going to need to be familiar with some of the themes of the Bible, as well as some hymns," Ian had further instructed. Don't worry; I will send you a few files to help you bone up. Essentially, they cover the standard tenets of the Christian faith: loving your neighbor as yourself; taking care of the widows, orphans, and the poor; and maybe giving your worldly possessions away. Just your usual selfless impulses!"

"Ian, you bloody bastard—I mean, jerk," Mac had gusted. "Now I have to sing, quote scripture, and become homeless? If you tell me any more, I'm taking my very legitimate retirement to Hawaii and sticking you with this whole shi—uh, mess."

Mac could only imagine that on the other end of the line, Ian had had his phone on mute and was laughing his ass off.

It was very rare that either of them was in a position to be laughing, and it felt good to think that Ian likely had been. But it was a brief moment of relief and they both knew it.

"JD, you know this is the perfect cover," Ian had said. "It's an orphanage, for bloody sakes. Who comes here except lost children and people wanting to make themselves feel good by doing good?"

Ian and Mac held a similar irreverence for God and his flock, and for many of the same reasons. Ian had slammed the door on the notion of any divine being the day his young wife had died in his arms, he'd told Mac, and for him, it had now become the simple question of, why did an orphanage even have to exist, if not because people and gods were not doing life right? Who would ever leave a kid like Molly on a doorstep? What God would allow that kind of debilitating rejection? Mac had agreed with everything Ian had shared in his moment of spiritual—or nonspiritual—frustration. But now, he thought back to the rest of his and Ian's conversation.

"The team is in place, complete with building materials, used clothing, food, etc. I think they even brought a bloody cow to donate to the village. Everyone is very kind, loving—"

"Okay, Ian. Cut the crap!" he remembered saying. "I get the picture."

Mac had been pushed as far as he was willing to go. If this operation required him to turn into a scripture-spouting, hymn-singing missionary, then that's what he'd do. He'd dress up as Tootsie if it made these maniac extremist bastards eat crow.

Chapter 50

YEMEN

Al-Zawahiri paced from room to room most of the night, his mind working its way, over and over, through the details of his glorious jihad. He could taste and smell the victory it would bring, and yet he sensed some unknown danger. His sense of foreboding was hazy at best, nothing credible or specific. And so, he paced, with sleep chasing after him but never managing to snag him.

As time dragged slowly on, he allowed himself a rare journey into his past. He found himself going back, all the way to the beginning, to his childhood, and the first time he had felt the desire to take charge of his life.

It was during the years spent at a secluded boarding school in Europe. His Western education had been deliberately sought for him by his father, now dead for many years. It was intended to teach him a deeper reverence for Islam by revealing the flaws of Western ideology, as well as an understanding of his enemy.

He had been an avid student, devouring knowledge as if it were the sustenance of life. Secretly, he had wanted to make friends with the other students and fit in, but when that didn't happen, he began to observe his peers much like a scientist studies slides under a microscope. He couldn't understand why they had so little appreciation for their enormous material wealth and the powerful education to which they were being exposed.

This practice of observation made Al-Zawahiri feel increasingly isolated and lonely. It also created the space and fuel for a growing sense of superiority—not because he thought he had superior talent or intellect, but because he had become convinced that he possessed a deeper level of discipline and gratitude than his peers.

He also remembered the day he'd understood the bigger purpose of his life. Thinking back now, it seemed odd that the knowledge would stem from something out of Western philosophy.

It happened during a literature class near the end of his time at the boarding school. He was to return to his family in Saudi soon. The teacher had assigned a Robert Frost poem to be read and interpreted by each student. Al-Zawahiri had always found this type of schoolwork the most challenging. Physics, math, science, and even history were all subjects that made sense and posed challenges that were easy to master. Give him an equation or a set of facts, and he was in his element.

But to attempt to analyze a poem—someone's feelings, or thoughts driven by an obscure moral code that he did not share or comprehend—was excruciating.

He had leafed through the entire collection of Frost's works from cover to cover, trying to find something that would make itself known to him. "The Road Less Traveled" had come the closest to being decipherable. Unfortunately, the teacher, wise to the laziness of his students, had used this popular poem as an example in class.

Al-Zawahiri had become overwhelmed with anxiety at the possibility of failing this assignment. His entire universe at that time had revolved around pleasing his father by being successful in school and bringing honor to the family.

He'd still had the volume of Frost's works before him. As he'd scanned the table of contents one more time, a title had caught his eye. The poem was entitled "Hard Not to Be King."

That hadn't made any sense to him at all—either you *were* a king or you weren't. Nobody chose it. It was decreed by your station in life.

Curious, he had opened the book to the poem. As he reading its words, the powerful narrative had grabbed him, even as its memory did now, in the darkness of his rooms fifty years later.

The poem told the story of a young prince who raged against the confines of his duty and destiny. He was being groomed to be king despite the fact that he didn't want the position at all. He decided to run away.

For a time, the runaway prince lived among the common people, hiding his lineage in mediocrity, all until a situation arose in which he was pushed into leadership. Instinctively, the young royal knew how to lead, and in that process of leading, he discovered that he could not run from the very fiber of his identity, or his calling.

He returned home to become the king he was always destined to be.

As a young man reading this story for the first time, Al-Zawahiri had been stunned. It was as if the words had jumped off the page and lodged themselves in his heart. Here was *his* story! Here was an explanation for the deep yearning he had always felt to lead and to conquer.

He had presented the poem in class with uncharacteristic passion. It was lost on all but the teacher, who had remarked on his student's great interpretive skills in grasping the concept Frost had been trying to convey.

Al-Zawahiri had soon graduated and returned to his people and his own, much different culture. But the poem had returned with him, riding along in his heart and mind, a constant reminder of who he was meant to be.

The old man shook his head in wonder at this poignant memory and the path it had sent him down. Here he was now, so many years later, still leading and still yearning for the greatness to which he had always felt called. He certainly wasn't a king in the literal sense, yet his growing role as leader of this powerful jihadist movement as it birthed a new Caliphate would soon make kings and presidents alike bow down to him.

He had read the poem to Nazir often as a young boy, and also before sending him off to study in the West, reminding his son often of his lineage and of his own destiny.

Unfortunately, Al-Zawahiri had never seen the same fervor or light in the boy's eyes, nor the passion for a greatness beyond himself, as he himself had experienced. He wondered at the generational divide, and at how different his son was from him. Nazir had always had the more reserved temperament of his mother, and perhaps that was acceptable.

What he couldn't decipher was his son's level of commitment to anything beyond himself. He had excelled in school, never rebelled when told of his father's expectations, and had obviously accomplished much. He had also used his accomplishments to help both his father and the cause in significant and impactful ways. The intelligence he was able to gather in Washington, and his ability to strategize, had surpassed even his father's abilities.

Still, there was something.

It was the unspoken, the omissions, that worried Al-Zawahiri. Admittedly, his son had been seduced by the mindless consumption and power-mongering of the "American Dream." It saddened him to see his son's potential mired in a wasteland of debauchery: the rumored women, the endless partying, and a passion for rich food and richer possessions.

If only Nazir understood that personal ambition was not the same thing as a holy mission. He seemed incapable of choosing the path that would require the difficult choices and discipline of being king. For some reason, despite all of Al-Zawahiri's best efforts, Nazir had never wanted to be a leader at all.

His thoughts shifted to his nephew.

Now, Amir, on the other hand, was someone who had caught the fire of a calling. Al-Zawahiri had spotted it early in his nephew's childhood, and taken Amir under his wing, working to tool and refine it. Amir had quickly proven himself a willing student. Every decision and life choice was made with Islam and the Caliphate in mind. He was confident that Amir would be relentlessly driven by these ideals until his death.

Al-Zawahiri's role in Amir's life had been to fan that fire, using it for the good of the many. But he knew that when the flame burned hot and Allah was pleased, the ultimate call to martyrdom was often received.

Al-Zawahiri stopped his pacing and stood in the quiet of the early-morning light. He had now only the honesty of his own soul with which to contend. The pacing had been a type of wrestling with the truth, and he'd known it. In fact, his heart ached with the knowledge of the choice he would make.

The choice was as clear to him now as it had been at the beginning of the night, but he had needed this time to walk his heart toward accepting what he had already known.

His stillness was the embodiment of his acquiescence. Allah was indeed great and the mantle Al-Zawahiri had accepted heavy, but inevitable. This was the true burden of being king.

Chapter 51

Hotel Gellert, Budapest, Hungary

Mac stopped at the front desk to ask about the availability of his room for the third time. After leaving Langley, he'd flown to the UK to refuel and pick up some munitions as well as a couple of Ian's MI6 operatives. That had taken much longer than intended, and after sixteen hours, he was feeling his age.

"Any word yet, young lady?"

Mac must have displayed the right amount of "arrogant American snarl" because not only was the room ready; he had been upgraded as well. Or maybe it was the fact that he was on a government tab and the clerk was a political science geek, interested in improving relations with the US. Nope, one quick look up through his shaggy eyebrows at the clerk's glare of irritation confirmed that diplomacy had not been a factor.

Mac made a quick note to get something done with the damned hair above his eyes when he got home. *How is it that the stuff has all but disappeared from my head but is mysteriously thriving in my ears and across my forehead?* It reminded him of the buzz surrounding that new GMO corn; it was supposed to produce an amazing harvest and was nearly impossible to kill. He could just hear his barber now: *"Mac, we're gonna need a bigger combine!"* Okay. He had taken a slight digression here.

Still, his reflection in the mirror behind the front desk was not reassuring.

With his room key in hand, he turned and slowly scanned the lobby. *Old habits die hard*, he mused. He really didn't need to be scanning for anything. If Ian's intel was correct, the bad guys were headed for Romania. The Americans? That was a different story. Mac checked his watch, calculating the current time. Ian's operative was set to check in anytime to give them an updated status on where the two were headed. All Mac knew was that it could be anywhere between Croatia and the orphanage.

Mac made a quick assessment of the growing swarm of tourists, easily identified by their overpacked bags and bewildered, jet-lagged faces. It was also easy to peg the business travelers, with their obsession with their electronic gadgets. They barely managed to avoid walking into each other, bumbling about with various things hanging from their ears, heads, and even eyeglasses—talking to ghosts like mad scientists who had experienced too much exposure to the mysterious fluids bubbling away in the laboratory flasks.

That's when Mac noticed the Arab standing partially hidden by a pillar on the second floor.

He could only see his profile, but he looked to be somewhere in his early forties, immaculately dressed and well groomed.

Mac could see that the man, even partially concealed by the pillar, was staring intently down at the crowded lobby. He appeared to be looking at a couple standing in front of the concierge desk. They were deep in discussion—probably about something of national importance, like fitting in massages before dinner on the terrace at eight. Mac took a minute to study them as well. They looked monied and successful. Was the guy watching them envious of their status? Hard to tell. Maybe he was just relieved that he didn't have to negotiate with a wife over every damn thing in his life, like breathing.

He'd felt that way once, when he thought Gloria was controlling too much of his life. Now, he'd come to realize what a gift that had been. You spend your life complaining about what she spent at the market, or the mess in the kitchen after she tried a new recipe—and then suddenly it ends and you find yourself eating frozen dinners alone every night off paper plates. If only he'd known how much he really appreciated her. But he hadn't, and now he'd never have a chance to tell her.

He shook himself, as if to shake off the memory, and continued to take in the layout of the lobby, including exits, restaurants, and elevators—and then he looked back up at the Arab. For some reason the guy had caused a hair or two to stand at attention on the back of Mac's neck.

The man had disappeared, and the pillar was vacant. The couple had also moved on, arm in arm, oblivious to having been watched by at least two interested parties. Mac turned and headed for the elevator and his much-needed bed.

As the elevator doors closed and he punched the button for his floor, he wondered whether he had what it would take to get this thing done. He said a silent "Hail Moses," added an Abraham, and finally threw in a Jesus just for good measure. Mac was determined to see this thing through, but it would be helpful if a few of these dudes showed up as well.

Chapter 52

HOTEL GELLERT, BUDAPEST, HUNGARY

"You know, this room may be on the old and musty side, but that view of the Danube and the bridge is stunning!"

Bree walked over to their big picture window, pushed the drapes aside, and stood in awe of the magnificence in front of her. She could see the parliament building farther down the river, and the lights of the bridge shimmering off the water. It reminded her a little of Paris, although she was pretty sure that neither the folks in Budapest nor the citizens of Paris would appreciate that comparison.

"We don't really have anything this old-world back in LA, do we?" Ben asked, walking up behind her to take in the same view.

Bree turned to face him and put her arms on his shoulders. "Thank you, Ben. For everything. For saying yes to this trip, even with so many unknowns. I know you don't feel exactly like I do about our reasons for coming, but I'm hoping that—"

"Bree, I wish I could tell you what you want to hear," Ben interrupted. "I wish I could hear what you hear in Jayden's diary. I really do. It would make things so much easier for us. But I don't. I don't see a God at work in the story, and I don't believe Jayden saw one either. I think it was a fanciful young kid's imagination in a place called Transylvania. That's all."

Bree could tell that Ben felt tired and defeated, and that he hated being the one to reveal to her that the miraculous and powerful God she longed to meet was merely a little man pulling levers behind a curtain. And for those and many other reasons, she felt a wave of compassion for him. As a woman and mother, she had been able to spend much of the past two years grieving. There were no cultural expectations limiting her sorrow, only the ones she imposed upon herself. Ben was a man, however, and the rules were ever so subtly different for him. Hearing his explanation and response to the journal reminded her of how much grief he still carried. He was probably exhausted by the process of not going *through* the process. She hung her head.

At that very moment, she made a decision to let go of her need for Ben to experience their son's "God encounter" the way she had.

If this God really exists, isn't it up to Him to reveal Himself to Ben? He certainly convinced Jayden . . . "I hope You do." When she caught that last phrase—and realized she had said it under her breath—she was surprised. *Did I just say a prayer? Good grief.*

She shook it off and turned her attention back to Ben. "It's okay, sweetheart. I don't need you to feel or think anything other than your own thoughts and feelings. I'm thinking this God, whoever He is, is probably able to get His point across to us however He wants to. He certainly did with Jayden, and it was real enough to make our son change his life. I can live with the mystery of that experience. I can't live with the idea of it tearing us apart. And maybe, in the end, that was what I needed to learn from this."

Ben was visibly surprised, then moved by Bree's calm and eloquent acceptance. Bree could tell that what she had just shown him was not the usual "take charge and make it happen" Bree that he knew and had probably expected to see.

"Honey," he said soothingly, "this isn't going to tear us apart. We've come through too much for that to happen now." Then he kissed her with such a slow and gentle kiss that both of them had tears in their eyes. When he pulled away, he added, "And thank you for giving me the space to get my arms around all of this new life. It's been a lot of loss and change for this guy who'd planned a much different outcome."

His voice broke on the last few words, and Bree again felt a flood of compassion for this man she loved so deeply.

The air felt lighter between them afterwards. They went down to the spa, arm in arm, like newlyweds, abandoning themselves to the "hedonistic pleasures" of the ancient healing waters.

After they had soaked away the weariness of their travels, they experienced therapeutic if somewhat exuberant massages from who they would later describe as "Helga I" and "Helga II." Then, feeling renewed and surprisingly serene, they'd gone back up to their room with the intention of dressing for dinner.

Looking over at the bed and romantic views through the windows, Bree decided they needed a change of plans.

"Ben, would you mind terribly if—"

She never got the chance to finish her sentence. A man stepped out of the dark corner of the room, a powerful-looking gun aimed at her heart as she stared, transfixed, at his dark face.

She looked back at Ben.

He was lying on the floor, facedown and still.

Why hadn't she heard him fall?

She tried to scream, but before she could move or convert her terror into any sound at all, the man with the gun stepped forward. At the same time, she felt a sharp sting in the side of her neck.

After only the impulse of a struggle, she felt herself drifting away, a feeling eerily similar to her earlier experience of floating in the mineral waters of the spa. Her last conscious thought was the same question she had silently asked every day for the past two years.

Did Jayden suffer?

And before she could grasp the answer she was given, the world went dark.

Chapter 53

HOTEL GELLERT, BUDAPEST, HUNGARY

Nazir stopped pacing and looked out the large window of his hotel room down onto the Danube below. He knew he had been pacing for hours because the once-blue water had turned inky black, reflecting the now dark sky as well as his own mood.

The unexpected encounter in the lobby had left him feeling riled up and unsettled. As much as he tried to concentrate on developing a strategic plan to deal with Amir, his thoughts kept getting entangled with the memory of the American woman's eyes, some strange lines from his father's poem, and ancient Arab history involving Abraham, of all people. The combination was baffling to him.

I feel like I am being haunted, he admitted to himself. *Why now, when I need to be free of everything but my mission?*

The more he tried to calm down and concentrate, the worse his agitation became and the further his plans drifted from his grasp. The irony was, he'd never had trouble separating his work from his emotions in the past. This was unnerving and, for him, extremely ill-timed.

He continued to grapple with the standing order to kill his cousin, Amir, the moment that the surviving orphan was dead.

There had been no last-minute reprieve from the imperial will of Allah interpreted by Al-Zawahiri, and Nazir knew one would not be coming. In addition, and certainly compounding everything, was the pressing issue of time.

The reason Nazir had come to Budapest was to meet up with Amir so they could travel together to Romania. As far as Nazir knew, his cousin still intended to go to the orphanage tomorrow and take care of the child. Once the girl had been identified and eliminated, Nazir would make sure Amir was martyred.

The dilemma Nazir faced seemed daunting.

How can I avoid killing Amir—and still manage to appease both my father and Allah?

He was uncomfortable following an order he had not received directly from the source. Nazir couldn't figure out why he wasn't able to hear the voice of Allah or discern his will for himself. Why was his father the only one allowed into that inner circle?

To make matters worse, Nazir could not stop thinking about the dead son's journal and *her* voice as she had read aloud the story of a very different kind of God. A God willing to reveal himself to a teenage boy in an empty church. A God willing to martyr his *own son*—an unthinkable act of love.

What had earned Bree's son the rarified experience of a personal interaction with his God? Was there something special about that chapel? Was it the boy's exceptionally good character? Nazir wrestled with these questions and more.

And that's when an unbidden thought occurred to him:

What if I asked Jayden's God to show up for me? What if I asked Him to help me know what to do?

Nazir eventually lay down on the bed, his mind and body exhausted with the struggle of these unanswered questions. But sleep that begins in a fever can never bring respite. His dreams became an extension of his inner turmoil as he found himself running and fighting and struggling in different heroic and not-so-heroic scenarios—his brain attempting to work out the issues plaguing his subconscious mind and heart.

Heart.

Heart.

Heart. As the word pulsed through his dreams and broke through into his conscious thought, he jolted awake and yelled a single word.

"Noooooooooooo!"

It was a primal howl from a place so deep within him that it felt like a tearing of the tectonic plates of his soul.

The stillness that followed was like nothing he had ever experienced. It wrapped around him in the darkness like a heated robe, numbing the earlier pain and confusion and calming his nerves. His heart felt saturated with knowledge and clarity, and he instantly knew what he was being called to do.

Every question or doubt that followed faded into the background of this powerful stillness. He was haunted by words he had heard in his dreams: *Be still and know that I am God.*

Nazir yearned for that knowledge.

He could tell from his dreams that the will of God was counterintuitive. Rather than the heroic action or brutal strength his father embraced, the actual will of God required surrender and selflessness. For Nazir, that meant letting go of everything he thought of as his identity and his abilities. What remained was a transparent shell of himself, standing on unfamiliar but holy ground.

This must be the path Abraham was asking me to take, he realized with a start. *It is certainly not a path of my own making. And it feels like it was decided long before my birth.*

He waited for morning, watching as the faintest light of dawn inched its way into his room. How ironic, he thought, that his father's beloved poem would in the end be woven into God's will. Nazir now knew without a shadow of a doubt that he was being called to his destiny—and that he would take up a crown.

It just wouldn't be the crown his father was holding out to him.

Chapter 54

Hotel Gellert,
Budapest, Hungary

Wide-awake, Mac lay on top of the bedspread. It was still several hours before the alarm was set to go off.

Okay, if he were honest—and it seemed like a good day for honesty since he'd soon be playing a reverend and all that—he'd been ready the minute he'd laid his head down on the pillow the night before. He had tried to sleep for about three minutes and then given up.

Who needs sleep, anyway? he decided. *I'll have the rest of my fu—I mean, frickin'—glorious retirement to sleep.*

He kept thinking about the mission.

It was complicated because they still didn't know how, when, or where the jihadists were going to attack next. The world is a pretty damn big place when you start looking for a few hundred vials of something. Which meant Mac couldn't just kill the shitheads they would encounter at the orphanage and then call it a day. He and Ian were going to have to make them sing. To add to the drama, jihadists had a penchant for ending their own lives if they got close to being interrogated, which only complicated the whole damn process.

So, he and Ian were going to have to buy some time. Mac knew they couldn't spook the mastermind behind this plot—and hopefully it was the big fish himself, Al-Zawahiri—or he'd likely cave up or attack.

That meant this guy would have to be convinced that the mission to kill the girl had been successful.

Mac rolled over on his other side and tried coming at the problem from a different angle.

Who was he kidding? For all he knew, half the population of New York could already be walking around with little time bombs inside of them. As of this morning, Ian's MI6 guys still hadn't figured out what had killed those kids. They'd narrowed it down to this "nano" thing; a microscopic delivery vehicle that could be programmed or triggered to release its payload and then dissolve, literally leaving no trace of its existence. But they still had no idea what was in it.

For some reason it made Mac think about the bugs swimming around in the rice paddies in Nam, getting under his skin and moving through his body. At least he knew what they were. This new world of technology and biochemical shit blurred the lines and made it nearly impossible to decipher what he was fighting.

And as if that weren't enough, there was the loose cannon of a couple walking into the middle of this nightmare. Maybe Mac should have had Ian's people grab them after all.

Maybe it wasn't too late to rethink that part of the plan. The Stantons were just too unpredictable. He'd talk to Ian about it as soon as he had the chance.

Mac gave up on any attempt at sleep, got up, and splashed cold water on his face. He finished dressing, then struggled to fasten his clerical collar. The thing made him feel like he was wearing a noose. After a last glance at the room, he tucked his gun into his back holster and walked out the door.

The van was waiting for him in front of the hotel. Mac walked up to pay his bill. The desk clerk he'd terrorized last night was long gone. Too bad. He'd wanted to impress her with his newfound religion.

He reached into his inside pocket, searching for one of those goddamn—er, gosh-darn—tracts Ian had supplied him with, but couldn't find one.

"Sir," the new clerk said brightly, "we are sorry you had such a short stay with us, but hope everything was to your satisfaction." The young man's enthusiasm so early in the morning was especially grating to Mac's caffeine-deprived, jet-lagged brain.

"I'm sure it was." Mac could think of nothing else to say since he hadn't used the bed or showered or eaten anything. He had simply used the toilet and washed his hands. As far as he was concerned, both the toilet and the sink had worked fine.

"If there is nothing else we can help you with, the total for the one-night stay is seven hundred US dollars. Would you like this to be applied to the credit card on file?"

Mac had been thinking about Gloria—and whether she would have enjoyed staying in a place like this—when the amount of the bill finally registered with his brain.

"Young man, did you just say seven hundred US dollars?" Mac bellowed. "Are you shittin' me?" This time, he didn't let his newfound religion get in the way of one of his favorite expletives. "This isn't exactly the Taj Mahal, son," he continued ranting. "I used the goddamned toilet three times, washed my hands twice, and lay on top of the bed, fully clothed, for forty-six minutes. In my mind, that's worth about a buck seventy-five."

Mac glowered through his eyebrows, noticing with great pride how his crop of bushy hair had expanded overnight, while waiting for the full effect of his speech to sink in. He demanded, "What's the other $698 for?"

Without missing a beat, the kid bent forward across the counter and answered with a deadpan glare.

"For the one time you didn't wash your hands."

Smart-ass, Mac admitted to himself with a level of admiration. He could see a younger version of himself in the making and was about to go *mano a mano* with the young man when he heard someone behind him clear his throat. Glancing back, Mac saw his driver. The man pointed to his watch.

Mac reached in another pocket, found one of the tracts he'd been looking for a moment ago, and slapped it down on the counter. "God bless you, son," he growled. "You're gonna need it!"

Gratified by the stunned look on the young man's face, Mac turned and exited the grand entrance of the Gellert, stomped down the stairs, and climbed into the passenger seat of the idling white panel van. The sun was just starting to lighten the edges of the sky, but the Danube still looked dark and ominous. He'd always found dark water a little unnerving. No telling what was just under the surface. *Kind of like people.*

Chapter 55

BUDAPEST

Ben was surprised he had dived so deep into the water.

The light above him was weak, and the water felt cold and murky. It seemed odd that Bree was swimming this deep as well.

The strangest part was that one of his buildings was jutting past him toward the light. It was an exact duplicate of one of the World Trade towers, which had not been his design, yet somehow this one was.

As Ben swam past the building, he could see into the windows at people sitting at their desks, working. Several looked up at him with terror in their eyes, yelled something unintelligible, then went back to typing or whatever else they were doing.

Ben tried banging on a few windows, hoping to get in, but no one responded, and he realized he needed to keep swimming. At one point, it seemed he wasn't going to reach the surface. That's when he realized he was swimming with one arm, because he was holding on to Bree.

While he was contemplating whether to let her go or just let them both sink, he felt a hand grab his shoulder, and they were being suddenly propelled upward. When Ben looked over to see who it was, Jayden's face was smiling at him. Jayden seemed to be saying something encouraging, but again, Ben couldn't hear any sound.

His heart was pounding at the sight of his son, and he had renewed determination to get to the light. As he hit the surface, he felt his lungs explode with the breath he had held for so long, taking huge gasps of air as he turned to thank Jayden. But instead of seeing his son's face, he felt something cold and hard. It was then he realized he was lying on a cold, gray concrete floor. His arms and legs were bound tight to his body.

He opened his eyes and looked into the menacing eyes of a stranger.

What's going on? Where am I? Ben's mind was a dense fog of nothingness. It required an immense effort to even peel the layers of his own identity back, let alone try to figure out where he was or how he got there. He had been traveling . . . with his wife and son . . . No . . . his son was not there, although it seemed like they had just been together. Somewhere.

"Good morning, Mr. Stanton."

It was the stranger with the menacing eyes. When he spoke, Ben realized he had an equally menacing voice, shrouded with an unfamiliar accent.

Ben tried to talk, but his voice sounded like a frog, and the words came out slurred and indecipherable. He meant to ask, "How do I know you?" What he said instead sounded more like, "Shoooow, hooowsmdy nam hmm?"

"Why are you in Budapest, Mr. Stanton?" the man repeated, his voice a steely reflection of his eyes.

The accent was so thick that now Ben struggled to understand the question.

We are in Budapest, Ben remembered with a start.

He tried to shake his head to clear the cobwebs, only to wince in pain. He'd clearly bruised his head at some point.

When he tried speaking again, his voice seemed slightly more reliable.

"Who are you? Why am I tied up? Where is . . . my wife . . . and son?"

As he asked the last question, he felt an instant pressure in his chest and for a moment wondered if he were having a heart attack.

The menacing face grew closer. "We have Mrs. Stanton in another room. We are not aware of any son traveling with you."

Ben's heart lurched as the fog dissipated a bit more and he was beginning to remember the details his brain had momentarily forgotten.

"I would like to offer an arrangement to you before you see your wife," the man said smoothly. "Are you ready to listen?"

Ben's mind cleared at the mention of his wife. He was truly listening now. He decided this must be a kidnapping for ransom. If so, he knew that every detail in the next few hours would be significant.

Ben scanned his captor's face for any identifying marks, like scars or other unique traits. The accent and ethnicity were definitely Middle Eastern. The English was proper and formal, as if learned as a second language later in life. There was something about the man's demeanor that was authoritative, as if he were used to power and decision-making.

Ben had a fleeting thought about the ISIS jihadists who were killing Christians all over the news and wondered if his captor was affiliated with them. No way of knowing yet, but he was pretty sure no one would confuse him or Bree with devout believers worth martyring.

No, more than likely, these people were looking for money, Ben surmised. He wished that he and Bree had done more to conceal their wealth and nationality, but looking up into the eyes of the stranger, he wasn't sure it would have mattered.

"I'm listening," Ben said, "but I won't agree to anything until I have proof of life for my wife and son—" The chest pressure hit him again, and this time Ben knew what it was and what had triggered it. Jayden. There would be no proof of life for an already-dead son.

Jayden is dead. I must have been dreaming.

"All in good time," Ben's captor said. "But first, let us start by talking about your destination in Romania."

Chapter 56

Near the Orphanage in Transylvania

The drive from Budapest passed quickly and without a hitch. Mac had spent a good part of the ride briefing the team members in the van about the strange array of participants expected at the "OK Corral." Even in the more polished form, the story sounded ludicrous, even to Mac.

"And I'm the one telling this thing!" he muttered to himself. "Ian was right. Who could think this shit up?"

The van driver dropped Mac at a nondescript stucco house just off the main street of Alba Iulia.

Ian greeted him just inside the door.

After a quick handshake that turned into a bear hug, the men seated themselves at a faded linoleum table in the kitchen of the small house Ian had rented.

Despite the lateness in the day, Ian handed Mac a mug of hot coffee, which he accepted with a grateful grunt.

Mac jumped right in with the question that had been weighing on his mind. "Do you think we've made a tactical error in not reeling in the two Americans when we had the chance? For some crazy reason they—out of all the weird-ass players in this thing—are the ones who keep interrupting my sleep. That's never a good omen!"

"JD, we've known they were going to be a loose cannon from the beginning. We chose to let their story play out for political expediency. Bottom line, we did not have anything on them, and to detain them would have had its own set of complications." Ian had as usual, done a great job assuaging Mac's concerns.

"At this point," Ian added, "we should be asking only one question: what are we going to do if they get in the way?"

There was a moment of silence as both men stared at the same empty wall, deep in thought.

When Mac finally responded, he delivered the answer with his usual brusque intensity.

"We stay the course!" he bellowed. "I said from the first phone call that these Arab shits were coming after the Western world. I still believe that. I also believe this could be as pivotal as Pearl Harbor. The bomb that followed that horror has kept the world in order for nearly eighty years. Sometimes there's tremendous collateral damage. We have no choice but to win against this evil—at any cost."

Mac knew he was preaching to the choir, but it felt good to get worked up about something. With Ian nodding in agreement, Mac continued with his assessment.

"I've been thinking about the objectives and targets of this bioagent. It may not need to be triggered in a larger population. All these schmucks need to do is create the fear of a trigger, and that gets them a seat at the big table. Once that happens, we're all screwed! So, whatever and whoever it takes to stop this, is the ticket price this team is going to pay."

Mac had locked eyes with Ian during the last part of his pregame speech. He knew his friend was well aware of what was at stake.

Mac thought about saying something sentimental about all the battles the two of them had faced together, but he didn't know where to start in their thirty years of partnership. Then Gloria popped into his head, and he could literally hear the list of regrets he carried over not telling her how much she'd meant to him. He still longed to make that right but knew that ship had sailed. He didn't want to make that same mistake again.

"I want to thank you, Ian. For being a—"

"For being a bloody patient chap," Ian cut it, "while you drag me into God knows what. How long have we been doing this—thirty years?! I'm thinking after this we should hang it up and spend some serious time fishing!"

Mac smiled with unspoken appreciation. Ian had obviously seen the unexpected emotion on his face and had jumped in to rescue him. It had given Mac time to recover his equilibrium. "I can't think of anything more awful than an entire day in a boat, in the middle of some hot, smelly lake, with you trying to tell me how to fish!" he joked.

"Well, that's not a very kind thing to say, Reverend McFarland!"

Both men enjoyed a good chuckle; then they finished reviewing their plan. At last, they stood up, shook hands, and walked out the door together. Mac could feel the instantaneous adrenaline rush as he mentally heard the starting gun go off. *Bet your ass ole Ian can feel it too*, he thought.

Chapter 57

BUDAPEST

Nazir knocked at the door and quietly gave the password. The door swung inward, and he walked into the dark interior, his eyes already working to make sense of the faces, shapes, and sounds. It was clear from the nods and murmurs that he was both expected and revered. After all, he was the son of the great Al-Zawahiri, mastermind behind the impending jihad and savior of his people.

He'd anticipated a meeting with Amir, maybe a quick cup of tea and briefing before setting off for the orphanage. When they'd last spoken, Amir had been adamant that they get to the girl as quickly as possible so that the more important task of the first wave of US attacks could be set in motion.

Despite feeling slightly off-kilter from his restless night and disturbing dreams, Nazir was determined to follow through with what he now knew was his destiny.

Still, nothing could have prepared him for what happened next.

He was led into a dimly lit room, and immediately his senses went on high alert.

Instead of finding Amir, he saw Bree tied to a chair in the center of the room.

Nazir looked over at the two men guarding her. "*Ma aldhy yajri? Madha faeilt?*" Nazir barked, demanding to know what was going on.

"*Nahn natabie 'awamir Amir!*" they replied in unison, blaming Amir and his orders for the woman's capture.

"*Sawf tadfae thaman 'afealika. 'Ayn 'amiran?*" Nazir rebuked them, barely able to contain his rage as he demanded the whereabouts of his cousin.

The man closest to the door ran out, and Nazir could only assume it was to let Amir know he had arrived—and was not happy to see the hostage.

For the first time, Nazir allowed himself to look directly at the woman. She seemed startled by the recognition of his face. And why wouldn't she be startled, after their awkward but cordial encounter in the lobby? She certainly wouldn't have expected their chance encounter to result in her abduction.

A dozen questions raced through Nazir's mind as he stared into her eyes.

What had Amir done? This wasn't part of the plan.

Rage boiled up inside of Nazir. This was *so* like his cousin, always trying to look the better of the two and undoubtedly trying to get back into Al-Zawahiri's good graces.

Nazir moaned. Where was the husband? Bree looked confused, like she had been recently drugged. There was some swelling and discoloration forming around her cheek and eye. Seeing that, Nazir allowed the rage he had tried so hard to contain to finally escape.

Nazir's single punch landed on the guard's jaw, dropping him to the ground at the same moment Amir entered the room.

"Cousin. Nazir. What are you so worried about here, that you take out a good, faithful servant?" Amir's voice was purposefully smooth and low.

"What's going on, Amir? What have you done?" Nazir was unable to hide the anger and disdain smoldering in his eyes as the two men stared at each other.

"I have made a few changes to the plan," Amir said with a shrug. "We needed funds for our journey, and I happened upon these two at the Hotel Gellert. You know the place, don't you, cousin?" Amir paused to let his words—and the revelation they contained—sink in. "They seemed as good as any ATM I could find." Again, his voice seemed unnaturally smooth, and he had a sickening half-smile on his face.

Nazir's eyes narrowed. So, Amir had been at the Gellert. That meant Al-Zawahiri had sent him to watch Nazir. The double betrayal brought an unexpected twist of pain. Nazir had suspected his father did not trust him. But to go as far as betraying him? What had he ever done but what was asked of him? He'd never uttered a single question about Allah's will or his father's vision. He had never given his father any reason to doubt his allegiance or his intentions.

Before Nazir could begin to formulate answers to the swirling questions, Amir broke into his thoughts.

"I have much to discuss, cousin. Let us move into another room, and I will finish the details of this revised plan."

Amir turned to the door. Nazir, now suddenly the follower, turned and left as well. There was nothing he could say or do to comfort Bree Stanton. And he didn't want to see whatever was in her eyes. She would undoubtedly be pleading for her life, and he had no answers. Yet.

Chapter 58

THE ORPHANAGE AND VILLAGE, ROMANIA

Members of the Delta Force team, posing as missionaries, fanned out into the village. They busied themselves repairing property, offering food, and dispensing medical supplies. The work was real, and the villagers were grateful for the help. The fact that the locals were unaware of the high-level surveillance equipment being installed did not diminish what they perceived as Christian love.

"Pastor Mac," as everyone was now calling McFarland, had been introduced around the village. In just a couple of days, he had become a familiar face, known by his clerical collar and spiritual nature.

Mac had managed to cobble together some semblance of the sign of the cross, and now spent most of his time walking the streets and mumbling indiscernible blessings over curious villagers. They often followed him about, telling him about their problems and needs in a language he didn't know. It didn't matter. He'd nod, make that stupid-looking mishmash of a sign, and offer words of encouragement. In the meantime, Ian looked incredulously on, occasionally providing an interpretation for anything he thought serious enough for Mac to know. It was a show to marvel at. The weird thing was, it didn't feel like a show to anyone involved.

Nothing, however, had prepared Mac for his first visit to the orphanage, or meeting the little girl. The orphanage was such a humble setting filled with overwhelming need. Clearly, this little Molly was just the tip of the iceberg.

It was also clear to Mac that Ian had gotten himself emotionally entangled in this mess. He could tell by the soupy way Ian looked at the director. Mac didn't like seeing that. It made them all more vulnerable. In his experience, when people let emotions get involved, they tended to make stupid, irrational decisions. He vowed to keep an eye out for his friend.

In the meantime, the Delta team had the run of the place. As they spruced up the paint and repaired the woodwork, they planted small, undetectable surveillance devices. Mac marveled at the technology.

At one point, he looked over and saw Molly intently watching the construction crew and wondered if she were catching on. He remembered that she spoke English.

"Well, young lady, what do you think about all of this crazy activity?" Mac delivered the line with his most pastoral demeanor.

"Very nice, Pastor Mac." She said this as she watched one of the team members install something that Mac knew looked different to her than the light fixture that had been there before. Clearly, no one was pulling the wool over her eyes. Mac made a note to let Ian know. But in the meantime he thought maybe it was a good idea to take her for a walk in the yard. With all of this new surveillance equipment and the weapons he knew were stockpiled within the compound, Mac was certain the grounds were more than secure. Just in case, he reached back to make sure his gun was securely in place.

"How about you show me that building out there with the colorful windows?"

"You mean, the chapel?" She had pinned him up against the wall with a single question.

"Yes, that one. Just giving you a little test, young lady," Mac said with a small, nervous laugh as he walked toward the door.

When she didn't immediately follow, he looked back to see what she was doing. She had climbed on a stool and was lifting a large, rusty key from a hook on the wall.

"We're going to need the key. Mama Iona keeps it locked now. She says God needs to stay inside His house." She seemed totally unconcerned about God being content to live in a rundown village chapel in the middle of Romania, Mac thought. Actually, he kinda thought it was the perfect place for the guy.

They walked over the dried, unkept grass to the old chapel. Mac figured it was about a hundred feet or so from the main building. As he took a closer look, he could see the bell tower, and he knew from having been here now for two days that it occasionally rang—for what purpose, or who did the ringing, he had no idea.

He waited for Molly before climbing the short stairs to the door. She handed him the rusty ring and key. The door took some finessing. Mac tried the lock several times. Nothing seemed to work. Finally, Molly took the key, jerked it back and forth, kicked the bottom of the door, and the thing opened.

"I guess you've used that key before," Mac commented, trying to hide the smirk that was forming.

"Oh yes. Mama Iona doesn't know it, but I talk to God here all the time."

Mac considered delving into her discussions with God but thought better of it.

I'm way out of my league, and she knows it! he admitted to himself.

The dust was drifting down through the rafters and floating through the shafts of light coming in through the stained glass. The air felt cool and smelled faintly musty—kind of like what you would expect from a deserted chapel in the middle of Dracula country, Mac thought to himself. It wasn't the most comforting place he had ever been.

There was a small altar with a cross above it. The Christ on the cross didn't look like the beautiful, angelic Christs he'd seen in paintings. This guy was in some pretty intense pain, and it showed. Looking at the figure on the cross only increased Mac's level of discomfort.

He glanced over at Molly, or tried to, but she was nowhere to be found. Then he saw her on her face in the aisle toward the front. *What the hell—heck—is she up to?* He didn't quite know what to do, so he stood quietly in the back, waiting for her to move.

After several minutes, she stood up and walked back to where he was standing.

"Aren't you going to talk to God, Pastor Mac?" She seemed genuinely baffled by his behavior.

"Oh, well, you see, I . . ." Mac suddenly regretted that he hadn't read more of the fine print in the study materials Ian had given him. "I . . . um . . . Do you always talk to God on your face like that?"

"Ever since Jayden was here." She said it as if everyone knew about Jayden. "I watched him pray that way, and I know God heard him. So, now I do it too."

"And, does He hear you too?"

"Sometimes."

Mac saw a shadow cross over her face.

"He didn't hear me when I asked Him to bring Jayden back here," she explained. "But I think when I asked Him to help Mama Iona not worry so much, He did. That's why you are here, right? She is worried that the government people will take her away from the orphanage because of the dead kids. She doesn't want to leave me alone."

At this, Mac sat down on the nearest bench with a heavy thud. So much for this kid being clueless. He was formulating a measured response when she added one more thing.

"You aren't really a pastor, are you, Pastor Mac?"

"Now, why on earth would you say that?" Mac tried to feign genuine hurt in order to buy some time.

"Because you don't look like you have ever talked to God before. And—she paused for dramatic emphasis—"you don't look like you even want to!"

Mac didn't even bother to argue. This kid was sharp as a tack. Now he and Ian would have to figure out how to keep her from blowing their cover when their friends, the Arabs, came calling.

"It's okay," Molly soothed, "God likes people like you who don't know Him yet. It gives Him something to do."

Mac laughed out loud before he could stop himself. He figured that was about as concise a statement about God as anything he had read in any book, including the Bible.

"You are probably right, kid. But let's get out of here before I find out!"

He jumped up from the rough-hewn pew, and together, he and Molly exited the church. Molly reversed her entrance ritual to get the thing locked up. Mac didn't offer to help. It gave him time to consider which of the many questions that had flooded his brain made the most sense to ask.

In the end, he remained silent. *Sometimes, in the presence of this combination of wisdom and innocence, it's better to just shut your mouth. Less accountability later.*

Chapter 59

BUDAPEST

Amir turned to face Nazir and, as their eyes locked, it was clear that the lines of authority stretching back to Al-Zawahiri had already been crossed.

The two men sized each other up like two knights about to defend their kingdoms. Nazir had known this day would come, his fitful dreams from the night before a vivid reminder that the true battle was not over a child in an orphanage or even becoming the heir apparent of his father. This would be the epic battle between two very different worldviews and the men that held them.

There was a momentary flicker of recognition when both men understood this, yet still chose to draw their swords and close the face plates of their armor. There would be no turning back, no respite, until one of them was defeated. It was destiny woven into the fabric and design of their souls. For Nazir, it was the defining call to be king.

As if to prove his assumption of being the victor, Amir launched into the new details of his plan.

"I have a brilliant plan, Nazir. It came to me as I watched you spying on them at the hotel. Why not use their grief and the husband's instinct of protection to our advantage? I was having a difficult time figuring out how to get the girl isolated without just blasting the whole place apart. These two will work as an excellent cover."

His speech was fast and clipped, with the slightly British accent they had all acquired during their years of private education. Nazir wondered why Amir was explaining his plan in English over their native tongue. But Amir was strange like that. Just like his matter-of-fact statement about watching Nazir—no preface or follow-up. Just one sentence to let the hammer drop.

"How do you intend to do this, exactly?" Nazir had regained his composure and hid his wariness beneath a calm demeanor.

"I have explained to the man that his wife must think this is a kidnapping for ransom. I told him that she must not know of anything other than that. I have also made it clear that her life will depend on it. He, in turn, must help us access the child at the orphanage."

"Do you honestly believe that after losing their own child, they are going to hand another one over to a bunch of Arab thugs?" Nazir made sure the emphasis was on the last word. It wasn't hard to do. In his own mind, this latest act proved that was all Amir and his group had become.

"I am far ahead of you, cousin. I have explained to the husband that the girl is my dead sister's child, abducted by a band of gypsies while she and her eastern European husband were traveling a few years ago in the area. It has taken this long and my dear sister's own early, grief-driven death to locate the girl. You see, I have thought of everything!" Amir could hardly contain his feeling of superiority.

"And then you plan to let these two continue on their vacation?"

Nazir had no faith in whatever answer Amir was going to give him. He knew in his heart that this couple had the mark of death already written on their foreheads.

"Of course, of course. They will provide money and the girl, and we will have closure. I will leave it to Allah to decide their fate beyond that."

Nazir had to admit that in theory, it was a good plan. However, he knew exactly how Allah was likely to fall concerning the couple's survival. His troubled dreams of last night were beginning to make more sense, and just for a moment, he allowed himself to think about Bree.

Chapter 60

BUDAPEST

Bree's first sensation was pain. Everything hurt. With her eyes still shut, she concentrated on each part of her body, trying to identify the source of her pain. It felt like her muscles were on fire. and any slight movement on her part sent her nerves firing up into her skull.

Where am I, and what has happened?

She could sense light but was terrified to open her eyes, afraid she was on some gurney and had been injured in some traumatic event. Had she and Ben been in an accident? She didn't remember driving anywhere. Finally, after what seemed like hours, she pried her eyes open, only to be bombarded by intense paranoia and fear. Several bearded men took turns peering into her face, increasing her terror, and making her heart pound in her chest like a sledgehammer hitting a spike. She tried to make sense of her unfamiliar surroundings. Where were Ben and Jayden? Why was she alone?

As she gained more lucidity and eventually her bearings, she realized that far from being on any gurney, she was actually strapped to a chair in the middle of a room that looked like it could have come from every spy movie she'd ever seen. Despite her initial terror, she almost laughed at the irony as she strained to look up for the proverbial naked light bulb and then down for the dank, musty concrete. Yep, both were there. Only, this wasn't a movie, and the guys guarding her looked like something more ominous than movie extras.

She stayed silent, keeping her eyes half-closed as she attempted to take in every detail of her surroundings without drawing attention to herself. Other than a slightly sore cheek, she was now pretty sure she was okay physically.

Mentally, she was definitely coming off a very strong tranquilizer.

Spiritually, well, forget spiritually—what kind of God lets this happen to someone who has already been through so much?

These thugs, Arab and somewhere in their twenties, did not attempt English. That meant there were long periods of silence, interrupted briefly with a spat of Arabic, which she couldn't begin to understand.

She made a mental note that if she ever made it home again, she would learn the basics of the top ten world languages. She couldn't help but think that if she could say, "Hello. How are you? Where are the bathrooms?" in their native language, the outcome in this scenario might be different. But who was she kidding?

Thankfully, from her treatment so far, it would appear they wanted her alive. Probably for ransom. Hopefully, wherever they were holding Ben, he was at this very moment agreeing to empty out their savings account so they could return safely to their island and pretend this never happened.

But what if he wasn't alive? She tried not to let her mind wander to the terrifying outcomes if that were true. She'd be at the mercy of her own limited abilities. How could she possibly defend herself? She looked around the room for any clue as to where she was, or for something she could use as a potential weapon later. Just then, a door behind her opened and someone new walked in. He spoke in clipped Arabic sentences, and she could tell by the tone of his voice that he seemed agitated or angry.

While he had started his conversation from behind her, he'd slowly moved forward toward the men who were guarding her, and she was able to catch a glimpse of the back of him. He was wearing a tailored suit and expensive shoes and seemed to carry himself with a high level of authority.

Whoever he was, her guards were not thrilled to see him. As she continued to watch the interaction between all three men, she couldn't get over the idea that there was something familiar about his walk and movements. It wasn't until he turned toward her and their eyes locked that she realized who he was and where they had met.

It had been in the lobby of the Hotel Gellert, yesterday! She had turned and plowed into him, and he had reached out to steady her. His behavior had seemed overly chivalrous, catching her arm to keep her from falling. She'd felt a surprising connection between them.

Now, fewer than twenty-four hours later, here he was, apparently her captor. *Some connection,* Bree thought. It had all probably been a well-choreographed trap. Still, she wasn't usually so wrong about people or her feelings.

She couldn't hide her surprise and disappointment as she looked up into his eyes now. His response was a vacant stare that seemed to land at the top of her head. She shook her head and looked away, as if to jar the memory until it yielded up the truth of the man.

He didn't appear to be struggling with the dichotomy of the situation. Just then, another man entered the room, and she had a fleeting thought about whether or not she and Ben's life savings split among her captors would amount to enough to save their lives.

Her thoughts were interrupted by the sound of a fist connecting with a face, then the thud of a body falling to the floor. This was followed by more urgent words, spoken in Arabic.

She watched the two men leave the room. The man she had met at the Hotel Gellert was rubbing his hand, which meant he had probably knocked out the man now lying on the floor. Maybe there was more to this mysterious man than she knew.

Chapter 61

ROMANIAN ORPHANAGE

The two operatives on duty watched the monitor with rapt fascination. As sentinels for perimeter security, part of their role was to keep an eye on the interior surveillance cameras that had been installed that day. They had run through all the other views and were focused on the ones in the dining hall, watching as some of the members of their team joined the director of the orphanage for the evening meal.

"This looks like something out of *Beetlejuice*, doesn't it?" One of the men laughed as he referenced the strange menagerie of characters visible on the screen.

There were eight special ops members dressed in an array of construction clothes, still covered with dust from their day of sprucing up the village.

Then there was the disheveled-looking pastor at the head of the table—who kept pulling on his clerical collar as if it were choking him.

There was the young orphan girl, clearly taking it all in and not missing a beat.

Finally, there was the spinster orphanage director and her companion, both deep into the "third act" of their lives. A couple of characters who, while trying to maintain the serious demeanor befitting the situation, were actually busy acting like the leads from *West Side Story*.

"Geez, it looks like a strange group to be taking on terrorists. Hope we know what we are doing!" the other operative quipped.

And it only got stranger when Mac rose to his feet to bless the food. The prayer meandered through so many Bible stories, it started to resemble a lost sheep looking for the promised land. In the end, Mac brought it home with a brief reference to the eerily similar "Last Supper." At the reference, everyone snickered with their heads still bowed. But after Mac's amen, when his dinner companions raised their heads and realized there were, indeed, twelve individuals around their table filled with bread and wine, a hush fell over the room.

As dinner wound down and Iona drew Molly away to get her ready for bed, Mac drew a breath of relief. They'd pulled it off. For now.

He addressed Ian and the special ops members around the table.

"First of all, thanks for being here. This initial op may seem small, but the bigger picture—should the outcome be unsuccessful—could be globally significant. Our objective is to capture, not kill. We'll need information—the type that's extremely difficult to extract from dead body fragments."

Everyone chuckled at the gallows humor that was always present at these types of intense, one-shot scenarios.

"As you are aware from our earlier briefings," Mac continued, "the terrorists have one objective: to kill the girl, and therefore get rid of the last trace of evidence of their test. To recap, our mission regarding Molly's safety is twofold. They must not have a chance to get close to her in any way or fly a trigger drone anywhere near her. The challenge for all of us will be, at the same time, allowing them to see her and think they have a chance."

The group was silent. They had just eaten dinner with Molly. Suddenly, it became a much more personal mission. Now that Mac had their undivided attention, he continued.

"I'm warning you now," he said, "these are some slippery, cunning bastards. Let's not lose sight of that. Ever. The stuff they've injected into those kids is ultimately meant for you and me. If we don't stop this shit now, we may not get another chance. Questions?"

The incongruity of the clerical collar mixed with Mac's expletives barely caused a ripple among his listeners.

For the next hour, the group mapped out possible scenarios, exit and entrance strategies, and talked through contingency plans.

After the group dispersed, Mac and Ian headed to the rooms Iona had prepared for her guests. In each room, four children's beds had been pushed aside to make room for a military cot. As Mac climbed onto his, he laid his gun on the floor, close at hand. As he heard the metal touch the concrete floor, he thought about the children who lived humbly in this room. Glancing around, he could see the children's meager belongings carefully folded and put away on a single shelf.

For some reason, this humble setting evoked a flood of anger, as if some internal dam inside of Mac had finally broken. He was unable to hold back the fury of seeing innocence and trust so violated by evil. This should have been sacred! Not the religious crap stuffed in that old chapel outside. This place! If God wanted to be God, why hadn't He shown up here?! What could have been more important than protecting these children?

Mac was hardly surprised when he didn't hear a response to his questions. He and God had gone a few rounds when Gloria died, and he hadn't heard anything from the Big Guy then either. Maybe the transmission frequency had been changed, and Mac hadn't gotten the memo.

Whatever the case, he wasn't going to hold his breath. What he was going to do instead was hand out justice. If God was busy, then Mac and Ian would get it done for Him. One way or another, these bastards were going to pay.

Maybe there was something to the idea of "an eye for an eye" after all, because just the idea of sending these jihadists to their fate calmed his earlier rage. He could feel his white-hot anger turning into a steel rod of determination.

Ironically, as he was finally drifting off to sleep, his last thoughts were about his own favorite childhood game, hide-and-seek. He began slowly counting, as he had as a child.

One . . . two . . . three . . . four . . . five . . . six . . . seven.
Ready or not, here I come.

Chapter 62

ROMANIAN ORPHANAGE

Iona tossed and turned in her bed.

Looking at the twin bed across the room, she could see that Molly was finally asleep. The little girl looked so peaceful.

"Am I doing what is best for this child?" she asked the question of herself in a low voice, so as not to wake Molly.

After Ian had revealed his identity and the proposed plan, there had seemed to be little choice. While the main objective was Molly's safety, Iona could not ignore the global implications of this deadly vaccine. After all, she was the only one involved who had actually seen the horrific results.

In the midst of this terrible challenge had come another dilemma: she was undeniably attracted to Ian.

She'd never imagined that, long past an age when she should be thinking about romance or love, such a caring, sensitive, and intelligent man would come into her life. She was baffled by his arrival, shocked by her own reactions, and now felt like she was being tossed by the stormy seas of decisions and change.

This orphanage and these children had been all she had ever known. To leave them seemed impossible. And yet, the idea of spending the remaining years of her life sharing meals, a home, and even a bed with Ian made her heart sing. She could barely hide her joy, even with her mind and heart fighting for supremacy.

And she didn't think she was in this alone.

Ian had feelings for her; she was certain. What if something happened to one of them before they had a chance to talk about this?

She had to talk to Ian. Now.

She checked quickly to see that Molly was still deep in sleep, then grabbed her shawl and quietly, on bare feet, slipped from the room.

Once in the hallway, it was a short distance to the room she had set up for Ian. She thought about knocking, but in the end simply opened the door and slipped in.

The moment she stepped forward, a hand slapped over her mouth and a gun barrel was jammed to her temple.

She didn't scream, but her heart jumped from her chest and stuck in her throat. As her eyes grew accustomed to the room, lit only by the early-morning light, she noticed the bed was empty. She also knew by the faint scent of his familiar cologne that it was Ian behind her.

As soon as he knew she was calm, he uncovered her mouth and spun her around.

"What the bloody hell do you think you are doing?" he blurted in a low whisper "Are you trying to get yourself killed?"

The line sounded like it had come from every American western Iona had ever seen. He sounded a bit like a British John Wayne. She almost laughed. Instead she said—revealing only part of the reason she was standing in his room—"I'm . . . I'm worried about tomorrow."

"Iona," Ian said softly, in a reassuring tone, "if you'd like, I can tell you again about the strategies and the protections we have put into place—"

"I don't want to talk about those," Iona interrupted, surprising even herself.

"Then what—"

"I want to talk about something else."

"Iona, fear is very normal in situations like this. I can understand—"

"Ian, stop." Iona wondered if all men were this clueless. "If something were to happen tomorrow to you, I would be devastated."

Suddenly, she felt like her heart would beat right out of her chest. Looking at Ian's bewildered face, she was certain now that she had imagined anything between them.

As she turned to leave for her room, Ian caught her arm and turned her so that he was looking into her eyes.

"Lady, you have absurd timing," he said roughly. "But if you want to do this here and now, then so be it."

"Ian, I'm sorry. I think I may have assumed—"

"You have assumed nothing and discerned everything," he said, his voice now softer. "I must confess that I have lost my heart to you, dear Iona."

"I—I didn't know. But I had hoped. And I was afraid because if something happens to either one of us tomorrow, I didn't want my feelings to be left unsaid."

Ian took both of her hands in his. "Nor mine." Then he smiled. "Coming here tonight was a brave move, my love." His smile broadened into a grin, and Iona's breath caught at the boyish charm of him.

"Of course I'll need you to marry me when this is over—and I think that we are going to need a bigger bed!" That last part was said as he glanced over at the single army cot and then back at her. He leaned close, kissed her cheek, and whispered, "It's the only thing saving you from a rather sleepless night."

Iona blushed, grateful for the dim light. She folded herself into his arms, and they stood cradled together.

Far too soon, they were interrupted by a gruff voice from the next room.

"Okay. Well, isn't that special," Mac bellowed from the other side of the paper-thin wall. "Some of us are trying to sleep before a fairly important day. I'd say get a room, but apparently you have one. I suggest you use it!"

Ian couldn't help himself. He found himself grinning from ear to ear—Mac hadn't even tried to hide the delight in his voice at Ian's good luck.

Iona and Ian laughed, and it felt therapeutic. Then they heard Mac's voice one more time.

"And by the way, now that I'm a minister, I'd be honored to perform the ceremony. Just let me know the date, and I'll put it on my rather crowded calendar."

Ian grinned and let out a few "bloody hells." The visual of Mac performing a wedding ceremony was more than anyone could handle.

By now, Mac's voice had awakened the whole place, and Ian and Iona heard doors open and people convening in the hallway between the bedrooms. Ian and Iona quickly joined them, trying to convince everyone to return to bed, but there was no use.

Arm in arm and still wearing their pajamas, they sheepishly resigned themselves to accepting the congratulatory hugs, sly winks, and bawdy comments of the Delta Force team.

Eventually, even Molly padded down the hallway to see what all the commotion was about. Judging from the laughter and smiles, she decided someone must have told a pretty good joke. She also decided it was going to be a great day.

Chapter 63

BUDAPEST

Nazir felt a strange sense of calm and clarity today. He had slept very well the night before and had awakened with a new strategy: Let his cousin get the girl, as originally planned. She was living on borrowed time, anyway. After all, she was supposed to have died in the initial attack, and as far as he was aware, she still had the vaccine inside her body. These weeks of life she'd been given were a gift.

But what Nazir couldn't and wouldn't let happen was for the woman, his woman, to feel any more sorrow or pain.

It seemed odd to think about everything in such honest terms. And yet, the truth was somehow liberating; he felt free from the oppressive confusion he had felt for most of his adult life.

With newfound clarity, he could see that his father had indeed betrayed him and had set this rivalry with Amir into motion. Al-Zawahiri had not only ordered Nazir to martyr his cousin, but Amir's demeanor seemed to indicate that he had received similar orders to take the life of Nazir.

So be it.

Later, as he entered the containment area, he saw the couple together. The woman was leaning against the man's shoulder, and he appeared to be holding her and talking softly at the same time. While Nazir wished he could be the one she was leaning on, he was strangely glad she was being comforted and was no longer alone.

Amir was already there, issuing orders in Arabic. He merely nodded to Nazir and then continued giving instructions to his henchmen. When he was sure they understood all that he was asking them to do, he turned to the couple and began speaking in English.

"I trust you have been able to sleep on my proposal and have made a decision regarding our demands?" Amir directed his question to Ben.

The husband spoke, and the strength of his voice again comforted Nazir.

"We have agreed to the demand for money in exchange for our safety," the American said boldly. "It will take some time and access to an international bank. I would like my wife to be freed now, and then I will continue securing the money."

Nazir admired the man's bravado in attempting to negotiate from such a powerless position.

"My plan is slightly different," Amir said while looking directly at the woman. "You will stay together, for now. I will travel with you as your driver. Another auto will follow us, but at some distance. We will first visit the bank."

Amir bent toward Bree until his face was inches from hers.

"Make sure you understand that there will be no tolerance for any cries for help or a scene of any kind. I will have a weapon trained on you at all times. I will shoot your husband in front of you."

Nazir's fists curled, and it was all he could do to control his emotions and his actions. He could see the renewed terror in Bree Stanton's eyes, and he yearned only to kill Amir with his bare hands and drive off with her to safety.

"After visiting the bank, we will travel on to the orphanage," Amir continued. "Once I have ascertained that the money has been successfully wired and you have been welcomed for your visit with the children, I will leave you there." Amir had such a smooth but icy delivery that for a minute the room was as still as death.

"What do we have as a guarantee that you will do as you say?" the husband asked, attempting once again to leverage security without any real bargaining chips.

"There is no guarantee. I could just kill you now. Would you prefer that?" Amir's arrogance and contempt seeped through his previously thin veneer of civility.

As Nazir looked on, he thought that his cousin's last words had cracked the Americans' facade of confidence. His capitulation was nothing more than a formality.

"When are we leaving?" the husband asked. Looking down at his stained clothing and over at his wife's equally disheveled appearance, he paused and then added, "We will need to return to our rooms to clean up for the trip."

Nazir had to hand it to him; the man had looked Amir up and down and without saying a word made it clear that, if not for the presence of his wife, he would have made a stand.

"Your room was swept clean, and you have officially checked out of the hotel," Amir said nonchalantly. "Your bags have been moved, and you can now shower and change here. As soon as you are finished, we will leave for the bank, and then journey to the orphanage and the rendezvous with your dead son's memories."

Without further ado, Amir turned and left, leaving the Stantons in such genuine shock that neither even attempted to speak. Ben's and Bree's faces were gray with fear at the realization that this was not a random kidnapping.

Nazir watched all this knowing there was little he could do at this point. He could do nothing at the moment except follow Amir's directions and be ready to intervene if the opportunity arose—and he was going to make sure it did.

He could hear Bree's quiet sobs as he left the room.

Chapter 64

BUDAPEST

Bree kept looking at Ben, and then at their driver. She was startled to see the Arab man named Amir staring back at her through the rearview mirror.

Now that she had calmed a bit, and they were no longer being manhandled, Bree felt her steely determination returning. She whispered to Ben under her breath, "Does this guy ever look at the road while he drives?"

Ben didn't bother to respond. He knew Amir had a loaded handgun in his lap, and that the men following them in a van were just as armed and dangerous.

So far, the man—Ben, too, had heard the others call him Amir—had kept his word. Ben and Bree were still alive.

The bank experience had been surprisingly easy. It turns out there are a plethora of major banks with branches in Budapest. Amir had given Ben account numbers and wiring details right before they entered the building, and Ben had gotten a private banker to help him with the transfer. He'd used the story of purchasing a vacation property overlooking the Danube. It had been a tedious process, but in the end, Ben had been assured that the money could be wired.

Despite their success, Amir had not warmed up to them, remaining stone-faced and intense.

Now that they were back in the car and heading to their next destination, Ben had some time to let his rational mind catch up to his adrenaline-fueled body.

They weren't out of danger, not by a long shot.

Even if they made it to the orphanage and Amir was able to locate the girl he claimed was his long-lost niece (and Ben was quite certain that was far from the truth), Ben and Bree's survival seemed doubtful. Why would Amir keep them alive? He and Bree were now witnesses to everything, with the ability to identify Amir and his cronies by their faces, cars, names—and even their bank accounts.

That didn't spell "safety" in Ben's mind. More like "expendable liability."

Chapter 65

BUDAPEST

From behind the heavily tinted window of his Mercedes sedan, Nazir watched the husband walk toward the door of the bank, Amir at his elbow. Even behind mirrored sunglasses, Amir's expression was dark and brooding.

Who does he think he is, this cousin of mine? Nazir wondered, *Allah?*

Once they were inside, Nazir turned his gaze back to Amir's car. The windows were dark enough that he could not detect any movement, but he knew Bree was inside. Two of Amir's men from the van now stood guard by the doors of the sedan.

Nazir opened his car door, hesitated, then slammed it shut again. He wanted to comfort her, but what words could he possibly say that would change what she must think of him now? Besides, how could he be comforting and yet truthful? Even he did not know how this journey would end. In fact, if Nazir were honest, it really didn't look promising for the American couple—or for himself.

This realization was fueled by the subtle change in Amir's demeanor toward him. Even when they were children, Amir had never forgotten that Nazir was the son of Al-Zawahiri. There had always been an unspoken line that was never crossed, a respectful deference to Nazir's status. Nazir's opinion had always mattered.

Now something had shifted.

It felt uncomfortable to be the one left out of the planning and decision-making process. Especially since this was the one time Nazir wanted to have a say in how things went down. The change was not just in Amir's demeanor. The power shift was palpable.

Nazir knew that his father had become disappointed with him and now distrusted him. It was a major and unexpected shift. Especially since he was Al-Zawahiri's only son.

It seemed ironic in the face of what he knew about the American couple and their grief over the loss of *their* only son. Having seen how they grieved, he tried to imagine a scenario in which their son could have done anything that would have led his parents to betray him. He could not.

Then he thought about the Americans' God. He'd had a son too. And that story seemed to include a colossal betrayal as well, one that resulted in the son's agonizing death on a cross. Again, the story of a father turning away from his only son. Apparently, this betrayal had been necessary for the good of the many—an assassination leading to salvation. Nazir was moved by the concept, and yet, he could feel the lingering pain of that betrayed son.

Of course, that's not how Bree's son had described it in his journal. He'd described the death of the Christ as the ultimate act of love in its purest form.

Nazir closed his eyes. He did not think his father's decision was motivated by love. His father was motivated only by what he deemed necessary for the survival of the caliphate. He had clearly decided that Amir was the man for that role, and that Nazir, with his Western influence and ideals, was not.

Yet, Nazir knew he was destined to be a leader. He also knew his life and choices were governed by a larger vision of life. In his heart, now forever changed by what he had seen and heard while watching the Americans, he wondered what that ultimately meant. If he wasn't to serve the Caliphate—and he knew he wouldn't—then what kingdom or set of ideals would he serve?

Whatever it was, Nazir was convinced it would require a new way of thinking. It would feel counterintuitive, like the hands of an analog clock moving in the wrong direction.

Which was why he was sitting in his car instead of comforting Bree, as he yearned to do.

Chapter 66

ROAD TO ROMANIA

After leaving the bank and returning to the car, Ben slid into the backseat next to Bree. He patted her hand and gave her a reassuring look before leaning his head back and closing his eyes. He needed to concentrate to figure out their next move.

Ben had no doubt they would be killed as soon as the girl was found. He needed some way to let Bree know they were facing trouble, and he wanted her to stay ready and stay close—without alerting their captor, of course.

He had an idea.

He opened his eyes and cleared his throat.

"Sweetheart, I've been thinking."

Bree looked at him. "About?"

"Jayden, of course. Remembering quirky things about his personality, things we loved."

Bree's eyes welled with emotion.

"Remember what a great storyteller he was?" Ben asked.

She nodded.

"How much he loved sci-fi stuff?"

At this Bree looked slightly baffled. Ben knew why. Jayden had never been one for space movies or books, preferring Harry Potter and nonfiction explorer biographies. And Bree knew this. Would she catch on?

"Remember his favorite movie?" he continued. "The one with the pig-faced people who had that strange language? Jayden spent months learning it. He actually got pretty fluent."

While he let that sink in, he glanced up to see if Amir was watching or listening. He was listening but didn't seem overly interested now that their money had been transferred. Good.

"How would he say good night again?" Ben mused. "I'm trying to remember. Oh wait . . . wasn't it something like *Eway areway acingfay angerday*? Er, no, wait—that's not right. It was *Aystay eadyray aystay oseclay*."

He could see Bree's expression tighten for an instant; then she chuckled and said, "Something like that, yes. I remember now. And 'I love you' was *Eadyray, oldgay eaderlay!*"

Ben couldn't help but be amazed at how quickly she'd caught on. She winked at him, and they both forced another, much louder chuckle, and Amir turned and told them to shut up.

Bree turned to look at the countryside as it sped past her window. She seemed serene, but Ben could tell by the way she gripped his hand that she was anything but calm.

Ready, Gold Leader?

He knew she'd gotten the message.

The countryside was ablaze with glorious fields of sunflowers and rolling hills of hay and other crops. Despite Ben's warning that they were facing danger and that she should stay ready and stay close, she felt herself falling under the spell of the bucolic beauty.

There was a vivid intensity to the shades of yellows and greens. At the same time, it had a sultry stillness that made it feel like a Van Gogh painting. In fact, it looked like a scene from one of her grandmother's old china plates that had hung on her walls. Dotted across the fields were small, white stucco houses with faded tile roofs. Each yard held an assortment of fruit trees, gardens, farm animals, and hanging wash.

She could see men in the fields and a few women around the homes, apparently washing and cooking and caring for the children playing nearby. It was as if the modern world had passed them by.

Bree felt a deep sadness she couldn't explain wash over her. Jayden had loved this place and these people, and she wished she had known earlier. Most important, she wished they could have experienced this together.

She hoped their arrival—with armed thugs in tow—wouldn't interrupt this idyllic setting.

Before long, they drove into a small village. The Mercedes maneuvered down the main street, around horse-drawn carts loaded with hay, a wagon train of Gypsies, and several cars, the makes of which Bree had never seen. There was even what appeared to be a wedding processional walking down a side street, headed back from the local church, its steeple clearly the tallest point in the village.

How odd that they were all in the same place, but with such different stories. Bree realized her story, and Ben's, had taken quite the unexpected twist. Now, instead of coming to this beautiful place to understand Jayden's experiences here, she and Ben were arriving as hostages.

But why?

And how had Amir known about their dead son?

Chapter 67

THE ORPHANAGE

Ian climbed the stairs to the second floor of the orphanage's staff dormitory, where Mac was holed up with the surveillance team. He knocked and then entered, glancing at the array of sophisticated equipment and the serious demeanor of the officers before addressing Mac.

"What do we have, JD? "

"Our worst possible nightmare coming true. The American couple have apparently grown tired of their honeymoon already. They were just spotted rolling through town. I'd bet we are going to have visitors in about ten minutes."

Ian stepped forward to get a better view of the surveillance monitors.

"To make matters worse," Mac added, "they are not alone. They're being tailed by a white van carrying who knows what, and another car further back." Mac delivered the grim news while staring down at the screens showing the vehicles moving through the village streets.

"So, the bastards are coming in under the cover of the Americans, who are most likely unwilling participants." Ian voiced the thoughts of many in the room.

"It's the collateral damage we'd most hoped to avoid," Mac said, shaking his head.

"Let's get the crew up."

Mac reached for his radio transmitter.

"Listen up. The Americans are being escorted into the village by what appear to be our Arab targets. We are expecting their arrival here within minutes. We can only assume the Americans are hostages at this point and are now a complication to our initial mission. Hold fire until further notice."

Mac's order was delivered with the sound and precision of a general in battle. He turned to Ian.

"Those bastards. Better get Iona and Molly into an interior room. I have a feeling our party crashers—and their hostages—are about to walk right up to the front damn door!"

Chapter 68

THE ORPHANAGE

Amir, speaking into a radio, ordered a halt to the procession just outside the long drive into the orphanage. He turned to Ben and Bree and launched quickly into his requirements from them.

"We are here to find my lost niece. Here is her picture and name. You will go to the front door and insist to see her. I will be behind you with a weapon. You will not take no for an answer. She is here, and you must take my word for that."

Ben looked at the photo before offering it to Bree. As she tried to take it, he gripped it tightly so that once again she was forced to make eye contact with him. He held her gaze for a moment before letting go.

When she looked down at the photo, she gasped. She was staring into the face of little Molly.

"But this is—"

Ben quickly squeezed her hand, and she stopped mid-sentence.

"What if they won't let us see her?" Ben addressed Amir, giving Bree a moment to collect her thoughts. "After all, they don't know us. We didn't get a chance to announce our arrival or set up a visitation."

"You will not need an appointment," Amir scoffed. "This is a small, rural home run by a single old woman. She will be happy to see you. When you are let in to the facility, just refer to me as your driver and guide. That will make my presence with you less awkward and yet necessary. "

Ben was amazed at the detail that had gone into the bullshit story. Amir and his cohorts were desperate to get to this girl, but why? This whole thing made absolutely no sense. Did this have anything to do with Jayden? Now Ben wished he'd paid more attention to Jayden's conversations about this place, as well as the journal Bree had tried so hard to get him to listen to.

"Courage, my love," Ben whispered to Bree. She could only nod, her expression going from puzzled to fierce. He could see Bree's mama-bear instincts rise at the thought that Molly could be in danger as well.

"What did you say?" Amir turned in his seat and glared at Ben. There was a moment when Ben was pretty sure he was looking into the face of pure evil.

"I was just talking to my wife," Ben said this with the calm of Buddha himself. His own thoughts ran closer to *Better watch your back, you bastard!* and he was hoping for an opportunity to clock this creep before it was all over.

Driver and guide, my ass, Ben thought as he set his jaw. *No one in their right mind will think this Arab thug is up to anything but bad news.*

Amir barked what sounded like orders in Arabic into the radio and put the car into gear. The Mercedes began rolling down the drive toward the orphanage. The surrounding grounds were heavily treed, which only increased the tension Ben felt. Seclusion meant vulnerability. With a quick glance back through the rear window, Ben saw that Amir must have ordered the van and car to stay behind. He wasn't sure if that made him feel better or worse about their odds of survival.

♛

Despite the weeks she'd spent anticipating this moment, Bree had never really thought about what it would be like to drive up to the actual door of the orphanage where Jayden had volunteered. She swallowed back tears as the gravel drive ended and the car swung in a wide arc to park next to the front door.

The main building itself looked like it had recently received a fresh coat of white paint, and pots of vibrantly colored flowers stood on either side of the door. It was smaller than she had imagined, and older for sure.

Amir had already stepped from the car and come around to open her door,

"Lady, let's go," he said coldly, his words interrupting her thoughts and increasing her already pounding heart rate. Ben squeezed her hand again, and she looked over in time for him to kiss her and whisper, "Be careful."

Absorbing some of his strength, she stepped out of the car and into the late afternoon sunlight.

Looking back over the top of the car, she quickly surveyed their surroundings. Across the drive and to the left was a two-story building with several doors lining the upper and lower floors. It looked like a type of small motel or rooming house. She thought maybe it was used for employees or visitors. She spotted two more nondescript buildings.

And then she saw what she'd been searching for.

At the far end of the property stood what could only be the chapel— Jayden's chapel, as she had come to call it since reading his journal.

It was much larger than she had visualized. In fact, it dawned on her that she'd caught a glimpse of the chapel's bell tower and steeple when they were winding through the village. The idea that they were so close to a whole village of people gave her comfort, and she felt a strange sense of peace wash over her.

Bree could have stood absorbing this scene and place for much longer, but Amir interrupted her thoughts. "Lady. This way," he repeated his order.

She could tell now that he was talking through clenched teeth, playing the solicitous guide but clearly not enjoying the role.

She looked back to make sure Ben was easing out of the car before moving toward the front door. There was a heavy, metal knocker in the middle, and before she could decide whether to use it or not, Amir stepped in front of her and banged it heavily several times. Just the sound of his intense impatience was enough to drive home the ominous reality of what they were up against.

After a moment, the door opened, and they were greeted by a tentative woman in her sixties. Bree noticed her smooth, high cheekbones and luminous blue eyes. She suspected this must be the director Jayden had grown so fond of during his stay here.

"*Buna. Pot sa te ajut?*" The woman's voice was at once soothing and authoritative.

Bree had to keep from reaching out to hug her for all that she knew about her heart and sacrifice for the children of the area. Instead, she smiled warmly and asked, "Do you speak English?"

Bree looked over at Ben and back at Amir, wondering if either had any intentions of helping her out of this awkward situation.

Just then, the door opened wider and a slightly older gentleman appeared next to the woman. He offered his hand to Bree.

"Hello. Welcome. I'm Ian. Mrs. Dalca is just learning the language. What can we help you with?"

Before Bree could answer, Ian looked past her at Ben and Amir and said, "My, you have quite an unusual entourage."

"My name is Bree Stanton, and this is my husband Ben and our driver, Mr . . . uh . . . Amir. We have been on a rather lengthy trip through eastern Europe, having started near Santorini. Well, actually, an island near there. But really, we started from Rome, I suppose. . . "

The man named Ian must have seen that she was getting flustered and jumped in to help. "Excuse me, and I don't mean to be rude, but how on earth did you two decide to come to this out-of-the-way orphanage, of all places?"

"Our driver . . ." Bree suddenly had a terrifying moment when she blanked on his name and looked back at both Amir and Ben before remembering. "Our driver, Amir, suggested that, since we were so close, we stop here to look for his sister's child. She was lost in this area over two years ago, and he has reason to believe she may be here at this orphanage. By any chance"—Bree handed Ian a picture of Molly—"is there a young girl here by the name of Maria?"

Ian and Iona both looked down at the face they knew and loved so much. Ian heard Iona's breath catch in her throat.

Ian handed the photo back to Bree before answering. "Unfortunately, we have many children who come through this facility. The girl does not look familiar to me, but I will be happy to check our records. We will do whatever we can to help you locate your lost . . . niece, is it?" He looked at the "driver" when he said this.

♕

Iona took this opportunity to study the American woman's face. She could see Jayden reflected in his mother's features. Then she looked at the woman's husband, standing behind her. Yes, Jayden had definitely inherited his father's blue eyes.

It was suddenly too much for her. She stepped back slightly, behind Ian's arm, still holding the upper part of the heavy door.

The one named Amir spoke up. "Perhaps we can visit with the children who are here."

Iona was too rattled to respond. She was grateful when, out of the corner of her eye, she saw Ian shake his head. "Unfortunately, they are not here this week," he told the Arab. "They are staying temporarily in private homes nearby. As you can see by the scaffolding and equipment, the property is currently under repair."

♕

Ian watched the Arab's reaction to this news and was not surprised by the anger that was clearly simmering just beneath the surface.

In the meantime, the fact that Bree had failed to mention her own connection to the orphanage through her son was all Ian needed to confirm that the Americans were indeed hostages. He could see the husband gazing intently around the buildings and property, undoubtedly looking for either an escape route or shelter, or maybe both.

That's what I would be doing, Ian thought.

He addressed the visitors. "Please, excuse the mess, and come inside. I'm sure you have had a long day of travel. Would you like some tea, or perhaps some of the local pálinka ?"

Amir answered authoritatively for the group. "Yes. We would."

Awfully commanding for a "driver," Ian thought.

"Mrs. Dalca will show you to a small sitting room," he said politely.

Giving Iona a reassuring smile, Ian swung the door open and motioned the group inside. Before closing the door, he looked across the grounds at the second story of the dormitory, where he knew Mac and the team were positioned.

I hope you are locked and loaded up there, old chap. This is going to be one hell of a ride.

Iona led the way down a short hallway and stopped at the doorway of the sitting area. She gestured for the visitors to go on into the room, then said in broken English, "I make tea."

Bree wanted to offer to help the older woman with the refreshments, but glancing over at Amir, she wasn't sure how to go about it without getting him riled up. She looked around briefly at the group and thought everyone seemed stiff and unnaturally tense.

Once they were seated, the man who'd introduced himself as Ian turned again to Amir. "Tell me: how is it that your sister's daughter came to be lost in this part of the country? I don't recall the last time a child went missing here."

"They were vacationing near here, and she was abducted by Gypsies. We thought she was lost forever, until we learned recently that she may have been abandoned by her kidnappers and brought here." Amir said this with a convincing air of authority. It sounded believable even to Bree, who knew the truth was much different.

"I am sorry for your loss," Ian said. "She looks like a lovely girl. She must take after her father, as I do not see the family resemblance."

Amir answered smoothly. "She is my half sister, and her mother is European. In fact, my sister was traveling through Romania taking Maria to visit relatives."

♕

As Ben watched the tête-à-tête between Amir and Ian, something felt off. He couldn't tell if Ian believed Amir or was merely buying time. And if so, buying time until what?

Iona walked into the room just then with a tray of assorted drinks and food. "Tea or pálinka?" she asked brightly.

Amir nodded toward the pálinka. Ian opted for tea, as did Ben and Bree.

♕

Iona smiled warmly as she handed a cup of tea to Bree. Her eyes caught and held Bree's gaze for a longer moment than necessary. Bree's heart skipped a beat. She wondered briefly if the woman somehow knew why she was really here.

In fact, Bree couldn't figure out what anyone knew and why. For that matter, how did Amir know about Jayden? It wasn't as if she and Ben had discussed Jayden's journal—or this trip—with anyone. Had the caretakers on Folegandros somehow spoken to Amir? How could they possibly know each other?

And even more important, what about Molly? If she wasn't here . . . where was she?

Bree was deep in thought when the director spoke directly to her in halting English.

"Mrs. Stanton, would you like to freshen up before you eat?"

It felt as if this woman were staring directly into Bree's very soul.

"Yes, I believe I would. It's been a long day, and an even longer journey." Bree let the words linger over the room, intending for her captor to hear her displeasure. But Amir was busy answering a barrage of questions, and Ben seemed a million miles away, in thought.

Bree stood and followed Iona out of the room and down the hall.

The moment they were out of hearing range of Amir, Bree moved closer to Iona and whispered, "I don't have time to explain, and I hope you can understand my English enough to know what I'm telling you. I am the mother of Jayden Stanton. He was here on a mission trip several years ago . . ."

Just then, they reached a bend in the hallway, and Iona turned swiftly to Bree and said compassionately, "I know who you are, Mrs. Stanton." She reached for Bree's hands and took them in her own.

Bree glanced over her shoulder but was relieved to see that they were out of earshot of her captor.

"I also know that you are here to follow your son's footsteps in hopes that you can ease the pain of your loss," the older woman continued. "Unfortunately, I must tell you two things, and neither will be easy to hear. First, the loss of a son, especially someone like Jayden, is beyond what the heart is prepared to bear. I know. I have recently lost *twenty-two* children to a horrible murderous incident, and I will never be the same. Unfortunately, your coming here may open new wounds before the old ones can be healed. I'm sorry."

Bree was trying to hold herself in utter stillness, so that even the sound of her breath would not intrude on this moment. The ache in her chest was so heavy she felt faint.

Before going any further, Iona opened a door off the hallway and steered Bree into what seemed like a small storage room.

"Second, and I wish I didn't have to share this with you"—she paused to lower her voice even further—"we believe the murderer of those children is the same gentleman you have arrived with today. He is here because of Molly. She was not with the other children that day. She was ill, and I kept her here with me. However, she carries within her body something that makes her the only living connection to the murders of my children. These men are here to erase that connection."

Horror spread across Bree's face.

"Mrs. Stanton," the woman went on, "they have used you and your husband's quest to lead them right to her. There is no time to explain all that has happened. You must trust me."

Bree gasped as she tried to understand what the woman was saying through her thick, whispered accent. This new information felt like a sharp kick to her stomach, and she was finding it hard to breathe.

She had thought this visit would bring some encounter with Jayden's God and that there would be a beautiful, peaceful resolution to their journey of grief.

Now she was being told that her need to connect with Jayden's life had been used in a diabolical plan of evil—and could result in Molly's death.

Bree shook her head, trying to clear both the confusion and the overwhelming emotions.

"There's something I need to show you, and we don't have much time," Iona said quickly. She led Bree back across the hall to another closed door. She knocked once and opened the door to the kitchen, then walked in swiftly, closing the door softly behind Bree once she was across the threshold.

"Molly, I'd like to introduce you to Mrs. Stanton," she said. "Sweetheart, this is Jayden's mother. Mrs. Stanton, this is Maria, but we call her Molly."

The shock for both of them was palpable. No one moved, as the knowledge and the history of events swept over them.

Molly made the first move, running toward Bree and squeezing her waist in a giant bear hug. The hug was so filled with love and emotion that it took Bree a second to respond.

"Oh, darling. What a wonderful welcome." These were the first words that Bree could think of. She leaned back from the little girl so she could take a better look at her face.

Molly was more mature than the little girl pictured in Jayden's photo, for sure. But she still had that beautiful, angelic look, and her curls were wild and even longer then before. Looking into Molly's eyes, Bree could see that there was something "old soul" about the girl that you couldn't see in a mere snapshot.

"No one had to tell me you were his mother. I knew when I first saw you!" Molly's declaration made the room go quiet. "You smile just like he did."

The past tense wasn't lost on Bree.

"Well, I knew who you were too!" Bree smiled and hugged the child again, smoothing back the bangs from her face and planting a gentle kiss on her forehead. This instant sense of familiarity and warm affection felt strange. This was not Bree's usual MO . . . even with Ben and Jayden.

"Molly, why don't you take Mrs. Stanton for a walk. Perhaps you could show her Jayden's old room in the dormitory," Iona said with a sense of urgency.

Bree looked at Iona, her eyes filled with questions.

"Trust me."

Bree nodded numbly.

"Molly," Iona continued, if you take Mrs. Stanton to the dormitory, she can also meet Pastor Mac and the other mission team members." Iona made sure Molly acknowledged her statement. One of the optional plans Ian and Mac had worked on with her was to get these two to safety if the opportunity presented itself, and Iona knew the timing would never get better than this. Once Jayden's mother—and Molly—reached the dorm, they'd *both* be safe.

Molly nodded solemnly before turning to Bree. "Please let me show you."

The child reached out her small hand and firmly grasped Bree's adult one, and as Iona looked on, the younger woman suddenly seemed overwhelmed with emotion. But when Molly gave Bree's hand an insistent tug, the two headed out the back door of the kitchen.

Once they were safely away, Iona smoothed her skirt, took a deep breath, and slowly began the walk back to the sitting room and the scene she knew was about to unfold.

Chapter 69

JAYDEN'S CHAPEL

As soon as they were out of the building and walking toward the back of the yard, Molly launched into conversation as if she and Bree had known each other forever.

"I knew you would come! Jayden talked all the time about you and his father. He wanted you to visit, and he told me you would." Molly explained all this while looking up at Bree with such pure joy that Bree could feel tears welling up. She looked away to keep them from falling down her cheeks.

"He also said he might not be with you when you came, and that I would need to help you feel welcome."

Bree felt the girl's words bump against her heart and travel through her body, making her legs weak and her head disoriented.

"He told you that?" Bree's voice shook, and she was unable to hide her shock.

Why would he have said something like that, unless he had a premonition that he was going to die?

"I was little then. I didn't understand everything, but Mama Iona explained some of it to me when I was older."

Bree was overwhelmed by the thought of her son being aware of something so horrible. Maybe he hadn't written in his journal everything he'd seen and heard. She wanted desperately to go back and unearth every conversation they had shared from the moment he'd returned home, but she was struggling to concentrate, and little Molly was insistent on moving on with her story.

"Mama Iona wants me to take you to Pastor Mac in the dormitory, but first I want to show you the chapel. That's where it all happened. Jayden said you would want to know about it. He told me the whole story over and over like he was reading a book to me. He even made me a book so that I could remember everything for you. I'll show it to you when we get back."

Bree was softly crying now, and there was no stopping the tears. Iona had been right: her heart was not ready for this.

Molly took Bree along the back edge of the property, skirting a long, low building that looked like a dining hall before arriving at the chapel. The child tugged her hand, taking her around the far corner of the building to the front, where they climbed the few steps up to the heavy front doors.

Bree tried to take a quick look back at the main building, but the chapel was angled in a way that kept her from seeing that building from where she stood.

If I can't see them, then they can't see us! That thought gave Bree her first feeling of peace since they had arrived at the orphanage.

She and Molly worked together, first to pry open the heavy doors, and then to force them shut once they were inside. Bree smiled and gave Molly a hug before they turned in unison toward the interior of the dimly lit chapel.

Bree hesitated and then slowly moved forward toward the nave, her footsteps echoing off the stone floor and toward the rafters high above.

Behind an elevated pulpit, dusty, stained-glass windows let in the feeble afternoon light, just as Jayden had described. As Bree's eyes adjusted to the dim light, she scanned the sanctuary, searching for the large crucifix. When she saw it, she, too, was taken aback by the anguished figure.

How could something so gruesome be in a place for young children? she thought.

She looked around for Molly, who seemed oblivious to the ambiance. In fact, Molly looked happy and peaceful, which was perplexing to Bree.

As Bree surveyed the chapel, the first words that came to her mind were *old* and *musty*. It certainly didn't have that golden hue of godly presence she had expected to find. But worse—and it was too devastating to say out loud—it didn't have Jayden.

Somehow, through all the planning, journal reading, traveling, and even danger, a part of her must have been hanging on to the irrational hope of finding him here—or at least his spirit.

But no. Instead, rows of pews filled the sanctuary. Bree walked past a third of them while taking it all in, and then, unable to go any further, slumped into a nearby pew, suddenly heartbroken and defeated. The feeling of desolation cracked open her grief, and it poured over her like the sudden melt of a mountain glacier. Somehow, Bree had thought that getting here would relieve the anguish from which she had been running for so long. She had hoped to find the answer to the relentless question of her heart: "But why Jayden?"

It was only the sensation of small hands insistently patting her on the shoulder that brought her back from stepping off the ledge of grief and into the abyss.

"Mama B, I have more of the story to tell you," Molly's pleading voice interrupted Bree's despair. "Jayden told me to call you Mama B. Is that okay?"

Bree could not raise her head to respond. "Yes . . . it is okay." She was staring down at her hands, folded in her lap and wet with tears.

"Oh, good. So, the story starts like this. In the beginning . . ."

Chapter 70

Inside the Orphanage

"**W**e've got a visual, sir," the man sitting in front of the monitor hollered to Mac. "Two cars and a van rolling up to the driveway. One car is continuing to the entrance of the building. The other two are sitting just in from the road."

Mac and his team were watching from inside the second story of the dormitory. It was located across and slightly north of the main orphanage building. He'd added this location in the early setup phase of their planning because of the logistical advantages. He didn't want to add, "In case the terrorists decide to take out the whole main building," which was exactly what they could be planning. There was no real way of knowing.

Mac walked quickly to the monitors to watch the anticipated arrival of the Americans and the jihadists.

Mac's role was to provide intel and protection. He would be responsible for monitoring the exterior of the property, sending in ground support, and ordering any necessary airstrikes. The drones were loaded and ready and the twelve special ops team members evenly divided between the property, entrance road, and village.

Ian, on the other hand, would be interacting with the terrorists and calling the shots from within the main building. With his fluent Romanian and his European accent, he was less likely to cause alarm or suspicion. He would need to assess and respond to whatever developed with the Americans and their escorts, as well as communicate with Iona in keeping Molly safe.

Tall orders for both men.

In Mac's mind, they had two clear and distinct missions: first, to protect the child, and then, to lure, capture, and torture the key players (*okay, maybe not torture, maybe just ply them with leftover Halloween candy or Amazon gift cards*) in order to extract the intel necessary to stop the "bio shit show" they were planning.

"Sir," someone interrupted Mac's thoughts, "both the van and the car are now backing out onto the main road."

"What the hell? Sam, keep your eye on them," Mac growled before addressing a second man studying an adjacent monitor. "And Ted, you stay with the group coming to the door. They are probably setting up some type of perimeter. Notify our field people. Let's get them teed up and ready. I may need them to close in."

The surveillance equipment the team had installed appeared to be providing more than enough visual intel. The visuals on the Americans and their "companion" at the door were practically high-def and gave the CIA analysts back in Langley more than they needed to identify the man accompanying the Stantons to the front door of the main building.

Mac leaned in closer to the monitor and studied the odd group standing on the porch. He thought the couple looked familiar. The thug behind them was another story. Mac was about to say something when he was interrupted by one of his team.

"Sir, we have confirmation from Langley," Ted called out excited, his eyes glued to a computer screen. "The man with the Americans is Amir Mohamed Zawahiri . . . nephew of Al-Zawahiri!"

Mac was stunned. Amir was not who they had expected to arrive with the Americans. They were expecting the Nazir character who had been tailing the couple in Croatia. Mac took a quick moment to high-five with his team before returning to their monitors—they were about to snag a direct link to the big kahuna.

Within minutes, their contact at Langley emailed Mac an electronic file. The details were ominous but included little he hadn't known from his own research on Al-Zawahiri.

"Gentlemen, our mission remains the same," Mac announced. "As you already know, all the players are considered extremely dangerous. Amir is on our list of the top ten most dangerous terrorists. He is thought to be behind several recent terrorist attacks in Spain and France, and now of course may be part of the team that killed these children."

Mac paused to let the gravity of Amir's involvement sink in before continuing.

"The fact that Al-Zawahiri has sent one of his own relatives places a much higher level of importance on this mission from their standpoint . . . and now from ours."

Mac could feel the tension increase in the room. He only wished he could let Ian know. It was too late. Mac could see from another monitor that Ian was already sitting down to tea with the kid-killing bastard.

Mac had little time to mull over that situation. With the first Mercedes still parked in front of the main building, the other vehicles—a white, nondescript panel van and a second black Mercedes sedan with dark, tinted windows—were once again in play. The van had backed out, driven on, and then turned in to another entrance closer to the outer edge of the property. As Mac watched, two men climbed out of the van. Within minutes, they had positioned themselves with rifles trained on the front door of the main building. Both men were heavily armed with everything from sniper rifles to grenades, and Mac could see that their belts were loaded with ammo.

Mac grabbed a radio and alerted the team about the location of the snipers. Immediately, four of the special forces team moved closer until they had a visual of the threat. They remained ready to take out the men as soon as Mac gave them the order.

Meanwhile, Mac turned his attention back to the second Mercedes. It had not stayed with the van. Apparently, while all eyes had been on the van and snipers, the second Mercedes had continued along the main road and disappeared. At that point, it was beyond the range of the property's perimeter cameras. Sam and Ted re-upped the satellite images, but by then the car was nowhere to be seen.

Mac said a few expletives under his breath, pulling at his clerical collar, which was beginning to feel like a noose.

"Dammit, I want this car found, gentlemen, and found fast!" Mac barked into the radio with such force that every team member listening had to pull their earbuds or head gear away from their ears. Neither the village team nor the team assigned to the orphanage had seen the second Mercedes. That meant it was somewhere between the orphanage and the village. Mac ordered both teams to start moving toward each other on foot. They would locate whoever was in the Mercedes in an inescapable squeeze and, more important, identify who he was and what he was up to.

Mac felt a quiet sense of relief. Knowing who the players were and having them spread out like this made capturing them alive a hell of a lot easier.

I may not need the hellfire drones after all, Mac thought, vaguely disappointed.

What worried him most now was that Ian and the Americans were chatting politely with an unpredictable killer holding a glass of pálinka in one hand and the fate of the world in the other.

Chapter 71

THE CHURCHYARD

With a fierce mixture of emotions, Nazir watched Amir's Mercedes move up the drive toward the door of the orphanage. He knew he couldn't intervene, that he had no choice but to watch and wait as Amir's plan to get inside the orphanage using the Americans unfolded. Still, it was difficult to leave the couple's fate to . . . well, fate. Nazir's best opportunity would come later.

As Al-Zawahiri had dictated, this was to be a quiet, covert mission. His orders to Amir had been "no scene or carnage." It was supposed to be a simple elimination of the girl. But now, having added in a kidnapping and ransom, Amir had escalated this into a much more complicated scenario.

And what really troubled Nazir was the thought of what would happen after the mission was completed. Undoubtedly, the Americans would be killed. Amir would not leave any witnesses, no matter what he had promised Al-Zawahiri or Nazir.

Nazir backed his sedan out of the main entrance and back onto the road. The van followed close behind. Nazir had studied the layout of the property using Google Earth and knew that less than a kilometer back toward the village was a smaller, less obvious turnoff that would bring them in at the back of the property, closer to the chapel.

A moment later, Nazir pulled over on the main road long enough to wave the van forward.

The van pulled ahead and took the turnoff toward the front of the chapel. Once the van had rolled to a stop, two men climbed out, carrying sniper rifles, and positioned themselves within range of the front door of the main building.

In the meantime, Nazir drove the Mercedes a kilometer or so further down the main road and turned off in a wooded area, parking his car deep in the foliage under the trees.

He quietly climbed out, grabbed a Dragunov rifle and some ammunition from a case under a blanket in the back seat, then quietly clicked the door shut. He stopped briefly to make sure the .22 pistol and silencer were both still inside the holster under his jacket. He crouched down and moved slowly through the trees so that no one would see him from the road. As he got closer to the property, he scanned the buildings and rooflines for any possible security cameras. From what he could see, the property seemed to be unsecured.

Still, he continued to take precautions, moving at an angle to the compound until he reached a point near the chapel where he had a clear view of the yard. Beyond the yard, he could see Amir's two snipers from the van.

Nazir crouched under a large group of overgrown trees and bushes and began slowing his breath and quieting his mind. He had made his decision regarding the showdown he knew would come with Amir. But first, he needed to eliminate Amir's two advantages.

The two men had followed Nazir's instructions perfectly. They were exactly where he needed them to be.

Nazir quietly raised his rifle, training the powerful scope on the first of Amir's men. Both of them were wearing earbuds, linked to Amir's radio. Nazir was glad for the extra level of sound protection. Once he had locked in on the first clueless team member, he began the instinctual routine of holding his breath and slowly feeling the trigger.

Then he pulled.

The silencer did not contain the entire sound of the rifle shot, and Nazir scanned for any response from the other sniper. He had not moved and didn't show any sign of having heard the first shot. The earbuds were Nazir's lucky break.

Again, Nazir went through the ritual of holding his breath and easing the trigger. Just as he was about to take the second shot, he thought he heard a child's voice. He glanced over just in time to see a girl and Bree round the backside of the chapel and head toward the chapel's large double doors, which were directly in front of Nazir.

He was caught off guard, forgetting about the shot he was about to take. He felt the cell phone vibrate in his pocket as he watched Bree climb the short steps to the door of the chapel, holding the girl's hand.

Bree looked sad and almost confused. It was only then that Nazir realized that this must be the chapel described in the journal from which Bree had read aloud that night in Vis.

Nazir watched the woman and child struggle for a minute with the heavy wooden doors before making their way inside.

He wondered what she was thinking and feeling as she walked into the place that had so impacted her son. The second vibration of his cell phone roused him from his thoughts. Maybe it was Amir, looking for the girl. Nazir was running out of time.

Nazir swung his scope around to the second man, who had repositioned himself closer to the chapel.

Nazir's second shot was clean and quick.

He put down the rifle and pulled out his phone.

He looked at the text thread between Amir, the two snipers, and himself.

He winced as he read the words.

"The girl and the American woman are by the chapel."

Before being dropped by Nazir, apparently the second sniper had been able to text Bree's location to Amir.

Amir would be coming for them now.

Nazir would be waiting for him.

He heard the click of a gun behind him.

He began slowly raising his arms behind his head, even before he heard a voice commanding him in Arabic to do so.

Nazir stood from his crouched position and turned slowly to face three men in camouflage. Clearly Western, but not European, he noted. These were American soldiers and probably special ops guys, he thought.

Good. We're all at the table now.

The journey to this moment had seemed like an epic battle, but now Nazir's decision was crystal clear, and his voice reflected his calm.

"I speak English. We don't have much time."

Chapter 72

THE UNRAVELING

"**A**re you telling me this was your sister's child?" Ian asked Amir for the third time. "And that they were traveling through THIS area two years ago when she was abducted?" He emphasized the word "this" with just a hint of suspicion.

"Yes," Amir said impatiently. "I have told you all of this. She was abducted during a visit with relatives to a thermal bath. Someone took her from inside the dressing area."

Ian knew there were baths within an hour of the orphanage. He had to hand it to the guy; it was a plausible story—except that it was an absolute lie. Ian tried to get a fix on Amir. He certainly wasn't like the sophisticated Nazir. This one was a bit rough around the edges.

"Ah, that's right," Ian feigned. "Excuse me for not remembering the particulars of the story. Have you traveled to this area before?"

👑

Ben had spent the last hour in almost complete silence. In part, because of Ian's ongoing questioning of Amir, but also because he knew that he and Bree—and possibly Molly—were going to need to find a way out of this mess. Ben was usually pretty good at figuring out how to solve logistical problems. In fact, Bree used to tease him about being "MacGyver," a character from an old show they used to watch. Ben really could fix, unravel, or create a replacement for just about anything. But it had always been engineering challenges, never anything remotely close to a life-or-death situation like this. He had to keep reminding himself to breathe and focus.

He casually glanced around the room. It offered little in the way of escape options. The single window was small and was not likely to lead anywhere useful. He couldn't see far enough down the hallway to get a clear sense of what it offered. And now apparently, Bree, who usually had the bladder of a large camel, had gone off to use the toilet and was taking her sweet time returning.

Ben thought again about Jayden and the time he had spent here. He tried to picture his son walking down the hallway or painting the fence outside. It seemed so far away from their home and life in LA. He could hear Bree's voice as she read Jayden's journal out loud. His descriptions of the village, this place, and even these people made more sense now.

Ben didn't remember Jayden mentioning Ian, though.

At that moment, Iona returned with more food and drink. She looked so tense that for a second, he wondered if she had been in the kitchen, poisoning the pálinka.

But where the hell is Bree?

Suddenly Amir stopped mid-sentence. "Where is the lady? Where is Mrs. Stanton?" His agitation increased with each question.

Iona seemed to deliberately take her time, setting all the glasses and plates down one at a time before turning to answer. "She has stepped outside for some fresh air."

As if on cue, all three men jumped to their feet. There was an awkward pause as each quietly sized up the others. The sound of a vibrating cell interrupted the silence. Amir reached into his pocket, grabbed the phone, and quickly read the incoming text.

In slow motion, Ben watched Ian reach into the inside of his jacket for what looked like a concealed weapon. He hadn't gotten to it before Amir's gun found the small of Iona's back.

"It's time we take a walk to the chapel."

♔

Ian caught Ben's eye. He wanted to make sure Ben didn't do anything rash.

As Amir began giving orders on how to line up for the march to the chapel, Ian could see that Ben had calmed down a bit and seemed more resolute than anything. Ben led the way out the door, with Ian behind him. Amir pushed Iona behind Ian, and his 9mm Glock, clearly visible now, rode along against her back.

Ian glanced up at the hidden surveillance cameras as they headed out the main entrance. He hoped JD wasn't taking a nap over in the dormitory control room—and that help was on the way.

Chapter 73

THE ROLL CALL

Mac stood watching a monitor as the special forces team moved in toward the roadside perimeter of the property. The four men in camouflage worked their way over to where the two thugs from the van had last been seen. As Mac was getting ready to direct their actions, one of the officers operating another surveillance monitor interrupted.

"Sir, we have more movement." He pointed to his screen in time for both of them to watch Bree and Molly struggling with the door of the church. It was more than Mac could take. He ripped at the collar hanging half off his neck and threw it onto the floor.

"What the fuck are they doing over there?" He watched as the two made it safely into the chapel, the heavy doors slamming shut behind them. They were supposed to head straight to the dormitory, and now the kid he was supposed to protect was out taking a Sunday stroll. What was going on?

Before he could answer his own questions, his team on the ground broke their radio silence.

"We've got a problem down here. Over."

Mac teed up his mic. "What is it? Over."

"We've got a couple of dead targets. Over." The soldier's inflection hovered between a question and statement.

"Say again?" Mac yelled into the mic.

"We've got two dead targets, sir. Both head shots, but we have not discharged our weapons, per your orders. Over."

Mac moved in to get a closer look on the computer monitor. He could see the two bodies, one slumped against the far corner of the dormitory and the other near the dining hall. He guessed they were probably about a hundred feet apart.

For a moment, he wondered if he had just led the entire group into some kind of elaborate trap. Was this another orchestrated attack? How was he supposed to protect these unarmed innocents when they were busy wandering around the grounds, mixing it up with the terrorists who, apparently, were now shooting each other? He was about to pull his team back when Ted, studying another monitor, interrupted his thoughts.

"Sir, I have some movement on this screen."

Mac told the soldiers to stay alert and hold for further instructions and then looked over to where the officer was pointing. It was difficult, but in the darkest part of the shadows under a group of trees, he could see what looked like a man crouched down. His first thought was that this must be the missing guy from the Mercedes.

The two officers monitoring the cameras and satellite footage confirmed that there was no sign of any other visitors in the area. That could only mean that for some unknown reason, this guy, whoever he was, had apparently taken out his own men.

"Okay, team. Listen up. Back out and leave the area. Repeat, do not move those bodies. Make sure it's a clean exit. Once out near the road, head north about three hundred feet and come in toward the chapel. There is a third target, in those trees near the back perimeter. Do not fire. Repeat, do not fire unless defending. Use caution. Package is armed and obviously dangerous. I want this one delivered! Over."

"Copy, that!" one of the special ops team members responded.

Mac watched as they backed slowly away from the dead men.

Mac continued watching the shadow in the trees. The man hidden there remained completely still. He had not done the one thing Mac was pretty sure he was there to do, which was eliminate the girl.

Why not?

Who was this guy and why had he taken out his own men? He had clearly traveled with them. Was he the missing Nazir, who both Mac and Ian had assumed would be at the door with the couple? If so, as Al-Zawahiri's high-ranking Washington mole, he should have been leading this team, not slinking around the trees, killing his teammates. Had there been some power struggle, some coup? And what was he waiting for now? A goddamned marching band?

None of these latest developments made any sense, and the answers continued to elude him. But what Mac knew for sure was that he wasn't going to get the luxury of those answers before he would need to make some pretty tough calls. He thought about looking around for the collar he had thrown, but then he let the thought pass—religion in the face of murderers with guns did not begin to even the playing field for him.

While he was congratulating himself on this epiphany, Sam, the officer at monitor one interrupted his thoughts once again.

"Sir, you are going to need to see this right away!" Sam didn't attempt to hide his distress.

Mac bent closer to the monitor, not believing what he was seeing. Walking out the door of the main building in single file were all the guests of Ian's parlor pálinka party. The part that kept it from being truly comical was the Glock gleaming in Amir's hand and buried in Iona's back.

"This is not looking good, my friend!" Mac said, as if Ian could hear him. "How the hell did this happen?" He threw up his hands and shook his head in total disbelief. "*And* they're headed straight for the chapel!" he bellowed. "How the hell can I drop the mother of all bombs on a chapel full of people I was sent here to protect?!"

The room was silent as the officers feigned intense attention to their duties.

"Where are we with the spook in the shadows?" Mac shouted.

More silence greeted him.

Just as Mac was ready to orbit a nearby planet, the radio broke in with the first good news he had received that day.

"Sir, we have made contact. Package has surrendered. We are delivering. Over."

Chapter 74

THE OK CORRAL

M olly was chomping at the bit to launch into the story she had waited half of her life to tell. She started at the very beginning, with Jayden's arrival.

Looking at her beautiful face and trusting smile, Bree was torn between letting Molly tell the story at her own pace or encouraging her to get to the critical parts. Bree suspected there wasn't much time before Amir came looking for them.

In the end, the choice was taken out of her hands. The doors of the chapel crashed open with such ferocity, both Bree and Molly jumped and turned in unison at the sound.

Ben was the first through the door, followed by Ian, and then Iona. Bree felt a flood of relief until she saw Amir—and the gun against Iona's back.

Iona stumbled, unable to tear her eyes away from Molly.

Suddenly, the whole picture became much clearer to Bree. She remembered the quickly whispered warning from Iona about the murdered children. Instinctively, Bree turned to reach out for Molly when Molly dived toward her, wrapping both of her arms tightly around Bree's waist. Bree could hear and feel the pounding of the little heart against her side. Or maybe it was her own heart; she couldn't really tell. She did know that she had never been so terrified. All she could think about was this monster, and silently vowed that this child-killing animal was not going to hurt Molly, ever.

Ben had been pushed along the aisle until he was standing next to Bree and Molly. He put his arm around both of them and whispered, "It's okay. Just stay calm."

♕

Standing near Iona, Ian caught Ben's eye again and mouthed the word "camera." He watched Ben wait a few seconds, then covertly scan the ceiling and walls. Ian could tell from his blank expression that Ben hadn't seen anything. But he could see a certain resolve in Ben's eyes. Ben would be helpful, when the opportunity arose.

Ian was fairly confident that Amir had no idea who he was, or about the gun hidden in his jacket. It certainly gave him an advantage, but he also knew that, realistically, his small-caliber pistol against Amir's Glock meant he would only get one shot. There were also a lot of unarmed innocent people in a confined space, or as JD liked to say, unfortunate collateral.

Thinking of JD now, Ian hoped his friend had been watching all of this and was now circling the wagons.

Turning to see how Iona was holding up, Ian was as proud of her stoicism as he had ever been of anyone in any situation. She looked like the winged Nike coming down the aisle. He could see every struggle and trauma she'd experienced running this orphanage etched in her face, as if they were all gathering together inside of her, to forge the courage this moment required. *My God*, he thought. *She really is magnificent.* He mouthed the words "I love you" to her, but wasn't sure if she'd caught them or not.

♕

Iona would have laughed had she known that Ian was likening her to a Greek goddess. She felt as wobbly as a wet noodle as she felt another shove from behind, wishing that she had sipped a pálinka shot or two herself.

The feel of the metal against her back and the sound of Amir breathing behind her filled her with absolute terror. To keep from fainting dead away, she kept thinking about Jayden and how joyful he would be to know that his parents had made their way to the orphanage. However this ended, little Molly would finally know that she had not been willingly abandoned once again. More important, she would know that Jayden had told their story—Molly's story—and that it was a story of love. Love, with a capital *L*, that had reached halfway across the world.

♕

Amir shoved Iona over to the group and pulled out another gun, setting it on the seat of the pew next to where he was standing.

He took a second to glance around the chapel. It was an environment that was truly alien to anything in his own religious training. He motioned to the Christ figure hanging on the cross near the front altar and sneered.

"So, this is the god that was supposed to save you, the pathetic infidels? How is he doing so far?" His laugh echoed through the high ceilings.

♕

Bree could feel Molly stifle a sob against her side. She reached down and began gently rubbing Molly's shoulder and arm, smoothing the mound of wild curls across her forehead and whispering to her like a mother.

"Shhhh . . . .It's okay, sweetie. We are okay. I'm here with you. Always." Then Bree caught her own sob. She was comforting Molly like a mother, promising to always be there for her. But was it a promise she could keep? She'd made that promise once before, to Jayden. And that promise had been obliterated by another evil man with a gun—another random spin of the dial of fate.

Oh, Jayden, my lovely son.

Now the tears were running freely. There was no stopping the grief. Rather than healing her, this place, and especially this chapel building, were opening up the deepest parts of her soul. As much as she tried to be strong in the moment, she could not get the cork back into the bottle of her emotions.

Ben watched a menagerie of emotions play out across Bree's face. Whatever she was experiencing in this moment, it looked like it was cracking her wide-open. At the same time he pulled her closer to comfort her, he was also aware of the serious turn in the dynamics of the situation.

Amir was not here to convert to Christianity. He was here for Molly, although Ben still had no idea why.

While Amir was busy pacing and taunting Ian and Iona, Ben took the opportunity to stealthily pass a message to Bree. "Honey," he whispered, "I'm here now, and I can't explain, but I think we are going to be okay. Whatever happens, the two of you need to dive for cover under a pew. Got it?" He felt encouraged when Bree managed a slight nod, but he could also tell she was still on shaky ground.

Ben turned back to their captor, who was still pacing and pontificating in the aisle near them, like some kind of maniac. Ben had no idea what was going to go down, but he could tell that Amir was getting increasingly agitated. Now he was ranting loudly about Allah, then damning some cousin of his, then declaring his allegiance to some Al-Zawahiri character. He yelled in English and then in Arabic and then again in English. It was a bizarre, psychological unraveling to witness.

Ben glanced over at Ian, who seemed to be casually watching the scene unfold, but whose body language resembled a coiled spring. Ben wasn't sure if this was a good sign or not. To him, it all felt like danger.

Chapter 75

THE SURRENDER

Mac's men cuffed Nazir's hands behind his back and shoved him into the back of a dark-windowed black SUV. There were at least two automatic weapons trained on him. Nazir hoped he would be taken to speak to someone in charge quickly. Otherwise, his surrender would be wasted.

He spent the quick ride trying to figure out the shortest version of the truth he could provide, and still have time to save Bree and the child. As the SUV pulled up to the dormitory, the armed men shoved Nazir out of the vehicle. Precious minutes ticked by as they guided him up a flight of stairs, then shuffled him down a hallway to his date with destiny.

The irony of this decision and this moment in his life was not lost on him. He knew that his father would have fierce disdain for Nazir for embracing the ideas of Christianity. However, he couldn't help but think that, in a small, hidden part of Al-Zawahiri's heart, he would be proud that Nazir had finally found something about which he felt fiercely passionate. Something worth taking up the mantle of his destiny.

Love.

Love from God.

Love for a woman.

These were what he believed in now. These would be what compelled him to lay down his life to his destiny as a "king."

Nazir was escorted into a room next to the command center and pushed into a folding metal chair.

Mac, holding a file on Nazir, was waiting for him in the dormitory. When his men pushed him into the room and into a chair, Mac didn't hesitate.

"Mr. Nazir, I presume?" Mac stepped forward and stood over him, looking like a cross between Warren Buffett and the late Billy Graham.

"I am Nazir. Son of your most hated and wanted enemy, Al-Zawahiri."

Mac had been surprised by this guy's immediate surrender and now was equally shocked by this admission.

He's the goddamned son? How did we miss that one? Mac chided himself, tossing the useless file in a nearby trash can.

"What brings you to the lovely area of Transylvania, Mr. Nazir?"

"I'm afraid we don't have much time for small talk. My cousin, Amir, has come here to eliminate the child. Her body contains a remnant of a bioagent my father tested on this orphanage a few months ago. Something he doesn't want known by your intelligence agencies."

"We know this already. And we know about the plan to unleash it onto some unsuspecting population. I want to know the target and the time frame."

"I can provide you with details in good time. But first, we must save the people who are in the chapel with Amir. He is planning to do more than just kill the child. For some reason, even though my father instructed him to do otherwise, he has decided to create an act of carnage here in order to bring honor to our cause and to my father."

"Why are you telling me this?" Mac asked, skeptically. "Why should I trust you?" At the same time, he had the sense that there was something strangely noble about this guy.

"Let's just say I have had a change of heart," Nazir said gently.

Mac pondered that for a moment. "I agree about saving the folks in the church, but you know I can't leave here until I have some specifics about the planned attack. My best friend is in that church. And I'm still not moving—until I hear about the target."

"My father's men are in the process of hijacking shipments of the Zika vaccination developed by your CDC for the purpose of replacing the vaccine with the bioagent. The shipments going to Houston, Atlanta, and Miami have been subverted, and some have already been replaced. The bioagent was never meant to be a mass-killing mechanism, but a powerful negotiating tool. Your government officials are not going to know which cities are affected. My father is going to use the fear this generates to extract a large sum of both money and power from your congress."

Mac wasn't quite sure what he'd expected to hear, but this one was a stunner. *Of course! Kill a few people to prove how lethal it is, and then leverage the hell out of the remaining 350 million people. Hell, why stop there? Why not the whole world?*

Mac excused himself and stepped back into the command center.

"Did you get that on tape?" he asked.

The officers at the monitors and around the room nodded in stunned silence.

"Send it to the assistant director in Langley right now. Make sure it's encrypted and sent as highest priority. "

Mac turned the radio up and issued his last command. "This is Mac. Surround that goddamn chapel and wait for me. I'm on my way. Over." He unsnapped the safety on his Glock in his shoulder holster, then pulled on his jacket.

Then he reached down to the floor, picked up his clerical collar, and buttoned it back in place. What he had just heard in the other room was so diabolical, so evil, that he decided he might as well invite the God of the universe to the game. After all, He'd created these shitheads.

Chapter 76

THE "COME TO JESUS" MEETING

Amir continued to pace up and down the aisle, the effects of the pálinka now loosening his tentative grip on his thoughts and emotions. The hostages found themselves flinching in unison as Amir gestured with his loaded gun, ranting about Allah, Nazir, and his uncle.

When Ian looked at Ben, he could see the American was coming to the end of his tolerance for being bullied—not unexpected considering Ben was a man used to being in charge. Ian was thinking about how to end this standoff with Amir, but in all honesty, he did not want to shoot someone in front of Molly.

Most important, Ian didn't want to risk Amir getting a lucky shot off and injuring—or, God forbid, killing—one of the hostages. Ian kept looking around for alternatives. It was during one of these visual forays that he thought he saw a shadow move in the upper balcony. He checked again a minute later but didn't see anything. He hoped it was JD closing in with the special forces team.

It was during another loud rant, this time in Arabic, that the door swung open and another Arab man walked into the church. Amir swung around and fired off a warning shot, narrowly missing the man and hitting the wall behind him.

The group was silent, as the echo of the Glock's powerful shot rebounded up through the high ceilings and back down to the marble floor.

👑

"Are you fucking crazy, Amir?" Nazir yelled at his cousin. "You could have killed me!" He tried to show annoyance, not the fear he felt in the face of his cousin's obviously irrational state.

"Where have you been?" Amir asked accusingly. "I have been dealing with all of this myself. I must shoot the girl so that we can get out of here. I'm tired of this now." He delivered the last part in Arabic. Nazir could see that something had clearly snapped within Amir.

"Let's not do that. She will not harm anyone. The plan is in motion. The vaccines have been delivered. We can leave now and we will be remembered as courageous men. Men with honor." Nazir spoke with authority, hoping that he might get through to Amir using reason. But that would be a miracle, and it was not to be.

Amir shook his head at the suggestion of walking away. Nazir knew his cousin felt obligated to show his ability to complete the jihad as *he* had declared. Since Nazir had, from Amir's perspective, shown a lack of courage, Amir would feel that he was now forced to take action. Nazir shook his head in disgust at his cousin's fatal irrationality.

♛

Ben had been watching the interaction between the two Arabs with a mixture of alarm and disgust. From the little that was delivered in English, it seemed these two men were not on the same page. They were arguing like kids on a school playground. This might be his captive party's only chance. He tried to catch Ian's attention to see if he was going to make a move, but the space between the two of them was blocked by Iona and Bree. He was not able to connect with him. He felt a rage build within him that he could barely contain. All he could think about was that these bastards were not going to take his family down without a fight. He had experienced that when he'd lost Jayden on a freeway, and he was not going to experience it now, in the middle of a church in Transylvania.

Suddenly, in one fluid motion, Amir spun away from Nazir and fired a series of shots in the direction of Molly. At the same time, Ben launched himself into the air toward Bree and Molly. His only thought was that he needed to protect them.

Nazir watched everything in slow motion. He would not hear the gunshots or the screams, or see the chaos of bodies flying or people dying. He would only remember that he had looked once more directly into Bree Stanton's eyes, and what he saw there was worth everything it would cost him.

Several bullets hit Ben's body. Ian winced at the realization.

More shots rang out.

Both Arabs jerked as their bodies, briefly suspended in space, absorbed the impact of bullets raining down from above.

Near the altar, wood splintered as the remaining bullets found a mark.

Ian pushed Iona to the floor between two rows of pews. Bree and Molly were also crouched down on the floor in between pews. Bree had flung her own body over Molly's.

After what seemed like an eternity, both Nazir and Amir fell to the floor.

Silence fell over the chapel. No one moved, paralyzed with shock and disbelief.

It took a few seconds before Ian was on his feet, checking Iona, who was shaken but otherwise unharmed. He glanced over to confirm that their captor and his partner were dead before moving toward Bree and Molly. He could hear Molly crying, and it was so pitiful that his heart ached in response. It was then that he saw Bree kneeling by Ben, who was lying in a growing pool of his own blood. She was trying to get him to open his eyes, but it looked like it was too late.

Another horrendous loss for this family, Ian thought.

By this time, Mac and the special forces team had moved down from the balcony. As Mac approached, Ian said dryly, "I was beginning to think you weren't going to show. What took you so long? Stop and do some shopping first?"

Before his friend could respond, a voice called out, "We've got a live one, here, sir!"

Ian turned to see one of the team members doing compressions on Ben's chest. Bree was sitting on her knees near Ben's head, caressing his forehead and whispering, "I love you" over and over again.

The military helicopter landed outside the chapel within twelve minutes. As the medics wheeled her husband to the chopper, Bree followed behind, Ian and Iona supporting her on either side. Before climbing into the chopper behind Ben, Bree turned to Molly. "I need to go with Jayden's father. But I will be back. I promise. Do you believe me?"

Molly nodded, her face streaked with tears. "I love you, Molly. We're going to get through this together."

Bree kissed the little girl and gave her a quick hug. She wasn't sure how much if any of what she said had gotten through the shock and trauma Molly was experiencing.

Iona reached for Bree's arm and Bree turned to face her. "I will be praying for you and for your husband," the older woman said.

Bree squeezed Iona's hand and nodded. She was too close to tears to speak. She took one look back at the bloody horror and the two men lying dead on the floor; then her eyes fell on the crucifix. She felt overwhelmed at what this chapel had brought into her family's life, and the pivotal role it had played in her own life. It seemed incredible that Jayden had found such peace, purpose, and joy in a place now marred by so much evil and carnage. She had no idea what to think about this juxtaposition or how she could possibly fit any kind of a God into this scenario.

With that thought, she climbed aboard the waiting helicopter.

Ben had not regained consciousness. Bree watched the faces of the medics working on her husband, seeking any assurance that Ben was still alive. One of the medics nodded at Bree and said, "We're doing everything we can, Mrs. Stanton," but the words weren't reflected in his eyes, and Bree sensed little hope. She looked back down at Ben. Would those bright-blue eyes of his ever look at her again?

She and Ben had started this journey with such high hopes, thinking they could survive and maybe even thrive after Jayden's death. They had worked so hard, and it had taken so much to get this far.

Now it all felt impossible. And worse . . . irreparable.

Chapter 77

THE DEBRIEFING

"Let me take a look at you two brave girls."

Ian forced a reassuring smile as he knelt to look Molly in the eyes. He smoothed her wild, dark curls as he looked her quickly over for physical injuries. He knew the emotional ones weren't even registering yet.

Once he was confident she had not been hurt, he stood and put his arms around Iona, letting her briefly lay her head on his shoulder.

He whispered, "Have you been injured, love?" He could feel her body tremble, still dealing with everything she had just experienced.

"No . . . I'm actually fine."

"You, my dear Iona, are my new heroine—a Joan of Arc in every way. We owe the success of this operation to you. You also have my heart, but we will discuss that later. In the meantime, why don't you and Molly go back to the orphanage and have a cup of tea? I'll be along as soon as we finish here." He motioned both of them toward the back exit.

Iona was grateful for Ian's wisdom as she took Molly out of the chapel through the back door so she would not have to walk by the dead bodies or see any more blood. Molly had not let go of Iona's hand since she had clasped it, and she was still trembling.

But Iona was simply grateful that Molly was alive. She knew that, with time, there was hope of recovery and life again. Maybe not in this moment, but eventually. If there was one thing she had learned in all the years running the orphanage, it was that children are very resilient. Love and time do bring eventual healing.

She couldn't help wondering if the Stantons would be so lucky. Mr. Stanton had clearly lost much blood and been gravely injured. She wondered if Mrs. Stanton, Bree to her now, could possibly survive another loss. Iona said a silent prayer for them both.

The impulse to pray made her think of their beloved Jayden. He had not only taught her to pray, but also to believe in the power of prayer. She had learned that those were two entirely different things.

He had said to her once, "Most people send up a prayer like a balloon, hoping that if it goes high enough and is pretty enough, it will eventually bump into something good. Iona, prayer is more like writing a thank-you letter to God for a gift you have already received. Prayer has power in it already, because God has promised to answer. If He doesn't, then He isn't God. Once you know that, then it's more like having Luke Skywalker's light saber with a lifetime battery."

She chuckled at the memory of Jayden trying to explain the *Star Wars* trilogy and its characters, complete with some acting and even humming of the movie's theme song. He had been quite a young man.

One day, when Molly felt a bit better, Iona would remind her about the courage of Princess Leia. Molly would like that.

♛

Meanwhile, Ian, Mac, and the team were working the crime scene inside the chapel. Mac spent some time getting Ian up to speed on what Nazir had shared, and how getting that time-sensitive information off to Langley had been the reason for their late arrival.

Ian marveled at how diabolical the whole plan had been, and how close the jihadists had come to implementing it.

"It was the damnedest thing, Ian. Nazir literally took out Amir's men, surrendered, and then spilled the beans on everything we needed to know. This was Al-Zawahiri's son! What are the odds?!" Mac couldn't get over the windfall it represented.

"Do you know why he did it?" Ian asked.

"I have no idea. It makes no sense given the powerful position he stood to inherit. But I do know that after we brought him in he offered up the coordinates for the Yemen compound and gave us details about the bio agent. So something was going on. We'll probably never know for sure." Mac glanced down at his watch. "But here's something we *do* know: The US government is sending a special gift basket to Mr. Al-Zawahiri right about now!"

Ian couldn't get over what his old friend looked like, with the soiled clerical collar hanging half on, shirt untucked. But it was the fire in his eyes, that look of being fully alive, that pleased Ian the most. JD had bagged a big fish and, in the process, stepped out of the small, self-imposed world he had inhabited for so long. Good on him.

Ian patted Mac's shoulder and congratulated him on a job well done. But he still couldn't resist a friendly jab.

"Oh, bloody hell, JD. Now your head will be too big for your knickers! More important, how are we going to go back to fishing after all this excitement? Stirs up the old flames a bit, doesn't it?"

Ian and Mac looked at each other, reflecting on the richness of thirty years of friendship, a deep mutual respect, and an even deeper desire to open an expensive bottle of scotch—together.

Chapter 78

THE HEALING

Ben awoke with the sense that he was swimming up from the bottom of some ocean. He felt exhausted, which made him think he'd been swimming for a long time. Looking up, he could see the surface and light—he just couldn't reach it.

Had he fallen overboard from a ship? He wasn't sure. He kept working hard, stroke after stroke, kicking and reaching for the light. But he felt stuck, as if he were tied to an anchor, swimming hard but never getting any closer.

At times he would tire out and give up, spreading his arms and legs like a parachute jumper, letting his body float and the cool, dark water pull him deeper and away from the light.

It felt like a dance, or some elaborate game of tug-of-war, only he could never see the other team.

When he gave up for the very last time, his body descended into the darkest and coldest water yet. This was the end, and Ben knew it.

That's when he saw his son. He couldn't remember his name at first, but he knew in his heart that the young man swimming toward him was his son. So handsome and strong.

The young man swam up beside Ben and squeezed his arm.

"I love you," he said.

The touch and the words made Ben cry, and the pain was overwhelming.

"Dad, it's Jayden."

"I know. I know!" was all Ben could croak out, his throat dry and parched even though he was floating far beneath the surface of the ocean.

"Dad, remember when you taught me how to swim? Who would have thought I'd be your swim coach one day, but here I am. And Dad, you need to try swimming some more."

"I don't want to, Jayden. I think I'm going to rest now." Ben spread his arms a bit wider as if to prove his point.

"No, Dad. That's not the plan. I wish it were, because I miss you and Mom a lot, but it isn't. You still have things to accomplish here. Important things. And you can't do them if you don't start swimming!" Jayden said this with a bit more emphasis.

It worked. Ben looked up at the barely visible light and started kicking.

"That's it, Dad. You are doing great. Mind if I swim along with you for a while, and we can catch up a bit?"

Ben was so out of breath from the exertion of swimming that he could only manage to nod.

"Great. You keep swimming and I'll go first. I'm going to start with the big question, Dad, because I think the answer will help you swim better. Here it is. Why did I leave? That's the one, right?"

Ben stopped mid-stroke, his face a contorted mixture of pain and fear.

"I know, Dad. We think we want to know the answers, but we are actually afraid of the answers, right? I was afraid too. Let me make this clear: I didn't want to leave you and mom and the life I had with you. But we ALL leave. It's just a matter of timing."

"Timing?" Ben asked, for the first time wondering why he was able to talk underwater.

"I'll tell you more, but let's keep moving."

Ben began kicking weakly. His heart still wasn't in it.

"If I hadn't left when I did," Jayden explained, "you and Mom wouldn't have come to the orphanage—and it was necessary for you to come. Just think about Molly."

Ben pictured a little girl with wild, dark curls. He remembered.

"And now it's necessary for you to understand that right now you are swimming for your life. But you have to decide how bad you want to live."

Ben's strokes were becoming a bit smoother and stronger.

"Dad, five years ago in the chapel, I saw all that would happen after my death. I knew you and Mom would come—and that your lives would be changed—if I had the courage to leave. God asked me to have the courage."

They swam in silence as Ben attempted to absorb Jayden's words.

After a few moments Ben asked, "What about your mother? How could any God do this to your mother, Jayden? You have no idea how she has suffered."

"This is the most important piece, Dad. We suffer because we think leaving is the end. A bad thing. Leaving is not a bad thing if you look at the bigger picture. Look at how much you and mom have changed, your priorities, your view of the suffering of others. Look where you are right now! At an orphanage in Romania, not a social event in Beverly Hills. My death moved you to look for more purpose, more meaning—and that search has led you to new choices."

Ben wanted to say, "No shit!" but thought better of it in case this was some kind of celestial entrance exam.

"And these new choices will in turn lead you to impact many people's lives because of your suffering, not in spite of it." Jayden's voice was full of passion with this last sentence.

Ben nodded. He was overwhelmed by his son's wisdom and the truth. Jayden's words felt like a searing hot knife slicing through the bitterness Ben had held in his heart for so long over his son's death. Ben felt his resentment and anger toward God begin to melt.

"I'm okay, Dad. Better than okay. I'm exactly where I need to be: within the will of God. And so are you! Keep swimming and know that God's love and mine will power you to the top. Give Mom a big hug from me."

And with those words, Jayden was gone. Again. But this time, Ben didn't feel the rage and despondency he'd felt the first time Jayden had left. This time, Ben felt free.

Chapter 79

THE AWAKENING

For days, Bree's life had consisted of little but waiting.

First, in the helicopter and transport plane, then in the waiting rooms of the trauma and surgical units, and now by Ben's side in the ICU unit at the Landstuhl Regional Medical Center in Germany.

She took what must have been her thousandth slow, calming breath. The day after the shooting, Ben had slipped in and out of cardiac arrest for hours. Bree sat holding his hand and talking to him through most of that day and into the evening. Every time he would code, a trauma team would rush in and work on him, sometimes almost to the point of losing him, but somehow, his heart would regain a sinus rhythm, and a few hours of calm would follow. Eventually, he'd have another cardiac event, and the drama would be repeated.

Ben had also gone through emergency surgery to remove two of the three bullets, repair tissue, and stop internal bleeding. Once again, the surgeons had struggled to keep him alive while dealing with his grave injuries.

Ben had yet to regain consciousness, although once he spontaneously said, "I know. I know!" as if he could hear every word she whispered to him.

The third day after the shooting, the thoracic surgeon arrived, looked sternly at Ben's chart before slapping it shut, then turned to Bree.

"Mrs. Stanton, I wanted to wait a bit longer, but we can't. Your husband's heart just isn't functioning well enough, and he continues to lose ground. I need to go in and attempt to repair some arterial damage caused by the bullet still lodged near his heart. I'm not going to beat around the bush here; this will be a tough one!"

Nothing could have prepared Bree for the worried look on the surgeon's face.

She nodded slowly, her eyes misting over for the hundredth time.

The nurses took Ben away and relegated Bree to yet another waiting room. As she looked around the nearly empty waiting room, she couldn't help but experience a feeling of déjà vu from the time, two and a half years ago, when Jayden had lost his battle for life on another operating table, in a hospital halfway across the world.

Back then, she had no thoughts of God or faith or anything that could help her. She had held on to Ben's arm that night, hoping he would be the savior, the guy who could make it all better—he and the surgeons. Only, as smart and capable as they were, they hadn't been able to stop death from arriving at her doorstep.

Once she and Ben had kissed Jayden, said their final goodbyes, and walked out of the hospital into the night, she had felt terrifyingly vulnerable. She kept thinking, *If everything is random, and it appears that it is, then I will never be safe again.* The weight of that knowledge had buried itself in her heart.

At least until the night in Vis, when she had vicariously experienced Jayden's journey with God. Jayden's words and that story had reached down into the deepest levels of her heartache and terror. Somehow, his words had turned into a light that shined into the blackness of her grief, lifting the weight of fear from her heart, and replacing it with hope. And that hope had given her courage.

Now, Bree was once again in a waiting room with no idea of the outcome. But this time, she had all that she had experienced since Jayden's death to keep her company. She had the journal. She had the mysterious sense of God's presence. She had hope buried deep where once there had only been fear. She had courage, strangely born from suffering.

She didn't have the answers to every "why" question. Certainly not. But she had received peace. Trust. Love. None of those things could be taken from her by death. She knew that now.

As she reflected on these things, she could feel a warmth radiating from her heart and out into her body. With it was the quiet, dawning realization that it was time to let Jayden's memory move into its rightful place in her life. Not to leave her, but to motivate her to use that heartache to help others. The big question for her was no longer *Why?* but *How?* She remembered Ben talking about the word "thrive." What did that even mean? What *could* that mean?

As Bree sat and waited for a report on Ben's surgery, her thoughts returned again and again to the orphanage. And to Molly in particular. Bree felt an inexplicable bond with that girl. Was it just because both Bree and Molly had loved Jayden? She didn't think so. Jayden may have been the catalyst that brought them together, but Bree had loved Molly from their first meeting. Bree finally had to acknowledge that whatever she and Ben did with their lives after this, she wanted Molly to be a part of it.

She spent the remainder of the night trying to make sense of what that would mean for their lives. Could they adopt her? If so, would that mean living in Romania? The US? How would all of this affect Iona? What if Molly didn't want to be with Ben and Bree as much as Bree wanted to be with her?

Ben survived the heart surgery that night and continued to beat the odds. Almost immediately, his coloring improved, and the pain etched across his face seemed to ease. In fact, he appeared to be peaceful and almost happy. His only stumbling block was that he had yet to regain consciousness. At times, Bree thought she caught his eyes opening, but he still seemed a long way away from his hospital bed.

One morning, two weeks after the shooting, Bree looked up from the paperwork she was reviewing for his long-term care. Through the glass wall of Ben's room, Bree was shocked to see Ian, Iona, and Molly standing at the ICU nurses' station.

Molly looked up and spotted Bree.

Before anyone could stop her, the child had squeezed past the RN in charge and run into Ben's room. She ran right up to Bree, wrapping her arms around Bree's middle with such force that she almost knocked them both over.

"Mama B! We've come to cheer you up and to check on Papa B," Molly exclaimed, breathless and flushed with excitement.

Bree didn't know exactly how to respond. That didn't seem to faze Molly, who just kept hugging Bree's waist, even when she turned to greet Ian and Iona.

"Thank you so much for coming," Bree said, and the relief in her voice was nearly palpable. "It's nice to have people here I'm familiar with. We've been surrounded by strangers for two weeks now."

"Bree, sorry . . . it took a while to wrap everything up in Romania and to make sure substitute staffing was established before we left," Ian explained, stepping forward to shake her hand.

Bree, however, ignored his outstretched hand and launched herself into his arms, tears spilling down her face. She sensed Ian hesitate before patting her on the back. She looked over his shoulder at Iona.

Smiling, Iona gently pushed Ian aside to wrap her arms around both Bree and Molly.

"There, there, dears," Iona said in her broken English.. "We are all right to have a little cry. It's been . . . dificil . . . um, difficult, but we will all be well now."

Just then, a nurse came in and gently ushered the group out to a small, quiet waiting room, where Iona directed Bree to a nearby chair.

"Ben has had three major operations," Bree said weakly, "one on his heart and two for internal bleeding."

"Is he awake?" Ian asked.

"No. He has not regained consciousness. The irony is that he was not struck in the head by a bullet. The head injury that is causing this is a mystery. The doctors are not sure if it is a clot, a stroke, or if he has a closed head injury from falling." Bree sighed, ready to think of something else. "But tell me about what happened after the shooting."

"Ian, why don't you fill Bree in while Molly and I visit the cafeteria? I think Molly is starving, right, little one?"

Ian waited until Molly and Iona had left before providing some of the more troubling details regarding their Arab captors.

"Those bloody bastards were intent on getting rid of all of us and then blackmailing the world with their little cocktail of evil. If not for Iona's courageous report and JD's bloodhound instincts, no telling what would have happened."

"JD?" Bree echoed?

"Er, 'Pastor Mac,'" Ian clarified. He cleared his throat. "And then there's the part about the Bergmans."

"Oh my God! The Bergmans! I just learned a few days ago about the fire at our property and their deaths. It's shocking. What a tragic accident."

"Bree, I know you were told the fire was an accident, but that's not quite true. Turns out your property swap mates were actually working with the jihadists involved in your kidnapping. They really never stood a chance. Unfortunately, we weren't able to make the connection with your story until it was too late to help them."

Dazed, Bree shook her head. "Oh my God. I didn't know."

"Switching properties was their attempt to put the jihadists onto your trail instead of theirs. You were being followed by the Arabs from the moment you landed in Rome. We were watching them watch you. That's how we narrowed the playing field."

After Ian, Iona, and Molly left, Bree recounted the entire dramatic story to Ben, who was still asleep in his coma. As for the coincidental tie to the orphanage and Jayden and their own lives, it was still too mind-blowing to comprehend, so Bree just stopped trying.

She wondered briefly about the man they'd referred to as Nazir and remembered her encounter with him in the lobby of the Hotel Gellert in Budapest. Now she realized why he had acted so strangely. And yet, she remembered looking into his eyes and feeling a strong connection with him. Under different circumstances, she felt there might have been conversations or common ground. After trying to make more sense of it, she decided to let that go as well. She might never know. Instead, she tried to focus on Ben's great progress and her own clarity regarding what she felt called to do.

In the week that followed, Bree, Iona, and Molly settled into a routine of sorts. At least once a day, Iona would sit with Ben so Bree could take Molly for an afternoon walk. The two would often get ice cream, and while they walked, they talked about everything from life in the United States to what they had both loved about Jayden. On one of their outings, Bree bought Molly some coloring books and gel pens so she would have something to do during the long hours spent in Ben's room.

Meanwhile Ian and JD were being called up to help finish the job involving the dead terrorists.

As Molly sat coloring and playing with her iPad, Bree's to-do lists slowly morphed from loose paper to notepads to a binder, complete with tabs. Personalities don't change, after all, she mused; she was still her daddy's overly prepared girl.

Bree wanted to create a nonprofit organization in Jayden's name to bring medical care to orphanages. It was the perfect blend of the things he was most passionate about and somehow, given the deceptive way this had all started with the jihadists' intent, it seemed fitting.

But this project made her feel revitalized, passionate and . . . strangely content. She passed her ideas by Molly and others, and they were all quick to encourage her to keep moving forward.

But first, Bree had to get her man to wake up.

One evening she decided to try reading Jayden's journal to Ben again. She chose a passage where Jayden had written about a memory he had of the three of them on a beach in Hawaii. A memory of Ben and Jayden throwing the football.

It was the same memory Bree had relived on the beach on Vis.

She wondered what had made Jayden remember this experience while halfway across the world in Romania. *Come to think of it,* she thought, *why did I remember it?*

Even now, she could feel the breeze of that memory stirring her heart, moving her from despair to hope.

In the end, that memory had made her feel close to Jayden, helped her remember his precious face, and ultimately had given her the courage to read his journal that night.

"Maybe it will give you courage, too, my precious love."

And with that, she settled down close to Ben's bed and began reading to him.

Chapter 80

I'm so glad I came to this place. It was really on a whim, kind of in reaction to my dad's wanting me to do some boring internship. I really didn't want to spend my summer in some stupid mail room or something.

"What are you going to do for SIX weeks in the middle of nowhere, without the internet, TV and a basketball hoop?" he asked me. I didn't really have a good answer.

What I wanted to say was something like, "Running away from being you . . . or your version of me," but in the end I just hugged him and left. I love my dad, and I don't want to disappoint him. But now I know I'm not going to be a business guy. My heart's not in it.

Something has changed me here. Sure, the chapel and God experience, but also this place and these kids. It's good to know that God loves me, but He showed me that it's worthless if it's not used to make the world better. Like this place. This director has worked her whole life just to get these kids through each day. It's not easy. They need a lot of help. I like helping them. It makes me feel better than anything else I've ever done.

That's how I discovered what I'm going to do. I've decided I want to go back to the States and get some medical training so that I can really make a difference here. Can't wait to tell my parents. Ha-ha! Dad has this thing about Grandpa Stanton, but oh well . . .

I try not to think about leaving here, leaving Jona and Molly. I'm crazy about that kid, and I like helping Jona figure out how to beat this screwed-up orphanage system. They feel like family. Funny, speaking of family, I had a dream last night. It was a memory, really, of a vacation in Hawaii with my family. I'd forgotten about it. The dream was so vivid. I'm still half in it even now.

We are all down on the beach. I can literally see the sunshine as it sparkles off the water and feel the trade winds as they blow across my shoulders. There's this great moment when I just stand looking out at the ocean, letting my toes sink into the warm sand. What a feeling!

Anyway, my dad and I are playing one of our goofy football games, where we throw long, high spirals in an attempt to make each other run like crazy and make zany, impossible catches. After one throw, my dad does this hilarious end zone dance. It's so ridiculous that I can't stop laughing at him. My mom is sitting on a lounge chair, holding up score cards with her rating of our performances, like in the Olympics. It's one of those perfect, perfect memories.

Not sure why I had that dream, especially here, where kids will never have that opportunity, never know what it's like to play a football game on a sandy beach with their parents. I'm homesick for sure, but maybe I'm supposed to do something with this. Maybe, in addition to medicine, I'm supposed to help them find that kind of joy. Love. Family. I'll have to think about some of this once I'm back home. Gosh, I have a ton of stuff to talk to Mom and Dad about, and some of it won't be easy.

But I think I know now that families don't happen by accident. I think God chooses us to be a part of each other's lives.

Sometimes it's easy, and we spend a day in the sunshine, throwing footballs, eating great food, and laughing together.

Other times, it's rough seas. We find ourselves floundering, trying to keep from drowning in whatever storm has found us. Then we need family to swim next to us, to encourage us, and to help us have hope.

My mom and dad are that family for me, and I hope I can someday be that for them as well.

Chapter 81

THE CHOICE

Bree stopped reading and studied Ben to see if he was responding to any of Jayden's thoughts.

Was she imagining things, or did she see Ben's eyelids flutter a bit?

She looked back at the page filled with Jayden's handwriting, and could feel herself being drawn back to that beach scene.

Her son could have been a great writer. The thought broke her heart, and for a moment Bree had to stop and sit with that grief again, letting it wash over her. He could have been so much.

And then it hit her, like striking a match in a dark cave.

But he was so much already. In fact, he had been everything he needed to be, for his own life, for the orphanage and children, and for her and Ben. Jayden hadn't lived a moment less than he needed to. Bree was the one who couldn't accept this.

Gratitude flooded her heart as she realized that her dead son's words were helping her finally acknowledge her greatest fear, that bad things just "happen" without any purpose or meaning. She allowed the thought of being constantly vulnerable to rise to the surface, letting the light of awareness bounce off its frayed edges.

How long have I been a prisoner to this terror?

As she read on, it was also his description of the three of them and the bond they shared as a family that gave her what she needed to finally move forward. Jayden had believed they were together by design—there was no randomness in why the three of them were a family.

If that were true, and she felt to the core of her being that it was, then his death couldn't be random either. Design was design. Faith was an all-or-nothing game. Either everything fit into God's design, or nothing did. At that moment, Bree realized she would need to trust in a plan she might not always fully see or grasp. No matter the circumstances.

Even in these circumstances, she thought, looking at Ben's still form and then around the hospital room, as if seeing these things for the first time.

Tears streamed down Bree's face, but this time she knew they were tears of relief at finally understanding the omniscient and omnipotent nature of God.

Her lack of faith had clouded her view.

I was so determined to see only the dark side of what happened that I missed the design. I couldn't see that everything has been leading me to this moment, to this appreciation for life, to this new purpose—and to Molly.

Suddenly she heard Ben gasp and suck in one long, deep breath. Almost as if he'd been swimming underwater for too long and had managed to surface just in time.

Awake, he looked wildly around the room as if he were shocked to be alive.

He croaked the word, "Swim."

In a heartbeat, Bree was leaning over him, his hands in hers. "Yes, honey, I was reading you part of Jayden's journal about a time on the beach together. We did go swimming, remember? Everything is fine. You are going to be just great. Wait until you hear what you have missed these past few weeks!"

She laughed as she kissed him all over his face, all the while thinking, *You have no idea!*

EPILOGUE

SIX MONTHS LATER

The donkeys seemed disinterested in making their way up the steep stone switchbacks. Their braying protests mingled with the wisecracks and laughter of the tourists they carried, creating a cacophony of sound and confusion. The more they balked, the more laughter could be heard from other tourists waiting in line for their turn.

One of the more stubborn donkeys decided to abruptly break rank and circle back down to the back of the group, the man on its back nearly getting tossed off in the process. This caused the next donkey in line to do the same thing.

Soon there was complete chaos as the whole line-up appeared to play musical chairs rather than progress up the winding stone pathway to the clifftop village overlooking the harbor. Several of the riders either slid off or were dumped off and found themselves sitting on the ground in shock as the smell of dung and dirt and heat wafted up from around them.

Molly's laughter grew louder as she watched the scene unfold. By the time the line had dissolved into a mob of sorts, she was laughing so hard that tears were running down her face, and she bent over, grabbing her stomach in an attempt to catch her breath. Her laughter was contagious, and soon Ben and Bree were chuckling and then convulsing with their own belly laughs. They were joined by others in their party, until everyone in their group was wiping away tears and slapping each other's backs.

The animals were eventually brought back into some semblance of order, and it was now time for Ben and Bree and their group to mount up for the climb up the incline.

"Hell, no!" Mac bellowed. "There's a limit to the kind of danger I'm willing to face, and getting done in by a jackass is it!"

Still laughing and gasping for air, the group agreed to bypass the donkeys and take the gondola instead.

As the cables pulled them up the side of the cliff, the breathtaking view of the famous Santorini harbor unfurled beneath them. Bree didn't think there could be a more stunning view of the Mediterranean. She was overcome with gratitude and joy to be alive—and to be making this memory as a newly created family. She looked over Molly's head at Ben and wasn't surprised to see his eyes brimming with tears of joy.

That is my man now, openhearted and willing to show emotion.

So much had happened since they had last been in this gondola. It seemed like a lifetime had passed by. In some ways it had. They were certainly changed as people; their lives turned upside down in every possible way.

Bree looked over at Mac and then Ian and Iona. What a precious group of friends. It still seemed incredible that their lives had crossed paths and that their journeys would now be forever entwined.

So much had happened to all of them since that horrific scene in the church.

Because of their heroic efforts thwarting the terrorists, Mac and Ian had been given honors from their respective agencies.

And while Al-Zawahiri might have been taken out, there were still plenty of new players willing to step into his shoes, which is why Ian and Mac had been appointed as liaisons to a new joint terrorism task force between the US and British intelligence communities. Their roles were described as high-level "think tank" operatives, which meant they would have plenty of time to enjoy perks, like unlimited fishing trips and very expensive scotch. It seemed like a supreme sacrifice but, as Mac so eloquently put it, "Some poor bastards are going to have to do it. It might as well be us!"

The renovation of the orphanage had been completed by a very grateful international community. Renovations included not only the chapel, but all of the living quarters, dining hall, main building, and the grounds. Most important, a memorial was created for the children who had lost their lives, moving them from anonymity to the light, never to be forgotten.

As for Iona and Ian, they had found their soul mates in each other.

They were married in the chapel.

Mac had officiated the ceremony, having secured an official ministerial license and wearing a new collar. Bree and Ben stood up for them as their witnesses, and Molly had served as their flower girl.

All evidence of the past violence in the chapel had been erased, and it was a truly beautiful and moving ceremony. The entire village attended the reception, including the new director of the orphanage. The couple had honeymooned on the island of Folegandros.

And finally, Bree and Ben. According to his doctors, Ben was a "walking miracle." Extensive rehab had helped him regain his health and his strength.

The doctors had warned Bree that everything Ben had gone through—the traumatic injuries, blood loss, and surgeries—could create an unpredictable change in his personality. She had prepared herself for what that could mean.

And they were right. Ben's personality *had* changed.

For the better.

There was a new softness, compassion, and peace about Ben that Bree had never seen or experienced in him before. She asked him once if he noticed the changes, and he had smirked and said he'd learned a few things while swimming laps during rehab.

Whatever it was, she was glad for the results and grateful that his life had been spared.

And as for Bree, Molly, the nonprofit, and learning to thrive? Bree had to laugh at the extraordinary ways all of her wildest dreams had come true. Molly now lived with Bree and Ben as their adopted daughter. And every day Bree spent bringing help to needy children gave her a day to remember and honor Jayden, as well as to love and be grateful for Molly and Ben.

Halfway through their honeymoon, Ian and Iona had insisted that Bree, Ben, Molly, and Mac meet up with them in Santorini.

"On your honeymoon?" Mac had howled when he got the call from his old friend. "What's wrong? Your equipment fail?" Bree had laughed when Iona had told her about their conversation.

Of course, Mac would never give Ian the satisfaction of knowing that the call wasn't a surprise at all—to any of them. Through everything they'd been through, the little group had indeed become a family.

As the gondola drew near to its destination at the top of the island, Bree sent up a silent prayer of gratitude. She was so grateful she hadn't known ahead of time about the loss of Jayden, the journey of grief, and Ben's near death. If she'd known, she couldn't have faced any of it.

But now she was overwhelmed by all the wonderful, amazing things that had happened since those awful experiences. It reminded her of a line from a Carole King song she used to listen to as a teenager: "You've got to take the bitter with the sweet."

She hadn't known what that meant back then. Now it seemed to reflect the true nature of life.

As if on cue, the sun dropped low over the water and the resulting explosion of color created a sunset so glorious that Bree sat motionless, unable to even blink.

Jayden's words seem to float down through the glow and into her own thoughts:

Sometimes it's those "rough seas" that bring the most unexpected gifts.

♛

The group of six stepped out of the gondola and walked to an overview where they could stand and drink in the view and the sunset. Without even being aware of it, they found themselves linking arms and gathering in to get closer together, each sending out their own version of a prayer of gratitude.

Someone stopped to ask if they would like a picture to capture their "family reunion," and they all laughed but happily agreed to pose.

Bree and Ben looked wistfully out at the sea. It seemed that Jayden was there in that moment; they could feel him in the warm glow of the fading light, and in the connection with each other. There was still loss, but somehow it felt different, like a badge of courage—courage they had earned by daring to move forward in life.

And the big question? Where was God during all this human mayhem?

In everything, or He isn't God.

AUTHOR'S NOTE

Dear Reader,

I love a good story. Thank goodness I've been blessed with supporting family and friends who have graciously and patiently listened to me while I've regaled them with many dramatic tales, both real and imagined. I am deeply grateful for each of you.

And who knew there are actually people who *have* to listen to stories as part of their profession! Thank you to my editor and now friend, Karen Scalf Bouchard. Your talent is jaw dropping, and I am still unpacking all of the wisdom and insight I garnered from our work together. I'm also fairly certain it was our epic hours spent dissecting this manuscript over Zoom that not only moved my story into an actual novel but also propelled Zoom's recent stock IPO. They should be thanking us, Karen!

I first read Robert Frost's poem, "Hard Not to Be King" in 1984 in an American poetry class while attending Whitworth University. Frost had written the poem in 1949, thirty-five years before I stumbled across it in that class. Unbeknownst to me, it imbedded itself in my heart and rode along quietly for another thirty years before resurfacing to become the foundational theme of this novel.

As soon as I caught my first glimpse of Bree and Ben on the distant horizon, dragging along their load of grief, it was as if the poem leaped from my chest to declare itself the anthem of their struggles. In helping them find their way through their loss and grief, I discovered that it isn't only a prince who is called to be king. We are all called to be kings

at some point in our lives. Sometimes, it's a single dramatic ɑ as Nazir's, but more often than not, it is the more courageoυ daily choosing hope in the face of great challenges, just like F Ben did.

Finally, there is the larger question of Who is calling. Ide that voice was the ultimate journey for each character in this ι is our journey also. God is the author of the truth that runs Frost's poem, through the lives of these characters—and if courageous enough, through our own lives as well.

Thank you for taking this journey with me.

Dana
www.danahallin.com